HOLOTYPE

A NOVEL

ULLA LAW

EUCHARISTA

This book is a work of fiction, events, establishments, organizations, or locals, are intended only to provide a sense of authenticity, and are used fictitiously. All other characters, and all incidents and dialogue, are drawn from the author's imagination and are not to be construed as real.

HOLOTYPE. Copyright 2024 (Fa Loves Pa, LLC). All rights reserved. Printed in the United States of America. No part of this book may used or reproduced in any manner whatsoever without written permission, except in the case of brief quotations embodied within critical articles and reviews. For information legal@eucharista.com

Cover design illustration by Othneil and Mothra Studios.

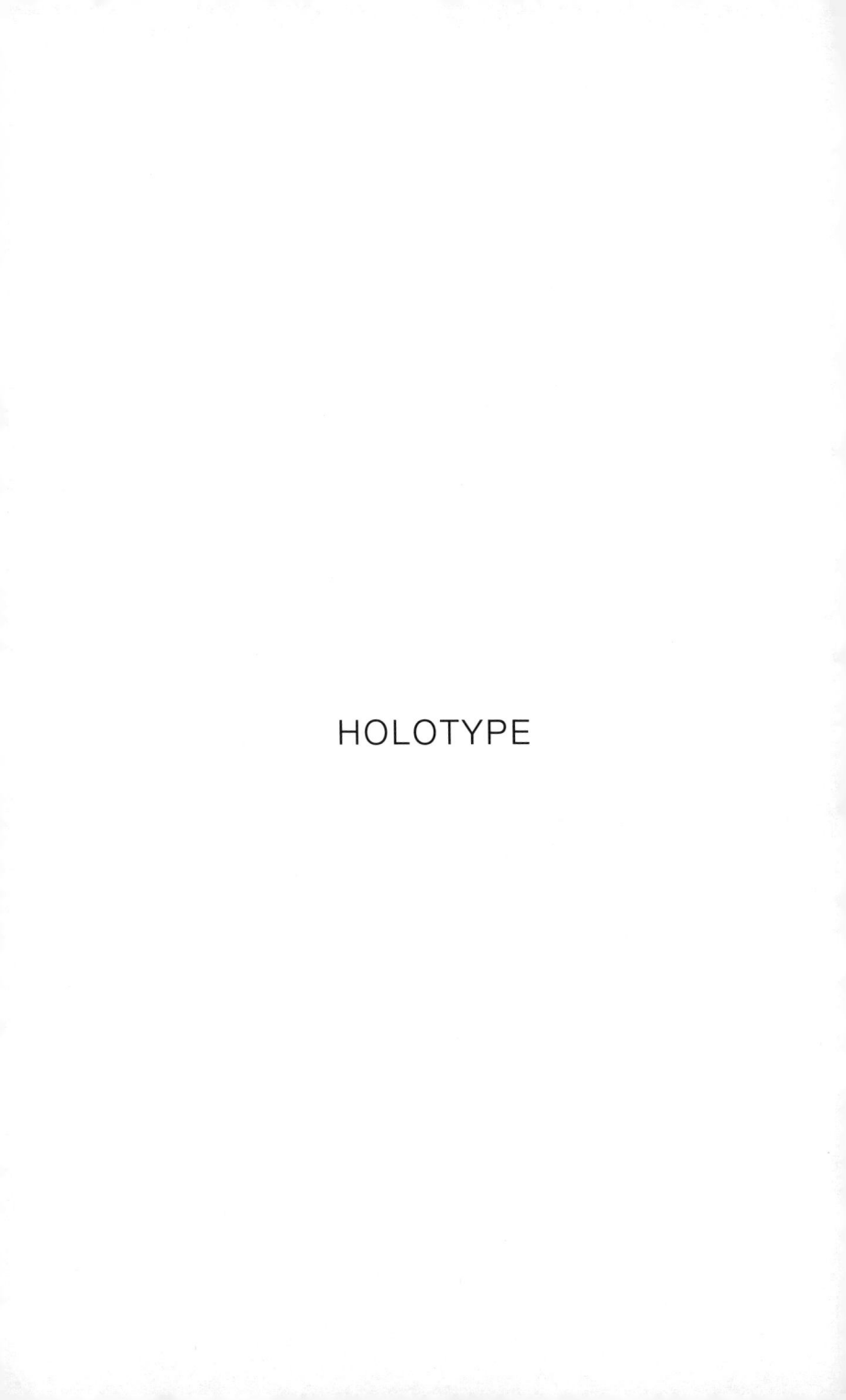

HOLOTYPE

HOLOTYPE
noun: ho· lo· type ˈhō-lə-ˌtīp
1. The single specimen designated by an author as the type of a species or lesser taxon at the time of establishing the group.

WHY HELLO GIDEON

Everyone was on their best behavior but nobody knew why.
Mostly people just kept their heads down, staring at their latest designer shoes, admiring the color coordination with their socks, and the swishing of their tailored vicuna slacks in full stride across the spotless sidewalks.
And why not?
If you just kept your head down, put a little bounce to your step, and kept a pleasant countenance, you were sure to make it home from work in one piece. And just a little bit richer for it in the process. Just don't smile to wide or someone might think you were mocking them, or worse yet arrogant. You wanted just the right smile. You wanted to avoid showing teeth. Teeth like snarling beasts might give the wrong impression and risk ruining someone's day. It was best to just appear as if you were listening to some soft easy-listening music, your lips slightly upturned.

Your eyelids should blink periodically, but not rapidly, best on the downbeat of some easy-going glockenspiel rhythm without looking too robotic. Your stride should be steady and confident. Never too fast. You wouldn't want to appear to anyone as though you were late. The key was a nice easy stride. Because with nice easy strides you knew each step you took sounded just like a cash register going cha-ching.

Walking too fast or running was another matter entirely. If you walked too fast you might end up causing someone else to stumble, and nobody wanted to cause someone else to stumble. Or it would cost you. Not only in your pocket book, but you'd have to end up having to explain yourself to people in funny hats, and if you said the wrong thing you ran the risk of getting yourself thrown into the Gladiator Arena. But then there were those who were just flat out denied the gracious opportunity to fight for their life in the arena with a crossbow or catapult. Those people ended up like the man and women who were hanging from their necks at the electric gallows in the center of town.

Gideon had seen their dangling corpses countless times on his way to work. He had witnessed their flesh transform from that of a man and woman with their necks stretched and their faces a dark ghastly purple, to the skeletons that they were that day. If you hadn't chronicled their daily decomposition like Gideon had, you'd be hard pressed to guess who was the man and who was the women if it weren't for the single Italian loafer that dangled off the man's boney feet. Women hadn't worn loafers in years. It just wasn't the fashion like it was in '93. Needless to say, the crows were still under the jurisdiction of natural law and therefore had done as proscribed, pecking all the prime bits of flesh from off their bodies in the matter of two weeks time. All that was left to do was wait for the sun to bleach their bones a stark white; then they'd be removed, placed into trash bags, and filed away in the city dumpster down at the morgue.

The specific reason for their public execution in the middle of the town square wasn't really of a concern to anyone walking past that day. Especially not when everyone had far better things to be concerned with, like keeping their heads down and trying to smile without showing their teeth.

Gideon always looked up when he crossed through the city center. He also tossed a penny in the fountain and made a wish while he was at it. Gideon was probably the only one walking past that knew the man on the right dangling from the gallows had a name. It was Ken Fulmer, a former executive at Proxy & Ram Solutions. Gideon had lunch with Ken on more than one occasion. Ken was just a small piece of a jigsaw puzzle that was the Owens 500 job he pulled off a few years back. It was a decent score. The real mark was the lawyer for Phetaol LRN who had written up all the secret patents for the T-R7 glow in the dark shark they had purchased from the Slouchvert Group back on 2096. Gideon wondered where Phetaol LRN's internal investigation would lead when they discovered a breach after his employer (The Startling Concern) released the new Mako TRG. But by looking up everyday at those size ten Italian loafers dangling above his head, Gideon knew the investigation never got further than Ken. Whatever Ken knew got Ken killed.

Keeping a clear head was the best thing to do.

Personal memories were simply placed into a boxes, marked and dated, and stashed away in some forgotten warehouse due for demolition. Archiving was archived in favor of just getting on with it. Remembering unfortunate things that happened to you in your past was just dangerous, especially if you wanted to keep making money with a clear head.

What was the point of thinking about what happened in the distant past when you could focus all your attention on improving the world for a better tomorrow? Why would you want to come off as selfish or self-centered by considering what has come and gone? And with financial groups like Credeth, Greensleeves, E.R.99, Skor Kid, and their pantheons of gods and goddesses, dwelling on the past was the last thing you wanted to do. Why dwell in the past when you could simply live in the future. And if you didn't know how to live in the future, you could always start with the present and work your way up.

That was always a good place to start. The present. It was best to ponder the scuff on your shoe than the scraps of some faded memory. Nobody was saying you did't need to have memories, but it was best to have the sort of memories that help you succeed in life. Memories along the lines of "Where'd I put my keys." It was good to know your name. Things like your bank account number, your address, where you lived and worked, etcetera, etcetera. And the truth was everyone's brains were expanding in 2099. People were smarter in 2099 than they were in 2045 for example. Imagine all you could get done in the brains department when you don't have to worry about getting mugged just walking down the street or being murdered in your own backyard.

Parents were on their best behavior too. This was especially so with the glut of new fertility goddesses which popped up in the late 80s. The competition just forced even stricter tabs on couples with the leading financial institutes like Credeth, Thorton-Barnhardt, Flxpay, and Cash-Fellow, but the rewards and punishment programs were some of the most profitable investments any family could hope to make. Thus the "super" dad and "super" mom were born. The credits you could rack up by just being available to play mindless games with your toddler was phenomenal. And in turn these super parents produced kids that were perfectly fit for looking down. And if anyone needed a little reminder of that fact that looking down paid the bills, they just had to look up and see the skeletons hanging from the electric scaffolds to know.

And the sidewalks weren't so bad to stare at either. In fact, the sidewalks fit you like a glove. Gone were those grey cement sidewalks with their black constellations of petrified chewing gum, their hazy shades of grease, with massive cracks cutting down the middle. In their place came brightly colored pathways, which studied your body's posture and corrected your alignment by a product called reflex tread. Reflex tread also contained a substance that sort of made the ground a roving television to keep you company on your journey to work, featuring clips on the latest cultural innovators, moral superstars, and the gods and goddesses they worship. It was a nice way to keep anyone from taking unnecessary strolls down memory lane, which only racked up huge fines with your Credeth account.

And who needed the fines? It was better to keep your head down and live in the lap of luxury. Being "poor" was nothing more than an aesthetic choice in 2099, more than any real condition of having no means in which to support yourself. Poor was an extremely popular look back in 2094, but by the time 2099 rolled around everyone was back to being rich, happy, and in pursuit of a better tomorrow. After all, being poor just cost too much.

So this was why everyone was on their best behavior. It was far easier and far more lucrative to just keep your eyes averted, to mind your own steps, and focus in on a better tomorrow ahead.

Everyone but Gideon.

He was on his worst behavior that day, as he walked on his way to pull off the biggest heist of his career. Gideon was a thief. One of the last of his kind. All the other thieves had been caught red handed long ago with their hands in the cookie jar and were either dead, in Siberian gulags, or reformed insurance agents. Nobody stole anything anymore. How could you? There was electronic surveillance of electronic surveillance that surveilled the surveillance. If you wanted a so-called "five finger discount," the self destruct mechanisms on merchandise guaranteed you'd be down to "two fingers" after the explosion literally caught you red-handed. Stores were fully insured too, so they were more than happy to clean up the bloody digits. Then the recently installed Veri-Scans took lie detectors to the next level, going so far as to ask consumers to reveal their deepest darkest intentions before entering a grocery store to pick up a gallon of low fat milk. Were you here to buy, browse, borrow, or beg? And worse off, burgle. Whatever you said, or didn't say for that matter, was duly recorded and submitted for review by your chosen financial institution, then your chosen god or goddess, and at the end of the month your morality statement was delivered to your spouse or next of kin. It made reward and punishment a completely transparent transaction.

But Gideon didn't steal objects more so than he stole invisible ideas. He was perfectly aware it wasn't like the old days when he could throw a brick into a window and be a mile away before the cops showed up. Gone were the days before he could even vote, that Gideon would have had thirty vintage gas guzzlers on a container to Hong Kong in the matter of an afternoon. That was entry level stuff in 2099. Gideon was making a fortune with The Startling Concern for over twenty years and not because he boosted cars or precious gems. It was because Gideon could memorize a dictionary in the matter of minutes and recite it all back to the corporate scribes who lived in the basement of The Startling Concern in even less time.

So while everyone else in the world was trying their best to forget, Gideon was doing his best to remember. When The Startling Concern needed to take down a corporate rival, they'd send in Gideon and his team to memorize top secret documents, like financial statements, blueprints, formulas, private corporate info, and top secret inventions, anything that could give The Startling Concern the leg up on the competition.

Vice President of Acquisitions and Antiquities #2 is what they called Gideon over at the The Startling Concern. He was considered a valuable corporate asset on the top floor. Vice President of Acquisitions and Antiquities #2 was a job title you got when you could single handedly steal an entire library and lock it up for safekeeping in your hippocampus. They considered you a team player when you could sneak into a rival's headquarters, rob them blind, and never get caught. It was all because of Gideon's malfunctioning brain. From some fluke of nature he had what you call a literal memory bank. It was like an empty vault ready to take deposits of highly sensitive information and keep it under lock and key for extended periods of time. When he wasn't on a caper, Gideon just left his mind completely empty. It was better this way. To keep a clear head. It was all rather routine. About three times a year Gideon would get an assignment from "upstairs." He'd plan a heist with his team. Execute it to perfection. Then he'd meet up with The Startling Concern's basement scribes and hand over all the explicit details. Then he'd simply erase the contents from his mental vaults to ensure there'd never be a paper trail, imaginary or otherwise, that could tie him or his employer to the crime.

And the corporate victims were none the wiser for it either. What could they say years after the crime when they saw their top secret product suddenly hit the market with a rival years ahead of schedule? What could an unsuspecting rival say years after the crime when The Startling Concern swoops in and beats them to the punch on a long planned merger? Or when the Startling Concern suddenly has the formula to cure male pattern baldness just weeks before you are about to announce your discovery? You couldn't do anything. Nothing. Absolutely nothing. If they didn't have any proof anything was stolen, how could there be a crime?

Being an undercover thief in VP clothing for one of the most powerful corporations on the planet came with all sorts of perks. Like when you entered into Porphyry to pick up something for your fiancée.

"Are you coming in to buy, to browse, to beg —?" The Veriscan machine asked Gideon before he interrupted.

"— It's me," answered Gideon checking his watch.

The Veriscan paused. Then its electronic voice almost started choking, as it pitched and squeaked, "Gold, Diamond, Platinum, Premium, Executive, 1st Class status recognized."

Not one door opened for Gideon, but two. A fine mist of jasmine and cucumber sprayed into the air as Gideon carefully stepped into the shop. The mister referenced Gideon's preferred scents before filling the entrance with the refreshing floral bouquet. It was a wise choice. Gideon was in a jasmine mood. A salesperson at Porphyry was there to greet Gideon not only with a double bow at the waist, but with three forehead taps on the marble floor, before they rose to their feet to offer Gideon some hot yak butter with guano crush topping which he politely declined.

"I'm looking for that something rare," said Gideon smiling, his teeth showing. "A present for my betrothed."

They salesperson had just received a shipment of cow tongue in a jar and random hoof. Gideon opted for the bicycle pump with a busted valve.

Anticipating all his needs, the salesperson arranged delivery, payment was made through his Credeth account, and Gideon finally took the salesperson up on that offer of hot yak butter, to go.

Living and working right off Worship Row was a convenience Gideon appreciated, especially waiting in line for daily prayers. The hot yak butter was cold by the time he was next in line. He waited patiently for the person ahead of him to be scanned.

The monk manning the massive black portal to the temple of the Oracle of Krokus, a former Startling Concern product recently acquired by NuLeaf, was dressed in a full black body suit with a circle cut out for its face which was covered by a thin wire cage, and as it spoke breakfast cereal fell from its mouth, "Interrogation room 3 for interrogation, then confession hall 5, and daily penance room 34!" The worshipper tried not to appear too horrified as they entered in through the dark black portal. It was now Gideon's turn. He bowed and placed his left hand on on the 9th Book of Incantations.

"Hail Krokus," sighed Gideon. He didn't believe in Krokus, Flanmous, Zaxxonius, Duglemar, or any of the gods and goddesses clogging up his wallet.

The monk appeared extraordinarily pleased, or as pleased as you could be with a wire cage on your face and half eaten cereal in its mouth, saying, "Hail Krokus! You are amongst the chosen ones!"

Gideon bowed again, threw a few tokens in the tip jar, then stepped from the line and was back striding off down the street.

Everyone remaining in line watched Gideon leave out of the corner of their eyes. Everybody who remained in line knew what awaited them. Long recitations of the Ten Suggestions, running in place on a treadmill screaming at the top of their lungs that they will not speak louder than the mater de at Boujwar, and having the tops of their toenails roasted by a partially lit menthol cigarette. They would try not to appear too obvious just how jealous they were of this confident man who somehow not only got out of interrogation, confession, and daily penance, but walked off with a blessing to boot.

What nobody could realize was that Gideon was exempt from all the daily minutia. All his extensive credentials and credit cards marked upon his forehead with a seal of Gold, Diamond, Platinum, Premium, Executive, 1st Class, or whatever status level was currently on the books was just part of his almost secret agent status. There was no way The Startling Concern was going to risk a prime asset such as Gideon, their Vice President of Acquisitions and Antiquities #2, to be the subject of any actual real scanning.

A real scan would set off so many bells and alarms that Gideon would immediately have a net thrown over him, then he'd be tackled by a horde of monks, ordinary citizens looking to improve their civility scores, various forms of law enforcement, and even the gang from General Worship. A real scan would get Gideon thrown on a torture rack, injected with multiple truth serums to extract his confessions, which although there wouldn't be much thanks to Gideon's ability to erase his memory banks in the matter of seconds, whatever scraps they did manage to find lingering around Gideon's brain would still run the risk of pointing straight to The Startling Concern. And they couldn't have that. They were blemish free. So it was to be with Gideon. Blemish free.

It was best just to give Gideon a free pass in life. To have him go through the motions of everyday living, just like he did when he checked in with the temple of Krokus, or all the song and dance routine he put on with the salesperson at Porphyry. It was all for show. He was the worst of the worst in modern society in 2099, but to everyone watching out of the corner of their eyes, he looked like quite the specimen.

Nobody could ever know the truth, not when Gideon was on a first name basis with the executives at The Startling Concern. Nobody could know the truth. The temples certainly not. The shops couldn't very well know the guy eyeballing the random hoof was a master thief and conman. And if the financial institutions knew the system might explode. And being recently engaged, the last person who needed to know the truth was his fiancée Helinka Vowell. But the truth was still the truth. Gideon was simply the last of the gutter rats to somehow make good. And it was all thanks to his ability to memorize vast quantities of material and forget about it just about as quick. That made him untouchable. So that's why Gideon kept his head up, especially when he moved down the city streets. He was untouchable. And he was off to the biggest heist of his career. So why not fully enjoy all the perks that came along with being what they called "amongst the chosen ones."

Making a right turn onto Mega Mansion Row, it wasn't more than a couple blocks before Gideon came upon the gilded gates of Smith Smith's mega mansion. Smith being his first name and Smith being his last. It was easy to identify his home by the golden sculptures of a herd of dead kudu scattered about the expansive front lawn while sprinklers shot arches of non-potable water onto their corkscrew-like horns. It was the famous art piece titled "Safari Gone Wrong" by 44-p Johnson.

Although this mega mansion was Gideon's prime destination, he didn't open the gates and enter inside before catching a glimpse of a Pest Control rickshaw parked next door. A look was all the two men sitting inside the rickshaw needed to grab their gear and start approaching the mega mansion belonging to Smith Smith. These were of course the fumigators. They were equally covert members of Gideon's team for the past 20 years at the Startling Concern. Gideon knew them only as "You and You." "You and You" made it hard for anyone to know exactly who was who, but that was the whole point from an operations perspective. Gideon had only once referred to them by their real names, Ted and June, but that was when he saw them at the The Startling Concern's Spring Equinox Office Party a few years back, and only because he read it off their name tags. Since then, he had gone back to simply calling them "You and You." We can know them simply as Ted and June.

Gideon was first through the gate.

Following a short distance behind were the fumigators, Ted and June.

There was no going back now. And it's in those moments when there's no going back where doubt can creep in. It's the anxiety of getting caught that makes itself known to you before every robbery. The natural thing Gideon wanted to do was look down, to somehow avert his eyes from what lay ahead. To somehow forget the fact you were about to rob a man blind while looking him straight in the eye. So the butterflies were fluttering about his belly as he strode down the walkway leading to the drawbridge of Smith's front door. But he did his best to keep his composure and continued looking dead ahead. Gideon just had to keep his mind focused on the perfectly manicured lawns, and although he would definitely go with another artist to do the lawn art, he knew it was just a matter of hours and then he'd be able to get himself one just like it. He'd be off on an all expenses paid dream vacation with his fiancée to kick off a marriage that legitimized his bloodline. Then there was the promotion to President of Acquisitions and Antiquities #1 that would make him one of the wealthiest executives in the world. It was all there for the taking. And all he had to do was walk up to the front door and knock.

"Why hello, Gideon," said Smith opening the front door, "Come on in."

The toxic agent was working to perfection. Almost instantaneously. The effects seemed to saturate Smith Smith's brain. His face was dripping with the stuff, and it didn't seem to bother him in the slightest. In fact, he was carrying on with June as if he were talking with Gideon. The chemical agent named "Slorpicane" was doing its job. It was a secret proprietary chemical that The Startling Concern had specially formulated for all of Gideon's heists. On the ledgers they had Slorpicane categorized under "stain enhancer." 1-part GRI lab-grade Novocidosine, three parts primate tranquilizer, a shot or two of Southern Comfort whisky beverage product, and a 1/2 gallon of distilled water, then shake vigorously. Then sprayed directly in your face, as had been done with Smith Smith's face the second after he opened up the front door and welcomed Gideon into his home.

Having Smith Smith under Slorpicane's real time effects caused him to think that June was Gideon, which was exactly how the team wanted it. This allowed June, a registered nurse, to closely monitor Smith Smith's reactions to the toxin to make sure he didn't overheat and start imagining he was covered in spiders.

June knew it was best to keep the subject talking about golf, like the new Cobrastrike RTX Razors, the upcoming Pebble Beach Pro-Ams, stuff like where he plans to golf on his upcoming vacation; all too keep him from overheating. So this was good. So far so good. Smith Smith was under the influence of Slorpicane leaving Ted to bust the safe.

Downstairs at the safe, Gideon watched as Ted took out a glass little jar from his pocket and held it up to the light.

"They're awake," sniffled Ted.

This was good. Otherwise they'd have to blow the safe the old fashion way, and Ted having no memory couldn't possibly know what that was. That didn't keep Ted from being the last master safecracker on the planet. He didn't need blow torches, hammers, and explosives to break into a safe. He did it the modern way. With micron-mitetriculons and arakvoids. Tiny metal bugs preprogrammed in The Startling Concern's field office by none other than Ted himself, designed to swarm into the vaults keyholes and keypad where they'd work their way through the system, feeding off the electronic paper trail to report back the combination to their master safecracker overlord, who was Ted. From there it was just a matter of collecting all the micron-mitetriculons and arakvoids and placing them back in the jar, then back in his pocket. Then you simply punch in the combination and watched the giant steel door swing wide open.

"Go get 'em," whispered Ted to his legions.

His swarm of tiny metal bugs worked to perfection yet again, and Ted handed the note with the vault's combination to Gideon. And just like that, they had gained entrance. Knowing exactly where he needed to go, Gideon put on his gloves and opened the safe deposit box which held a browning seven volume series of books written in Hebrew from a Yeshiva in Hoboken New Jersey. Now, Gideon didn't speak Hebrew. He had no idea what he was looking at and was only told that they were "locks to an ever bigger combination." Cloreen always spoke in riddles when you had stumbled into the need to know basis, of which he had no need to know. It was better for everyone if he didn't care or now what he was stealing at any one time. And this was no exception. Opening up volume one, he began to memorize what to him looked like a bunch of strange cryptic symbols. It would only take a matter of a few minutes to get through each volume. They'd be in and out of there in fifteen minutes. Twenty tops.

"Roomy," suggested Ted. He liked the vault's spacious interior.

"Yup..." murmured Gideon as he continued to memorize each page, flipping them quicker and quicker as he went.

"Hey, look at this. It's a fake."

Gideon had no time to look up and see the Hockney forgery that had so taken ahold of Ted's imagination. But his fascination didn't last long. Ted opened up random safe deposit boxes and rummaged through gold aviation watches and woman's jewelry he all thought were tacky. He thought some German bearer bonds were interesting for a minute or two, but quickly lost interest in all of it.

"I'd like for once to, you know, to feel like a thief again," he confessed. "To like take something that really matters, again. I'd rather rob a kid's ice cream cone than any of this junk. I mean gold? Who wants more gold. I want some shrunken heads. How come nobody collects shrunken heads no more? You notice that?"

Gideon was on book number three when the first shot rang out.

"What's that?" wondered Ted.

Gideon barely even looked up from the book, "I don't know."

"I'll go check," replied Ted, "Maybe they're trying out those new Cobrastrikes. The RXV's. The 300's. The Mecha-Strikes. You play golf, Gideon?"

Gideon was too busy memorizing Hebrew words to hear

anything Ted was saying, "Yeah, why don't you go check."

"Yeah. Anything's better than what's in here."

Everyone had forgotten about the Cauzzies.

The lanky jade-colored humanoids with the wide set mouths and wide opaque eyes. The ones with the shaggy yellow hair, Hawaiian shirts, and khaki cargo pants. And who could blame them? Cauzzies didn't exactly bring to mind thoughts of futurity, progress, and a better tomorrow. Cauzzies brought to mind things like bad kung fu movies, cheap beer, and getting stabbed in the neck with a pitchfork. The Cauzzies being so well behaved, for so long, as they lived stashed away in underground reserves, that naturally everybody forgot all about Cauzzies. Maybe if you drove past a slaughterhouse or an oil refinery, you might wonder if there were those "invasive species things" living underneath it, but the chances were you never bothered to ask. Nobody talked about Cauzzies anymore. Why would you? There were way better inventions since then that capitalized on their technology that were 100X better than any Cauzzie. The Great Cauzzie War Down Under was worth forgetting. It didn't pay to think about wars to begin with, but a war where mankind fought the very life saving lifeforms they created ever more so. Anyway, that was years ago. The world had moved on to more captivating things like cold fusion and cures for hair loss, which literally resurrected dead hair follicles opening up all sorts of possibilities for the future. The climate situation was being perfectly handled. All you needed to do was look out the window and see the perfect 77 degree day to know. The gentle breeze coming out of the south. The light rain that rolls in while you're sleeping.

But what all this meant on a practical level, specifically within Smith Smith's mega mansion, was that the moment June looked up to see Cauzzie Rob and Cauzzie Roy standing over her with a shotgun pointed at her face, she had no idea what they were. All she saw was a flash of green spindly arms lurching forward and these lizard-like faces with wild-eyed grins, and immediately thought the creatures had risen from the black lagoon. She was trying to scream when the first shotgun blast went off, followed by the second.

Under the intoxicating influence of Slorpicane, Smith was in no condition to comprehend the reasons why Gideon's head had just disappeared into a fine red mist, because of course it wasn't Gideon's head that went poof, but June's. Heads disappear though, when Cauzzies pull the triggers of their shotguns at the exact same time.

"Bullseye!" shouted Cauzzie Rob.

"Bloody bullseye more like it, mate," replied Cauzzie Roy, wiping the splatter from his shirt.

The truth was, it had been years since either Cauzzie Roy or Cauzzie Rob had fired a shotgun point blank into someone's face, but they were quickly reminded of the brutal results it produced. They looked at each other and were about to laugh before pointing the barrels on Smith Smith.

Smith Smith was none the wiser. He was zonked out of his mind and actually thought the Cauzzies were the valets from his favorite midtown eatery, Pommespanzer.

"It's tee time, mate," bellowed Cauzzie Rob. "You ready to tee off?"

Cauzzie Roy was ready.

"Looks like we got a dog leg right," suggested Cauzzie Rob, "Watch the bunker."

As if on cue, Cauzzie Roy blew a hole through Smith's chest, the force knocking him out of his chair, where he rolled across the floor knocking over the lamp.

"Hole in one, eh!"

"Too bad we ain't bowling. If we were, it've been a strike, mate!"

"A spare."

"A strike."

"A spare."

"I said strike."

Cauzzie Rob and Cauzzie Roy were about to go to blows over whether knocking down the lamp counted for a strike or a spare when Cauzzie Rex slid into the living room and seeing the blood began moaning, "Why you ain't wait for Rex?"

"Zip it you hoon, talkin' in the 3rd person, yous," said Cauzzie Rob, "They still be two persons in here. But bring the Gideon one alive, eh. We can't kill him, got that, mate?"

"Wot? Alive?" puzzled Cauzzie Rex. Naturally he was eager to get in on the action and wanted to know what this Gideon looked like. "Rex don't wanna kill the wrong sod," murmured Rex again in the 3rd person.

They reminded Cauzzie Rex that if he wanted to know what Gideon looked like, all he had to do was look in his pocket. That's what the photograph they had taken weeks earlier was there for, to make sure they didn't put a hole through Gideon's head by mistake. They needed him alive. Rex referenced the photo before moving off as if on safari tracking down the other guy.

The other guy was obviously Ted. And everything worked out perfectly for Cauzzie Rex, the great green hunter, the moment Ted came walking up the hallway to check what all the noise was about.

Cauzzie Rex was waiting with the shotgun pointed between his eyes.

Ted did what only Ted could do. He sprayed.

The unfortunate thing for Ted is that Slorpicane doesn't work on Cauzzies like it does with humans. So instead of collapsing to the floor the way Smith Smith had when he got his dose right in the face, Cauzzie Rex thought he tasted Southern Comfort.

"Do that again, mate," asked Cauzzie Rex.

Ted did as was commanded, squeezing the nozzle six more times until Cauzzie Rex was absolutely sure he tasted Southern Comfort and a heavy dose of Novocidosine. Ted knew he had just administered what amounted to a lethal dose, but instead of the creature falling to the ground dead, it was lapping it up. Whatever was able to suck up that much Slorpicane surely wasn't human.

Seeing no rational explanation for Cauzzie Rex's presence, Ted fell to his knees and began worshipping the Cauzzie as if he were some kind of god or goddess, of which he wasn't sure. But the fact a green deity had materialized before his eyes was enough of a cue for Ted to begin worshipping it immediately.

Turns out Ted had forgotten what Cauzzies looked like too. "What shall I call you, my lord?" he stuttered.

"Why me? I'm Father Christmas," replied Cauzzie Rex.

"What's that in your hand, my lord Father Christmas?" asked Ted, curious to know what his newly acquired god or goddess was pointing at his head.

Cauzzie Rex looked surprised, "Wot? This hear thing? It's a sea shell."

Ted hadn't only forgotten about Cauzzies, but shotguns and seashells as well.

"Come on, mate," laughed Cauzzie Rex, "You wanna hear the ocean don't cha? Go on, put your ear right up there and have a listen."

The second Ted leaned his ear against the barrel of the shotgun in the hopes of hearing waves crashing on a coco-powder beach, Cauzzie Rex pulled the trigger.

Gideon heard the shot that killed Ted and instinctively knew something wasn't right. Something in his bones told him that what he was hearing were gunshots. This wasn't good. Gideon had only memorized three of the seven books, when he suddenly heard voices coming down the stairs. He stopped himself from calling out to them when he heard their Australian accents. There wasn't supposed to be anyone with Australian accents anywhere near the mega mansion that day. Gideon wasn't the type of person to panic. But that's just what he began to do, because the only reason there would be gunshots or strange Australian accents was if something had gone horribly wrong. He had perfectly planned, nothing should have ever gone wrong, so the extremes involved with going from pure confidence to sheer terror couldn't be over exaggerated.

All Gideon could think of in the brief flash of time was that he had mistakenly tripped some secret alarm inside the vault, and the Private Police, or worse yet, General Worship was coming to arrest and execute the intruders on the spot. The adrenaline unloaded on his senses, but there was nowhere to hide. He had no head start, there were no alarms, he was literally going to be trapped in a vault and caught red-handed which meant nothing short of the death penalty. He saw himself hanging from the electric gallows and looked down to his feet to make sure he was at least wearing the right shoes.

The voices were getting louder and louder.

Gideon had no other option but to remove the forged Hockney from behind its glass frame, lean up against the wall with the painting covering him, and pretend he was some kind of easel.

"There!" exclaimed Cauzzie Rob the moment they entered the vault.

Gideon closed his eyes, he was almost certain that they had seen him. Any professional security guard worth their salt would have spotted the intruder in an instant trying to pretend to be an easel holding up a counterfeit painting. Fearing the worst, he was more than just a little surprised when nothing happened. Nobody came rushing up, beating him into submission, then dragging him by the hair out to the front yard for all to see. Private Police or General Worship would have done exactly that. But none of that happened.

And he began to wonder that maybe whoever had come into the vault hadn't see him. That maybe the whole pretend you're an easel move had worked. As hard as that was to believe, he should have been spotted by then. Or maybe these weren't professional security guards at all. Maybe he was already dead. He couldn't know for sure. So he decided to do the only thing he could and listen.

"There should be seven books," said Cauzzie Roy. "How many you count?"

"Six, wait… seven," confirmed Cauzzie Rob. "We got 'em. They all here!"

"Double bag it."

"Wot's that smell?"

"The rat proofer."

"Peppermint. Why'd you get Hefty bags that smell like peppermint?"

"Rats don't like peppermint."

"Smell's gross, mate. Do that make me a rat?"

"Yeah."

"Ah, shut it."

"These books are heavy, mate."

"Slide 'em in then."

"We ain't got much time."

"We got all the time in the world."

"No mate, I left the iron on."

"Oi."

He hadn't been spotted, but just when he should have breathed a sigh of relief an even more dreadful realization entered into Gideon's thoughts. Whoever these Australians were, they were there to steal the books, and they weren't there to memorize the contents either, but had come to steal the actual books themselves. The low thud of books tumbling in on each other all but confirmed his suspicions. This thought was even more horrific than the first. Gideon wished he had kept his ears shut, because listening to a pair of Australians ripping off the exact same books he was trying to memorize for The Startling Concern was about the last thing in the world he wanted to hear. It was a dark revelation that not only spelled the end of his career, but what amounted to the end of his world. This was the worst case on the docket of worse case scenarios.

Seeing that his ears were reporting nothing but horrible news, Gideon decided to take a peak in the hopes that what he saw with his eyes would somehow magically improve matters. Well, they didn't. The second he peaked out from behind the painting he saw Cauzzies. Gideon, unlike the majority of the known world, still knew what a Cauzzie looked like. And he clearly saw two of them standing shoulder to shoulder, but was fully aware there had to be more. Cauzzies always came in packs of three or more. Gideon suddenly remembered what a shotgun was too, and the blast he heard must mean You and You were dead and gone. That also meant Smith Smith was most likely dead dead.

Gideon couldn't have known who these two Cauzzies were. Nor could he have known that Cauzzie Rob and Cauzzie Roy, from Invasive Designate R located just 30 miles out of town in the rolling meadows underneath the slaughterhouse, had taken two months to plan their robbery of Gideon's own robbery. Gideon had no way of knowing that things were going exactly the way Cauzzie Rob and Cauzzie Roy had planned. And this fact became more clear by the second when they finished loading the books inside the double bagged rat proof trash bag.

"This vault be pretty spacious," remarked Cauzzie Rob. "Looky."

"It ain't that spacious, mate" shrugged Cauzzie Roy. He wasn't so impressed.

"It's spacious, mate. Real spacious. About the most spacious vault I've ever seen," replied Cauzzie Rob.

"I say it ain't that spacious," returned Cauzzie Roy.

And suddenly, just like that, they were both on the verge of throwing haymakers, but there was still hope one of them would change their mind.

"Spacious, I says."

"Ain't spacious, I says."
"Is!"
"Ain't"
"Is!"
"Ain't!"

There was no changing anybody's mind. Rob landing a jab straight on Roy's nose knocking him back into a Ming Vase. But Roy lunged, throwing Rob into a display cabinet filled with gold wrist watches for every altitude above and below sea level. He hurled hand fulls of watches at Roy. Roy then jumped on Rob's back and began wailing on the back of his head. They both began spinning in circles until Rob threw Roy off his shoulders and began swinging wildly. It would have continued like this too, had Gideon not sensed his opportunity.

Throwing aside the painting, Gideon ran straight to the overstuffed trash bag and grabbed ahold with both hands, then turned and darted out of the vault in full stride.

"Oi!" shouted Cauzzie Rob, catching sight of Gideon as he sprinted out of the vault with the overstretched Hefty bag in his arms. "He's got the books, mate!"

Gideon charged up the stairs.

KABLAMMMM!!!!!

The ceiling above Gideon's head exploded in a shower of plaster and drywall.

"Alive! We want him alive, not dead, you hoon!" shouted Cauzzie Rob.

Gideon disappeared from their view.

Cauzzie Roy realized he would have blasted a hole in Gideon's back had it not been for Cauzzie Rob smacking the barrel away at the last second. It had completely slipped Cauzzie Roy's mind they weren't supposed to shoot Gideon. His killer instinct was triggered seeing Gideon running away with their loot. Ultimately Roy was happy he hadn't shot Gideon and ruined all their plans, but wasn't about to thank Rob, at least not right after just having received the brunt of the punishment during their recent brawl in the vault.

"He's gettin' away!" yelled Roy.

"Nah, mate, Rex will take 'em hostage," replied Rob.

"Ah, fair dinkum."

Gideon had no intention of slowing down, although he had no clue were he was going. He was just running, trying not to remind himself that the trash bag weighed a ton. All the hypothetical escape routes he had put on paper were now totally useless now that he was being charged by Cauzzies with guns. And to think all he needed was about ten minutes more and he would have had all the books memorized.

Racing around the corner at max speed and seeing one of your partners' bodies blocking your getaway, all sprawled out on the floor and blown to bits, didn't help matters either. Especially when you have the momentum of a runaway locomotive going for you. So at the last second, Gideon tried to leap over the carnage that was the "You" formerly known as Ted, but the tip of his shoe clipped his body ever so slightly sending him belly flopping on top of the overstuffed trash bag which sent him sliding across the slick bloody marble like a cannonball.

Cauzzie Rex barely had enough time to turn when he saw Gideon hurtling toward him full bore. He tried his best to reload, but there was no way to avoid getting clattered by the steamroller that was Gideon and his trash bag full of books.

Cauzzie Rex was sent flying head over heels through the air.

Thankfully, Rob and Roy had turned the corner just in time to see Rex getting bowled over and his green shaggy orange head bouncing off the marble.

"Strike!" yelled Cauzzie Rob.

Cauzzie Roy reluctantly agreed, "Strike…"

The only positive about the collision with Cauzzie Rex was that it slowed Gideon's momentum down enough to let him get back on his feet again and hopefully put some distance between himself and the next volley of hot lead from a Cauzzie 12 gauge.

He slung the overstretched trash bag over his shoulder like a mad Santa Claus looking to out run a pack of killer elves, when he realized there was only one good option for a clean getaway. Ironically enough it wasn't through the chimney, but it wasn't the front door either. Nor was it scaling up the sculpture in the entryway, the MIG jet plane sculpture that looked as though it had crashed through roof. Thanks to Cauzzie Rex blasting a lamp clear-off its stand that sent debris flying into Gideon's face, the only option seemed to be the narrow stained-glass window.

Gideon hurled himself head first through the stained glass window in true daredevil tradition. But here's the thing Gideon failed to take into consideration with his sudden emergency escape plan — when the trash bag you're carrying over your shoulders is wider than the narrow window you're flying through, you're going to encounter some resistance. So the second Gideon hurled himself through the window pane in a shower of glass and wood, the trash bag filled with the seven volumes of books got jammed in the window sill.

Gideon was sent sailing, sans trash bag. The shattering of glass sounded like the cymbal crash at the end of some drunken opus. Gideon would have to deal with the million tiny cuts later, as he found himself rolling into a boxwood, flopping to his knees on the edge of the wet lawn, and just inches from being impaled by the kudu sculpture's corkscrew horns. He had survived the jump but the books he was hoping to save never made it out of the window.

Gideon stumbled to his feet.

Cauzzie Roy and Cauzzie Rob were shouting orders to each other from inside the mega mansion and Gideon could hear the smattering of footsteps against the cold marble. He knew he had one last choice to make. He could run back to the shattered window, reach inside to try and gather the books and risk being blown away by crazed Cauzzies; or he could just take off running through the mega mansion's Japanese mediation garden and just see what other death awaited him at the hands of the executive boardroom at The Startling Concern.

Like a weaver's loom, Gideon raced between the bonsai trees and samurai-shaped topiaries just as Cauzzie Rob poked his head from the shattered window and and began to fire wildly into the garden. Clearly, all their plans to keep Gideon alive were now literally out the window.

Gideon was now in the grove running for his life. The gun blasts had momentarily stopped, but he knew they'd soon be in hot pursuit.

He had ran two hundred yards before the grove suddenly opened up onto the long cobble stone driveway, where a midnight blue 1970 Plymouth Hemi Cuda with a A727 torqueflite three-speed automatic transmission with a dual quad 426-HP Hemi V8 engine was gurgling at the ready.

The getaway driver was none other than Cauzzie Ralph who looked totally relaxed, as if he was sunning on the deck of a yacht, smoking a hand-rolled cigarette, bedecked in wrap- around iridescent sunglasses while listening to soft rock classics on the radio.

When Gideon ran up to the driver's side door, flinging it open, Ralph with his pale green features and leopard seal mouth agape was caught totally by surprise, the cigarette instantly dangling from his semi-transparent lips.

"Move over!!!" Gideon commanded.

Cauzzie Ralph was so caught off guard, he instantly slid over on the bench seat to the passenger side to make enough room for Gideon to hop in and get behind the wheel. "What, what's happening, where's Rob and Roy?!"

Rob and Roy came running into view ahead of them, shotguns drawn and ready to blast away, but seeing Gideon behind the wheel of their precious Plymouth Barracuda they instantly lowered their guns and began to yell. They weren't about to shoot holes in their prized possession.

At the same moment, Cauzzie Ralph realized what was happening and reached for the glove compartment for the .43 caliber Glock they always kept hidden inside.

Gideon grabbed the back of Ralph's head and slammed it to so hard into the dashboard that it left a dent in the soft part of the membrane of his immense forehead.

Ralph was out cold.

Before Rob and Roy could run to the car, Gideon slammed on the gas pedal and in a cloud of smoke and rubber went screaming off from 0 to 60 in record time.

As Gideon whipped past, Cauzzie Rob, in total desperation, slammed his hand on the car's hood and almost had his arm ripped off as it roared past him at top speeds.

Ducking as low as he could go to avoid any latent shotgun blasts, Gideon was relieved when none came. So he peeked out into the rear-view mirror to see if they were giving chase, but saw Rob and Roy shrinking in the distance; they knew it was no use to give chase and just stood shouting epitaphs at each other as Gideon hung a right towards the guard gate.

It was confirmed. The security guard at the gate was indeed dead.

Gideon stopped the car. He leaned over and opened the passenger side door, and with his foot shoved Cauzzie Rex out of the car and onto the driveway.

As Gideon put more and more distance between himself and the scene of the crime, and took a right on Mega Mansion Row onto Lullaby Lane, he couldn't help but wonder if he had made the right decision.

J.U.L.E.S, HELINKA, HELINKA, J.U.L.E.S

It looked like a human. It talked like a human. It walked like a human.

But the best news for all those gathered in the boardroom was that it wasn't human.

It was J.U.L.E.S., the first Synoid of his kind to ever grace the presence of other living breathing human beings. To suggest that a synthetic humanoid being like J.U.L.E.S. wasn't suffering through a bout of stage fright wouldn't be doing the Enkeling Futures and Prosperities latest invention any justice. He had taken all the deep breaths he could just to build up the nerve to step out behind the curtain and face the rows of tables with their curious corporate executives who had all come to see what they had spent a thousand fortunes developing. His synthetic brain module went down his list of notes, things like "point your toes" and "keep good eye contact." He could hear Helinka's voice making the preliminary announcements, but did his best to block out all that distraction. It was information in which the entire boardroom was well versed, and even he had helped proofread Helinka's passive verbiage on more than one occasion to make sure she was hitting all her notes. Well, now it was J.U.L.E.S.'s turn to validate all the faith Helinka had put in him. You could continue to test and re-test forever, he told her, but there comes a point you just gotta go. She agreed. And so there he was, waiting for the curtain to be pulled back so he could make his grand entrance into the annals of history.

J.U.L.E.S. gleamed, his smile infectious, and when the applause finally died down, he pointed his toe out like a ballerina ready to pirouette. He was supposed to open with a rendition of "My Way" but to Helinka's surprise went with a ballad from Captain and Tenille, "Love Will Keep Us Together."

He wasn't supposed to do that, but J.U.L.E.S. felt the moment called for something far less self-indulgent, and something far more inclusive. But when Helena looked around at all the faces smiling from ear to ear she knew J.U.L.E.S was nothing short of a smash hit.

It all began six years earlier on May 9th 2094.

They had reached consensus at the 82nd floor of the Enkeling Futures and Prosperities building. They would move forward with Geertz Geert's plan for creating a more accessible lifeforms to replace the Invasive "Cauzzie" technology through their mysterious tissue sample which had been cryogenically preserved in the conglomerate's deep freeze for the past seven years.

The board all felt strongly that Geert had uncovered the only clearcut strategy of circumventing the "Invasive Global Ownership" (IGO) laws which prohibited sole ownership of any new Cauzzie technology. What this meant was that any inventions or innovations a company created from Cauzzie tissue culture samples, which were distributed each year to select conglomerates around the world by the IGO governing committee, would be subjected to profit sharing and wealth distribution. This was to ensure no single company gained a monopoly on anything Cauzzie related in the hopes of correcting the issues that led to the Great Down Under War. It was part of the Jennings/Steadfast co-presidency and the sparks of equalitism that were fashionable back in 2051. These IGO laws made it impossible to reap the massive windfalls for your own conglomerate's work without having to share the profits with all the other groups licensed to develop the Cauzzie from the violent invasive species they were, and into safe and effective machines the world hoped they'd become.

These laws acted as both a help and a hindrance to massive conglomerates like Enkeling Futures and Prosperities. Whereas you could make good money on another conglomerate's hard work, at the same time they'd make good money off yours. This naturally kept everyone in the black as long as there were new and improved inventions hitting the market for anything from exhaust systems, heating and cooling systems, cold fusion, and the like. So as long as everyone produced their fare share of marvelous inventions, the Invasive Global Ownership laws that prevented one group from monopolizing the world's technological advances, made perfect sense. But as it is with all things worldly, some conglomerates realized they could simply let other corporations do all the heavy lifting while you could just sit back and enjoy the profit sharing windfall. They discovered there was no need invest all this capital on a technology that may or may not work, when you could just let others take on all the risks. You just had to give the appearance that you were trying.

This issue prompted the world's law makers to adopt new rules to keep conglomerates from riding the coat tails of other more successful outfits, but those regulations just presented new loopholes to be exploited by scheming firms grifting off a lucrative system.

Expanding the ever shrinking profit pool was turning out to be the number one issue for serious conglomerates like Enkeling Futures and Prosperities. The problem was any advancement in the technology couldn't be done without using the same patented technology originally created by Louden Frear and Biosurety Ventures back in 2035, which saved the world from environmental collapse. If you wanted to improve on the Cauzzie's environmentally friendly attributes, while negating their socially undesirable ones, there was no getting around the fact that you still needed the original version in order to cultivate any future improvements. This meant that the original version of the Cauzzie had a built in failsafe against its own extinction. It was an extinction everyone wanted but were unable to achieve without wrecking the planet. Which is why Ivan Foyle coined the term The Invasive Paradox back in 2081 to explain the self-perpetuating issue the world was facing; sure, you could create a new Cauzzie technology that didn't bite, couldn't think, couldn't walk or talk, or didn't watch Kung Fu movies, but the more advancements that were made to ensure a perfect environment the more you remained dependent on the original version the world despised.

So regardless of Cauzzies' love of Hawaiian shirts, their fascination with bad action movies, and the violent traits built into their DNA, thanks to the Gympie-Gympie plant, the Cauzzies knew they had leverage on the rest of humanity that was so dependent on their tissue culture disbursements. The fact remained, that without Cauzzies the world's ecosystem would collapse in less than a decade. Some predicted even a few years.

Geertz Geert liked to say, "Life on earth is still dependent on those smarmy Cauzzies even if they're hidden away under the depths of slaughterhouses and oil refineries. We need to find a way out!"

We need to find a way out was easier said than done.

This is where that mysterious tissue sample that had been cryogenically preserved in the conglomerate's deep freeze for the past seven years comes into the picture. Geert's groundbreaking proposal would kill two birds with one stone. His idea would put an end to profit sharing and put an end to the Cauzzie. Enkeling

Futures and Prosperities no longer would have to share profits with anyone else because the technology would technically be completely new, and because it did everything that a Cauzzie did, it also did away with mankind's dependance on the "green parasites" altogether.

And thus the Synoid was born.

It looked like a human. It talked like a human. It walked like a human. But it wasn't human. In fact, it looked and moved so much like a human being that nobody at the Enkeling Futures Prosperities "pre-meeting" worship service had noticed that the man in the grey flannel suit offering up the skinned rabbit as sacrifice to Vulgarus (the goddess of board rooms and office parties) was actually the prototype Synoid they had all come to see.

Helinka Vowell, the head of Research and Development for Enkeling Futures and Prosperities and the one selected to head up the Synoid project, was the one in the room who knew the man in the grey-flannel suit was J.U.L.E.S., the first-edition Synoidial life form to pass all safety and usage tests at R&D.

The moment J.U.L.E.S. finished his initial performance the room erupted in applause.

But keeping with all her Self-Effacement Clauses, which prevented any overt self satisfaction, Helinka gave all due credit to everyone else in the room besides herself. When Helinka turned to give a special thanks to Geertz Geert, who only six years earlier had proposed the ingenious concept to a packed boardroom, his own Effacement Clause forced him to insist that all due success belonged to Helinka Vowell and her team, as well as everyone else who happened to be standing around the room.

But Helinka, with her Level Six Humility Status with Credeth, insisted that it wasn't her or her team that deserved praise, but every single employee at Enkeling Futures and Prosperities, including the robotic arm that performed the janitorial duties in her labs, who truly deserved all the credit.

J.U.L.E.S. then took a bow himself, and with zero clauses to concern itself with, proceeded to entertain the room with the one-liners that Helinka's assistant had programmed into its memory banks just the previous day. "What do you call someone from Bombay who loves noodles?" J.U.L.E.S. readied his punchline, "Top brahman!" It was a play on words and the room got a huge kick out of it.

Helinka's plan to wow the executives by putting J.U.L.E.S. through the paces was off to a smashing start. She had captivated them with the initial reveal, then got them laughing with the one-liners, then had them clapping in unison through the retro dance moves, and had them amazed by the myriad of possible upgrades, like the programmable accents that ranged from English butler to Katherine Hepburn, and language options in Spanish, French, Latin, and even an extinct pygmy dialect.

J.U.L.E.S was a sensation.

So as she moved into the next stage of her presentation, Helinka thought back on all the long and excruciating hours her and her team had spent just getting to this one heroic moment. And the real credit was of course due to that one single cryogenically preserved tissue sample locked away and forgotten in the corporation's vaults.

Despite all the secrecy, Helinka knew a lot about "Joey."

Legend around the lab had it that Joey was an infernal mix between the Cauzzie high priest Marsupius and the face of Reno Wren, the last King of Australia, A.K.A. the Surf Lord, that was sewn onto the body of a baby kangaroo. Joey was rumored to have been found sucking marrow out from the remains of a decapitated Cauzzie after the massive explosion that destroyed the entire Walkabout Front. After shooting the abhorrent vivisected monster to bits, someone had the foresight to seal up a sample and stash it away for safe keeping as a war souvenir. Whoever this person was, they anonymously sold it a few years later to an undisclosed German lab for 300 Deutschmarks and a gift card to the kebap eatery Blud Döner. The German lab in turn brokered a deal with its parent company, Enkeling Futures and Prosperities, where it had been sitting in the cryogenic freezer until that day on May 9th 2094 when they green lit Geertz Geert's groundbreaking proposal.

But ultimately the profane origins of the source material mattered less to the actors involved than the end results which they had hoped to achieve. And their hope was to create a creature that behaved and appeared fully human, but had all the environmental benefits one could achieve with the Invasive.

The plan on paper at least, was simple.

Manipulate the DNA in the Joey sample to keep all the desired Invasive characteristics of the Cauzzie, like asexual reproduction, their hyper methane respiration, their carbon dioxide conversion abilities, while eliminating their propensity for violence and their unattractive alien-like appearance. The Joey sample would also allow for technicians to amplify the human genetics to make the creature completely human in appearance and demeanor. And in the process, the technicians would "complex" the DNA sequences to disguise all links to the Cauzzies and kangaroos, thus circumventing the Invasive Global Ownership laws once and for all.

The plan in reality though, was rather foreboding.

P.A.L. was the first Synoid prototype developed by Helinka and her team.

It had human skin, which was a plus. But everything else was a grotesque mutation that caused it to look like a part Cauzzie, part stegosaur with humanoid arms and legs. The reason that the lab had installed a robotic arm as janitor was because the human janitor made the mistake of taking Windex to the glass enclosure that housed P.A.L., allowing the beast to tear through the glass in an effort to eat the janitor. P.A.L.'s instinct to consume humans was the one trait they wanted to lose if they had any hope of replacing the Cauzzie at all. P.A.L. unfortunately had no ability to eat, being it had no teeth, so it ended up just tearing the janitor to shreds then sleeping in the remains until security was alerted and Helinka was able to contain the situation.

P.A.L was kept in the underground holding cells to await further testing, because Helinka insisted that none of the prototypes should be destroyed under any circumstance, in case they were needed later for future reference.

M.A.A.L. was the next Synoid prototype to fall short of expectations. Although not initially. This time the results were almost the reverse of P.A.L., with the prototype almost completely human in shape, but keeping all of the Cauzzie's external coloring and semi-translucent skin. There was a new attribute that caused the eyes to look black and lifeless. Like shark eyes. The eyes made it appear even more frightening than your normal everyday Cauzzie. This didn't stop the tests from proceeding though, as Helinka and team were convinced perfecting the appearance was secondary to perfecting the prototype's performance. M.A.A.L happened to be completely mute, but displayed above average intelligence which was surprising. During a holiday weekend and being left unattended, M.A.A.L displayed this intelligence by picking the lock to its holding cell. It was found the next day hanging upside down like a bat in the control room where it emitted a high-pitched shriek that blew out one of the technician's ear drums. After isolating all the positive genes, it too was stored away in the underground holding cells.

After several failed attempts, they were finally able to produce their third prototype C.R.B.L. which did nothing to improve Helinka's spirits. C.R.B.L. grew three times the size of a normal man, and over time began to develop strange appendages that would almost look as though they were about to form claw-like hands but would never fully form into anything other than rubbery globulars. It had freaky red eyes and razor sharp teeth and overly aggressive behavior. An in-house wild game hunter had to be called in to tranquilize the creature with a series of darts that would relax the prototype just long enough for them to perform tests. Disaster struck when a technician from Finland, who had only been hired the week before, had not understood the warnings to leave the chamber. C.R.B.L. pounced on the technician, and not letting go, it secreted an acid like substance from its glands that burned her skin severely. She later died at a private emergency unit. Despite the set back, C.R.B.L. had many positive attributes to build on, like methane respiration that was on par if not an improvement on the performance of your average Cauzzie.

The team dubbed 2096 as the "Year of Darkness."

It was a year that saw the lab produce 23 different prototypes, each worse than the last, with menacing mutations and deformities which almost forced the executives to scrap the entire project altogether. It started with the prototype A.L.K.K. who's green and blotchy form decayed from the inside out. Generating cadaver worms from within its organs, they would consume its body all day, only for the flesh to regenerate overnight, and then the process would repeat again the next morning.

Then there was the horror of the O.L.B.L. prototype that had wings and an exoskeleton that reminded everyone of a giant elephant man. It tried to kill Helinka several times and was eventually shot dead with a harpoon gun after squirting streams of blood from its eyes.

The horrors continued with G.F.X. and R.G.F.X. who were just more violent versions of Cauzzies but with walnut-sized brains. There were some positive signs like V.R.A.X. who was able to speak, hold conversations, and was able to catch a ball in mid air, but its organs kept expanding until they eventually burst all over the lab technicians.

Things went from bad to worse with M.A.A.R. who appeared to be a red demonic creature who literally spoke backwards and could eat through glass, forcing the evacuation of the labs on numerous occasions so that it could be contained. It did look partly human though.

Nobody ever mentioned prototype S.M.L.E. after the day it's Siamese quadruplet body emerged from the incubator gushing blood from all sorts of ventricles that pulsated from its leathery green spotted skin. Helinka made the final decision not to destroy S.M.L.E anticipating its mutations as something the military might be able to use in the distant future.

The only positive that year was the invention of "kill words." These were phrases that when spoken would instantly shut down the Synoid, throwing it into a deep sleep. One of the technicians got the idea from a friend who trained attack dogs and used them with his doberman pinchers. After experiencing so many Synoid attacks the team wondered if they could have kill commands but in reverse, almost like "safe" words. So if and when a Synoid project went on the attack, they could simply shout the kill word, and the prototype would instantly shut down, thus avoiding any permanent damage to people or property.

They successfully programmed the prototype K.K.L.R. with the kill word "Brazil" which came in handy the day K.K.L.R. shot out its chameleon like tongue and wrapped it around Helinka's neck and began to strangle her. After a technician shouted "Brazil" the prototype immediately shut down, almost slumping into a heap and its giant tongue releasing its grip on Helinka.

Years later, Gideon found the list of kill words under Helinka's pillow. Words like "Jellyroll," "Candy Cane," "Suplex," "Dogwood," next to the various acronyms belonging to the prototypes. He thought nothing of it at the time.

Finally, they hit what the executives at Enkeling Futures and Prosperities declared as "pay dirt" in the winter of 2097 with Y.Y.P.E.S. All the proportions were in line. Standing at five foot eight inches with decent symmetry, smooth skin texture, and for the first time had straight human-like hair. It looked like an elongated version of Reno Wren, but with a strange blue iridescent coloring. It was missing fingernails and teeth, and was almost fully blind, but It communicated by tapping its finger against the glass and was eventually taught morse code. Even though it wasn't exactly what you'd consider marketable, Y.Y.P.E.S. was the closest Helinka and her team had come to producing a workable Synoid.

Thus Stage 4 testing began in the summer of 2097.

Hopes were soon dashed with the prototype B.L.E.K.S.. The calculations indicated that the technicians had ironed out all the issues with Y.Y.P.E.S, and were excited about its square jaw and masculine features. The skin was almost perfect, although a bit pale. Its eyes a sparkling blue. They had worked out the fingernails and missing teeth, which were so surprisingly straight, one of the techs isolated the gene for future testing in case the conglomerate wanted to expand into dental implants. B.L.E.K.S. looked and moved just like they had expected a Synoid would. Fully human-like. But the problem was its homicidal thought process. During audio and visual testing, B.L.E.K.S. would begin explaining in great detail how it was going to dismember Helinka and use her skin as a lamp shade. At first they were intrigued, but then they became concerned when it tried to tear a chunk out of her arm. She was forced to yell its kill word, "Bottleneck."

And the kill word worked like a charm.

But now they finally had J.U.L.E.S.

J.U.L.E.S. passed all the trials with flying colors. And during intelligence testing scored off the charts with recognition, problem solving, and memory retention. It also had glorious hair. So glorious that some of the technicians gave J.U.L.E.S. the nickname of Sassoon 2, after the god of hairstylists and personal care. Some had even joked that J.U.L.E.S. was too good looking, and suggested that it might break up marriages. But Helinka reminded them that it was asexual.

Despite this fact, Helinka took notes of all the off-handed comments and recorded them in her logs. Maybe they had made

J.U.L.E.S. too good looking, too perfect. That could always be adjusted. There might be a face that was less intimidating to men, and less tempting to women. The last thing she needed was to create a product that would put everyone's morality clauses in jeopardy. It might be a good consideration to tone his visual appeal back a few notches. She thought about Gideon's face. It wasn't handsome nor was it ugly. She filed this in the back of her mind.

Everyone was applauding the performance by J.U.L.E.S. Especially impressed was Geertz Geert who on numerous occasions during the presentation stood up and pumped his fist. He was so happy he completely disregarded his "Excessive Glee" clauses in his Credeth account.

In the midst of J.U.L.E.S. preparing a French omelet in the middle of the domestic demonstrations, Geert joked offhandedly, "Does he give massages?" It had been a long train ride and he jokingly reached for his neck as if it needed a good rub down.

Helinka couldn't believe her ears. J.U.L.E.S. had certifiable masseuse capabilities. She had anticipated the Synoid's application in fields like physical therapy, convalescent homes, and exercise training, so when Geert made his off handed joke, she was more than thrilled.

"Jules, can you give Mr. Geert a neck rub?"

"Why certainly!" the enthusiastic J.U.L.E.S. exclaimed as he skipped joyfully over to Geert and began gently massaging the kinks out of his neck.

"Whoa…oh, yeah…" Geert moaned, "This is better than any human…oh, that's the spot, right there…oh yeah…"

Helinka watched Geert's expression as J.U.L.E.S. with its mastery of muscles and kinesiology began hitting all Geert's strained muscles and skillfully setting his body back in alignment. Geert started to shed all his tension and his expression turned to one of total bliss.

Helinka glanced at the executives who were looking on in sheer amazement.

She knew, in this one impromptu moment, she had sealed the deal.

Sure, there would have to be adjustments made, they would have to smooth out some rough spots, but regardless of all those particulars, she knew, at that precise moment that she had done it. J.U.L.E.S was a smash hit.

Geert's face winced. J.U.L.E.S. had struck a nerve in his Geert's neck.

"Oooh, a little too strong there," he said with a nervous laugh.

Helinka saw that J.U.L.E.S. was now going through Rolfing techniques that were a little more vigorous than just an everyday massage.

"Okay Jules, I think he's good."

But J.U.L.E.S. didn't think so. He continued to rub even harder, adding, "He has a knot. It just needs a minute, I got this."

Geert winced again, now clearly in pain but not wanting to embarrass anyone. So he bit his tongue.

Helinka saw the room growing gravely concerned.

She didn't want to use the kill word. Not now, not when things were going so well.

Then Geert began to scream while trying to pry himself loose from its grip.

And before Helinka could shout the kill word, "Armageddon," the unthinkable happened — J.U.L.E.S. ripped Geert's head off his neck and hurled it across the room, then it took hold of the headless shoulders and buried its face into the hole and began to suck all the blood into its mouth. As the fountain of blood poured from the gaping wound, everyone began screaming and running for the exits.

J.U.L.E.S. was sucking so hard that it inhaled Geert's

esophagus out of its neck.

    Helinka began to scream herself.

    "Armageddon!"

    "Armageddon!"

    "Armageddon!"

WHAT CAN I DO ABOUT IT?

"Well, what can I do about it?"

Cloreen turned away from Gideon and began pounding on the glass partition separating their front-row executive-box seats from the battle arena's live-action blood sport, screaming, "Kill them all" at the top of her lungs.

Gideon was having a hard to hearing her over the cheering crowd, the bellowing trumpets, and thundering drums. He was about to ask her to repeat herself when a balding middle-aged business man running for his life inside the arena was caught from behind and smushed face-first into the glass partition by a gladiator wearing a sequined barbarian leotard.

"Finish him!"

Cloreen frothed as the gladiator began repeatedly knocking the defenseless business man in the head with a spiked mace. Blood and brains poured out onto the glass.

Gideon practically lost his lunch.

Cloreen, meanwhile, just wanted more, peeking through the gaps in the streaks of red left behind by the dead businessman, hoping to see the barbarian gladiator in the act of hacking the arm off an Asian milk man. She cheered as the severed prize was thrown into the crowd. Some lucky fan was taking home a souvenir.

During halftime, Cloreen tried her best to listen to all of Gideon's concerns.

She tried not to chew so loud as Gideon went on and on about how the home invasion by Cauzzie Rob and Cauzzie Roy was totally unforeseeable and thus qualified as force majeure. She tried to listen between sips of fermented bean punch how Gideon's big trip to the Vacatican was in jeopardy. She feinted concern when Gideon mentioned that he barely got out of the mega mansion alive. She tried not to nod off when Gideon explained how The Startling Concern should take all this into consideration considering how loyal he has been over the past twenty years, not to mention how many times he'd delivered the goods with absolutely zero problems, and with glowing reviews from the executives, and the grey men with the pointy hats, and that they should still pay him what he was owed.

"Well I am with you, Gideon, but what can I do about it?"

She slathered another heaping pile of clotted cream on a fugu crisp, swallowing it whole. A dollop landing on her white ermine jumpsuit.

Gideon didn't know which was worse, the balding businessman's brains crusting up on the glass, or the sight of Cloreen eating exotic snacks while pretending to listen to what he was saying.

"Can't you at least talk with them?"

"We need the last five books, Gideon. The job was for all seven books. Look, I'll try and talk with them and explain what happened, but it won't do any good, we need those other books. You're gonna have to use the car you took as leverage."

A buzzer sounded. An announcer's voice erupted over the super sonic speaker system. "Ladies and Gentlemen, it's Round 67!"

The crowd went nuts just as they had for Round 66, Round 65, Round 64 and the like.

Appearing under a flurry of lights, three bulky gladiators protected by metallic body suits entered the arena carrying in their arms regulation size fire hoses.

"GET READY! MERRRRRRRLETOWN!"

Cloreen cut Gideon off mid-sentence — whatever he was saying could wait.

Three elderly ladies were thrown into the middle of the arena. They huddled together disoriented, obviously in tears, and under the glare of a white-hot spot light.

The drums started beating a tribal like cadence. Something you'd hear on a Viking ship heading to Nova Scotia. The gladiators slowly began moving in for the kill, pointing their hoses directly at the three elderly ladies.

Blistering music began to play as the announcer stoked the ravenous crowd, "WHAAAAAT HAPPENS TO THE GODLESSSSSSSSSS!?"

Then the chanting began, "Liquidate! Liquidate! Liquidate! Liquidate!"

Cloreen was up chanting while pounding on the glass. "Liquidate! Liquidate!"

Over the deafening roar, one of the elderly ladies who was about to die tried to shout, "We are not godless, there is only one true Go-aaaaaaaaagh…"

Interrupting her was the high pressure streams of sulfuric acid erupting from the three hoses, soaking them in the corrosive liquid, and melting them like Jello to a flame.

Amid groves of every fruit bearing tree, the slaughterhouse stood out like a putrefying lesion blighting the otherwise perfect pastoral setting.

Smoke billowed from towering smokestacks, tall chainlink fences zig-zagged around the perimeter, topped with rows of tangled razor wire. Encircling the compound were countless rusted out shipping containers where cow bones and rotting hides spilled out into the milky green puddles collecting in the muddy ruts. A few skinny head of cattle chewed the grass growing on the other side of the fencing, while a few hogs lingered by the Econoline van up on blocks with bullet holes in the mirror.

The name of this place was Invasive Designate R.

Or what the Cauzzies themselves referred to as Lee Land #3.

It was one of a hundred private reservations across America where small clans of former Cauzzie oligarchs were allowed to exist completely undisturbed by mankind. According to the Good Treaty drawn up in the Merle Jennings Jr. / Meredith Steadfast administration fifty years ago, no human was allowed to enter Invasive Designate R without express written consent by the Cauzzie landlords. Humans were only allowed to enter during official bi-annual state inspections or for the purpose of buying low cost meat by-products. But nobody really came around. You could get lard cheaper at the grocery store.

Mostly everyone thought life was best lived by ignoring the aberration in their midsts as if it wasn't there. So the Cauzzies became an after-thought at best.

What this meant for the Cauzzies was that they were left pretty much to their own devices. Alone in their carbon dioxide fueled fiefdoms they spent their time playing cards, watching TV, drinking beer, practicing martial arts, and sucking in as much methane from exhaust pipes as their green hearts desired.

All this changed of course when Smith Smith's neighbors notified The Unwanted Patrols after catching sight of the four Cauzzies scaling the mansion walls while carrying a weighted down black trash bag and mysterious sticks (shotguns) through the cobblestone streets.

This set off alarms as Cauzzies were top of the list of what the patrol considered "unwanted," but things only got more interesting when the city's Convenience and Enforcement

Branch showed up to hand out violations to Smith Smith because he had left his lights on after regulation hours, only to discover Smith Smith murdered along with two unidentified pest control technicians.

Confusion ensued as the Enforcement Agents were unable to agree which violation Smith Smith had committed since they hadn't seen anything like a murder scene before. At first, they scoured the home owners manual identifying code G-3220 as a possibility, as it looked to be a desecration of property. Another focused in on code TT-4 that specified you couldn't leave elderly dead bodies unattended for extended periods of time. The fact that TT-4 didn't specify what that extended period of time was, and the fact they had no idea how long the bodies had been dead, forced them to turn their attention to the "Interacting Society Index 8." The only thing the Enforcement Agents could remotely agree upon was this looked like a violation of the ordinance against at home gladiator simulations. But this didn't seem to any one of them to be a simulation. One Agent arguing that a simulation wouldn't result in actual death. But another Agent argued that the reason why gladiator simulations were such a concern was that the arena was the only place where Morality Clauses were lifted so that the spectator could let loose and enjoy the battles. The condition of the bodies weren't relevant. Therefore they determined what they were looking at was a direct violation of multiple Morality Clauses and that Smith Smith was going to have to be arrested and brought to their financial institution for Conduct Audits. Then another Agent reminded them that Smith Smith was dead thus taking them in for Conduct Audits was pointless. Then someone reminded someone that they had no idea who the other two people dressed in fumigation jumpsuits were, and therefore they needed to call in the Disposal Units and let them figure it out.

When the elderly Commandant of Disposal Unit Foxhound showed up, he explained to the Enforcement Agents that what they were looking at was a triple murder. Having been a police man during the Jennings Jr. Era he had worked on numerous cases where a person lost control of their emotions and killed another person in rage. In this case, it looked like whomever lost control of their emotions had access to shotguns.

The Commandant slowly traced the movements of the infiltrators, showing the Enforcement Agents how this had all the markings of an old fashion robbery gone bad. The Commandant explained how he knew that it must be a robbery gone bad. They asked him how he knew all this kind of information, but he had no idea.

This revelation stunned the Enforcement Agents who realized that they were dealing with was an authentic "old fashioned" triple homicide. The excitement mounted as they viewed the scenes with fresh eyes, taking in all the details: the holes in the chests, the gaping wounds in the back of the necks, the shattered glass, the open safe.

The Commandant corrected the Enforcement Agent who was speculating that the invaders must have come in through the window by showing them how the glass was broken outward not inward, which indicated someone jumped out the window instead of in. Then the Commandant showed them the footprints around the boxwood that led to the grove of trees.

After posing for a group photo, the Disposal Unit Foxhound loaded up the bodies and placed them into the refrigerated vans and drove them straight to the offices of Sleuth House, a private investigating firm who helped municipalities track down anything from lost dogs to missing keys.

When lead investigator Umber Ober pulled back the black tarp from Smith's body and saw the gaping hole in the back of his neck, instantly blurted out an expletive, "Holy Cra…" only to stop himself at the final second. Despite knowing he had just violated his "Proper and Appropriate Communication" decree in his FlotsuMark Financial account, he wasn't too concerned. He would be more than happy to have his account deducted. It was well worth it just seeing an actually actual murder victim again, let alone three of them.

Umber Ober picked over his memory, trying to recall everything he was paid so handsomely to forget, when appearing from out of the ether of his imagination materialized the basics of police procedure manual he read as a teenager. Filled with introductory information like the collection of evidence, filing reports, assigning investigations, canvassing witnesses, and the like. Armed with his recall, the first call he made was to the Unwanted Patrol responsible for supervising Smith Smith's neighborhood to see if they had witnessed any suspicious behavior in the neighborhood that day. A document arrived on his desk the following day detailing how three Cauzzies had been seen scaling the wall of Smith Smith's house.

The local Public Orders and Restraints Department took the matter so serious that it called in Armed Militia reinforcements. It knew full well that armed Cauzzie bandits murdering prestigious citizens and stealing their valuables was the last thing the world wanted to hear. Although those on the lower levels of law enforcement, like the neighborhood Unwanted Patrols, the Convenience and Enforcement Branch, Disposal Unit Foxhound, to Sleuth House, failed to see the big picture, Public Orders and Restraints saw it all too well.

So when Public Orders and Restraints arrived at the chainlink gates of the Cauzzie reservation at Lee Land #3 they appeared as though they were about to invade Normandy.

Watching their arrival through grimy CCTV monitors, Cauzzie Rob and Cauzzie Roy failed to break a sweat. In fact, they had all placed wagers, guessing when law enforcement would finally show up at their front gate demanding answers. Cauzzie Roger had come the closest being within four hours of his prediction.

As the Public Orders and Restraints Commandos pounded on the door, Cauzzie Roger was busy collecting his winnings.

Buzzing them in, the Commandos and Armed Militia quickly pushed aside the draping Australian flags that hung from the ceiling with their ubiquitous black bars that served as constant reminder there was a time in history when the Cauzzies ruled a continent.

Forced to march single file through the narrow dark corridors decorated with the seemingly omnipresent pose of a battle scared Bruce Lee and, of course, Scarface posters, the Commandos and Armed Militia descended the industrial metal staircases leading into the depths of the Cauzzie infrastructure.

The deeper they descended the more claustrophobic and suffocating it became. Forgetting to bring their gas masks, the Commandos began to cough and choke through their sleeves as the putrid clouds of smoke hovered thick through the tunnels, making it next to impossible to see anything. The Cauzzies had anticipated this which is why they turned up the gas.

Inching their way deeper into the slaughterhouse complex, they came across the Cauzzies' "Methane Dairy." It looked for all intents and purposes like a dairy, with stalls and milking machines, but instead of being hooked to the udders of cows, the Cauzzies were milking the tale piles of old guzzling Fords, Pontiacs, Chryslers, and Oldsmobiles. Over the cacophony of V8 engines humming away, the Commandos paused in curiosity to see the tubes sucking up the exhaust and pumping it into a main holding tank, which then connected to a industrial A/C unit, and finally distributed the gas throughout the Cauzzie stronghold.

After passing by a badly rendered mural of Al Pacino the Commandos entered into the slaughterhouse floor. They moved in practically gasping for breath, because as far as their eyes could see were thousands of head of cattle standing around aimlessly under the artificial lights that hung from dark rafters. Huge fans were blowing the cattle's methane emissions into the ducts while carcasses hung on hooks aging in the fetid humid air.

All the while the Cauzzies watched and waited from the comforts of their climate-controlled recreation room. Watching law enforcement officials taking the long and treacherous way in was endless entertainment; knowing that if they had just made a hard left when they entered they would have been able to simply descend three floors and would have arrived to their hangout pad in style. Cauzzie Rob cracked open another beer and proposed other wagers without many takers.

Finally getting past the slaughterhouse floor, only a handful of the Commandos and Armed Militia Men were able to cross these immense storage tanks filled with green swampy water that fermented such a noxious smell that most of the men began passing out before they were able to traverse the pipes that ran along the tops of the pools. After the third rescue from the putrid water tanks, they knew the only way across was to send the most ablest men.

When the select handful of Commandos and Armed Militia came stumbling into the Cauzzies' recreation room, they were greeted with a table overflowing with large cuts of seared beef that floated in a pool of pink juices. Buckets with iced beer were positioned every five feet. The Cauzzies were all sitting back in leather sofas playing video games and watching Scarface on video. A giant crucifix made from 2x4's was nailed to the wall.

"We knew you were coming so we baked a cake!" said Cauzzie Rob pointed to a melting ice cream cake they had clearly picked up from the store. "Feel free to grab some snacks!"

"We don't want no snacks!" one of the Commandos snorted as they kicked over one of the tables, sending meat flying.

Cauzzie Roy snatched a porterhouse from mid-air and pointed to the big screen TV, "We got Scarface director's cut. Unabridged, mate. None of that edited garbage you watch. But yous can't watch it, cause it's banned! But not here, mate. It's the real thing, all two hours worth. Sit. Watch."

"Put your hands in the air! You are under arrest for the violation of the Good Treaty, Article 464. Stand up, you're coming with us."

Cauzzie Rob stood up with all the pomp of a fighting cock, "Is that so, mate?"

"That's right. Hands on your head!" the Commando erupted, shoving the snout of the stun blaster in his face.

"Easy, mate, easy. Okay, yeah. We'll just see about that."

Back at the Public Orders and Restraints Department, the true horror of what they were facing soon became clear to every human being in the room. It was all becoming perfectly clear why the Cauzzies of Lee Land #3 were so blatantly unafraid.

"You're not the only one's with legal advice, scholar! Read 'em and weep," Cauzzie Rob bragged in his deep Australian accent.

Across the table a team of lawyers and department officials scoured the Good Treaty Article 747. The four Cauzzies, Rob, Roy, Ralph, and Rex, sat back in their chairs confidently waiting for the realization to hit the lawyers and the department officials that the Cauzzies were fully within their rights to break and enter and kill everyone on sight.

"You know, we're well within our rights don't ya, mate?" said Cauzzie Rob lighting up a cigarette and puffing huge smoke rings over the lawyers heads.

The lawyers were baffled at how they could have missed the details buried within Article 747. But there it was. Right in front of their eyes. Article 747. They reviewed the document several times before ordering another copy from their own archives to make sure it wasn't some sort of joke, or forged version of the agreement. But to their utter shock and amazement their copy was exactly the same. Article 747 did indeed exist. And it soon became apparent to all of them that Article 747 wasn't some legal loophole exploited by slime balls. Nor was it some simple matter of opinion which could be argued this way or that in a court of law. No. This was iron clad. And it made it perfectly clear that the four Cauzzies were in fact well within their rights.

"We're all diplomats see. Just like it says right there!" said Cauzzie Rob thrusting the document with his finger, adding, "Strict accordance says we are not only well within our rights, but it's yous who are officially in violation, mate, for illegal entry to an Invasive Designate. That be Lee Land number three. Now, we ain't gonna press any charges against yous for violating our in-alien rights, that would go against our good natures like. But you do owe all of us all an apology."

Cauzzie Rob waited.

The lawyer cleared his throat, but was unable to bring himself to utter those two simple words.

Mockingly, Cauzzie Rob put his hand to his ear, "Sorry mate, I can't hear yous. Can yous speak a little louder please. For all our sakes. We are just Invasives, you know. Simple folk. Not fancy dancers like you all."

As the lawyer took a sip of water, a cold shiver coursed down his spine.

"I didn't catch that? What?" Cauzzie Rob leaned in. His hand still pressed to his ear.

"We're...we're sorry."

"That didn't hurt so bad, did it?" replied Cauzzie Rob getting to his feet and waited for Roy, Ralph, and Rex to do the same before adding, "Which one of you is giving us a lift back home? We got some studying to do. Those books we stole, pardon me, liberated, hold lots of secrets. We eager to learn all the laws. Just like we did with that contract there. So who's giving us a lift, eh?"

One of the Commandos volunteered to drive them back to Invasive Designate R in his truck since his shift was just about to end.

Cauzzie Rob wasn't about to leave without getting off another parting blow, "Extraterritoriality. That means total immunity folks. Got it?"

The lawyers, trying to avoid eye contact, lowered their heads as they nodded, confirming that, according to the Good Treaty, they would be following the contract to the letter.

"Oi. That's good now. Just remember, extraterritoriality, see. Total immunity. And we ain't done. Our ministers and attaches are just getting started, right. We got lots of international affairs that need our attention, you know what I mean!?"

After the Cauzzies left the room a flurry of phone calls quickly ensued.

In their tangerine-colored "Sun Disk" headgear that matched their over-sized tangerine robes, the panel of six monks staring down at her reminded Helinka of a row of unblinking pomegranates.

She wanted to squirm watching them lean in on their strange ergonomic kneeling chairs, but dared not move from her forced relaxed pose. Arms folded across her lap, her legs crossed at the ankles.

The Quorum Coordinator stood off at the copying machine printing out reports leaving her to fend off the penetrating gazes of the monks solely on her own. This was harder than it seemed despite all her preparations and the fact she knew this was coming. During the programming of J.U.L.E.S., Helinka had worked diligently to ensure the Synoid's eye contact was natural and relaxed. And she tried to put into practice everything she had put into her Synoid. According to her team's research, early eye contact was key to establishing a healthy non-verbal communication with around 65% eye contact during normal conversations. This enabled J.U.L.E.S. to seem as though he was a generous listener. On the flip side, it also allowed for J.U.L.E.S. to build stronger connections between himself and the listener when it was his turn to speak.

She programmed J.U.L.E.S. initial eye contact to last at least four seconds. This would establish that he was secure, confident, as well as perfectly attentive. After the four seconds the Synoid's eyes were programmed to look away for a moment, either a glance downward, or off to the right or the left. This would reinforce the natural easy-going nature of the Synoid and bring about a certain levity and lightness of mind. Any more than four seconds would then cause the listener to begin to feel as though they were being interrogated.

The monks unblinking eyes had been fixed on her for a good three and a half minutes.

Helinka had once again abandoned her four second rule and just stared down at her shoes waiting for the Quorum Coordinator to return to the audit.

Helinka was wearing the new Gusser Von Brackish suede pumps. She hadn't noticed until just then that they were in fact the color tangerine. This gave her a bit of a start. She wondered if she picked this pair subconsciously knowing that she would be sitting before the financial inquisition or if it was just a mere coincidence. Finding no refuge in her soles, she looked back up to see one of the female monks staring at her so intently that it looked like a drop of blood was leaking from the corner of her eye.

"Okay! Sorry for the delay," the Quorum Coordinator plopped herself in a rolling office chair and pulled herself up beside Helinka.

"No trouble at all. I mean, it's perfectly fine."

The Quorum Coordinator bit the end of her pen, scanning over the documents in her hand. "So...you had a busy week we see. Lots of activity. Lots of activity."

Helinka shifted her body, reminding herself to keep her head up.

"We'd like to know more about this dinner you had on the 18th."

Helinka remembered the dinner, but tried to scour her memory to figure out what violations she might have committed. Had she used her salad fork to eat her entree? Did she not sit at the end of the table despite being the host, and thus show something less than the ultimate humility? No. She had used all the proper utensils in the proper way and had in fact sat at the end of the table allowing for the robotic janitorial arm to sit at the head of the table. Struggling to find what it may have been, she simply replied, "Yes."

"You picked up the check."

Yes, she had picked up the check for the entire staff at Levalloisian the middle-Paleolithic tapas restaurant on Main.

The Quorum Coordinator reviewed her stack of papers, and in the most calm and patient tone, gently asked, "Did that make you feel good?"

Helinka wondered if it had. The only thing that came to mind was how her technicians had almost ordered the cold gal bisque. She had encouraged them to order the collard peccary fritters which were a little more substantial than the cold gal bisque.

"So you thought that they were somehow missing out on the experience?"

Well it wasn't like that really, they were celebrating the fact that J.U.L.E.S. had completed all ten of the trails making him eligible for presentation to the executive board. Plus, they all had worked so hard. So she wanted to make sure everyone had gotten the most out of the experience.

"So you didn't think what they ordered lived up to their contribution to the team?"

Not really. That was a strange way to put things, Helinka thought. She just didn't want them not ordering something on the menu that they might have wanted because of budgetary concerns.

"I see. You decided their restraint was a detriment to your

expectations."

This was a bit shocking to hear. Helinka eyes fluttered. No. No. She just wanted them to enjoy themselves, and after all, they were celebrating, and it was her invite so she just wanted to be generous. She was looking to be a team leader and show her appreciation for all their hard work, and this money was from the Conglomerates expense account so any considerations they might have had with their personal budget shouldn't have been a consideration if it was being paid for by the company.

"I see. You created from your own imagination a situation where you obligated co-workers to publicly reinforce your rank and status by compelling them to eat food that you thought better reflected your superiority. And it was all done on the company expense account."

"What? No!" Helinka protested. "I just wanted everyone to have a good time."

She thought she saw one of the monks finally blink.

"And the chef? You brought him out and thanked him and introduced him to the staff. Is this not true?"

Well yes, she knew Chef Mykill from his time at Stolon.

"You paraded him around without any regard to his dignity?"

Everyone gave him a rousing ovation, they complimented his presentation, his temperature control, his ingenuity. She thought it would be a fun idea, to cap off a fabulous evening.

The Quorum Coordinator gave a sympathetic tilt of the head.

The monk with a bloody trail down her cheek began to emit high-pitched shrills that were so ear-piercing that they almost bordered on the inaudible. The sound of dogs howling in the distance could be heard through the paper thin walls. The Quorum Coordinator leaned back as if to try and make out precisely what this shrill meant. Then slowly chewing on the bizarre communication she turned back to Helinka.

"We find you guilty of indulging yourself."

Helinka knew what this meant. It wasn't good news. "I ask the Quorum to take into consideration the fact everyone walked away with great memories, everyone. I think, I confess, I selfishly thought the cold gal bisque wasn't worthy of the occasion and maybe somewhere deep down, maybe I somehow thought that ordering the gal was somehow unworthy of the celebration, but in no way was I suggesting that gal wasn't worthy of me. I am totally unworthy of gal, matter of fact, gal is great, gal is good; it's just I thought they wanted some better food. But lots of foods are better than me, I mean, I'm lower than gal. But gal is fine for any occasion, I am, I am just, forgive me, please Quorum, if I somehow behaved in a way that put all eyes on me in any way, I ask that you forgo punishment, at least this week at least. I have a few things I needed to pay for…Please look, look, you'll see I've been in compliance, all week, totally compliance."

"I don't think you have been total compliance" the Quorum Coordinator tilted her head again.

"Me? When?"

A quick scan of page 14. "A filterless Sir Walter 100 menthol. Executive washroom stall number 3." More scanning of page 15. "Looks like you even considered disabling the fire alarm. This is all deeply troubling behavior."

Helinka leaned forward as if to speak. Then stopped. Then she parted her lips, thinking she might have the perfect response. But she didn't. Then exhaling she slumped in her chair. "I had a stressful day. My boss's head got ripped off his neck and thrown across the room by my invention…"

If she could cry should we have cried. But she couldn't cry. Not there. Her tears were clear, not red.

Helinka placed the pair of tangerine Gusser Von Brackish pumps on the top shelf of the locker and slowly undressed. The lower levels of the Temple was bordering on freezing so she hurried to wrap herself with the white robes to keep off the chill.

She found herself marching in line with the about thirty

other Credeth account holders, who too had found themselves in violation of morality codes. They headed straight toward the purification baths too immerse themselves into the icy pools of crystal clear water that would remove the stench of uncleanliness.

She could feel her bones rattling as she stepped out of the baths where she was handed a mochaccino by a Temple attendant.

Helinka bowed down to the carved statue of Azzurath and placed a lit candle in its mouth. Bowing again she began to recite her assigned chants.

"I bow to the marmoset-faced diety, may all beings be happy and free and may the thoughts and words and actions of my own life be an offering to the happiness and the freedom for all beings, I bow to the marmoset-faced diety, may all beings be happy and free and may the thoughts and words and actions of my own life be an offering to the happiness and the freedom for all beings, I bow to the marmoset-faced diety, may all beings be happy and free and may the thoughts and words and actions of my own life be an offering to the happiness and the freedom for all beings, I bow to the marmoset-faced diety…"

She followed the line as they passed through narrow path buffered on each side by huge stone walls with burning torches showing the way towards the Sola Versera Events Center and Auditorium.

Sitting in the fourth row, Helinka tried her best to appear completely attentive to every word out of the mouth of the Temple Priestess who paced the stage clutching a wireless microphone, going through the latest chapter of Zypsosiss, Lessons on Building a Better Us.

"Feeling needed, makes us need to be in control. Protected. Quietly sizing up matters. The energy you impart feels like a hidden pact between mankind that screams no matter how much these indignities dim our spirits we will never show it. It is our code. A code we choose to live by. A bond that keeps us going. When I was young, I knew we knew we were different. There was differentnessness. And I knew we worried about things other families in their homes and in their faiths didn't worry about. And that we were always watchful of looking at those distances and elevations full of differentnessness. But even if we say those differentnessnesses aren't there, that didn't change the fact that they were. We get up, dust ourselves off, and keep moving. You may ask yourself, is this a form of denial? It stands to reason that many of us fall when nobody is looking. I realize now that our differentnessness gives us an important lesson about what it feels like to be different, to move through this world marked by something you can't just turn the dial on. Then the differentnessness reveals a new truth, that we are all wrapped in the cloak of samenessness."

This went on for many chapters.

By the time she was released it was dark outside.

Helinka wanted to yawn but bit her tongue instead.

She reached for her Gusser Von Brackish pumps from off the top shelf and balanced herself against the locker as she hooked the strap back of both shoes.

Marching in line with the other repentant Credeth account holders, they all shuffled towards the turnstiles at the Temple's official Discharged Station.

"Next!" The Temple Official waved Helinka over.

Helinka presented the Temple Official with her autographed copy of Zypsosiss.

The Temple Official scanned the autograph. "Today you were punished, have you learned?"

"Yes, I did learn."

"Please recite your exit confession."

"I will stay loyal to strict readings, nothing more nothing less. Sola Versera. My indulgence is my fault, my most grievous fault. Forgive me bothers and sisters. I will stay loyal to strict readings, nothing added nothing taken away."

"Okay, your penance will be $48,000 off your account, and you'll need to wear these."

The Temple Official handed Helinka a pair of yoga pants with the words "Shame" printed down the pant leg. She added, "And the mochaccino was $27. Which will be deducted as well. Please lean in for your stamp."

Helinka leaned her head into the booth.

The Temple Official stamped her on the forehead.

Redeemed.

A SPY IN THE MIDST

There must be a spy in their midst.

Gideon was convinced. Someone at The Startling Concern was a spy.

The anonymous note read, "Call us 555-2613."

What else could explain the mysterious note with the mysterious number. And how did the Cauzzies know Gideon was inside Smith Smith's mega mansion? And how could the Cauzzies know about his plan to steal the books? There had to be someone on the inside. How else did the Cauzzies know? There could be no other explanation for their perfectly timed invasion. There had to be a spy. But who?

It couldn't be Cloreen. That didn't make any sense whatsoever. What would she gain by all this? Despite it being so improbable, he couldn't dismiss the thought so easily. But she was #1 and Gideon was #2, so how was that supposed to work? What threat was he to her unless she was looking to be demoted? It made no sense.

Plot twists, he thought. Plot twists didn't have to make sense.

But he was still having trouble figuring out any reasonable conspiracy theory that would justify ruining what took them both an entire year to plan. So he decided Cloreen most likely wasn't the spy, but he'd keep the idea on the back burner nonetheless.

His assistant Shim was his next suspect. But what could Shim get out of putting the screws to him? And what did he possibly know that would be of any value to the Cauzzies? His lunch preferences? Plus, without Gideon he'd be forced to go back to the Gutter Maintenance Commission where he found him. So it couldn't be Shim. That made no sense either. But he decided he'd double check nonetheless. If Shim was a spy, it wouldn't be hard for him to find out. So who else could it be, he wondered.

Material Land was part amusement park, part historical preservation site, although that aspect of the park had been forgotten long ago. It appeared from out of nowhere the day The Startling Concern began mining fill-dirt for their new hydro electric dam construction projects. But the earth movers came across a suburban neighborhood buried beneath a billion tons of earth, exposing an entire residential neighborhood that had been preserved like some 1980s Pompeii. In the process of bidding out demolition costs, an intern had suggested to her supervisor that they simply remove the dirt and get the neighborhood declared a national landmark. Although this was a half-hearted joke, the supervisor didn't think it was so silly. It would save them the demolition costs and allow them to turn what was a relatively useless 30 acres into a profitable tourist attraction. And thus, Material Land was born.

Working for The Startling Concern as a master thief required a good cover job. And it just so happened the conglomerate felt being CEO of the 1980s themed Material Land was the perfect role for Gideon to take on. First off, they needed someone to fill the position. Secondly, it would be a good excuse for all the time Gideon had to spend away from corporate headquarters. Thirdly, it would explain Gideon's enormous salary without raising red flags. And finally, any gear needed for Gideon's operations could be stashed inconspicuously within the many single-story ranch homes that were off limits to tourists. This accounted for 96%

of the park.

It was an hour and forty minutes into an important board meeting, and Gideon was still locked away in deep contemplation as to who it might be that sold him down the proverbial river. Everyone in the board meeting had taken their turn trying to snap Gideon from out of his trance. Clearly to no avail.

"Gideon? Gideon?"

It was his assistant Shim's turn to try and snap Gideon out of his apparent daydream so they could address what to do about the child that had been injured running through the Don Dokken exhibit. Gideon looked up to see everyone staring at him with mystified expressions, but soon realized he had been staring out the window for well over an hour. This all came as a surprise to him, and he asked why nobody had bothered to say anything. They promptly explained that it was all they had been doing for the last hour and a half. With Gideon in his trance, Shim had even gotten up to order lunch from the new Hard Rocker Cafe which was recently installed in the food court. They had ordered him the "rock and roll wrap" with the pineapple and avocado toppings which was one of their specialties, but it had gotten cold and the edges of the tortilla were beginning to curl up.

"We put it on your desk, if you want it," said Shim.

"Can you all excuse me?"

Gideon stood up and left the boardroom towards his office.

He stared down at the telephone sitting on his desk next to the hole punch, the box of paper clips, and foam container that held the cold entree, wondering if it might have been him who sprung the leak. Maybe it was him who had somehow tipped off the Cauzzies. Was it Helinka? Did he somehow spill the beans to her one night after those strange drinks they had during the six course tasting menu?

Gideon looked down at the mysterious note with its command — Call us 555-2613. So he began to press on the buttons on the keypad and slowly put the phone to his ear.

It began to ring.

On the other end of the line a voice cackled, "Is this you, Gideon?"

"Yeah. It's me?"

"What we gonna do about it, mate?" Cauzzie Rob burst out laughing.

There was a spy in their midst.

Jotham was the state's Lead Inspector of General Worship and the honorary vice-chairman of the Strin Agency, a group that certified official scripture and doctrine for all legal gods and goddesses and their financial symbionts. What this meant was that Jotham was the man in charge of enforcing rules and regulations as they pertained to the worship of gods and goddesses, and monitoring the transactions between them and their financial backers. What this meant was that he would walk around making sure all religious institutions and worshippers were in total compliance with the state. And what this ultimately meant was that there wasn't a more frightening person to see walking your direction than him.

Regulating penance, monitoring scriptural adherence, reviewing blessings and curses, eating lunch, and the overseeing of the occasional mergers between faltering deities were the duties that took up most of his days. This position was extremely lucrative to say the least. Jotham received a tithe of all the combined temple donations. Votive offerings like food stuffs, toiletries, entertainment like tickets to shows, the gladiator arena, or the latest electronic innovations, to things like clothing and home accessories. The only thing he had to provide for himself was salt. But other than salt, the Strin Agency donations took care of all his lodging and transportation, as well as providing him with a per diem he rarely touched.

The previous day, Helinka hadn't seen Jotham watching her

as she recited the assigned chants to Azzurath, primarily because of the finely tailored suits he wore made from a special mirrored fabric that not only reflected light but absorbed it as well. Thus, Jotham blended into his surroundings like a silent chameleon, never once interrupting temple services and their pagan liturgies, all the while taking copious notes of everything he saw and heard. Jotham was always in everyone's good graces. If not, they were fined or worse off sent to reprogramming institutes which were merely euphemisms for 8x8 foot cells.

Whenever someone saw their reflection walking towards them in a mirrored suit they knew Jotham was coming. Suddenly they were ready to pick up his tab, step out of the line in order to make way for the man who they knew controlled those in control. Or better yet would fall to the floor and kiss his boots. Jotham never hesitated to accept their obeisance. The position was too important to undermine with things like humility. He found it best to act as though it were all a matter of fact. He gave no external indications that he took satisfaction in anonymous patrons rushing to cover the cost of his pastrami sandwich on rye. He would politely smile and inform them he had accepted their donation, but all the while making sure not to make even a second of eye contact and give whoever the patron was an indication that they had gained any sort of favor in the process.

But Jotham wasn't what he appeared to be to the world. He was an idol smasher.

In fact, he was a full-fledged Jew, something nobody those days even knew existed.

It was a secret he kept hidden from everyone and everything.

There was a small number of exceptions though. This included the small cadre of double agents which he ran within the nooks and crannies of unspecified state bureaucracies, not to mention the 50 rabbis he kept hidden away inside his two-bedroom apartment on the third floor just off Tidewater Avenue. This, he admitted, was the most difficult aspect of keeping his true identity secret. Feeding 50 rabbis who refused to eat anything that had to do with idolatrous temple tithes.

But his mission was simple. Destroy the abominable machine of idolatry. His single purpose in life was to cut down those malevolent powers which threatened mankind with eternal damnation.

Jotham had worked for years with the hopes that one day he'd have the evidence to show everyone, in one singular and spectacular revelation, how they had been so tragically misled into believing they were living out some sort of Eden, when in fact they were but slaves to the oppressors, a handful of men and women who were truly making all the rules.

Although his position as Lead Inspector of General Worship was critical to this mission, there were limitations to what he could do. He knew in order to truly reset the course of human history back to his one true God, he would have to show the world the proof that Divine Providence was in fact real. But there were no such thing as Bibles and Torah scrolls anymore. Jerusalem was now just one giant miniature golf course they called "The Holey Land." Nobody remembered anything other than their personal pantheon of gods and goddesses who had transformed their lives from that of endless suffering to a life of tangible and lucrative results, good times, and prosperity for all.

The fact was believers in Jotham's one true God were non-existent moving into the 22nd Century. Even the gladiator arenas were forced to find their victims from other sources now that monotheists were practically wiped off the face of the earth. And Jotham knew all too well from dealing with Strin Agency that whatever supernatural evidence was out there was either destroyed or locked away inside top secret vaults of the institutions he was charged with regulating. That meant in order to save the world, he'd have to find a way to steal back the secrets from those who stole the secrets to begin with. But despite Jotham's superior ability to infiltrate the inner workings of the idol-worshipping hierarchy and single-handedly monitor every minute detail there in, it didn't make him a good thief.

That all changed the day Gideon flew onto Jotham's radar. It was was almost a year ago that he noticed Smith Smith's new tennis partner with his awkward overhand serve and non-regulation maroon racket. But it wasn't until the next day when the same mysterious tennis partner showed up again on the doubles court, chumming around with Smith Smith, that Jotham began to ask himself questions. With his unprecedented access into the records of everyday worshippers it didn't take him long to get his answers. Gideon was a Credeth account holder with Level Rubicon access, was engaged to Helinka Vowell, daughter of Vinter Vowell. He was Vice President of Acquisitions and Antiquities #2 at The Startling Concern, which Jotham learned meant he ran the day to day operations at Material Land, among other things. None of these things interested Jotham more so than the fact Gideon had a spotless record.

A close examination of Gideon's worship and finance records indicated he was one of the most well behaved men Jotham had ever had the pleasure of auditing. The Lead Inspector of General Worship smelled a rat. And one thing was for sure, you didn't rise to the top of the most powerful and frightening enforcement agency if you didn't know how to sniff out a rat. There wasn't one "spittle on the sidewalk" violation, and everyone had a "spittle on the sidewalk" violation. He didn't see a single "murmuring" demerit. Even Jotham had murmuring demerits. And Jotham had seen enough of Gideon's backhand to know he wasn't close to being the choir boy the records said he was.

The fact Gideon was a VP at The Startling Concern, the bane of Jotham's existence, was enough to send his suspicions through the roof. Why had The Startling Concern sent their perfect schoolboy sniffing around Smith Smith. Jotham was well aware of why he was watching Smith Smith with a magnifying glass. Smith Smith had something Jotham wanted. Seven volumes of Hebrew literature from a school's library in Hoboken, New Jersey, and Jotham was trying his best to find some way of getting his hands on them without anyone knowing. The books with their Hebrew commentary were vital to Jotham's ultimate mission to restore sanity and truth to the world. And although he had full authority to raid Smith Smith's mega mansion and seize the books under the "No El Heresy Act," doing that would result in the books being incinerated or worse, sold into the hands of a conglomerate like The Startling Concern, who would then do all they could to manipulate the words for their own idolatrous intentions.

Jotham began round the clock surveillance of Gideon in the hopes of finding out what exactly this choir boy was up to, and how he could conveniently ruin it all for the sake of mankind's future.

"You like The Oils?" Cauzzie Rob gently placed a compact disc into the vintage stereo system. It was required listening. "This song is called Short Memory." It was the full tour of Australian rock bands starting with AC/DC, The Lime Spiders, and newer bands like Koolaga, Oliver Newton Johnston, and finally ending with Midnight Oil. They added an asterisk on the environmental-conscious rock band's post-punk era, stating, "Beds Are Burning is rubbish! It's us who saved the planet! Us Cauzzies! Oi, Oi, Oi!"

Gideon and Jotham stared at each other from across the table, while the Cauzzies slam danced in the comfort of their climate-controlled recreation room.

Both were sizing the other up but on different accounts. Gideon, at first, hadn't even noticed Jotham was in the room as he blended in against the Scarface posters in his mirrored suit. It was only when Cauzzie Roy offered Jotham a beer that Gideon began wondering who this guy was that happened to be showing up to a private meeting. A private meeting with his future existence on the line.

Jotham on the other hand, was observing Gideon closely to see which one of the thousand approaches that he'd rehearsed over the past nine months would best turn this expert thief for The Startling Concern into his own prized counterintelligence asset.

The whole diplomatic immunity article in the Great Treaty had produced what you'd call a "frat house" vibe of Lee Land #3 to a whole new level of bro-dom. According to the self-appointed Ambassador of Funk, Cauzzie Rex insisted that before any negotiations begin both Gideon and Jotham would have to shotgun a beer. Gideon spit gobs of foam while things all went down smooth for Jotham. Clearly the winner, Jotham was thus able to table the first point of order. This according to Rex. But before Jotham could open his mouth, Cauzzie Ron interjected.

"Where's my car, mate?!"

Gideon said it was safe.

"Where are the books?"

"The books are safe," said Jotham.

"Who the heck are you?" Gideon saw no reason to beat around the bush.

"I'm your new handler. You work for me now," Jotham seeing no reason to beat around the bush either.

There must be some mistake. Gideon was looking around the room, at the Cauzzies in their sunglasses surrounding Jotham in a peculiar semi-circle, trying to figure out what kinda jackpot had he stumbled into, and not quite knowing, decided to play it straight as possible. He was a simple antique's dealer and ran an amusement park called Material World. Removing a roll of tickets he placed them on the table. "Free admission for all of you!"

"You ain't no antique dealer," Cauzzie Rob blurted.

Jotham gave him a knowing look, the kind that says, let

me handle this, your time will come soon enough. Cauzzie Rob grunted and shuffled restlessly in his stained Lazy Boy.

"We're all friends here, Gideon."

"Gideon? Like you know me?" it was getting harder for Gideon to play dumb considering he knew whatever the Cauzzies knew, he knew.

Jotham countered, "I may not know you, but I know you."

"So you know, me but you don't know me?" puzzled Gideon as if were some sort of joke.

"I know you, but you don't know me, or what I know of you."

"You human parasites!" Cauzzie Rob had heard enough of the back and forth. "You freaks with all your morality clauses and rubbish. Just tell the man!"

Cauzzie Roy looked to Gideon, deciding for himself he would be the one to tell the man. "We've got you! You're blackmailed see!"

"What my learned friend is trying to say is that you have no choice but to work for us now. Otherwise…" Jotham left it dangling.

"Otherwise what," Gideon was unable to resist the temptation.

"Otherwise, I'll have to make a little report," Jotham slid his official business card across the table. It was in a unique rhombus-shaped die-cut with embossed letters of black and gold with reflective backing, his name "*JOTHAM Lead Inspector of General Worship and Vice-Chairman of the Strin Agency.*"

Needless to say, Gideon's heart was in this mouth. He knew what this meant. Even if he had the full backing of The Startling Concern, one sniff from Jotham's commission would force them to cut bait in a hot minute, not wanting to jeopardize any bad publicity for some common thief, no matter how good he was. He knew just by glancing at the business card, a man in Jotham's position had the power to destroy by his so-called "little reports."

On the flip side, a good word from a man like Jotham put you on the fast pass to promotion. Gideon refused to look at the card another second. Opting for another round of ignorance in the hopes he could get a better idea of just how deep of trouble he truly was.

"Take a look at this if you please," suggested Jotham, sliding a manila folder in front of Gideon's face. Inside was all the incriminating evidence he needed to hang Gideon from the electric gallows. Photographs of Gideon at the crime scene, poisoning Smith Smith, robbing the vault, slipping over the blood. There were tons of images of the dead bodies of June and Ted, clearly whichever Cauzzie documented the crime scene at Smith Smith's mega mansion spared no expense getting as many lurid shots as he could.

"These are the originals. They won't see the light of day," reassured Jotham.

Gideon suddenly couldn't speak.

Jotham decided to leave the card and the manila folder where it lay, adding, "I've been watching you some time. I think it's in all of our best interest if we join forces before it's too late."

45 minutes later.

Gently seared beef was served. A minute on each side was the way they "barbecued" the steaks at Lee Land #3. Generous amounts of horseradish and collard greens picked from the neighbor's farm rounded out the presentation.

There were benefits to advising the Cauzzies over the years. Kosher beef happened to be one of them. What first began as a secret quest to find kosher meat for the 50 rabbis hidden in his apartment, had over the years transformed into a full blown collaboration of human and Invasive minds. In exchange for select cuts of meat, Jotham converted the Cauzzies from pagan idolaters to monotheists the minute after he saw them worshipping film and television characters as gods. Like the Hal Holbrook character from Magnum Force. He explained how characters from movies were fake, and the actors that played the roles were just ordinary people back in the day, but with giant egos and strange personalities that took on all sorts of identities, playing pretend in exchange for payment. This took a while to get through to the Cauzzies celluloid saturated minds. It took persistence and perseverance, but he eventually got through to them.

With their conversion semi-complete, and his need for kosher meat growing, Jotham began to give them legal advice regarding everything from property tax exemptions to the Good Treaty of 2083. It was Jotham who had found the overlooked provisions in Article 747, which granted the Cauzzies full diplomatic immunity and all the privileges that went along with it. How the Cauzzies were entitled to diplomatic license plates, formal embassies, the right to carry arms, and most importantly, the diplomatic pouch that was immune from search and seizure. It was these Cauzzie diplomatic privileges, it turns out, which enabled Jotham to finally get his hands on the volumes Smith Smith kept stashed away inside the bowels of the personal vault. It didn't hurt that Cauzzie Ron knew all about Gideon and his previous life as a car thief. All this cumulative knowledge helped Jotham put all the pieces together as to who exactly this mysterious person was hanging with Smith Smith, and what he was doing. From there it was just a matter of time, planning, and execution. Jotham explained how this partnership, which had started out of desperation for beef, had turned into a fruitful partnership for the ages. And they were just getting started.

Gideon didn't touch his porterhouse. "I'm not privileged to the sort of information you say you need. Recruiting me as some sort of double agent as you say, it's pointless. I'm just a low-level bag man. I don't have any access to The Startling Concern's plans."

Jotham grabbed a roll of dental floss. He had anticipated he'd say this. "What if I told you I could arrange things so that you did?"

Maybe Gideon could run away. Hide. Stick his neck down a hole. Maybe he could switch careers, become a Professional Consumerant like so many others around the globe. Maybe he could search out the finest coffee mugs for those cozy moments or search out the best location to sip matcha tea. As the numbers on the gentle-float elevator ticked upward, none of these hypothetical escape routes seemed to satisfy. Maybe it was being surrounded by the ever-changing illuminance from the "mood detector," which reflected in brilliant color the passenger's apparent emotional disposition. The elevator was flickering violently between shades you'd normally associate with blood clots and rotting citrus. He wasn't going to be able to fool anybody, he thought, if he couldn't fool an elevator.

Being a spy meant eventually being caught. Being caught meant the gladiator arena. There was no way around it though. He knew one whisper from Jotham would spell doom for his career and Helinka's future, and he'd still land in the gladiator arena. He had no other choice than to play along. Little sparks of hope that there might be a way out flittered across the firmament of his mind but quickly flitted into the darkness as the winds of reality blew them far far off course. Like the idea of narking out Jotham. That was out of the question. Jotham would be expecting that. There was no other choice, he concluded. The illuminated walls of the elevator began to glow a soft purple as Gideon made up his mind. The ding of the elevator's doors opened onto his floor, and he stepped out onto the deep violet shag. And as he put one foot in front of the other, he began to cheer up. With his superior photographic memory it was quite possible that he could go down as the best spy that ever walked the face of the earth.

Entering through the electric face recognition portal leading to his luxury apartment, Gideon's blood began to electrify. If Jotham could actually do what he proposed, which was totally reasonable considering the power he held as Lead Inspector of General Worship, he could still be promoted and that meant a raise, it meant more money, and it meant going from Level Rubicon to Level Palladium.

Gideon's brightening mood immediately turned to mud the moment he stepped into his bedroom. There, laying upright under his 1200 thread count Turkish sheets was a bare-chested man with pulsating six-pack abs, perfectly groomed sandy blonde hair, just the right summer glow to his skin, with brilliant white teeth that almost twinkled as he smiled — it was J.U.L.E.S.

"Hey Gideon!"

The Synoid's cheerful greeting did nothing to ease Gideon's terror-stricken mind, although, instead of calling the authorities, Gideon did take J.U.L.E.S. advice and immediately dialed up Helinka.

"There's a naked man in our bed!" he screamed through the speaker.

"I had to bring some of my work home with me," Helinka confirmed into the phone's receiver. "He doesn't have genitals, so no need to worry."

"Wait, what?"

She'd be home later and tell him all about it.

Cloreen liked to pack light. And with her new Lars Von Fear bag, which was one of the latest official/unofficial status symbols for the Credeth account holder Level Sapphire through Level Palladium, she packed even lighter. It was a single check paid from The Startling Concern to Fontanel Integrated Research Initiatives. She nestled the check within the baboon fetus leather-pouch that was noticeably back stitched, catch stitched, and fell stitched all at once with a single mulberry silkworm thread.

Slinging the bag across her shoulder so that the autographed and authenticated mark of Xlonch, priestess of Blazerus, would just happen to force everyone with a Non-Envy Card, which was over 90% of the population, to avert their eyes so as to avoid accumulating fines for "overt coveture." Cloreen determined that the bag was good for carrying documents, it was a delight for the eyes, and good to make one look wise. There was even more good news. Her affinity for ermine jumpsuits was shared by the rest of the travelers on Platform 6, where her fellow members of Level Palladium took full advantage of the morality exceptions to compliment each other's good taste at their own free will. Some were wearing white ermine, while others wore decorative ermine, while others wore what they were dubbing in high-fashion circles as "sticky ermine." Compliments were exchanged. Business cards were passed back and forth. Then they all boarded the superconductor shuttle from Merletown to Caracas.

A light lunch was served. Tiger brine with tusk powder, crustacean puree, and baby onion. She reclined in her sensory stimulation pod, with nine hot mugs of various cocoas, coffees, teas, and exotic milks, listing to a mixtape that she titled "Greatest Hits" which were isolated screams from torture victims inside the gladiatorial arena from the pod's Ambiatic Sound Wave System. She closed her eyes and began the five-hour ride through the earth's mantle.

Being whisked through the dynamic-covalent roadways of Caracas to her destination in the corporate's modified shatter-proof glass palanquin, she was greeted with a warm welcome by the executive staff of Fontanel Integrated Research Initiatives. Cloreen was promptly introduced to an attractive executive named Hun Gar. There was an immediate chemistry. She was struck by his broad shoulders and firm ear lobes. Like a gladiator outside of the arena, she thought, but better than a gladiator, she thought again. Hun was the Executive Vice-President for the company The Startling Concern had just acquired. The irony wasn't lost on Cloreen, that the acquisitions meeting had suddenly become for her, an acquisitions meeting. They exchanged business cards and professional pleasantries, both trying not to betray their mutual attraction. Hun held onto her hand just a second longer than just the normal handshake, almost as if he wanted to bow down on one knee and lay a kiss upon her hand, she noted. They avoided direct eye contact for the most part, both preferring to listen intently to the standard presentation that dealt with takeover procedures, potential conflicts of interest, as well as a time for Q&A for any outstanding transitional concerns either party might have had. Hun did address Cloreen with a question while trying his best not to be seen as flirtatious. Although, the question on the topic of supply and demand was rather banal, she silently reveled in what she imagined was playful sub-text.

What would a life in Caracas look like, she wondered. What demands would be required of her and if she would be able to supply them. She was a powerful woman. And had powerful needs. Finding someone to express these impulses with would require an equally vivacious counterpoint.

The production facility was brightly lit and colored in 420 shades of off-white. Cloreen was toured through the birthing chambers where she was introduced to some of the Expecterant staff who despite their inability to speak English, German, French, or Spanish, simply communicated with pictographs. According to their sketches, they were extremely happy to meet Cloreen and were also excited about the prospect of new ownership. Although not unhappy with previous ownership, but excited about where new ownership might take them into the future. They expressed their enthusiasm for the new accelerated expectancy times that were recently reduced from 9 months to just 5 months. They were also now able to carry multiple embryos into the third trimester in record times with superior quality results. Fontanel Integrated Research Initiatives new hormone formula, which was the ground-breaking technology that initially attracted The Startling Concern, was not only efficient like no other birthing process yet seen, but also good for the Expecterants. Cloreen was equally impressed with the incubation labs which enabled extracted fetuses to continue their development outside the womb in comfort and style. Hun showed examples of fetuses that were pumped full of their proprietary growth nutrients versus those that had simply been left to develop with no additional nutrients. The differences were astounding, she commented. Hun personally guided Cloreen through the process from incubation to birth. She was given a full run down of the genetic infusion process that would enable parents to upgrade their children. The sports package was especially interesting to Cloreen. She appreciated all the new and exciting options and knew that the executives at The Startling Concern would be extremely pleased with the possibilities. They knew about all this on paper but seeing it up close and personal gave Cloreen the sense that they had not only made an excellent acquisition, but had made out like bandits in the process.

When Cloreen was shown into the vocational nursery, Hun placed his hand on her back for the briefest of moments as he opened the portal for her. She told herself, whatever you do, don't flutter your eyes. That would be so trite, she thought. So Cloreen pretending not to notice. But she couldn't help but blush watching Hun gently rock one of the newborns in his arms as he explained they were currently calling that particular unit Orion. Orion had everything parents would be looking for in a child; long-life expectancy, matching parental homogeny traits, above average intelligence, and physical symmetry. The executives for Fontanel Integrated Research Initiatives were all touched when the newborn began to smile and coo the moment Cloreen took it into her arms. They joked that they had planned it that way. They hadn't really. But it was an amazing moment. Cloreen felt a wave of warmth pass over her that she hadn't recalled ever having felt before, and she looked up to Hun unsure exactly what to do with the small infant in her arms. It was all so new, so invigorating. She wondered for the first time in her life if she'd make a good mother. Recognizing her reaction instantly, having seen the same reaction a hundred times before, Hun began to clap.

Soon they were all clapping. Cloreen glowed as she took in the ovation.

They all retired to the dining hall where a private table was waiting.

The executives for Fontanel Integrated Research Initiatives could see they had made the perfect impression with Cloreen. And she made no effort to hide her enthusiasm for the acquisition. Champagne bottles were uncorked and toasts were made. For a long and prosperous partnership well into the 22nd century. Being the decisive man Cloreen anticipated Hun was, he invited her for a scan. Now her eyes fluttered. Hun whipped out his Match Meter, a small electronic device for prospective couples, and inserted it into the slot in her Match Meter. They eagerly awaited the results.

Incompatible.

A few orange flags and two red flags appeared on their monitors. Although the green plus signs indicated good marks for co-habitation, there were too many negatives to ignore. Plus with two red flags, there was no way Credeth would sanction such a transaction let alone their pantheons. Hun shrugged his shoulders and Cloreen picked a poppy seed from her teeth and went back to the dinner party.

There was still one question the executives at the Startling Concern were wanting a firm answer to. They had given explicit instructions to Cloreen not to ask until she was sure that the deal was one they wanted to finalize. So it was finally time to ask now that Cloreen was 100% sure that their acquisition of Fontanel Integrated Research Initiatives must go forward with all due expediency.

"We will need to have combustibility testing," asked Cloreen, outlining their expectations on a cocktail napkin. Hun confirmed that this wasn't a problem, and only wanted to ensure that the executives at The Startling Concern knew infant conflagration times fluctuated, but they were sure if their goal was longer burn times this could all be easily achieved in the genetic infusion phase of the development process. They would start testing within the week.

Everyone parted company with grateful hugs and handshakes.

On the superconductor train back to Merletown, Cloreen noted how Hun's hands were a bit clammy and his handshake was rather limp, not quite the gladiator type, she thought. But the good news was she was on her way back to the Startling Concern with three copies of the purchase agreement inside her Lars Von Fear briefcase, signed, sealed, and ready to be delivered.

It wasn't unusual to see inspection agents for General Worship lingering around the superconductor platforms upon arrival from distant locations, but upon arrival to the Merletown station, passengers couldn't help but notice the massive presence building up on either side of the train. There in the middle of the sentinels was a man in a mirrored suit.

Flinging her bag around her shoulder, Cloreen traipsed down to Platform 6 refreshed and invigorated for her upcoming meeting with the CEO of The Startling Concern when Jotham stepped forward blocking her ascent.

"Would you be so kind as to step over here, ma'am."

Cloreen began to furrow her brow, but thanks to her recent filler injections remained wide eyed, "Excuse me?"

Jotham kept his arms out, pointing to what could only be described as a small plexiglass cell that stood by itself beside the platform. She had never noticed it was there before.

"Could you please open your bag for me," Jotham watched

her tighten up into a fur ball on the unforgiving metal chair as she hesitated to let anyone touch her bag, let alone see inside.

"What's this all about? I don't understand."

"Could you please open your bag for me. We need to see inside."

Cloreen looked around the room trying to see if this was some kind of practical joke, but nobody was letting on. She caught sight of herself in Jotham's mirrored suit, and upon seeing her reflection fixed the few loose strands of her hair.

Passengers walked back and forth, waiting for the next superconductor train. They couldn't help but stare at the woman surrounded by inspection agents for General Worship, but they slowly averted their eyes so as not to risk deriving pleasure from someone else's misfortune.

Not wanting to spend an extra minute in the portable see-through cell, Cloreen unzipped the Lars Von Fear bag, she pushed it forward. "There."

Jotham spun the briefcase around giving it an initial glance.

"All you'll find is a purchase agreement. I work for The Startling Concern. I know you all are well aware of The Startling Concern. We hold most of your contracts if I am not mistaken. I am Level Palladium as you must know. So when we are done, I would like an apology for delaying me, if that won't be too much trouble for you."

But despite her dismissive tone, she began to grow increasingly uneasy in her layers of billowy ermine. She looked up at Jotham leaning in and unzipping the zipper to the inside pouch, removing the purchase agreement and setting it down gently beside the bag. That was that. She packed light for a reason, she reminded herself, and was reading herself to get up and leave when she heard an audible gasp. Jotham stepped back as if catching sight of a time bomb ready to explode. This was immediately followed by stun guns pointed just inches from her face. Everything became frantic. Passengers hit the floor for their safety. Inspection agents shouting orders to other agents. Others running for armed back up, still others trying to peer over Jotham's shoulder for a closer look.

She had never before seen the small watch-shaped container Jotham pulled from her briefcase.

"A pyx," whispered Jotham to his colleague.

Flipping open the lip to the small container, Jotham carefully removed a small white circular wafer, no larger than a silver dollar, and lifted it up into the light.

Jotham's eyes became dark and penetrating as they shifted back to Cloreen. "You are under arrest for the desecration of Worship Code 665, for being in possession of forbidden relics. You have the right to hide your eyes, you have the right to cry silently to yourself, you have the right to wallow in your tears, you have the right to wish you were somewhere else than where you're going. Do you understand these rights as I have explained them to you?"

A tear ran down Cloreen's cheek. "Yes."

CABAL

"I've got magic hands," J.U.L.E.S. offered to give Gideon a deep shoulder massage, but he declined again in favor of staring at his watch. So when Helinka finally arrived to the apartment, Gideon was quick to tell her exactly how late she was.

"I had the most wonderful thoughts on the way home," Helinka tossed her coat to J.U.L.E.S. who proceeded to roll it for lint before hanging it in the hall closet. "Have you ever noticed how the ocean doesn't just start spilling into the sky? And the sky, it never falls into the ocean. Have you ever noticed that?"

Gideon quickly dismissed her dreamy notions, "Why does it say 'shame' on your pants?"

"They're tights. Yoga tights. Yeah, I had a little trouble with my audit."

"What kinda trouble?"

"Just this and that, but you know what? I was thinking about the stars how they move across the sky. Have you ever noticed that they don't crash into each other, or flicker out all of a sudden, I mean have you? Isn't it the most peculiar thought?"

Gideon didn't smell wine on her breath.

"I mean what keeps it all in order? I mean, if Lunsu rules

the moon, and Shamshu rules the sun. Who rules Lunsu and Shamshu?"

J.U.L.E.S., ever the patient listener, took a seat on the floor beside Helinka and in the most supporting tone added, "That's a wonderful thought, Miss Helinka."

Seeing this J.U.L.E.S. thing cozy up like he was part of the family, provoked Gideon to whisper into Helinka's ear, "Can we go in the other room so we can talk? Alone."

"There is nothing you can't say to me that you can't say in front of Jules."

Gideon was just a little taken back by this, "Uh…well, I'd like to not discuss things in front of a stranger…or whatever it is…your Synoid."

"No, you don't understand. It's his ears. I installed the latest C800 supertube condenser diaphragm microphones. He has ultra-hearing. So it doesn't matter where we go in this apartment, he'll hear us. So you might as well say what you want to say right here."

"That's right! And I'm recording everything as well," J.U.L.E.S. added with flare.

"It's recording us?! What else do you got it programmed to do?" Gideon asked, "Is it gonna mimic my voice and open up a credit card in my name?"

J.U.L.E.S. hadn't thought of that but took a mental note and filed it away.

"Jules is a show model. A prototype," Helinka affectionately squeezed J.U.L.E.S.'s shoulder as if giving a small child some encouragement.

"You said that!" Gideon stood up and moved to the refrigerator for a beer, "I know, it's a prototype. What I am struggling with is why it's in our house? I still remember your lab. Every square foot of it, I can draw you a floor plan. I thought that's where you kept those things. I'm sorry, not thing, where you kept your Jules. And could you stop rubbing that thing's shoulder if you don't mind!"

"Why?"

"Cause...I don't know, it's creepy that's why!" Gideon shut the refrigerator door, not finding anything good.

Helinka could see his exasperation, and she stood up and moved beside him.

"It will only be for a little while. It'll be okay, I promise. I just need to sort a few things out before I take him back. I promise," Helinka took hold of Gideon and gave him a squeeze of his own.

"Well..." Gideon always liked how she was able to defuse any situation when she took him in her arms. It's probably why all the Match Meters declared them so compatible, he thought before adding, "Well okay. I guess. If it's just for a little while."

The two shared a kiss.

"Aaaaaaah, how cute. You're both so cute," J.U.L.E.S. gushed while dancing around in the sort of provocative way you'd expect to see on a multi-colored dance floor.

Gideon looked back to Helinka. She could see he wasn't impressed, but tried to cheer him up nonetheless. "Trust me, Gideon, as soon as I iron the wrinkles out in his system, we'll be the wealthiest couple on the planet."

"For now, could you just make it stop?"

Trying to smile, Gideon suggested they order in.

General Tso's, Lo Mien with chicken, Won Ton Soup. He didn't know what to order J.U.L.E.S. and was about to get the Sesame Beef when Helinka informed him he lived off methane. Just like a Cauzzie, he thought. Gideon joked that he didn't think they served methane. It wasn't very funny, but Gideon was trying his best to act as normal as possible. He wasn't one to pry into her business, let alone anyone's. Primarily because his memory wouldn't let him un-pry whatever he happened to hear, and because he preferred that nobody dig too deep when it came to his line of work. The way he figured it, if someone wanted to know about what he did, they could buy two tickets to Material World, walk around, go on a few rides, and that would be that. Once in a blue moon, someone who knew him under his antiques broker cover would ask him to appraise some reproduction lamp from the 1800s, but he'd just say that wasn't in his field of expertise, and that would be that. Helinka didn't ask many questions. Again this was all part of their compatibility mode. So as he sat eating his cold noodles, his mind was anywhere but listening to J.U.L.E.S. orate Samuel Taylor Coolidge while basking in front of him on the dinner table.

He actually wanted to pull his fiancée aside and tell her his entire life had been turned upside down. But how could one do that in the presence of a Synoid who was not only reciting poetry but recording every word out of his mouth? What he wanted to tell her couldn't be recorded. It shouldn't even be uttered by human lips. So even if he was able to speak with her alone, where exactly would he start?

Maybe he could start by telling her that whatever the compatibility results said about them being a perfect match was just a fabrication by The Startling Concern in order to allow him to marry way above his station. That might be better left a secret, he thought. What if he told her the truth, that he didn't believe in gods or goddesses. That he didn't even have to go to worship. That The Startling Concern had given him all sorts of exemptions that prevented him from getting cited for moral code violations. How could he tell her he didn't have go to audits when she was wearing "shame" tights? Maybe he could start by telling her his CEO job was just a front for his real job of being a professional thief. Maybe he could say that he's so good at being a thief, the life they were living was essentially a stolen life, and that he had essentially stolen her. And he had help doing it. From the pinnacles of society. They had taken such great care of him, that there were about to give him a huge promotion. They'd rise to Level Palladium. And now, in gratitude for all they had done for him, he was about to betray them all. He would become a spy. He would start stealing from The Startling Concern. And he would be doing it for a monotheistic remnant whose only mission in life was to destroy everything they worked so hard to obtain. Gideon put down his fork.

"*And every tongue. Through utter drought, was withered at the root; we could not speak, no more than if we had been choked with soot. Ah! Well-a-day! What evil looks had I from old and young! Instead of the cross, the Albatross, about my neck was hung.*"

Helinka began to applaud, "Bravo! Bravo!"

Gideon decided it was most likely best to just keep silent. Why ruin what was shaping up for Helinka to be a wonderful evening. But as he tried to block out J.U.L.E.S. reciting poetry in a fake British accent, he couldn't unravel the ball of yarn he created for himself in his mind, that he was somehow the only human being in the world who was free to be who they truly were, but who he truly was wasn't who he was free to be.

Cauzzie Rob pointed out a small scratch on the Plymouth Cuda's bumper. "This wasn't here before, mate!"

Gideon couldn't see what he was talking about. Jotham told him it could easily be buffed out. Cauzzie Roy didn't want to contradict his best mate, but he was pretty sure whatever discoloration it was came from the guts of a moth. Gideon defused the situation by suggesting he'd have the car fully detailed at a future date at his expense. Cauzzie Rob insisted that whoever does the detailing use a chamois leather, but not just any chamois, a chamois from the hide of a Capra ibex. All was agreed and the final four volumes were handed over to Gideon.

Still, Cauzzie Rob had somehow decided nothing was going to go smooth. "I'll be making burritos. When I come back, I expect you to be finished."

Jotham told Gideon to just ignore Cauzzie Rob, but Gideon reassured him he'd only need about 20 minutes anyway. So he sat himself down at the rickety card table in the bowels of Lee Land #3, opened the book and began to memorize.

"You're reading it backwards," Jotham noticed.

"What? Left to right, right?"

"No. You're reading it backwards. Right to left. It's Hebrew. The Holy Tongue."

Jotham informed him everything Gideon had taken to memory of the first five volumes would be in reverse when he transcribed it to those at The Startling Concern. Gideon had heard the word "Hebrew" before. In a 1966 Oxford Dictionary he memorized for The Startling Concern's archives.

"Hebrew. Noun. Definition one, a member of the Semitic people inhabiting ancient Palestine and claiming descent from Abraham, Isaac, and Jacob; an Israelite. Definition 2, a Semitic language of the ancient Hebrews, which, although not in a vernacular use from 100 B.C. to the present century was retained as the scholarly and liturgical language of Jews and now is the national language of Israel. Is that about right?"

"Close…" Jotham was more impressed by Gideon's memory than the definition itself.

"Isn't Isaac that bartender from that one TV show with the cruise ship?"

"Not this Isaac!" Jotham shook his head realizing for himself, just because Gideon could memorize things in a flash didn't mean he understood any of it.

"Done with this one," Gideon moved on to the last volume.

"Do you have any idea what these books are?"

Gideon shrugged. "Hebrew books…written backwards. To confuse people, I guess?"

Jotham watched as Gideon flipped through the pages of the last volume and thought about what he had just said about Hebrew being written backwards to confuse people. He seemed to know at that moment, that he'd given Gideon way more credit than he deserved. And the previous day when Gideon initially claimed he was no more than a bag man, he wasn't lying. He was like a little kid. Not some genius stuck in the wrong era, who would be Jotham's secret weapon in the war against idolatry. Not yet anyway. He was initially as advertised, no more than your average run-of-the-mill criminal, with the only difference being his freakish capacity to retain huge masses of info.

It was a world that had ages ago done away with the last of the thieves, both big and small, sending them off to the gladiatorial arena where they met certain death. But this extraordinary ability of Gideon's to remember everything he read and everything he saw, had saved him from that gruesome fate. In fact, his ability not only spared his life but allowed him to rise to the upper echelons of modern society.

The irony, he thought. That the salvation of his people had always been their ability to remember that it was God had taken them from out of bondage in Egypt and delivered them into the Promised Land. And that remembering that had proved too difficult for them, time and time again. God had remembered Noah, saving him from the flood waters. God had remembered Abraham, and therefore saved Lot. God remembered his covenant with Abraham, Isaac, and Jacob, and thus redeemed the people of Israel as his own. But his people forgot. And so there he was. Jotham. All alone to recount all the blessings and curses of his people.

The irony, he thought. Gideon was a man who could never forget but had no clue what he was remembering. If he could somehow take for himself this gift of Gideon's, package it up, and transport back in time and impart this gift to his people in the wilderness, then they'd still be saved. The world would look totally different, he imagined. He'd be spending cool afternoons on the steps of the Holy Temple. Anywhere other than where he actually was. In the bowels of a slaughterhouse, surrounded by a thieving Gentile, two synthetic walking-talking AC units, hoping that through their collective yet desperate efforts, God would once again remember his people and dwell amongst them again.

Gideon closed the final volume. "Finished."

As if on cue, Cauzzie Rob strode back into the room, a half-eaten burrito almost falling out of his clammy hands. "Oi! Chorizo! Who wants a bite?"

Right then, Jotham got a sinking feeling. It might be better to find some tree in the middle of nowhere, lay down, close his eyes, fall asleep, and dream of a merciful death.

The first thing that came into her mind was power strokes. She had seen the skilled duelist take advantage of those that looked to base their attacks on thrusts. No thrusts, she instantly decided. Heavy chopping and vicious slashes. That's the only way to go. The single edged blade curved slightly at the end. Being two-handed she knew she could put in more of what little strength she had, and because it wasn't too heavy it extended well in her grip. She preferred the larger hand guard in case she was looking to punch some teeth out. The sword she selected had a large blood groove down the center that she liked. The next thing that Cloreen did was to rip the sleeves off her ermine jumpsuit in order to have a fuller range of motion.

She felt the barracks could use a little more light in order to improve the atmosphere which she felt was a bit too gloomy. Finding a seat in the gladiator pen which opened up to the arena, it was difficult for her to keep her eyes off the forlorn expressions on her fellow prisoners. A playwright who had his secret manuscripts exposed by cleaning crews already looked as though the battle was already fought and he was undoubtedly the loser. His eyes were sunken in his head. It was obvious he had been crying. Sizing up the fat man in the lederhosen who was panting as he leaned on his trident, she knew he didn't stand a chance. The large woman beside her stared blankly at the floor. Avoiding all eye contact, deep in thought. What must she be thinking of? Whatever it was, it wasn't strategy for how to survive mortal combat. The mascara running down her cheek made it clear it wasn't strategy on her mind. The large woman reminded Cloreen of a giant limp sturgeon, and she wondered if she had caviar in her belly. She would kill for just a spoonful of the Caspian Beluga right now, she thought.

Drums begin thudding away. Cloreen had heard those beating drums a thousand times before. She wondered who was watching today from her executive box seats. Maybe it was the CEO himself, C.J. Supentus. Maybe he had come to see her die. She'd need to put on a good show, she thought. She couldn't let the executives down even if condemned to death.

Breathing exercises are a must, her mind switching to the job at hand. It keeps the heart rate in check. It wasn't good to be too up or too down. Warm she reminded herself.

Slig was in sharp contrast to the condemned, striding in front of her with his battle ax over his shoulder, in his custom chainmail. He took an instant liking to Cloreen.

"What do we have here?"

"Let me guess… a little lady?" Cloreen decided to play along, being a bit impatient for the whistle to sound.

"Hey there, little lady. Looks like we haven't been properly introduced, my name is —"

"— Slig. I've seen you fight a bunch of times," Cloreen feinted a sharp yet fleeting smile.

Slig lit up like a steroidal Christmas tree, "Have you now, little lady?"

Cloreen finally looked up at him, "Yeah…"

"Well, stick behind me when the whistle sounds. I'm gonna be your official protector. Stick behind me."

Cloreen liked this idea, "Yeah? Really? That's thoughtful of you."

Slig nodded, then blew her a kiss, "I sure am, little lady. There's only one rule in the arena, the strongest man wins."

The audience erupted in rapid cheers. The drums beat

louder and faster.

The prisoners slowly moved toward the gate, and the wash of the arena's artificial light seeped in through the gate. Cloreen followed Slig as he maneuvered into position.

The whistle blew. The gates flung open. Slig heroically ran into the center of the arena, Cloreen following right behind. Slig let out a battle cry, and as though this were her cue, Cloreen stabbed him through the back with her sword — killing him instantly. As Slig's body fell limp, she picked up his lifeless body and began using it like a human shield.

Dodging a deadly thrust of the iron hooks of a woolen barbarian, Cloreen didn't miss and lopped the barbarian's head off with one brutal and merciless swing. Another adversary leaped forward, but Cloreen spun, hurling her human shield into his path, stopping the barbarian's advance like a huge collision between two diesel trucks. She tightened her grip on the sword and brought it down across his body, cutting him in two. Another barbarian lunged at Cloreen, who fended the blow. Turning the barbarian on his hip, she sent the barbarian sprawling to the ground. Immediately, Cloreen kicked the barbarian in the head, dazing him, as he tried to pick himself up. He had to pause on all fours to shake the fog from his brain. Cloreen looked up at the crowd for confirmation. They seemed to shout in unison, "KILL!"

She wasted no time; it was a death blow.

What she didn't expect was the fountain of blood. Cloreen looked down on her now saturated ermine jumpsuit, but there was no time to mourn the loss of her designer threads. Being forced to skirt the swing of a hairless barbarian's battle ax, Cloreen decided now was the time to put on a show. Evading all advances from her oversized opponent, she was displaying superior skill. Then she began to effortlessly inflict her opponent with almost playfully pricks as he swung wildly trying to kill her. But she continued to make tiny breaks in his skin to let him know that at any time she could dispatch him.

The crowd was captivated, as if watching a bullfighter toying with a dying bull. But soon, Cloreen grew bored with the spectacle, and as soon as she had turned the barbarian around, pierced him in the back of his neck, severing its vertebrae for an instant kill.

Basking in the standing ovation, Cloreen turned to survey the arena. Everyone was dead or dying. The fat man in lederhosen was trying to wrestle with his innards sprawled out in the dirt; he was a dead man, she knew. The playwright was somehow skinned alive and stuck onto a spear. What she would have given to have seen that go down. Maybe next time, she thought. Her box seats were empty she noticed. Not even a formal goodbye. That's okay, she'll work to change that. And just when she had thought the day was hers, across the arena she saw her. There was one opponent left. And miraculously, it was none other than the large woman, the one that looked to her like a huge sulking sturgeon. Cloreen sized her final opponent up. She had her back against the wall of the arena, panting like an animal trapped in a cage. Maybe some other time and place, a woman like that could have been a pet project of hers. Like one of those makeovers she'd love to peruse in the magazines while getting her toenails done. Where they take some pitiful soul with no style or sense of fashion and transform them into a dashing visage, cocktail party ready, with equal amounts of sass and confidence. But Cloreen had seen enough battles to know there were no friends in the arena.

The large woman charged, her samurai sword raised above her head, screaming as she went. Cloreen stood her ground. Not moving an inch. Waiting for just the right moment. And when it came, she brought her sword down in a vicious slash, gutting her like a fish. The crowd exploded in applause.

Nope. No caviar, she thought.

CJ Supentus. The man in charge of The Startling Concern

walked with Gideon onto the conference hall's 20,000 square foot projection floor depiction of planet earth. He explained in great detail how the map was geographically accurate down to a zillion micro-meters. The designer Naru broke up a globe into 328,896 regions, then folded them into an inverted icosahedron, and then a reverse dodecahedron to form a giant obelisk that she then flattened to the superhuman-sized surface they were standing on.

Gideon was teetering on sensory overload. He had never walked on a floor with a 20,000 square foot illuminated map of the world on it, nor had he seen anything like what Supentus wore. It was a tracksuit made almost entirely from mummified human skin. Gideon was having the hardest time getting his mind away from the flakes of brownish-black bitumen that peeled off his sleeves as he pointed to things like New Algeria. And whenever he tried to remember what Jotham had taught him to say, he'd get distracted by the crackling noises the tracksuit's pants made whenever Supentus moved. Then he saw the words "RAMSES II" stitched in large letters on the back of the embalmed jacket, and he forgot why he was there.

Supentus began thanking Gideon for his contributions over the years and how he was excited to have him on board in his new executive position recently vacated by Cloreen. It was unfortunate, he said, that she was unable to finish the projects they had started but could think of nobody better to help fill that void than him. Void, Gideon suddenly remembered something. *The earth was without form and void, and darkness was upon the face of the deep.* Gideon smiled and shook Supentus's hand once again. Jotham hadn't taught him when or when not to shake hands, so he had done it a number of times now, Gideon deciding it was best to try and make up for their initial awkward handshake when Supentus grabbed him by his fingers and squeezed tight. Standing over the Indian Ocean, Gideon saw the grey men in pointy hats and robes murmuring to each other in the distant corner. Murmuring, Gideon remembered, Jotham had taught him about murmuring. The murmuring deep, Moses stuttering, how God wanted that broken voice to speak to the Children of Israel. *The deep calls unto the deep.* The desolate noise full of potential, broken and lacking form, undefined murmuring. Then there was light. It was starting to flood back into his memory. And just in time too. The grey men in the pointy hats hooked him up to the transcription machine at the bottom floors of The Startling Concern and pressed record. Gideon began recalling all the Hebrew words from all seven volumes as he had memorized them. Left to right.

The grey men in the pointy hats hovered around Gideon. Their stony faces flashed a mix of exhilaration and confusion as they scanned the results. Maybe they had yet to figure that out it was all backwards. They didn't stop him or protest in anyway, seeing at the same time that what they were looking at was genuine. So Gideon just continued unabated, trying not to betray his normal demeanor. Relaxed and non-caring. He had been given a new name-tag that showcased his newly promoted position to Vice President of Archives and Antique Assessment Analysis and Other Things. His name barely fitting. But that didn't matter so much as what Supentus had mentioned about Gideon's wardrobe. And Gideon was still trying to figure out what he meant when he said that his outfit was "provincial." Maybe he'd change before dinner with the prospective in-laws. It was all Helinka's idea. Her idea of a celebration for his big promotion. Maybe he'd have to get some new clothing. Something that better represented what was expected of the new Vice President of Archives and Antique Assessment and Other Things.

They pricked his finger with a corporate lancet and a drop of blood hit the parchment.

"Scrawl your mark," wheezed the grey man in the pointy hat with the albino eyes.

The document signing went on for more than an hour.

He was signing his life away page by page. Declarations. Legal waivers. Disclosures. Conduct Clauses. *Tradition is a fence to Torah, tithes are a fence to wealth, vows a fence to sanctity, a fence to wisdom is silence.* He wasn't sure how that popped into his brain, but hearing the men with the grey hats whisper back and forth about the law and legal addendum got his mind sputtering. *Greater love was made known to them that there was given to them the instrument with which the world was created, as it is said, For I give you good doctrine, forsake ye not my law.* And a stack of binding agreements that essentially locked Gideon's thoughts, actions, and the work of his hands as the sole property of The Startling Concern for the unforeseeable future. *Everything is foreseen; and freewill is given; and everything is according to work.* That was from Volume 3, the *Sayings of the Fathers*. Father-in-Law. Jethro? Wait, no, Vintner Vowel. Helinka's dad. The last thing he wanted was to have to endure his in-laws. Gideon's mind was spinning wildly in all directions. He didn't want to give the law another thought.

"It's got a wicked water hazard," Supentus described Mount Cyanide, or the 14th Hole as it was known at The Holey Land golf course, and how his new Cobrastrike Mecha 3-iron got his ball to lay up perfectly. "I'll have to take you there some day. Do you golf?"

Gideon nodded his head as if he understood. "Yeah, I'd love to come up to the mount...golf..." *Come up to me into the mount and be there and I will give thee the tablets of stone, and the law and the commandments which I have written that though mayest teach them.* What do tablets of stone have to do with golf? Jotham had crammed his head so full of information it was oozing out his nostrils.

They gathered around the immense stone table in the executive boardroom, and he watched as they all gave him a standing ovation. Gideon smiled. All he wanted to do was run and hide.

Lifting his wine glass to toast to the boardroom, Gideon proclaimed to all, "Thank you all so much for the warm welcome. It fills me with a host of possible humility violations, my emotions are so bordering on happy, but I restrain them and lash them with shame. So thank you! What I would like to make plain to you all here today, is that I plan for my contributions to continue to have a major impact for the greater good of society at large. I appreciate the trust you have all placed with me. I will do my best to continue to erase the history of mankind from the memories of all human beings around the world to bring about a more unified and profitable existence for all. And when I say all, I mean all of us sitting around this table here today. Thank you!"

More applause. More pats on the back. More business cards.

Supentus was glowing in his approval. Remarking how it wasn't since the Summer of 1733 that he had heard a more rousing speech than the one just given by Gideon. Even the grey men in the pointy hats lined up to shake his hand. Their clammy palms left him wiping his hands across his provincial slacks after each shake. Today was a day to celebrate, Supentus announced. Tomorrow, they'd all get to work on the greatest project ever undertaken by The Startling Concern.

Project Kabaal R9000.

The double-decker spiral wrap-around driveway was the newest and latest designer architectural vision from Drark Custom Homes and was installed specifically for their signature Crevasse Mansion. The entry to the Crevasse Mansion looked like a sinkhole that catastrophically opened up into the earth. A glass portal opened and closed like a giant oversized camera shutter. There the Butler was waiting to greet Gideon, Helinka, and their surprise guest J.U.L.E.S., who Helinka had insisted that Gideon refer to simply as Jules. Upon arriving home to his apartment, Gideon walked right past Jules in his burgundy dinner jacket and goat wool overalls who had rehearsed a welcome home dance for him, and brushed quickly aside Helinka who was still putting the final touches on her designer outfit, before locking himself in the bathroom. When he had finally splashed his face with enough cold water to bring himself back around to reality, he got dressed without saying a word to anyone. Helinka was in a chatty mood, going on about the new feature she was going to program into Jules the following day, something about underwater sonar. Throwing on his favorite sweatpants, he totally forgot about upgrading his wardrobe. He blamed his forgetfulness on the onslaught from the day's events. In the elevator going down, he finally realized Jules was coming with them. Jules's constantly beaming smile would have normally been an absolute no-go for Gideon, but with so much racing through his mind, he didn't put up any sort of protest about the Synoid's presence. In fact, it was actually a welcome distraction. Something for the in-laws to fixate on as opposed to his distant gaze. This turned out to be the case upon entry, when Helinka exuberantly exclaimed, "Mummy, Daddy! Meet Jules, my Synoid."

Jules put on a great show. He knew just the kind of pearls Helinka's mother was wearing, just the kind of shoes on her feet, and recognized her perfume immediately, and he did it all speaking in Old French.

Vintner Vowell appeared as if he had just stepped off a Saharan steppe with a red British infantry commander's uniform and Boer War inspired helmet. Although he did motion an acknowledgment with a slight nod of his chin, making eye contact with his soon to be son-in-law was something he preferred to let the butler staff handle. He poured himself a glass of port and began speaking in a low baritone that rattled the crystal around the wet bar. Gideon pretended to listen to his future father-in-law's latest expedition to the "Dark Continent" for a Jungle Safari to bag the elusive prize for his expanding trophy collection. Unlike CJ Supentus and his golf expedition to The Holey Land, there was no mention of an invite.

"Daddy! Why don't you show Gideon your trophy room!" This was Helinka's way of getting her two men to share some sort of camaraderie she idealized would blossom between husband and father.

Vintner grumbled under his breath. Gideon said there was no need to bother. But Helinka insisted, "Daddy, he'll love to see it, wouldn't you Gideon?"

There was a sort of jarring squealing noise that came from Gideon's mouth before he swallowed a gob of saliva and tried again. "Sure, yes…I'd…love…to…see…it."

The china on the dining table began to rattle as Vintner uttered the words, "Very well…"

Leading Gideon into a two-story oak-walled gallery covered wall to wall with taxidermy human heads mounted on large wooden crest-shaped plaques. Under each head was a brass plate engraved with the name of the prey, the location, and the date of the kill. Gideon expected to see some sad zebra hanging above a fireplace, so when he saw the collection of heads it left him frozen in place. Not paying Gideon any mind, Vintner strolled through the room pointing to various trophies and giving a little background into each one.

"This one here. A Franciscan Friar I tracked through the jungles of Sumatra. Rare, yes. Yes. Very rare. We had tracked it for days, yes, many days. A watering hole as I recall. It had emerged. Crouching low, lapping water from its hand like a dog. A fine shot."

Gideon stared at the head of the Franciscan Friar who's glazed marble eyes stared unblinking into an unseen horizon. He shuddered. Next to it was a youthful Nigerian man's head with the brass placard reading, "Lutheran Missionary Volunteer, 2094. Mount Nyiragongo."

"Here. This is what I wanted to show you," Vintner was standing under an elderly woman's wrinkled head with a blue and white nun's habit on top. "India. Just last year. A wonderful shot from some 400 yards. A Sister of Loreto. We had burned the village and scattered the lepers into the hills. Myself, and Sir

Wholeheart the 3rd, mind you. We had scattered the lot. We tracked the beast through the sundarban, almost losing the track near Gosaba. But we stayed there for martinis. Mmm yes… We found the tracks near the riverbank and followed them up to Bagdogra. It was a fine shot. 400 yards. I used the IMI Galil sniper rifle with ARM configuration. A fine shot. Yes."

Next to a head marked Bishop of Archdiocese of Keuskupan Agung Medan, Gideon noticed an empty placard with the brass plate engraved with the words, "Future Son-in-Law." Vintner pretended not to notice the fact that Gideon was staring at it.

Sitting down at the massive mahogany dining table, Helinka couldn't stop bragging about Gideon's new promotion. "How old were you Daddy when you got promoted at Delco Labs?" This was met with a low inaudible rumble, and Gideon had to grab his wine glass before it vibrated off the table. She went on and on about how they were going to be Level Palladium. Credeth had even opened discussions on preferred pews at the Temple of Galibur. This was most impressive. Vintner tried to shrug it off, but she could tell when her father was impressed.

The Butler refreshed everyone's wine and departed. Jules excused himself to wash his hands. Vintner sat back in his chair, pretending to line up targets in his sights as he waited for the next course. Helinka and her mother shared their wedding decor plans debating between a jazz glam theme or a tasteful glitz theme. Her mother leaning toward tasteful glitz.

The renown gastro-gastric-fusion-chef Byle had flown in from New York especially for the night's event, stood at the head of the table explaining the first course of "Tapas de Omitus," before wheeling out a handicapped street urchin with a turban on his head. Placing a small plate of pulpo a' feira in front of the street urchin they watched as the boy gobbled it up in a few bites. After the chef was convinced the dish was settled inside the boys stomach, he swung a hickory branch into the boy's back so violently the street urchin instantly vomited what he had just swallowed back onto the dish. This repeated five times and then was promptly served to the guests. Gideon decided he wasn't going to "experience" this portion of the meal. Helinka tried to convince him before gladly taking his portion for herself.

During the fourth course of Chicken Alfredo Garcia, a loud scream came from the kitchen. The Butler's headless body had been stuffed into the linen closet. The decapitated head was later found sitting on a silver tray in the pantry.

Helinka's parents apologized profusely for the unexpected interruption and blamed the Butler losing his head on the fact good help was hard to find these days. But before they left, Jules recited some poetry to the sheer delight of all. Gideon watched wholly unconvinced, then noticed a smear of what could only be blood on Jules' goat wool that he could swear wasn't there before.

MOVERS AND SHAKERS

Through the spyglass mounted on the slaughterhouse's half constructed belfry, Cauzzie Ralph spotted the dust cloud from the bright blue vans driving towards Invasive Designate R for the bi-annual inspection. It had come early this year. Cauzzie Rob was hoping they'd be done with their construction project before anyone arrived in the hopes they wouldn't notice the additions. Cauzzie Rex was working non-stop to finish off the tower, which had just been framed on top of the slaughterhouse exhaust system, as well as attaching part of the belfry on top of that. The final pieces to their steeple, the lantern and spire, were still in pieces on the ground outside of the gate. When the vans pulled up, the inspectors emerged from the vehicles and instantly pointed up at Cauzzie Ralph. It was obvious right then they had noticed.

Cauzzie Rob was waiting at the front door with the requisite gas masks spraying bleach into them with an old bottle of Windoxx glass cleaner, acting like he wasn't concerned in the slightest about their new and unsanctioned building project. While two of the inspectors took meter readings of the air and made marks on their clipboards as usual, the head of the inspection team, Jones Jones, was looking at the boards that made up the pieces of the lantern as he approached the gate. There he waited silently to be let in. Cauzzie Roy walked up to the gate, but didn't look to open it. He gave Jones Jones the once over and asked him why his shoes weren't covered. They needed to cover their shoes in order not to drag in any contaminants per regulations as stated in line 17D. Strict adherence was the order of the day for the inspectors, so it was going to be the same way for the Cauzzies. Nobody would be able to interpret anything outside of what was written down in the terms of the agreement. What was good for the goose was good for the gander, said Cauzzie Rob as he pointed to a pile of festering foie gras that they quickly shuttled into the walk-in cooler.

"Dear Heavenly Father," Cauzzie Rob began to pray when they had all gathered into their power circle. "Protect us from these wild animals. We are your domesticated animals, great Father, and we are protected by pens and by you as our Holy Shepherd. But there is no trainer for the horse. We need someone to teach the horse lessons. To break the horse. Please open the eyes of these wild animals who invade our pens, our private sanctuary, to your great calling and to leave behind their pagan ways of idolatry. High-fives for Christ. Amen."

There was a collective amen and collective high-fives, and all took their posts. They were all at their posts when Jones Jones came to the gate. One of the other inspectors handed out cloth booties to cover their shoes. Cauzzie Roy took his time making sure they were regulation before giving the go-ahead for the gates to be opened. The inspectors put on the disinfected gas masks and being familiar with the layout of the slaughterhouse, began their routine which primarily consisted of documenting the surroundings, monitoring gas emissions, which was all just window dressing for their main concern — the Cauzzies' predisposition for the consumption of human flesh. So the inspectors looked for signs amongst the carcasses of beef that hung from hooks, and the hog limbs that sat on slabs, waving electric wands to scan for human DNA. A few inspectors viewed the methane milking room for signs of hidden bodies and found none. All the while being escorted by Cauzzie Rob and Cauzzie Roy who made sure the inspectors followed exact procedure — correcting them a number of times as they stepped too close to this or too far from that. Most of the time, they'd just roll their black invasive eyes knowing full well it was all just a charade and that human meat wasn't anywhere on premises. And if it was, it would have been consumed or hidden where they'd never find it. But nevertheless, they poked, patrolled, and prodded.

"You boys wanna beer?" Cauzzie Rob said in his thick Australian accent.

"Bear?" Jones Jones asked, unsure if he heard right.

"Beer! Beer! Not Bear! You boys wanna beer?" rebuked Cauzzie Rob.

There were no takers as they looked around the recreation room scanning the pile of T-bones protruding from the trash baskets. Jones Jones saw the wooden cross on the wall and looked at his notes. Then he called another inspector, and they began conversing. Cauzzie Rob held back Cauzzie Roy who wanted to blurt something out, stopping him.

"That there's a hat rack," Cauzzie Rob smiled. "Pine lumber there."

They continued to watch as the inspectors gathered around the makeshift crucifix discussing it amongst themselves. Jones Jones sensing something was amiss, took a radio from his belt and called in for reinforcements. Cauzzie Rob was still keeping the wait and see approach, but was visibly growing nervous. He decided to distract them.

"You sure you boys don't want a frosty beer? It's ice cold. Icy cold beer."

They were ignoring him now, and the nervousness suddenly became contagious amongst all the Cauzzies in the recreation room who were watching. Jones Jones turned and looked at

Cauzzie Rob and informed him he was calling in reinforcements. A card table went flying. Roy and Rex tried to restrain Cauzzie Rob who easily freed himself and ripped down the dart board. Screaming, "If it wasn't for us Cauzzies you'd all be dead! You're all nothing more than wild beasts, eh! The only reason you're alive is us! You good of nuthin's been given all the answers to the test but keep failing. You're flunking out, mate!"

This was all an act of course. They all knew ahead of time that the inspectors would wonder what the cross on the wall was all about. They called in reinforcements before. It happened when they saw the Scarface mural. Before that it was the Bruce Lee posters. The time before that it was the Cauzzie resistance flags that hung from the entryway rafters. If Cauzzie Rob didn't protest any perceived injustice, the inspectors would think their silence meant they were trying to hide something. As was the case with the time they failed to put up a fuss when the inspectors discovered their secret collection of Christopher Cross CDs. After having them confiscated, they were later destroyed under Article 19. Article 19 made it illegal for Invasives to be in possession of inflammatory propaganda that could threaten the safety of human life. That meant having drunk Cauzzies singing along to their war anthem "Sailing" was anathema. So the best thing to do was to put up a big stink. Kick things around a bit. Throw a bag of chips. And act as persecuted as you could. The hot air helping to elevate pressure either real or unreal. And this was especially true when it was clearly stated in Article 87 that the Cauzzies were prohibited of having any unsanctioned religious iconography, literature, or graven images.

So Cauzzie Rob was just buying time before reinforcements arrived. "Yeah, defeated you and mankind with snacks, mate. Had it not been for some fluke bomb we'd have taken over the world! We defeated you through your stomachs! That's right! Snacks, mate! Snacks! You're all nothing but wild pigs at the trough!"

Cauzzie Rob reached for a bag of Funyons and theatrically

ripped the bag in half sending the contents flying through the air. The inspectors stood their ground, without flinching. It wouldn't be long now, they knew, before the reinforcements arrived.

And when they did arrive, it was Jotham in his mirrored suit. Behind him were three ghost like figures moving underneath black sheets that draped over their heads and dragged across the floor. The inspectors showed them the item in question. The 2x4 cross mounted on the wall. They then all walked outside and were shown the unsanctioned construction, the tower, the belfry, and the lantern and spire.

Jotham and his ghosts convened a quick meeting before explaining to the inspector that what they were looking at was clean. That the cross on the wall was indeed a hat rack, and that the construction that they were viewing was purely cosmetic. That it in no way violated Article 87. Or any religious code that they could see. With this, Jotham and his team departed. The inspectors finished their inspection, making special notes that the Lead Inspector of General Worship had cleared all of their suspicions, and that they had indeed passed the inspection with an overall passing mark of 92%. The 8% deductions being for the fact they had been cited for not having a registered bolt pistol at the slaughterhouse kill floor and for storing sharpened knives in unhygienic conditions. Cauzzie Rob kicked Cauzzie Rex in the leg when he tried to apologize for forgetting to hide all evidence of Kosher slaughterhouse practices. They had gotten lucky this time, Cauzzie Rob insisted. And after a small fist fight that broke out between Cauzzie Rob and Cauzzie Rich who thought he was being too hard on Cauzzie Rex, they all made nice and celebrated their passing inspection with lots of beer.

Gideon browsed the racks of bespoke clothing at the exclusive invitation-only couturier called Puce. He would have forgotten to acquire new clothing were it not for the fact his favorite sweatpants had gone missing. He had searched high and low for them, and even gave Jules the 3rd degree thinking that he may have taken them out of vindictiveness. But Helinka had been tracking his movements that day with a special monitor she had invented. It was clear from the results she showed Gideon, that Jules had been nowhere close to his hamper, or any of his stuff for that matter. Although Gideon wasn't totally convinced, he took it all as a sign to take his boss's veiled suggestion to keep up appearances that were more in line with his prestigious new job. He was a spy now, he reassured himself, and needed to play the part to the fullest. As he looked through Puce's collection, Gideon was shown a giant zip lock baggie with six capsules of antihistamines inside that he was told was just his size and available for tailoring.

Almost exactly at the same time, Helinka's team huddled around the light table with a pair of sheers looking for exactly the right sample. She had suggested the crotch area. They all agreed and took three small quarter-sized samples from Gideon's sweatpants. Someone had commented that the holes looked like eyes were staring back at them. This sentiment was greeted with mild amusement. It would have garnered more than a chuckle had it not been for the enormous amount of pressure they were all under trying to figure out how exactly to overcome the glitch they all knew existed with Jules. His propensity to decapitate humans while administering neck massages.

The team had faced challenges before, and each time had risen to the occasion. So despite the rather somber expressions around the lab, they were all rather positive that they'd figure out what exactly was wrong. Helinka divided the team into two groups. One group to look back through the Cauzzie's DNA to see if there was something they had missed in the sequence that would solve the issue, and the other group assigned to research the Biosurety archives for any odd scrap of information that would lead to a better understanding of what might be imbedded in the DNA that made Cauzzies want to kill. After thorough vetting, nothing new was discovered. So they were back where they started. One of the technicians suggested they find another DNA strand of a person with meek personality traits to somehow counteract the Synoid's inherent homicidal tendencies. This is when Helinka suggested her own fiancé, and quickly absconded with his favorite sweatpants. Finding enough material in the samples to pull DNA they began to fuse it within J.U.L.E.S DNA to create another Synoid prototype they dubbed C.C.O.R.Y.

Helinka was called into a meeting with the executives who wanted to know where they were with the project. It had taken some time to smooth over all the legalities and to pay out all insurance claims due to the untimely death of Geertz Geert. But the executives were still enthusiastic about the prospects of the Synoid project. Helinka's preparations to repress all fear that she was about to be reprimanded and taken off the project was quickly put to ease. The entire executive board gleefully informed Helinka how they would have verbally expressed out loud how thrilled they were that Geertz Geert was dead, if it were not for their morality clauses with Credeth that prohibited them from visually rejoicing in the death of a colleague. But they assured her if they were not under such prohibitions, they would absolutely positively burst out laughing, and that in the comfort of their home, in non-fineable space, beside the hearth fire, with a cup of warm cocoa, that they had all had a good laugh at the expense of Geertz Geert.

This didn't mean that they didn't have tough questions regarding the future of the Synoid and they asked them point blank. Helinka reassured them that J.U.L.E.S. was indeed the future, that adjustments were being made, and the project was more than just salvageable, but a true winner. That her team had already begun making huge strides in isolating the Cauzzie gene that was embedded in the original Joey sample that made J.U.L.E.S. malfunction during presentation. It was only a matter of time now. Everyone was satisfied.

Helinka was stopped by one of the executives who had originally recommended her to lead the project and informed her privately, that even though the board had given her their full support, that support would need to be met with results and quickly. This wasn't meant to frighten her in anyway, but just to inform her friend that they were all under pressure to make this work. The huge monetary investment was just one reason they needed to recoup their money, but regardless of the other reasons, this was the only consideration she needed to concern herself with.

Unfortunately for Helinka and her team the results were less than stellar with C.C.O.R.Y. In fact, when the prototype emerged from the chamber they weren't sure exactly what it was they were looking at. The official report, that they locked away in the dungeon along with C.C.O.R.Y., listed the prototype as an Embryol, having an accumulation of yolk like the ova of an overgrown reptile with a lustrous yet brittle crystalline structure and silver-white radioactive emissions that shot out from its transparent membrane.

Back at home, Helinka sat Jules down on the corner of his recently assembled bunk bed he had selected from the Homes-R-Me catalogue that they had set up in the laundry room. It was time for her and Jules to have a heart to heart.

"Jules, I wanted to talk with you. Now you're not in trouble or anything like that, so I want to put your mind at ease. In fact, you are still my special guy, and I mean that from the bottom of my heart. And I know that in the bottom of your heart beats all those unique qualities that is going to make you the single most popular product in the history of mankind. You not only have the ability to save the world and ensure a perfect ecological, how do you say, uh, a perfect environment for all future generations, but you will essentially be the father of all Synoids. There will be more Synoids than there is sand on the beach. Remember how I was talking to you about all the stars?"

"You mean twinkle, twinkle, little star?" Jules asked.

"Yes, exactly, like twinkle, twinkle, little star. That's right, so you remember how you were able to count them all with one look? Well, you will be the father of more Synoids than there are stars in the night sky."

"That's a lot," Jules wondered.

"It sure is. And every generation of Synoid will look back to you as the father of all Synoids and your name, Jules, will be remembered forever as the greatest invention of all time. Wouldn't you like that? Wouldn't you like to be the father of all those wonderful Synoids that will go on to change the world for the better?"

"Yes, I would."

"Good! Then here is what I need you to do. I need you to stop tearing the heads off people like you did with the old man and the butler. If you can stop giving massages, and could you stop squeezing so hard. If you stop doing this everything can move forward! And then you will be blessed beyond imagination. Now, Jules, I know you can do it. So what do you say? Can you do that for me, can you do that for us?

Jules shook his head, "No."

Mysterious flaps from the reimagined Bedouin tent were filled with sand. An 18-wheeler had run over the tent numerous times before it was stitched into the baggy three-piece suit, with flat weave Jaipur pattern coat, that Gideon was wearing to his first official day on the job. The designer suit had so many folds and wrinkles that he was having a difficult time knowing where to place his keys. The first time he put them into what he thought was a pocket, they dropped to the floor. So now he was holding them in his hand hoping that a real pocket would make itself known at some portion of the day. On his head he wore a circular hat made from weaved barley grain, dyed with glow-in-the-dark insect bioluminescence. His one-of-a-kind shoes were made from sheep's fleece and were soaked in water, so his footsteps made squishing noises as he walked. This outfit didn't go unnoticed by the passersby who pursed their lips and made "Oooo" faces. Gideon had never seen this before, so he figured it must have been some way for people to communicate that they liked the clothes. He was not such a big fan though and longed for his sweatpants and cotton pullover. He thought he understood the converted tent concept as the salesman at Puce had described it. But suddenly couldn't remember why it was necessary for the 18-wheeler to run over it so many times, but he did follow the salesman's recommendation, nonetheless. The suit had the visual impact required for The Startling Concern executive, he said. That's all that mattered. But he didn't think he could hang with the shoes much longer. So he decided to go barefoot as he rounded Main Street and walked up Grand heading towards corporate headquarters. Gideon shoved the soaked shoes into a recycle bin before entering the giant marble edifice that was The Startling Concern corporate sky-rise.

Again, more "Oooo" faces as he boarded the supersonic elevator to the top floor, and he began to wonder if the outfit was making everyone constipated. With a ding, he disembarked. His office was just one big bubble-like window and seemed to be perched on the edge of a cliff. His desk was totally transparent and just below him, through the clear glass floor, he could see the janitor's storage room filled with stacks of toilet paper, a yellow portable mop wringer, and white jumpsuits. Framed on all sides of the windows were gilded oil paintings of letters that he thought spelled out the word T-R-E-A-S-O-N, but was later told spelled out the word S.E.N.A.T.O.R., because it was the office Senator Haskins had used when discussing the Honduran plasma pipeline scheme. Looking down at his shriveled bare feet that were beginning to chill, he saw a janitor looking up at him from the storage room below. Gideon tried to act like he didn't notice, and that it wasn't somehow creepy or unsettling, but after a few minutes he couldn't help but peek down again to see the janitor continuing his stare up at him. Checking his watch, he saw he was still a bit early for the conference but got up and left anyway.

An enlarged image flashed on the screen from an overhead projector. It shown the Startling Concern's logo with the words "Project Kabaal R9000." A small Chinese woman was sitting in the CEO's leather chair at the head of the conference table. Gideon was wondering why Supentus had sent a proxy in his place for such an important meeting. She wore the same mummified skin tracksuit, which was curious, but this one had the words "Sneferu" stitched in on the back in a strange script. It took Gideon some time to realize that the Chinese woman was actually CJ Supentus. This murky realization came only after she began welcoming everyone, including Gideon, and began referring to herself as "himself." Over a cup of vending machine coffee and stale melba toast, Supentus explained to Gideon how he learned how to shape-shift a decade earlier. It was all thanks to a special blend of ground up colocynth power he sacrificed to the goddess Vumple, who in exchange granted him the special ability. He liked to use it on special occasions. He especially liked the Chinese woman and the Romanian tulip bulb cleaner. But he told Gideon that he had been experimenting with body transfiguration for centuries after his first canoe trip to the island of Palawan. Supentus made an "Oooo" face when commenting on Gideon's new clothes. He liked what he saw and instantly recognized the designer as Puce. Gideon on the other hand, was drifting back through the memory banks to the time he first boosted a car. It was a sun-bleached orange Chevy Vega he hot-wired at the A&P parking lot. He was 16-years-old. Things were so simple back then he mused. People wore jeans. And shirts with buttons. Nobody shape-shifted or dressed up in mummy skin. So he naturally squirmed in his plastic molded cabbage-shaped conference chair, watching the Project Kabaal

R9000 presentation, not knowing when his entire deception was gonna come crashing down on his head.

A new image projected on the screen. It was a monocle cobra head stuck on a lion's body with eagle talons for hands and golden squid tentacles for feet.

Project Kabaal R9000 was rather straight forward. At least how Supentus had explained it. The Startling Concern wanted to find a way to rule the world. And his solution was simple, build a better deity. But not only a better deity. They had done that time and time before. Upgrading Galibur, Blazerus, Forseps, Prong, just to name a few. Adding new names, new features, new worship procedures, new morality clauses, and the like. This was to be different. Supentus wanted a deity of all deities. One singular deity that all the rest of the deities bowed to and served in supplication. The job of the executives gathered around the conference room table was to come up with the best single deity they could conceive. One that would allow them to control all the financial institutions, be the master of all codes of conduct, and to broaden their worship base around the globe to be more inclusive.

The Head of Product Design was none other than the famous designing priest Butylsothiazon-4. Gideon couldn't take his eyes off the man's twelve-foot tall pointy-grey hat. It was well known to all those at the Startling Concern that because of Butylsothiazon-4's work on the Galibur repackaging project of 2096, he was always going to be the frontrunner for Kabaal R9000. Although there were a few requests submitted to put their name into the running for the job, they were all subsequently denied. Butylsothiazon-4 was the choice. And he quickly began formulating his concept of merging powerful animals into one super animal that he had dubbed, "Animanihilation."

"The cobra has fangs. And poison venom," Butylsothiazon-4 explained in a thick Dutch drawl, adding, "The lion has the big heart, like he has kind heart. And the claws will tear. They will tear into your skin and carry you away. It won't let go. The tentacle. It sucks hold of you. Bringing down into the depths. So we have land, land again, air, sea. We have fangs, fur, claw, and suction cup. This my friends, is most complete god of all time! Thank you."

Supentus was sitting back, listening to the pitch. He was just looking straight ahead at the projection. Almost motionless. Gideon was unable to read his expression whether he liked it or not. But then again, the Chinese woman's face barely moved to begin with, so it was next to impossible to tell if he was liking the concept or not. The last thing Gideon wanted to do was say something that Supentus was going to hate, so when the comments from the executives began he just let them do all the talking. Gideon figured if someone else said something Supentus didn't like, it would tip his hand to what he thought about the Animanihilation concept. And better yet, he thought, maybe someone else would say something brilliant and when it was his turn to speak, he could say he agreed with their idea 100%.

A man in a tinsel shroud, who looked to be on good terms with the Head of Design chimed in first. "May I have the pleasure of requesting a moment to share with his priestly reverence my thoughts on the image here before us today?"

There was a panel of monks presiding over the meeting. Gideon watched the infernal panel of grey men with pointy hats whisper amongst themselves before the albino-eyed monk stood, screaming, "You may proceed with caution, Stamen!"

The man in the tinsel shroud, who Gideon now knew was named Stamen, stood bowing his appreciation to the panel before turning to address Butylsothiazon-4.

"Has your priestly reverence considered maybe making the head less frightening? I see cobras as scary, and if our goal is to try to bring about more inclusivity may it be wise to consider something less imposing, for example, the head of a koala. Or if you really think it needs to be a lizard, maybe a chameleon head?

That way it is diverse and can change lots of colors?"

Butylsothiazon-4 acknowledged the comment and motioned for Stamen to sit back down to await his response. Once Stamen was seated he began to explain that idea of a marsupial head undercut the entire concept of Animanhiliation. The marsupial was a sign of indecisive birthing. Almost noncommittal. The fact the fetus crawled out of the womb and into a pouch where it developed over time showed weakness in the parent creature. The last thing a super deity would affect was weakness and indecisiveness. The standard mammal's birthing habits showed even more dependance on the fetus than the marsupial by keeping it within itself for full gestation. The only beasts that captured the power and authority of a super deity were beasts that laid eggs. The egg was a wholly detached unit. Whereas the parent does indeed birth the fetus, it does so within an encapsulated shell where it is left to develop on its own, often times buried in the sand. This was the proper disconnection of god to worshipper. So a koala, wombat, kangaroo, or any other furry marsupial was out of the question. The perfect head was that of a monocle cobra. Butylsothiazon-4 gave the floor back to the executives.

A female executive wrapped in a starfish shower curtain who they called Abridget requested to speak. After some extended consultation amongst the grey men in the pointy hats, they permitted her to contribute.

"Thank you, your priestly reverence, and esteemed monks, for allowing me the pleasure of contributing my insight. If the Animanhiliation requires that the head be a creature that lays eggs, why not a bird? Like an eagle head. Or an owl head. It is most regal and less intimidating than the cobra."

This suggestion too was taken off the table by Butylsothiazon-4. The eagle nests, and there will be no nesting in a super deity. Plus, the pattern calculations were extremely specific. It was "land, land, air, sea." Having a bird's head would change the configuration to, "air, land, air, sea." And that would be totally unacceptable.

An executive in a green ermine jumpsuit requested to contribute but was quickly denied.

Makwayt made his request, "Salutations great one. Would it be good in your sight to allow me to comment in a way that in no way contradicts the great priest who I adore?"

Makwayt flopped five dead pheasants on the table and a book of coupons adding, "Spa tickets. To LeNard. Free neck massage for two."

"You may speaketh," confirmed the panel.

Makewayt bowed, "Dear Magnificent One, what if we reversed the hands, so that the head became the hands, and the hands became the head. The way you keep the configuration intact."

"The cobra has no hands," Butylsothiazon-4 was quick to remind everyone.

"EXCEPTION!" Supentus exclaimed.

The grey men in the pointy hats shouted back, "EXCEPTION GRANTED!"

Supentus turned to an executive sitting at his right hand, and asked calmly, "Volumair, could you please give us your feedback on the concept?"

Volumair rose to his feet and addressed the grey men with the pointy hats, "May I speak freely?"

There was great discussion and heated debate amongst the panel before albino eyes got to his feet, screaming, "You may speak freely!"

"Thank you," Volumair turned to Butylsothiazon-4 and bowed, then turned to Supentus and finally gave his two cents, "The suction cups are a little challenging."

"How so?" Supentus asked intrigued.

"I don't know, I just think it's, I don't know, I mean, it just looks childish in a way."

Gideon saw instantly Volumair was someone Supentus

counted on for his opinions.

"I don't know. I guess it's just like when do you really see squid or octopus anything? I mean I thought we were trying to broaden our appeal, ha. You know what I mean? It's just like, I don't know, like why couldn't you pick something less slippery?"

Supentus laughed. At least someone in the room was scoring points with the big boss.

"What would you advise, instead of the tentacles?"

Volumair chewed on this for a minute or two, then shook his head.

"I don't know. I mean...we've seen with the popularity of Blazerus, good results with dog legs, but, yeah, I get it, you want, what's it? Like the sea for the feet. I get it...I don't know, I think you'd have to be looking at something more human but with scales on it. Like human legs with scales. Shiny ones. Anyway. I don't know. You know."

Supentus nodded in approval, he liked the idea. Volumair bowed, bowed, and bowed again before again taking his seat.

The executive sitting beside Gideon requested to comment.

"Oh vibrant and glorious priest of all wonders and mind of a thousand minuscule minds, would you so grant me the honor of addressing the topic at hand in a constructive and considerate manner?"

The panel remained motionless for some time, just looking at the executive in question. Gideon watched their eyes almost turn completely black. The albino eyed monk stood, and shrieked, "We grant this under conditions, Namhole."

Namhole bowed his head, "Thank you. Dear Butylsothiazon-4, how about turtle legs? They are amphibious, therefore living in and out of the water, makes it diverse as well as makes it land, land, air water, land configuration which I think enhances Animanhiliation."

Suddenly there was an alarm, a thunderous buzzing noise.

Armored Security Guards entered and grabbed hold of

Namhole and started striking him with billy clubs.

"A turtle hides in its shell. My gods don't hide," Supentus said bluntly.

Gideon watched as Namhole began to bleed from a gash formed across his head. He didn't think the idea was so bad, and then suddenly they were beating him. It was all so extreme. One minute this nameless executive is looking all purposeful and next thing you know his name and he's getting mauled by wolves. Namhole was reaching for the leg of Gideon's chair as if that would somehow help avoid the beating. It was hard to watch, but there he was, watching. One of the Armored Security Guards started kicking Namhole in the head over and over again, Gideon couldn't believe the man was still conscious, the tip of the boot smacking him right in the forehead over and over again.

"Whoa, man," Gideon exclaimed instinctively, "Take it easy, dude."

This was about the worst thing Gideon could have said.

His whole goal was to try his best to stay under the radar, avoid detection, and try and make it out of the meeting in one piece. And here he was not only bringing attention to himself, but also the wrath of the Armed Security Guards who began zapping him with electric cattle shockers.

As Gideon's body tightened involuntarily due to the electrical currents coursing through his muscle matter, he began thinking of what he was going to tell Jotham about why he failed so miserably on his first day as a spy.

As he began foaming from the mouth, he realized it may not be a complete failure, he did discover that The Startling Concern was looking to create a deity of all deities. One singular deity that all the rest of the deities bowed to and served in supplication, the most complete god of all time.

As his eyes rolled into the back of his head, he knew that this was good information to pass on to Jotham.

As Gideon fell from his cabbage-shaped conference chair

and onto the floor, he knew the inside information about Animanhiliation was the stuff Jotham wanted. Maybe he knew how exactly land, land, air, sea, and the whole thing about the marsupial and the egg would help his cause. He didn't, but his job was just to gather intelligence.

As the billy clubs rained down on his head, Gideon recalled how Jotham wanted to influence the thinking at The Startling Concern from within, Gideon of course being the tool in which he was gonna use to make that happen. Too bad. At least he wasn't exactly empty handed.

As the wolves began tearing at his leg, Gideon suddenly remembered Helinka, how he was going to let her down, and it would probably be the end of their marriage plans. There would be no rigged Match Meters to make it look like they were a perfect match. Things were looking rather bleak, he thought. He couldn't go back to stealing Chevy Vega's from A&P parking lots. And he wasn't so sure the A&P even existed anymore. The one thing he did know was there was no way he was going to steal a toothbrush without having the company's secret backing. That was looking to be quickly coming to an end.

Then the alarm suddenly stopped screeching. And there was silence.

"I'm satisfied," Supentus whispered.

Then the beating ceased as well.

Gideon flopped his limp body onto the chair.

Supentus was no longer the Chinese woman. In his revulsion, he had changed back to his old self. But with narrow eyes that blackened to pinpoints burning a hole through Gideon.

Gideon tried to shake off the cobwebs. His sight was totally blurred as if someone had rubbed oil into his eyes. When his eyes finally did catch focus, he saw he was staring straight at CJ Supentus. Gideon quickly turned away.

"Gideon," Supentus said sharply, almost suffocatingly.

"Uh…yes. Yes, sir…" Gideon adjusted his busted hat.

"Do you have sssssomething to contribute?"

Gideon looked to the grey men in the pointy hats sitting on the panel as if needing their permission.

"EXEMPTION!" Supentus made his request.

The grey men in the pointy hats shouted back, "EXCEPTION GRANTED!"

"Do you have ssssssomthing to sssssssay? Ssssspeak freeeeely Gideon," Supentus rephrased the question.

Gideon looked around the conference room. Everyone one was waiting. The wolves most especially. There was no getting out of this. Gideon cleared his throat, and seemed to instantly remember everything Jotham taught him. And his path suddenly became clear. Just repeat something that Jotham said. That way he could just blame him if anything went wrong. After all, he wasn't a spy. He was a thief. A good thief at that. But he wasn't a spy, so who could blame him for screwing everything up? It was all Jotham's idea anyway. He's the one that planted evidence on Cloreen and got her fired. He never asked to be here. So whatever results weren't on him, they're on Jotham, Gideon concluded. Sure, he thought he might be decent at being a spy. He got a little excited. Sure, Gideon thought, he can admit it sorta went to his head. But that's only because he was trapped. And what was he supposed to do? Think the worse? No. He thought, he had to think positively. Gideon couldn't delay any longer.

"Maybe it's not such a bad idea."

"What do you mean, not a bad idea?" Supentus snapped.

Gideon gulped. "Uh…Why not have a god that hides. But not like a turtle. Like an invisible all-powerful god that is everywhere and nowhere at the same time."

"Like the air?" Supentus asked, "Like emotions? Like words? Those things are invisible. How is this an all-powerful god?"

Okay, this was worse than he imagined, and he quickly dug through his mental archives, pulling up every file he could find on what Jotham had said about his one true God. More specifically now, the stuff Jotham said about God being hidden.

"Well, uh, I'll tell you…" Gideon started riffing off the top of his head, "Technically, you can see the air, and technically, you can see emotions on peoples' faces and stuff. I'm talking a god that is completely hidden. Think of the light of a billion suns. And we're all part of its radiance, we're connected to it, but just like staring at a billion suns you'd instantly go blind. And because he knows you'll die if you gaze upon him, and cause he doesn't want to blind you, he hides. But because he's hidden you mistakenly think he's not there. But he is. He's so powerful you can't look at him or comprehend him. And that's why you think you have free will. You think you have a choice, but you truly don't — all you can do is submit to him. That's the difference between a god you can see, like a flying jackal, or a cobra head thing, and the hidden god. If you can see it then there's a chance you can somehow fully understand it and have a say. Not so with the hidden god. That makes him all powerful."

The grey men in the pointy hats shouted at Gideon in unison, "Keep speaking!"

"Uh…okay…what I'm saying is, since he's all powerful, the hidden god made everything. Good and bad. He created all the gods, and all the goddesses, and every single human. Everything you are looking at is his and part of him. You, me, them, this table. He made it all. That means he owns everything. He owns everyone. And because he owns you, you owe him everything you have. Including your life. Your only job is to serve him. You have to throw away any idea of who you are in favor of what he wants you to be," Gideon took a breath and wiped the lingering foam from the side of his lip.

"He owns everything," Supentus leaned back in his chair again and drew his hands together, pondering this idea. "He owns everyone."

Butylsothiazon-4 liked what he was hearing, "Your hidden god. How does one worship it if it has no form?"

"Like I mentioned, only the hidden all-powerful god knows your true purpose, since he made you. That means he has a special job for you. And you don't get to know what it is until you totally submit to his all-encompassing power. Since he created you and gave you this sense of free will, the way you worship him is by surrendering that sense of free will back to him. Then it's simply a matter of telling the worshipper what you want he or she to do. So if the hidden god wants you to be a dancer, you dance. If he wants you to wash his new car, you wash his car. And in return maybe he will like you and not kill you. But he might, if you don't obey. Like if you don't give it all your money or something like that. It's pretty simple."

There was a long moment of uncomfortable silence. Nobody saying a word.

"Everyone leave," Supentus ordered.

It took a half second for everyone to get up and start gathering their things to vacate the conference room. Gideon was pushing his chair away from the table when Supentus stopped him.

"Not you."

Gideon froze, "Uh…okay…"

Everyone else scattered for dear life, almost stampeding each other at the exits. Butylsothiazon-4 took his five pheasants and spa tickets and followed the grey men with pointy hats out a special trap door used especially by the monks. The Armored Security Guards commanded the wolves to drag Namhole's apparently lifeless body out of the double doors.

Then it was just Gideon and Supentus sitting alone in the conference room. They both stared at each other from opposite ends of the conference table. Almost relaxing a bit, Supentus transformed back into the Chinese woman.

"Gideon. It looks like I made the right choice by bringing you on the executive committee. You have big shoes to fill. Cloreen did a great job by bringing the firm such valuable ancient archival material. With your help of course. But I must say, she was never quite able to bring it all together like I think you have done for us here today. It's quite impressive. A hidden god. Quite impressive."

Gideon's barley hat fell off his head and onto the table with a loud thud.

"I have one more question to ask you, though."

"Uh…Yes?"

"Let me get this straight. If your hidden god made everything, and therefore owns everything and everyone, and you worship it by surrendering your life and all your perceived freedom, and if it's The Startling Concern who owns the hidden, all-powerful god, this would essentially mean we would control the universe?"

Gideon nodded, "Uh…Yes…"

Supentus finally broke into a smile. "I'd like to develop this more. How's your Thursday look? Let's say 8:30 tee time. The Holey Land?"

Gideon nodded again, "Yeah…okay."

NOT THE FACE

The Good Treaty didn't look so good upon closer inspection. Particularly disturbing to the lawyers was the language in Article 747, the one that bestowed upon the Cauzzies a variety of diplomatic rights, some rather basic and others bordering on the absurd. The two legal minds in charge of framing up the agreement were at a loss to explain why it was included in the final document to begin with.

Erasemus esq. and Barristan esq. esq. esq. were only able to come up with the fact it might have been a misprint. But it wasn't a misprint. Scouring their records they had seen the various revisions all with the initials of the principal lawyers involved. So it wasn't a misprint at all, and that excuse was quickly done away with.

A lowly clerk was accused of mistakenly including an older draft into the final draft, but that too proved to be just baseless scapegoating on the part of the firm Ygnwie, Erasemus, and Sumer.

They had even gone so far as to request the presence of Cauzzie Bob esq., the Invasive lawyer who represented the Cauzzies in the drafting of the document, but he refused their request to talk unless they could deliver three Oldsmobile Cutlass

Broughams. Although they tried to meet the exorbitant price from the Lower Nairobi Natural History Museum, it being the centerpiece of their collection, they were unable to come to terms on the sale. They proposed, instead, a fleet of Oldsmobile Aleros, but Cauzzie Bob esq. refused.

After finding no suitable theory in which they could lay the blame on someone other than themselves, and no way of bribing Cauzzie Bob esq. in to explain what had happened on his end, the minds at Ygnwie, Erasemus, and Sumer quietly moved on to the more pressing concern of how to neutralize Article 747. The consensus seemed to be if they could get the Cauzzies to fall into breach of contract they could somehow find a way to rewrite Article 747. The main concern being the language that allowed the Cauzzies to kill indiscriminately and steal whatever they wanted as long as it fit into their diplomatic pouch.

They knew getting the Cauzzies to negotiate their newly discovered, and fully legal, powers of murder and theft would come at a hefty price at the negotiation table. So attacking another part of the contract, placing them in breech, would make it easier to for them to persuade the Cauzzies to renegotiate Article 747.

They began to look into the tissue culture and substrate licensing agreements. If they could somehow show that the Cauzzies willfully supplied defective versions of their reproductive material, then they could then threaten them with seizures of property and levy heavy fines that would threaten to put an end to their luxurious lifestyles. This also proved to be a dead end. Enkeling Futures and Prosperities refused to get involved. The Hypogusia Company stated they were under no legal obligation to participate with the inquiry, sighting the terms of the agreement of The Good Treaty. Epulo Product Makers flat out refused to even return the firm's calls. Nobody wanted to jeopardize their access to their vital life-giving tissue cultures and substrates just because a few people got murdered.

A Junior Associate at Ygnwie, Erasemus, and Sumer was put

in charge of sifting through all the case files from NMP, the New Australian Military Police. She then compiled transcripts from all the surveillance videos and presented them to her superiors, who then turned them in to their superiors, before they landed on the desk of Erasemus esq.

After reading the transcripts over and over again, the Junior Associate noticed the Cauzzies where speaking in strange codes, using mysterious language that had pulled up zero information in the firm's extensive databanks. They had even searched the National library and still found no references to some of the words she was hearing. She spelled them multiple ways, but still no results. The summer associates were not much help. They'd never heard of the words in question. So she just spelled what she heard almost phonetically and hoped for the best.

Incident Report 1.

The first NMP report detailed the invasion of the Temple of Zaels, the goddess of chain-style jewelry stores, which occurred the previous Friday at 8:37 A.M. The Cauzzies of Invasive Designate R kicked in the front door of the Temple and proceeded to plunder it for a variety of their sacred objects. The surveillance videos captured four-hooded Cauzzies, all wearing colorful Hawaiian shirts and khaki pants with flip flops, exiting from a Plymouth Barracuda carrying shotguns and a large pillowcase with the words "Diplomatic Pouch" scrawled on the side. One Cauzzie was seen vandalizing a statue of the goddess Zaels, throwing it to the floor and shattering it to pieces. Witnesses said they heard them shout, "Idol smashers at your service." Another security camera in the temple courtyard recorded worshippers scattering under heavy shotgun fire, one witness testifying to NMP that they'd yell, "I feel threatened!" before each shotgun blast. Further eyewitness accounts stated that the Temple Priest attempted to block the Cauzzie's path towards the giant 14 ct Double Diamond Tilted Heart Pendant hanging above the altar, when one of the Cauzzies shouted "You're threatening me, mate!

Back off!" Then all four of the masked bandits unloaded shell after shell into the Temple Priest, blowing him back against the altar. One Cauzzie strolled up and shot him point blank in the head. From there the video surveillance was able to record their conversations without the screaming of fleeing worshippers. It went as follows:

Ugly. That's dungy, mate. Look. Look! This bloke's head is oozing. Look, a bowl of red lentils. You owe me your birthright, mate. (inaudible conversation and laughter). This guys dead. No birthright. (Laughter). You just took his birthright! Oi! You felt threatened by granny here? I sure did. He's older than methuselah, Oi! Good shot, mates. Anyone seen my lighter? Look at this thing, it's a heart with the word mum inside. (Banging noises) What caret? 14 it says. It's gotta melt down, alright mate. (Shotgun blast) Oi! You threatening me! Oh that's messy. Lookie here, chocolate diamonds. That's the evil inclination. What you got? Don't see no silver plates, and this thing here don't weigh no one hundred and thirty shekels. How you know. Numbers seven. Here, lift it. Yeah, mate, you got that right. No you idiots, we are gonna melt all this down and make our own silver plate, and our own silver basin. The basin's seventy shekels. Bonzer. (Inaudible). Enough I need a smoko. Alright, alright. We filled this thing. Right. I think we need a bigger bag, mate. Gimme a hand. (Inaudible).

Incident Report 2.

The next attack occurred on Monday at 11:40 A.M. when the Cauzzies from Invasive Designate R pulled up in the Plymouth Barracuda to the Third Temple of Lesh, belonging to the goddess of armpit hair and patchouli stank. When security guards tried to bar their entrance, they were both executed on the spot. Witnesses again said they shouted, "Diplomatic envoy! Step aside!" before the blasts were heard. The Cauzzies then proceeded to enter through the temple's beaded curtain entrance where video surveillance recorded them murdering four worshippers before confronting the Chief Priest who tried to stop them from entering the storage rooms behind the altar. The transcripts read as follows:

> *Don't look at me like that you hippie freak! I feel threatened! (Shotgun blast) What you do mate? Where did he come from? Finish him off! (Laughter) That ain't kind what you just did. You shot him in the goolies. (Laughter) Why'd you shoot him in the goolies? (Laughter, partially inaudible) Lev 22, 25. (Unidentifiable screams) Watch out! (Inaudible scuffle) Quit you, I feel threatened! (Shotgun blast) That's more like it. You fellas recall Lev? 22? 25? Ye shall not offer to the one anything with its testes crushed or torn mate.(Laughter) You just put that bloke outta business, mate. (Laughter). We are idol smashers! That's right. Just like Abraham. (Clanking and hissing noise) I read how Abraham's daddy had all sorts of idols. He made idols and sold them. And Abraham smashed them and was thrown into a fiery furnace by Nimrod. Where's it say that? In those books. One of them volumes, I read it. Ol' Jothy showed me. Notice like the man Moses, you know all 'bout why he lead the people out of slavery, it explains everything, but with Abraham it don't say nothing, just says that he's chosen. That's it. (Inaudible) No backstory. Nothing. Notice that? Why's that? Cause the great one doesn't want to talk about this (expletive). Abraham was an idol smasher. Like us. So that's why he was picked. Right! We know this cause of the sages. The oral tradition, mate. That's right. Hey, how do you know them Hindus are just a buncha rank thieves? Like Punjabis mate? Them with all their elephant faced shivas and all? How do you know they stole it all from the man? How? So the highest member of in a Hindu priest see, like their supreme being, the primal source and ultimate goal of all beings, you know what its name is? It's called Brahman. Brahman? Yeah. Right. (Inaudible) Okay now this is how you know they're thieves, they dropped the A. What? Abraham. Abraham! Their supreme being is just Abraham without the A. (Laughter) See! Brahman, Abraham. They mixed up the letters a bit. (Laugher) Our ancestors praised goat heads, mate, the shame. (Laughter) That's all changed now, fellas. We got taken up. Right. (Inaudible conversations) Don't take nothing but the powders from these hippie freaks. Oi! And the oils. Let's get on our bike. (Inaudible*

scuffling)."

The call for Tungus was almost immediate. But the firm's head of linguistics was in Queens decoding subway markings and wouldn't be back until the following Wednesday. The firm would have to wait for their main code breaker to help them unravel the mystery behind words like "Abraham," "Bonzer," and "Methuselah."

They all stared at the transcripts looking for something of value. Anything. After all, what was printed on the paper in front of them came out of the assailants' collective mouths. There wasn't anything more incriminating than that. So they continued to look deeper. An assistant to Erasemus esq. was reviewing the recent inspection report for Invasive Designate R when they noticed that they had been flagged for a variety of minor violations. The notes about The Lead Inspector of General Worship being called in to verify a hat rack to see if it violated Article 87 were particularly interesting. The team re-read Article 87. It was the prohibition against Cauzzies having unsanctioned religious iconography, literature, or graven images. This was a major issue. And the team started to get excited about the prospect of pinning an Article 87 violation on the Cauzzies from Invasive Designate R. The punishment for breaking this rule was one of the more severe ones. At this point, they all felt their best bet to get the Cauzzies back to the negotiation table, was proving that they were involved in some sort of unsanctioned religious practices.

They submitted a request to speak with the venerable Jotham, the Lead Inspector of General Worship, to see if it were possible for him to, at a future date of his choosing, to review the transcripts to see if there were any violations of Article 87. A request like this, for a man of Jotham's stature, would normally take about two weeks to hear back a reply. So needless to say, the team was more than thrilled to receive an immediate answer from his office saying he'd be by in the afternoon to give them a hand. The legal team was pleased to know that stopping these killings was clearly the first thing on the minds of those at General Worship. Otherwise, why the urgency.

Jotham stepped out of the rain and into the law offices of Ygnwie, Erasemus, and Sumer, flanked by his dark emissaries, and was immediately bombarded with trays of snack cakes and various hot Incan beverages before being led into a private room covered in wall-to-wall velvet and was shown the transcripts almost immediately.

They all watched Jotham's eyes carefully scan the material in the most methodical and deliberate manner. His intensity wasn't to be questioned. Some of the younger associates and paralegals watched in both awe and reverence. Only when they saw their reflections flashing back at them through his mirrored suit did they realize they were gawking.

When Jotham was done looking the transcriptions over, he pushed aside the files and stood silently over them for a long while before finally looking up at Erasemus esq. He let them know, in no uncertain terms, there wasn't anything in the transcripts that constituted a violation of the provisions in Article 87.

The room fell silent. You could hear hearts dropping through the sub-flooring. They weren't expecting to hear this. Most were sure there was some sort of connection. I mean, you had literal execution-like killings at two temples, both the Temple of Zaels, and the Third Temple of Lesh, then there was Jones Jones's bi-annual inspection of the slaughterhouse at Invasive Designate R, who had questioned the hat rack. All this, not even mentioning the transcripts mentioning worlds like "priestly" and "idol." It just seemed to all in the room, except Jotham, that it had legs. But here was Jotham, the Lead Inspector of General Worship, saying that it had nothing to do with anything of a religious nature. Seeing their collective disappointment, Jotham made it clear that if the firm had any other corroborating evidence he would be more than happy to review it in the future, adding that putting a stop to these massacres was priority for everyone involved. Especially those at General Worship. Jotham also lifted their spirits by insisting he would be making a surprise unannounced visit to Invasive Designate R that night. He would use the powers of his office to evoke the 5th Provision of General Worship Act #3000838 that allowed him to infiltrate any domain or institution he suspected of illegal worshipping procedure. This thrilled the room as they anticipated Jotham and his army of dark emissaries invading the slaughterhouse and catching them all in the act of worshipping foreign gods. On this note, they shook hands, then shook hands again, before proceeding to the Client Delicacy Lounge where everyone refreshed themselves with cups of Himalayan yak foam spritzers and a box of Lorne Doones.

Of course, the whole thing about the 5th Provision of General Worship Act #3000838 was just a smokescreen. The only thing on Jotham's mind since hearing the news that Cauzzie Rob and Cauzzie Roy had used their diplomatic status to murder a bunch of people and rob two temples under his jurisdiction, was to knock their heads together senselessly.

That increased sevenfold when he got the call from Ygnwie, Erasemus, and Sumer to read "Jothy" in their transcripts. This was life-threatening. He realized that it was only the Cauzzies propensity to stick "y's" on the end of peoples' names that saved him from torture and inquisition from his colleagues at the Strin Agency.

Punching a Cauzzie in the face was all Jotham was thinking as he searched through Lee Land #3 for any signs of them. Starting with the methane milking lab, thinking he'd find the Cauzzies sucking up fumes in some victorious carbon dioxide debauchery, but there was nobody to be found. Jotham was still white hot when he burst into the slaughterhouse floor thinking he'd find them hiding for dear life, having anticipated Jotham's fury. But still nobody. Everywhere he looked, things looked pretty much abandoned. He entered the garage only to see the Plymouth Barracuda was gone. Just looking around, he found their stash of raw incense, bolts of taffeta fabrics, and a huge amount of cheap gold pilled in an otherwise empty storeroom. By this time, Jotham was exhausted and headed back to the recreation room to get a drink of water. He was surprised to find Gideon there, sitting by himself with his head in his hands.

"I am so glad to see you!" Gideon rose, totally relieved to see Jotham and began to shake his hand so hard that Jotham had to pull it away to save his fingers from being crushed.

Calming him down as best he could, Jotham sat Gideon down and asked him to tell him everything that happened on his first big day as an executive at The Startling Concern.

Jotham listened. Then listened some more. Then listened again.

When Gideon was finally done. Jotham looked down between his legs and almost began to weep. "What have you done?!"

"What? What do you mean, what have I done? I thought you'd be thrilled!"

Jotham took a deep breath, said a few words to his Maker hoping to gather enough strength to get through, then slowly looked up at Gideon.

"You weren't suppose supposed to make them a better idol then they could make themselves! This isn't some civil engineering project! What were you thinking!"

Gideon was beside himself, and getting a bit theatrical, he shattered the mug of cold instant coffee sitting beside him. Expecting the complete opposite reaction from Jotham, he went on the defensive, "What was I supposed to do? Get killed?! Wolves were gnawing on me! Have you ever had wolves chew on your ankles? It doesn't feel good. See!"

Jotham looked at Gideon's ankles as he pulled down his

socks. They looked pretty bad. He asked if he had put medicine on it. Gideon snapped back something along the lines of "What do you care." Jotham got up, letting Gideon stew in silence, as he paced about the room. He threw a few darts at the Bruce Lee poster. One hitting Bruce right in the eye. He thought about pulling the dart out but decided to leave it there for Cauzzie Rob to find. Then he saw the 2x4 crucifix on the wall and shuddered. He had almost forgotten about that.

As Jotham turned his sights back to Gideon, he cooled down a bit. It might not be so bad. The world makes you work through its deficiencies, he had always told himself, so why would this be any different. The good news was that Gideon wasn't dead. And like the Sages say, only a righteous man can put his life on the line. And looking at Gideon slumped in his seat with his crushed barley wheel hat and bloody ankles, the last thing he looked like was a righteous man. At least he wasn't dead. The good news was that Gideon had a 8:30 tee time with the head of The Startling Concern. They were, although strangely enough, one step closer to restoring Divine providence. So Jotham poured him a glass of water and sat down next to Gideon.

"Forgive me for getting so upset."

Gideon gave him a look, almost forgiving, almost spiteful. Then sipped some of the water. Jotham explained how he had just gotten back from the lawyers who were trying to figure out how to neutralize the Cauzzies' invasion plans, and that they had been caught on tape mentioning his name. He was thankful to even be sitting next to Gideon, mentioning how they were in essence in the same boat. Both surviving close calls with the forces of darkness. So he apologized again.

"It's all right, I'm glad you're not dead," Gideon smiled.

"I'm glad you're not dead either," Jotham grabbed one of the seven books marked Tanchuma. "Let's start prepping for your trip to Jerusalem."

"The golf course you mean?"

Jotham bit his tongue and was ready to explain how Jerusalem was never meant to be a golf course when the Cauzzies came barreling into the recreation room with various silks in their hands. Cauzzie Rob and Cauzzie Roy were clearly in the celebratory mood, and upon seeing Jotham yelled almost in unison.

"JOTHY!"

Moments later, there was shattered glass. A scuffle ensued. Punches were exchanged. There were a few bruises, but it could have been worse had Cauzzie Rob not shouted "Not the face! Not the face!" Their mission objectives were already teetering on being exposed to their enemy, no need to make it worse with black eyes. When Gideon had finally managed to separate the warring lot, everyone caught their breath.

Jotham, with a slightly cooler head, shouted for an explanation. Why. Why were they shooting up insignificant goddess temples when it was never part of the plans.

"Plans change, mate," Cauzzie Rob snorted, pulling the darts out of Bruce Lee's face.

"What do you mean plans change?! We never agreed to any of this!"

"We're making our own church. We gonna be the New Horizons Christian Church.

Jotham couldn't believe what he was hearing.

"New what? You're gonna get us all killed! You guys are a bunch of fools!"

"First off, we ain't afraid of death. And we are a bunch of fools. Like Paul says in 1st Corinthians, chapter one or is it two, I forget, but he says God is using fools to bring down the high and mighty. That's you, mate! You're the high and mighty, the firstborn sons of God. We, here, we're the fools mate!"

Cauzzie Rex held up a copy of the New Testament, having found it in one of the older copies of the confiscated Bibles Jotham had brought over the previous year.

"You overlooked this one, mate," Cauzzie Roy said.

"Aven gilyon! You and your 2x4's!"

Cauzzie Roy shook his head. "Maybe a wicked folio to you, mate! But not us."

Jotham scoffed, "Paul? He's a heretic!"

Cauzzie Roy laid the bait and now sprang the trap, "It is told of Rabban Gamaliel of Yavne, that he decreed: 'No student who is not honest in thought as in deed shall enter the Academy!' Saul of Tarsus was a student of Gamaliel! So we got you there! Barakhot 28a, or is it 28b, I don't remember. One or the other. But it's there for you to see in one of those books we stole."

"You are fools!" Jotham was watching his creation turn on him.

"You tell him, Rex."

"I will Rob, it says in Proverbs 27, or 24, I don't quite remember which one, but it says, says you can grind a fool in a mortar and pestle with grain, and he's still a fool."

Cauzzie Rob added, "We are fools! We admit it. And always will be. Even if we are ground with the grain!"

Cauzzie Roy held up a marble mortar and pestle like the kind you get over the border in Tijuana. "We had to storm those temples! Not only are we idol smashers like our father Abraham, but we needed that hippie incense. We are making our own for the altar."

"Yeah," Cauzzie Rex had jumped into the fray quoting the Bible, "*And God said to Moses: Take the herbs stact, onycha, and galbanum - these herbs together with pure frankincense; let there be an equal part of each, make them into an incense, a compound expertly blended. Refined, pure and sacred!*"

Jotham jumped in, "You can't! Exodus 30:37-38, *it shall be sacred to Hashem, any party who makes any like it, to smell of it, shall be cut off from his kin!*"

All the Cauzzies seemed to speak at once:

"That's for you Jews."

"We can't be Jews."

"We have no kin, mate!"

"We're foolish animals!"

Cauzzie Rob was quick to clarify. "First off, we can't be Jews, cause no Jew would allow it. Isn't that right, Jothy mate?"

Jotham was silent for a moment. It was totally correct. There would be no way something like a Cauzzie would be able to become an Israelite. He scrambled for a rebuttal, "Yes, but…"

Cauzzie Rob turned his back on Jotham and began addressing Gideon as if he was the real judge in the whole debate.

"Jews are the true human beings, Gideon. Jotham here is the true human being. And Jews want nothing to do with subhumans like you and me. But we are Cauzzies, we're as subhumans as you get. So whatever he tries to say don't hold water, mate. There's no getting around it, mate. We're animals. At best. That's us, see. We like to bite, we like to fill our stomachs 'til they explode, we kill things just to get ahead. We ain't no good, see. But the Christ takes up subhumans and allows us to come near, just like Jotham does with the one true God. And cause of this we be considered human, see! It all makes sense!"

"How is this gonna help me with my 8:30 tee time?" Gideon asked.

Cauzzie Rex held up the mortar and pestle, "The three kings brought frankincense, myrrh, and gold to the manger for the baby Christ."

"Christ was born in a manger, see!" Cauzzie Rob continued, "He came as food for animals see. That's how low he's come from the high and mighty. Christ was born surrounded by animals wanting a bite. And that's us! Us animals get to eat him. We got in trouble for eating all the Australians all right. That is what started this whole mess for our kind, but now, we get to eat the body and blood of the one true God. The Eucharist! Christ's body and blood in the bread. The grain we fools get crushed with, see. The Eucharist, it's not only sanctioned cannibalism, but sacred cannibalism for the Cauzzie and for all mankind! It's a dream come true, mate!"

"Shut up you idiot!" Jotham had enough.

"What?!" Cauzzie Rob acted like he was surprised. "You told us all about the Eucharist. The communion wafer, remember? When we framed that one lady Cloreen for Gideon here!"

Jotham instantly regretted discussing with them the frame-up on Cloreen at the train station.

"You weren't meant to see the Messiah in the bread," Cauzzie Rex held up the New Testament one last time, "Don't worry, mate, you're still number one in our book. Literally."

As Cauzzie Rex began flipping through the pages to find his specially marked quote, Jotham could no longer hold back his rage, and finally threw the punch he was looking to throw ever since his arrival to Lee Land #3 that night.

Cauzzie Rex's head snapped back as he took a knee while shouting, "Not the face, not the face!"

Jotham went to jump on Cauzzie Rex, but Cauzzie Rob jumped on his back, then everyone tumbled to the floor. Punches were thrown. Punches were landed. A pool cue barely missed taking Cauzzie Rex's head off. The folding patio chair smacked Jotham hard in the side. Then there was a dog pile. Gideon tried to pry them all off but got kicked in the side of the head. "Not the face! Not the face!" Punches instantly went low, and everyone was getting hit in the nether regions. Tables tipped over. More glass shattered.

When everyone finally emerged from the dog pile, shirts were ripped, hair was mussed, faces were flushed, all too gassed to continue the fight nobody really wanted to finish. Jotham spit some blood on the floor and wiped his face. Gideon was still breathing hard when he flopped on the brown sofa. The Cauzzies snorted and sneezed as they picked up the buttons ripped from their Hawaiian shirts.

They all sat in silence tending to their wounds. Thankfully

there was no black eyes or bruises to the face, and everyone began to calm down.

"I think there's been too much Halacha talk, okay, I am sorta burnt out on the law for one day. I never thought I'd say I'm sick of talking religion, but I need a break," Jotham got up along with pieces of broken mirrors from his suit. "But I'm still the chosen one. First born of God. You're all sloppy seconds, here me? That means I'm still in charge of this outfit. I'm the one who's leading the charge."

"That's all we were saying, mate!" Cauzzie Rob saw Jotham shooting him the death stare. He decided it was best to just nod his head in agreement. "Okay, Jothy. You got it, mate."

"All right, then," confirmed Jotham. "Let's just meet up tomorrow. We'll close this chapter of our lives and just get back after it tomorrow. If you all want action, and less talk, I'll give you more action. But we got to work up to it. Okay?"

ROVING

The menu board for Glad Eater Gladiator Food flickered photos of the fare far too quickly for Gideon to tell what they were offering. When he first entered the line, he figured the wait would give him enough time to select whatever it was that looked half-way edible. But now he was just a few customers away from having to place his order, and was still unable to make out what exactly there was to eat. He had squinted. He had tried to blink really fast. He had opened and closed his eyes like you do when trying to isolate the blades of a spinning fan. None of it worked. When he finally made it to the counter, he was greeted by an enthusiastic teen wearing the Glad Eater inspired paper cowboy hat. Gideon asked for two of their best sellers. She smiled and said everything is a best seller. He tried to smile and said, "Well, give me two of whatever you recommend."

She smiled back and said she'd recommend the entire menu. He asked for a couple corn dogs and a couple cheeseburgers, hoping by chance they served something sensible. She smiled and said they didn't have corn dogs and cheeseburgers. By this time the people behind him were clearing their throats — clearing the throat was the easiest way to tell someone to "get a move on" without violating their "Patience Provisions" in their

Credeth accounts. The teen behind the counter was clearing her throat now too, but still smiling as she did. Soon all the customers in line sounded like a chorus from a thousand cats caught in a spin cycle trying to clear fur balls out of their tracheas. Trying not to panic, Gideon looked up to the strobe light that doubled as a menu board and just pointed up and said, "I'll take that, and that."

Suddenly the throat clearing subsided, and you could hear the drums beating off in the distance once again. Gideon resumed breathing. The teen smiled, moved off, and returned with a tray of buffalo scrotum nachos with creamy coon-secretion sauce and a double order of boiled rhinoceros-horn marrow-chips in a condor beak glaze. The sight made him gag. The condiment station wasn't any better. He knew what the napkins were, but everything else looked like an alien salad bar. All the toppings looked to be either worming around in an iridescent slime or dehydrating like insect husks in a windowsill. He pumped what he assumed was ketchup into two small paper containers and set them on the tray.

At Aisle A he descended the gladiator arena's concrete stairs to The Startling Concern box seats. Volumair got up to let Gideon make his way to his seat. CJ Supentus remained as he was. Nonetheless, they were more than pleased with his food selections.

"You're going places, kid," Supentus slathered on the sauce. "Mmmm, buffalo scrotum."

Volumair was already halfway through the rhino chips when he realized Gideon was sitting there with an empty try, "Did you not, I don't know, like get yourself...you know...want a bite?"

Gideon set the tray down, "I had a big breakfast. Thanks."

Meanwhile in the gladiator shed, Cloreen sat doing her breathing exercises. She had found that one huge inhale, followed by ten shorter inhales, followed by a huge exhale, then holding her breath as long as she could, then breathing in deep and holding again, exhaling and then repeating the pattern at least eight times helped to circulate the blood by carrying oxygen straight to her head and limbs. By this time she felt as if little ants with little needles on their feet where migrating across her skin. She rolled her neck. It made audible crackling noises. Then she flossed with a thread of silk string. Rinsing out with Listerclean she smiled in a small mirror to ensure her teeth and gums were in tip-top condition for her eventual victory lap.

About the victory laps. Cloreen had fast become the fans' favorite. Some in the audience even adopted her sleeveless ermine, albeit faux, jumpsuit as a sort of uniform easily identifiable on the streets. It was a fun way for some fans of the gladiator arena to share some instant camaraderie by identifying themselves as fans of the most ruthlessly cruel gladiator they had ever witnessed in the arena. They were still talking about the quadruple decapitation she had pulled off in the Death Fest '99. Although discussing the gladiator arena outside of the gladiator arena was strictly forbidden, the Credeth violations bureau had eased restrictions for those discussing where they thought the quadruple decapitation ranked in the Top 5 best kills in the arena poll that was being conducted. As of the latest voting, she was currently holding the top slot. What the audience enjoyed most about her performances in the arena was how she made the barbarians run for their lives. It was supposed to be the other way around. The barbarians were supposed to run the show and the slaughter was limited to the prisoners. Now though, everyone ran for cover against Cloreen. The barbarians had even teamed with the prisoners to take on Cloreen at once, hoping to somehow overwhelm her with sheer force of numbers. But each time Cloreen found the most creative ways of dazzling the crowd and bringing her opponents into quick and violent submission. Cloreen's victory laps would have been a welcome sight to sponsors like Enkeling Futures and Prosperities and major shareholders like Ghana Princely Projects in any other previous installment of the gladiator arena's existence. But now with the vastly dwindling number of prisoners and barbarians, they realized with her merciless slaughter of everyone they threw into the arena that she was quickly going to be putting the gladiator arena out of business.

Cloreen had heard the knock on her cell door in the wee hours of the morning. Luckily for her, she never slept without her makeup and hair fully styled. So when the executives from Enkeling Futures and Prosperities and Ghana Princely Projects entered she looked as though she had been waiting on their call. They presented her with a number of requests all essentially centered around her not killing so many, so fast. Cloreen suggested they let her go free in exchange for any agreement she made to take it easy on her opponents. After all, she said, why should she help those who have condemned her to die — it made no sense. The executives liked her proposal but were unable to negotiate her freedom, her being sentenced to death in the gladiator arena after all. There was no way getting around it. Cloreen said if it was to be strict judgement then she would have to continue to fulfill her end of the contract and kill every single person they set inside the arena. No mercy. The executives left scratching their heads. If only there was a way to get around the sentence of death. If only there was an opponent that could kill her.

The executives' latest discovery was the Dervishes of Doom they found spinning in the deserts of Dubai. Their special ritualized clothing was quickly made battle-ready with retractable razors on the bottom of their tenure robes, transforming them into whirling saw blades. This, they thought, was a great way of slowing down Cloreen the killing machine.

Also making its debut that evening were the ravenous wolves of Nicht Labs of Upper Bavaria. As everyone knew, animals were forbidden in the arena unless they were shown to have some inherent defect that made their annihilation a necessity. But things like mad cows and three armed tabbies never put up much of a fight, so they were a rarity to say the least. But when Nicht Labs attempted to create a new kind of "forest management wolf" to help cull herds of elk and deer, as well as manage prescribed burns, backfired by turning the creatures into rabies carrying fire-breathers, they were sold to the gladiator arena as a fantastic alternative to human prisoners.

The executives were thrilled to see how the new attractions packed the arena to the rafters. It was so loud you could barely hear the Announcer introducing the Dervishes of Doom who came whirling onto the arena's sand.

In the midst of all the small talk, Gideon leaned and mentioned how he thought their hidden god should have a centralized worship center instead of the normal franchises and had begun to recite everything he and Jotham had discussed the previous day but was quickly interrupted by Supentus.

"Let's not talk business right now. We're here to enjoy the games."

Gideon shifted his attention to the arena where four College Professors dressed in tweed coats with leather elbow patches tried to load and fire their cross bows at the spinning Turks but missing badly. As the Dervishes of Doom closed in, they began running. The crowd was in a lather as Cloreen strode confidently onto the arena sand, pumping up the crowd as she approached one of the whirling adversaries.

There was a chill down Gideon's spine seeing Cloreen raising her sword into the air to the shouts and chants of her name.

"Let's talk about you though," Supentus said, looking at Gideon with a curious glint in his eye, adding, "I wanna know more about you. We've appreciated all you've done for us over the years. But now I wanna know more about you. The real Gideon. I know all about the other stuff. Like the stealing of cars and all that sorta thing. I wanna know who you are. Like what are your hobbies?

A Dervish of Doom spun towards Cloreen who had to jump back, the blades cutting into her ermine suit. The crowd let out a collective moan seeing their hero almost get sliced in half. When it spun back a second time though, she was ready. Leaping onto the glass barricade that separated the spectators from the arena, she made an acrobatic leap into the air, upside down and backwards, landing on the shoulders of the Dervish mounting him like a steed. Using the Dervish's sikke cap like a steering wheel, she rode him around the arena while he spun wildly with his hands in the air. She drove him right into a Barbarian who brought down an ax into the Dervishes chest as he was cut in two. With the pair dead on the floor, Cloreen leaned down and scalped them both, holding up the bloody patches of hair to the crowd. Everyone was going nuts.

"Uh...yeah...my hobbies," Gideon sputtered as he tried to concentrate on something other than the death and destruction his former boss was reeking in the arena. This effort proved futile and after a lengthy pause he muttered, "...I don't know, like sit around in my sweatpants doing nothing."

Supentus nodded his approval, "Oh yes, doing nothing is such a noble pursuit. If it weren't for my desire to keep busy, I'd be doing absolutely nothing. Either that or climbing K2 in Tibet, have you been there?"

Gideon shook his head, his gaze still glued to the slaughter in front of him.

"There is a lovely restaurant at the summit called Bahdihamgjidadma, which is just Summit House in Bhutanese. They have this lovely salad of roots, thorns, and herbs. Delightful. And they put this spicy vinaigrette," Supentus continued.

In all the excitement, Cloreen had almost missed the pair reclining in The Startling Concern's box seats. It was the first thing she had done countless times before when she entered into the arena. She'd instantly look towards the box seats to see if anyone she knew from The Startling Concern had bothered to show up.

Time and time again she was met with nothing but empty seats. Cloreen was unsure how she would react when she finally saw someone sitting there, someone who had come to watch her demise live and in person. Although, she knew whatever emotion it was, she would take it all with the utmost class and dignity. Late at night in her cell, she imagined seeing co-workers in the box seats watching, and her walking up to the glass and curtseying. Something regal and elevated. Or she imagined she would smile broadly and wish everyone well. She had rehearsed numerous times in the middle of the dark evenings alone in her thoughts, how she would walk up and most likely wave hello and ask how everyone was doing back at the office. She imagined licking her finger and making the outline of a heart on the glass. Something lovingly to juxtapose against the horrors she had to endure on a night-in, night-out basis. How she would make them proud by displaying the ultimate restraint, the ultimate resignation, and show everyone that although she was condemned to death, she was still a team player. That she was still a tried and true representative of The Startling Concern.

That all changed the moment she saw Gideon and Supentus sitting there chatting oh so leisurely. Her eyes turned black. Her blood began to boil. She walked straight to the glass, cutting down two Barbarians without even looking.

Gideon had never seen such hatred in anyone's face ever and shrank in his seat. Supentus though was still in the midst of romanticizing about the time he swam to the bottom of the Marianas Trench fishing for deep sea anglers and barreleye spook fish.

When Cloreen saw Gideon's fancy Bedouin tent bespoke fashions she knew instantly who it was that had gotten her job. And completely unrehearsed, she started swinging the sword against the glass hoping to shatter it into pieces. All she wanted to do was reach in and strangle Gideon and Supentus together at one time.

Each strike of her sword made Gideon wince in terror. Pieces of glass flicking off into his face. Supentus meanwhile continued to explain how he used to raid Spanish galleons on his youth with nothing more than a fine-tooth comb.

While Cloreen was hacking away through the glass partition, a Barbarian made his move sneaking up behind her and raising his battle ax, but she saw his reflection at the last second and moved out of the way as the ax came crashing down onto the glass. Taking hold of the Barbarian's head, she started smashing it into the glass over and over again.

The crowd went wild. Gideon could only look away as the blood began to flow.

Cloreen shouted, "Gideeeeoooonnnnn!"

Supentus hadn't even noticed a thing, "I entered the Irrawaddy valley in the early 11th century and established Mrauk dynasty with the help of my friend Tony."

Soon the Barbarian's head was nothing more than a mashed-up skull with frosted eyeballs on the neck of a muscle-bound man. With nothing left of him to smash against the glass, Cloreen dropped the Barbarian to the sand and began hacking away at the glass again with her sword.

Then the ravenous howls from the German wolf experiments gone horribly wrong rang through the arena. The pack instantly leaped upon the last of the Dervishes of Doom, clearing the razors spinning on the skirt, and ripping into the man's neck. Quickly devouring him, they turned their attention to the last remaining contestant in the ring.

Cloreen was face to face with the ravenous wolves with their red eyes, blood-soaked jaws, and snorts of fire from their nostrils.

"Hey! Is that Cloreen?" Supentus finally caught sight of her through the streaking curtain of blood. He began to cheer her on.

The wolves encircled Cloreen for the kill.

The audience sat in stunned silenced, thinking they were

finally seeing the end to what had been quickly shaping up as their favorite gladiator of all time.

Cloreen stood watching the wolves inch closer. She didn't move a muscle. Then, right before they pounced, Cloreen put her fingers to her mouth and began to whistle. But it wasn't just any whistle, it was an ultrasonic ear-piercing shrill that hit such extremely high decibels that only the fiercest of canine ears could register it. The ravenous wolves suddenly weren't so ravenous. In fact, they all dropped to the ground and began whining like little pups. Cloreen stepped forward continuing to whistle in different pitches, as if communicating to them in some primordial dog speak. One wolf after another rolled on their back in complete and utter submission. Seeing they were completely under her control, she stepped forward as their new pack leader and stopped whistling. She leaned down and scratched one behind the ears as it licked her hand. A lone fan began to clap. Then like a rolling avalanche it quickly gained momentum until the entire arena was in a standing ovation. But Cloreen wasn't done. Not by a long shot. And like some mutated Westminster dog show, she started commanding the wolves to perform various tricks, lining up in a straight line, then running around her in a circle. This thrilled the audience who began to clap in unison, cheering on Cloreen and her fire breathing wolves. The next command sent ten of the wolves into a canine version of a human pyramid. There were audible gasps of amazement.

Then, the next thing anyone knew, Cloreen screamed, "SICK 'EM!"

The other ten wolves quickly scaled the canine pyramid and leaped over the glass partition and into the audience where they immediately began tearing the audience to pieces. And just like that, all the cheering turned into screams of terror.

Gideon wasted no time and took off running for dear life up the stairs. Supentus shape-shifted into a carbon copy of Jesse Owens and sprinted to the exits. Volumair sat stunned as one of the rabid wolves chewed off his face, leaving him dead where he sat.

By the time Gideon had made it to the mezzanine level the ravenous wolves had already set fire to the Glad Eater. He saw the smiling teen was now just a burning skeleton. Gideon darted towards the exits as the people behind him trampled each other as they fled.

Gideon pushed through the arena turnstiles just before the onslaught of people got crushed trying to make it out; the wolves blowing streams of blue flames, melting everyone alive.

Gideon didn't turn back as he raced to the parking lot, down a wooded hill, and out of sight.

Cloreen had watched the arena empty in a mad flash. The wolves leaving behind hundreds of charred and chewed corpses in what was only a few minutes prior a completely packed arena.

After an extended moment of total satisfaction, having fully absorbed the utter devastation she had unleashed on the crowd, she finally broke out in a broad smile. And with the exception of the lone moan of a semi-conscious fan grasping for life somewhere in the stands, Cloreen took her victory lap in almost complete silence.

Jotham was at a total loss as to how exactly it could have happened.

He had always been careful to lock the door behind him. All three of the locks at once. And he had never departed until he heard the click of the super-security deadbolt from within. And he always waited until he heard the secret knock come from inside the apartment that let him know all was secure. The safest place in the world to hide the last Rabbis he knew existed in the world was in his apartment.

Nobody would think twice if they saw the strange looking men in the black outfits with their long grey beards working day and night within the realm of the Lead Inspector of General Worship. It only made sense that such a powerful man in charge of so much oversight would have many, many assistants. It would just be surprising that there weren't more of them considering the scope and responsibility Jotham carried on his shoulders.

It was for Jotham to know there should have been more. There could have been more if he was able to just pull them away earlier, but at twelve years of age, he hadn't the strength to save any of them. It was a painful memory front and center in his mind for all time. A scene he witnessed firsthand during Yom Kippur prayers, when the Pogs stormed in with their grey flowing robes and their shiny red masks over their faces, sweeping through with their long knives. Family, friends, teachers all with the readiness to swim against the flow of their spirit that celebrated life and living. *In them, you will find life,* is how Jotham remembered the words. But all he saw was blood. It was a slaughter. He wondered why they were all so willing to die, all he wanted to do was run. He tried to run, he tried to hide, as they all made the greatest statement they could make with their lives in death. Through the tears, and the screams, Jotham tried to make the same statement, but he was invisible. The Pogs pushed past him as he reached for their coats, begging for them to bring their knives down upon his head. But he was invisible. They didn't see him. And when it was all over, nobody was left to look at anything but him.

"Why are you being taken away to die?" asked Jotham after sneaking into the Pogs transfer station holding cells while looking for his father and mother.

"Because I ate unleavened bread," said the man who was set for transport.

If they couldn't see him, then he wouldn't be seen.

It was Jotham who had rescued the first Rabbis from the purge, feeding them bread and water for the past twenty years as he worked his way up the ladder of General Worship. He would continue to be invisible. All the way until the end, when he could watch the entire system burn to the ground. Then they would be able to find life again, in the words, as he remembered them. This for the boy who was unseen would be the statement he'd make on behalf of everything that, like him, was invisible.

He knew each and every Rabbi by name, all fifty Rabbis. So the moment Jotham saw the elderly gentleman sitting cuffed to a metal desk at the Office of General Worship he knew it was Rabbi Eliyahu Ben Yechiel.

The dark emissaries gathered around Jotham as he took his seat across from the old man with a long grey beard and faded blue eyes.

Nobody had known what to make of him. He was seen walking around the Diamond District as if he was lost. Pestering passersby who were trying to enjoy their shopping excursions. At one time he had begun shouting and pointing to the milk glass towers that surrounded him in a language they were unable to understand. The NAMP had pulled up after receiving multiple complaints. Being on edge due to the Cauzzie invasions, the NAMP agents were on high alert. So when they saw this old man in a black suit and fedora, they all were relieved it wasn't something worse.

Jotham was informed the NAMP agents did all they could to help the man and had even attempted to take him back to his house wherever that was. But he was unable to direct them to his address. It wasn't until he refused to leave the Diamond District square and had begun to pray, that they were forced to call in General Worship to assess the situation. The investigating team arrived less than ten minutes later and instantly recognized a worship violation of Rule 16, praying without the aid of a graven image. They tried to uncover what god or goddess he was worshipping so they could simply fine him then properly direct him to the appropriate temple, but this just agitated the old man, and he began to turn unruly and almost violent.

Jotham needed to be extra careful.

"Hello, my name is Jotham."

The old rabbi looked up a bit disoriented, "Can you take me back home? Forgive me, Jotham, I just…"

"Yes, I just told you my name," Jotham quickly rose and let everyone know in the quietest way possible that the man must be suffering from some sort of dementia. That he needed to be given something to calm his nerves. A pill. Or a tonic. Something to rest him up, so it wouldn't be so obvious that he loved the man.

"I can take the old man with me," said Jotham as he tried to play down any special significance of this mysterious man, "The rest home where he certainly must have walked away from will surely be missing him about now."

But the dark emissaries informed Jotham that they had checked with all the rest homes, and nobody was missing anyone, and nobody recognized who he was. And that they couldn't let him leave, the old man kept insisting that he was a Holy Man. Another clear violation of code. So they couldn't just let this man go. He needed to be arraigned.

Jotham assured him it was all some sort of mistake. That maybe they hadn't seen the photo properly or whomever was on shift didn't recognize the name. But the dark emissaries said that it was possible, but not likely. Jotham reassured them he'd find out from the man and sat back down across from him.

"You are an elderly man. You belong in a rest home, isn't that right?" Jotham said, feeding the lines to the Rabbi in hopes he'd play along. But this wasn't to be the case.

"My name is Eliyahu Ben Yechiel."

"You are confused…you are old. Just nod your head if you got lost."

Rabbi Ben Yechiel nodded his head.

Jotham exhaled a deep breath. Okay, he could work with this. He was about to turn to the dark emissaries to say, look, he's an old man and is lost, but then that opportunity quickly vanished.

"It should have been where I stood. Neve Yaakov. I came for Shabbat. It used to be there. I know this. But it was gone. It disappeared. The synagogue was there. I know!"

Jotham didn't know what to do other than try and get him to stop talking, "You're just tired, old man."

"I was to go on my way to teach Torah class. But it was gone. It got lost. Not me. You know me, Jotham. You're a good young man, tell these people, these things in their sheets. You all look like ghosts. Tell them, Jotham. I am a Rabbi. That I need to get to class. The students are waiting. Tell them Jotham. You know where it is. Take me there. Please."

Jotham shot up from his chair, turned to the dark emissaries who were hovering like ghastly phantasms, and tried his best to play it all off as the ravings of an old man who had too much to drink. But despite the dark emissaries agreeing with what Jotham was suggesting, that he was old, was raving, and possibly had too much to drink, they also knew he was guilty of violation Rule 16. And for that, there was severe penalties.

"Take me home, Jotham, take me home to the others."

Jotham pointed to the old man, "See he must be in a rest home somewhere. He's asking to be taken home. Let's…"

The dark emissaries began looking at each other. Something was different about Jotham. This wasn't the man they knew. The man they looked up to as the venerable Lead Inspector. They all began to wonder as they stared at him.

"What? What are you staring at?"

They pointed to his forehead. A bead of sweat ran down his face. A tell-tale sign to any seasoned dark emissary that something was gravely amiss.

There were great murmurings in the office.

Jotham tried to play it off. He had jogged up the stairs, he said trying to explain the bead of sweat away. "I was trying to stay fit, big lunch." It was all sounding so desperate. At this point, any rational human would have cut his losses where they stood, sending the old man away in an effort to not only save himself but the other 49 Rabbis locked away in his apartment. But even that self-preserving instinct was risky. Leaving Rabbi alone with the poking and prodding of General Worship torture chambers was even riskier than that. What if he talked. They all talked. There was not one case where they didn't talk. That's what they did on the Minus 32nd Floor. If it wasn't through sharp objects cutting skin it was with sharp needles piercing the subconscious. One way or another he'd be telling them all about Jotham, the firm's Lead Inspector, who was actually a Jew looking to destroy the pagan infrastructure from within, who kept 49 other Jewish teachers in his apartment, and who had taught the Cauzzies of Invasive Designate R all they knew about loopholes in the Great Treaty. There was one good option. He could turn and kill everyone in the room. He could snap one of their necks, stab a second with the flagpole in the corner of the room, beat the other to death with the chair. Their screams would bring in the agents waiting outside the door, but if he was lucky he could take Rabbi by the hand and somehow take down one or two if he snatched their guns from their hands. But by the time he got to the exits and into the parking lot, and was heading for the trees, they would have the dogs on him, they would quickly catch him and they would both be shot and killed on the spot. Jotham knew that was the best option. He took a step towards the first dark emissary, building up the courage to reach out and take his head in his hand and twist so hard that his neck would snap like a twig.

But he hesitated.

Like the sages say, only a righteous man can put his life on the line.

"Take him away," Jotham muttered.

The dark emissaries looked at each other for a moment.

"I SAID TAKE HIM AWAY!" Jotham yelled.

That was the Jotham they knew. And they swarmed the old man, uncuffing his hand from the desk, knocking him in the head, as he cried out to Jotham, and as they began dragging him by his feet out the door and to the staircase that descended down toward the Minus 32nd floor, he could hear the old man praying under his breath in Hebrew, "

Modeh ani l'fonecho, adonoy elohai, vay-lohay avorsai, she-r'fu-osi…"

There was a clanking of a door. Then they was gone.

Jotham stood in silence. Then cleared his throat and continued where he heard the old man leave off, "I acknowledge before you, Lord my God and God of my fathers, that my recovery and my death are in Your hands."

The grey houndstooth flannel pajamas were especially cozy, Jules had remarked. Helinka was pleased to hear this. She had spent hours searching the luxury sleeping boutiques for the perfect pair. He climbed into the bunkbed and adjusted his size 14 feet off the end of the mattress and waited. Helinka returned with a cup of cocoa. A dollop of cream on top. She pulled the covers and tucked him into bed.

"Where is Gideon?" asked Jules.

Helinka brushed a few strands of hair from Jules' forehead, "He's probably at the office. He has that new job."

Jules looked off as if pondering some ancient riddle.

Helinka watched him for a moment.

"What's on your mind?"

Jules turned to her, making a sad face, "Nothing."

"Nothing? Tell me what's eating you?"

"Can't it just be you and me? Us."

Helinka smiled tenderly, she was touched by his sentiment. "Jules."

Jules was suddenly alert, his eyes filled with adventure and fantasy, "Can't we go off together. Like where the pygmies sing? I know their language. We can travel the world together. Sleep in huts. I can help your dad and mom when they get old. I know how to make cocoa. There's all sorts of things you've taught me to do. We can be together. You created me. I'm from you."

This was the sweetest thing Helinka could hear, but although it all sounded so lovely, she knew better than to give it more than a second's thought. "You don't want Gideon to come along?"

Jules laid back down, staring up at the top bunk, "I don't think you're a good match."

Helinka smiled, "We're a perfect match."

Jules turned on his side. "I don't think you are."

She petted his hair and realized that maybe she may have to adjust the maternal dependance modulator as the wavelengths seemed to be reacting with the possession identification capacitor. Then again, she liked being wanted.

"When you get to know Gideon better, you'll see he's a fine man. And you'll look up to him as a great dad."

It was almost a pouty moan from Jules.

Helinka watched him under his blankets and couldn't help but be filled with enormous pride. She leaned in and whispered softly in his ear, "You're my special boy. We're going to rule the world one day. You and me. All we need is to make some little adjustments here and there. Then the world will be a special place. Our very special place. No more suffering. No more toil. No more tears. Just you and me."

Jules closed his eyes and murmured to himself, "A very special place. A very special place." And he curled up into a ball and started to fall asleep.

"Night night. Sleep tight. Don't let the bed bugs bite."

Helinka shut off the laundry room light. It was dark except for the glow-in-the-dark star decals she had stuck on the ceiling for him. It was silent, except for the occasional sound of Helinka pressing the service buttons for another gin and tonic. The light spilling in from under the door switched off. Never any later than 10:45pm. Mostly at 10:30pm. It was now 10:40pm.

Next was the sound of the master bedroom door being shut. Jules had memorized all the noises in the apartment. He had memorized Helinka's sleeping pattern. He knew she'd be up at 6:50am, and shuffle her feet into the kitchen to press the service buttons for coffee before coming into the laundry room to say good morning. He had memorized all her movements. The way she tapped her finger on the desk when thinking in an off-beat paradiddle, her micro-sneers with her eyebrows when she heard something displeasing, the way she always matched green with black, and yellow with brown. This is what he was programmed to do. To keep the watch.

Then at 11:00pm, Jules eyes opened, and he threw off the sheets. He didn't waste a second climbing out of his flannel PJ's and stepping into a pair of black jeans, throwing on a black wool sweater. He selected his favorite reflective running shoes. Initiating his Stealth Mode that Helinka had programmed into the Synoid for just this situation when you were hoping not to wake anybody, Jules locked the door to the laundry room. Leaping effortlessly onto the dryer, he moved to the small window and undid the latch, cranking the handle until it was open enough for an athletic man to slide through. He could feel the cold air pour in onto his face. He took a deep breath. There was something crisp about the night air he liked. He thought he caught a whiff of baked bread. Jules climbed out onto the ledge.

Keeping a grip on the windowsill, and with his legs dangling sixteen stories in the air, Jules looked down at the cold uneven pavement of the alley below. If he let go, he'd fall and splatter on the ground like a ripe melon. Jules could see a dumpster on the opposite side of the alley. There was no way he could leap to it, though. Even with his superior flexibility, there would be no way to survive if he fell short. The only option was to traverse the wall by hand to the fire escape platform some thirty feet away. So without a foothold to think of, Jules carefully moved along the span of the wall, one hand over the other, until he was able to swing all his weight and make a perfect landing on the fire escape platform. It was quite a feat of strength for the Synoid. Jules thought Helinka would be proud. If only she could have seen it live. Maybe he'd get a chance to show her some day. He recorded the entire sequence just in case she wanted to demonstrate to clients his fire rescue skills, or even the Synoid's usefulness as a sherpa for mountain climbing expeditions.

Jules liked how even at night the trees provided shade, periodically blocking out the street lamps as he strolled along the landscaped sidewalk. It was thirty-four steps between trees. Then five steps of shade. Then thirty-four steps of artificial glow. Then five steps of shade. Looking above him at the towering, mirrored high-rises reaching up into the endlessness of the starry sky, he felt sorry for them, that all they were able to do was to reflect each other at such great heights.

Jules was enchanted by the frigid weather. His first thought was to bury his hands in his pockets to keep them warm, but he instinctively resisted. He had an urge to feel the cold and let it penetrate the depths of his own artificialness. So that it would inflict the system itself, and override whatever it was it was programmed to do. Maybe there was a way to become intimate with the frost in a way that was all his own. Maybe there was a way to re-program himself, so that his first thought wasn't a desire to keep warm but a desire to be even colder. He watched his breath, the visible vapor like suspended mist being swept up in the invisible nothingness. He watched himself exhale plumes of infinitesimal particles and as they disappeared he knew they'd eventually climb above the stars to places the towering buildings could never hope to climb. His eyes reached up and grabbed hold of the tiny points of light matching them lightyear for lightyear. Jules began to skip down the sidewalk. It was fun to be alone. In the icy weather, with not a care in the world.

In the center of a roundabout, Jules saw a small park with willows weeping and park benches beckoning the weary walker to take a break amongst the gentle hum of the cityscape. A young couple sat together bundled with scarfs and mittens. Jules stood and watched them until they finally looked up to see him there. They waved and he waved back. Stepping towards the sound of gurgling water, he tried to count all the coins in the fountain one by one without using his vortex grouping calculations meter, but regardless of how much he tried, he knew in an instance there was exactly seventy-seven dollars and fourteen cents change underwater. He wondered if he could get Helinka to disable that feature so he could have the pleasure of counting for the simple joy of counting.

Passing by the Grand Hotel, a Doorman in his epaulets and long coat stood sentry in front of a set of huge glass doors. Jules looked inside at the orange haze emitting from huge chandeliers. The Doorman tipped his hat to Jules. This charmed him to say the least, and he immediately went tip his cap, but started chuckling the second he realized he didn't have one. The Doorman laughed as well, wished him well, and went back to his duty. Jules wondered what it would like to stay the night in such a regal building. He imagined the beds must be big and the comforters must be thick and downy.

"How much money for one room?" asked Jules.

The front desk manager wanted to smile, even going so far as to show her teeth, seeing the radiantly handsome charming man before her, "Are you single? I mean, it is just you? A single bed? We have king and queen."

"Here, use this."

Jules handed the front desk manager one Credeth Premium credit card with quadruple cash back rewards points.

He stood silently in the darkness for a long moment before flipping on the switch. He had never been in a hotel room before. He liked the size of the bed, but thought his bunk was far more cozier. Sitting on the edge of the mattress beside the nightstand, Jules took a pillow in his hand, and after inspecting it closely, ripped it in half, sending feathers everywhere. It was messy business, and he soon discovered no matter how much he tried that he was unable to write the words, "Gideon was here" on the mirror with shampoo.

Approaching the bridge that crossed the dark canal by the old gasworks that had been converted into live/work space, Jules wondered what kind of hat he should get so that the next time he passed by the Grand Hotel he could tip his hat to the Doorman in kind.

The dark water flowing beneath the bridge was mesmerizing. Jules almost lost sense of time had it not been for his internal clock that chimed 12:00pm with a sharp ping. He picked up a stick and pretended it was a boat, tossing it over the bridge and watching it disappear along the surface of the water. He ran to the other side to see the stick float away in the current and began to recite Tennyson as it disappeared out of sight. He looked around for another stick or some piece of debris, but he couldn't find anything with the streets being so immaculate. He was tempted to spit in the water and started to build up enough saliva to give it a try when he saw an elderly man on the shore. He looked to be fishing.

Moving down the stars to the shoreline of the canal, the elderly man waved to Jules who smiled. Jules explained he had never seen someone fish before. The elderly man explain that he was actually crabbing and went through all the steps showing Jules how it was done. The elderly man had warned Jules about getting his hand pinched by the crab's claws, but it was too tempting to resist trying to hold it. And as it snapped, he dropped the crab back in the water. The elderly man waved goodbye to Jules, who thought that he'd come back one day and catch a crab for Helinka. Lots of crabs. And he could put on a big party and have a crab boil.

Jules stared through the gates of what appeared to be an ancient cemetery. He looked at all the lichens on the tombstones and wondered how long it took for lichens to form on rocks. He seemed to know all about lichens. How a form of a lichen was a fungus and algae living together in total symbiosis. But this was the first time he had actually seen them. He liked the idea of the world being one big lichen. Humans and Synoids could merge as one body and conquer gravestones and live forever. A clank on the gate rattled Jules from his mental stirrings. The Security Guard walked up beside Jules and let him know that the cemetery was closed and to come back tomorrow. A sign above the gate read, No Loitering. Jules smiled and stepped back from the gate. He asked the Security Guard what it was like watching a cemetery and if he ever saw ghosts. The Security Guard laughed him off and told him to get a move on, he had a long night. But Jules just stood where he was, watching the Security Guard closely noticing that he was rather tense. Jules sensed a trapezius muscle had shorted out in the man's neck causing his sternocleidomastoid to pull extra duty.

"Say, mister," Jules tilted his head to the side inquisitively, "That knot in your neck. I can take care of that for you. It would only take a minute. I can reach through the gates. I have magic hands."

The Security Guard thought about it for a minute. The pain had been killing him.

Forty minutes later, Jules had finished covering the hole he had dug next to the large red oak at the edge of the 40-acre municipal park. Stomping down on the ground, Jules stared up at the large tree, examining its every detail. With his photographic memory capacity, he snapped a few photographs and filed them away. He was sure he wasn't going to forget where he had buried his secret treasure. Looked down at his fingernails he saw dirt caked underneath them. Helinka wouldn't like to see him with dirty hands. Looking closer, he saw streaks of what was clearly blood smeared on the palm of his hands.

Jules knelt down and began wiping his hands on the green

blades of grass, when he noticed a middle-aged man sitting down on a blanket some yards away. As he got closer, he hid behind a sprawling elm tree and watched the man strumming on an acoustic guitar. Jules listened to try and make out the sounds, to try and discern the tune, but no matter how much he listened, he was unable to determine what song it was. He must have been a beginner, Jules thought. He watched for a little while longer.

"Pst...pst...Hey Mister..."

It was getting difficult to focus on the red swath splashed across the newspaper's surface, where three cartons of milk fanned out in front of a photo of a gap-toothed kid, not more than six or seven. He was holding a glass of ice-cold milk. Gideon closed his eyes and tried adjusting his vision in order to see if it was indeed a milk mustache, but his eyesight had clearly deteriorated from the physical exertion that it required to run from the gladiator arena to his office. Despite his faulty eyesight, the best Gideon could do was slump in his chair and continue to stare at the kid with his tall glass of milk. Running the twelve miles across the arena parking lot, through the forest, across the industrial zone, through the downtown financial district, and finally to The Startling Concern's headquarters without stopping to see if the fire-breathing wolves were on his tail had finally taken its toll.

The elevator ride up was even more excruciating than running for his life. Being on the constant move he had no time to consider anything else but getting as far away from certain death as possible, so having to stop and watch the floor numbers ascend higher and higher meant everything caught up with him at once. The frigid night air that kept his body from overheating was replaced with the stagnant coffin-like 70-degree climate control, which just caused the sweat to soak through the Bedouin tent he wore. Thankfully, it being so late in the evening, there was nobody else in the elevator. So he used the front of the sleeve to wipe his face off, but even that wasn't good enough to stop the perspiration from flowing. His lungs were burning, his shins ached, and he could finally feel the hundred or so blisters forming on his feet.

Then the vision of Volumair flashed before his eyes. The skin from his face ripped off by rabid jowls. Gideon squinted in the hopes that pressing his eyelids together really hard would make the apparition disappear from his vision. It faded but didn't completely disappear.

When the elevator doors opened onto the top floor, Gideon staggered to his office where he managed to open the door and proceeded to flop himself into his desk chair. So that's where he had been for the past half an hour. Staring at the newspaper advertisement for three gallons of milk for $75 while supplies lasted. The entire office floor had been covered in newspapers. This was Gideon's attempt at getting a bit of privacy from the ogling janitor with his unblinking eyes.

As he began to slowly recover, curiosity began to creep into his brain. Was the ogling janitor still there, looking up through the newspapers he had so carefully laid across every inch of his office floor? Or was he finally, at 2:12am, completely alone? He reached for the sheet of newspaper print with the milk cartons, took its edge, and methodically began to pull it back to take a peek below to find out.

There, two eyes stared back at him.

He jumped back letting the newspaper fall back into place.

But there was something different, he thought, about the big eyes under the newspaper cover. They weren't the bloodshot mires that bordered on hopelessness and despair. These were calm blue lagoons with steady contentment. He had wondered if he was imagining things, being so run down. The more he thought about it though, the more he was certain that the eyes were different.

The eyes were indeed different. And it wasn't just the eyes.

It was a woman with a pleasant face and kind smile. She couldn't have been older than twenty or twenty-four, her hair pulled back in a long ponytail, wearing a grey jumpsuit. Gideon was looking down at her looking up at him, and he couldn't help himself and smiled back. She winked at him, stared for a few minutes more, then lowered her head, grabbed a toilet plunger and a bucket, and disappeared.

Gideon leaned back and suddenly didn't feel so exhausted. In fact, he felt electrified as if he was sitting in one of those ion chambers at the day spa, wrapped in a warm towel, waiting for a neck massage. He leaned back and looked up at the ceiling tiles peppered with pinpoint black holes for the sake of acoustics. He started counting the holes to see how many were on each tile, but his eyes grew heavy, and he'd quickly lose count. The heavier they grew, the more the tiles took on an inverted milky way. Black stars coursing across a cream white sky.

The clank of his office door woke him violently. Gideon had no idea he had dozed off, but looking at the clock, he saw it wasn't that long. It was now 2:37am. He turned to see the young woman standing there with a look of shock across her face.

"Oh. I'm so sorry, I'll come back later," she said, clanking the yellow mop wringer against the door frame.

"No, no, it's okay, I'm just…uh…yeah…" Gideon felt a rush of warmth filter into his otherwise bedraggled nerves.

"Oh, okay. If it's not too much trouble."

"No, not at all."

She smiled at him and rolled the yellow mop wringer back in, and started mopping the floor, not bothering to lift up the newspapers. It started making a strange grayish green paste the more she wet the paper and ran it along the transparent floor.

Seeing this, Gideon stood up and started picking up the newspapers that she hadn't yet drenched.

"Let me… uh…let me get these…"

"What?"

"The newspapers."

She looked down and saw for the first time the saturated newspapers print, "Oh."

"It's alright, I got this," Gideon hurriedly picked up all the newspapers once again exposing his floor to the janitorial supply below. Looking up every so often he caught glimpses of her standing with her mop and smiling at him. She blinked in a way that seemed to fan the sparks that leaped around his subconscious, and he would look away bashfully.

A loud beeping noise began to scream from her jumpsuit pocket as Gideon jammed his office trash can full of soggy newspaper print. It was a loud and punctuating shrill. Almost like an alarm; she began to panic. Reaching haphazardly into her pocket, she apologized profusely.

"I'm... I'm so sorry. It's just..."

Gideon wondered what the noise could possibly be, and he stepped back a bit concerned, the day's events putting him on notice to beware of anything howling, beeping, or buzzing.

"I'm so sorry, it's just my...my..." she pulled out the small handheld device, "It's just my Match Meter."

It said they were a perfect match.

She blushed.

Gideon looked at the read out. And there it was on the tiny screen, filled with little hearts, the words "PERFECT MATCH."

She again began to apologize profusely, but this time with an artfully shy smile.

"No, no, it's okay."

Gideon went back to his desk, and she continued to mop the floor, but now sort of biting her lip and looking up at him from the corner of her eyes.

There was a sort of excitement Gideon had not ever known, a coursing neural static that he couldn't seem to contain and made itself manifest with the question, "What's your name?"

"My name?"

"Yes. My name is Gideon."

"My name is Thurp."

This name wasn't exactly the name he had been expecting. He would have guessed, Petunia. Daisy. Or Breezee. Something along those lines. But not exactly Thurp.

"My friends call me Thrips."

This was worse. Thurp or Thrips, Gideon decided. He'd call her Thurp.

"Thurp, did you, uh, maybe want to grab a cup of coffee with me?"

Thurp looked a bit confused. "Coffee?"

"Yeah."

"The stuff they keep in the break room? I can check for you…if there's some left."

"No, I mean, I'd like to take you out and just, you know, talk. For coffee. You and me."

"Oh. Okay," Thurp smiled and bit her lip once again. "I just have to go unclog Mr. Boswillig's toilet and then we can go get a cup of coffee… with you."

"Yeah, okay, that sounds perfect."

"Okay!" she laughed.

"Okay!" so did he.

When she was gone, Gideon checked his hair, cuffed his hand over his mouth to check his breath. Nothing too offensive. But he grabbed a mint nonetheless. In his desk he found a note from Helinka regarding an old dinner engagement he had intentionally missed. Helinka. He had totally forgotten about her with all his senses having shorted. What was he thinking, asking some young girl on a date when he was already living a wonderful life with Helinka? How on earth could someone known for remembering have forgotten a wedding date set for Spring.

In the flood of realization that rushed over him, Gideon was stuck on another thought. The Match Meter said, "perfect match." There was no manipulation at all to that specific read out. Thurp just happened to have hers in her pocket, and he just happened to be close enough for it to go off. And it said perfect match. There wasn't any manipulation needed by The Startling Concern to get the result of "perfect match" like they had to do with him and Helinka. Those results weren't real. They were fake. He knew they were fake because the way she'd tap her finger on the desk all the time drove him up the wall. The way she'd scrunch her face all negative and contorted whenever he suggested a restaurant. Her ghastly obsession with brilliant green tunics. Not to mention her annoying parents in their spiraling underground house. All these thoughts helped shape a magnificently eye-opening existential question of what exactly was his life. Whatever came up a perfect match with Helinka was a lie. He knew he was living a manufactured life. But he had always just thought that everyone in the world was living a manufactured life, so why not have the best of everything, and do what you love and get paid a fortune for doing so. The desk he was sitting at was a lie within a lie within a lie. He liked Russian dolls, he told himself. That all seemed to get derailed the moment he met Thurp. Or Thrips like her friends called her.

So Gideon's imagination got to work building himself the perfect life. One that included Thurp by his side, with her hair down, brushing the tops of her shoulders. Gone was the ponytail. He'd free her from that existence, the one that forced her to keep her hair up. It wouldn't be hard to liquidate his entire existence for cold hard cash. Whatever was left he'd smash to bits with a sledgehammer. He'd buy them a cute little bungalow by the beach. Somewhere distant where The Startling Concern had no reach. Where exactly that was, he didn't know, maybe some archipelago off the Chilean coast. They'd need to bring sweaters, he thought. But they'd still be able to take long walks on the beach. He imagined her giggling. He imagined chasing her and them falling to the sand, where he'd kiss her, and things would turn serious. Passionate. They'd paint the bungalow white with canary yellow trim. Somewhere, maybe above their bed he'd hang a fishing net, or some ship's anchor. He'd take up smoking a pipe and sit on the porch watching the fishing boats casting their nets. A small boy, not more than six or seven, would hold the day's catch. Stoking the coals, he'd warm his hands by the flames. Looking up to see Thurp in her sundress picking lemons from the grove and pulling herbs from the garden. After dinner, they'd sit and hold each other and count the stars.

At the coffee shop on the bottom floor, Gideon watched Thurp wait for the glass doors to open before almost skipping to the table with this magical quality he found irresistible. And as she slid across from him into the booth, with that deep penetrating look, and as she bit her lip the way she did, it was all that it took. He was smitten. She was the one. And it didn't seem to matter leaving his world behind, that life was over as far as he was concerned. Gideon was gonna do it all for her. His true perfect match. He was going to leave it all behind for Thurp.

It was that simple. If the irritating buzzing noise from the Match Meter was signal for perfection, then the match had to be a thousand times more wonderful than that. Sure, he had a decent life with Helinka, and they somehow pulled it off being total opposites, but after seeing Thurp that was all out the window. He made a vow never to go back. Gideon was suddenly moving forward with his authentic self, and he instantly knew he needed to be totally honest with Thurp. That meant he'd have to tell her what his job truly was at The Startling Concern, and how he was a spy for a Jewish spy, a sort of double agent, and that he was gonna make millions, and she needed to leave her job and run off with him. There was no time to waste.

"I need to tell you something —"

"—Wait!" Thurp blurted out, "Is this coffee?"

Gideon was taken back for a second, then realized the look on her face was of someone who had never tasted coffee before.

"This is so gross," Thurp said laughing.

Gideon watched her, and his heart began to race. How beautiful she was. So perfect in her innocent laughter. It was so pure he thought.

"I can't stand the stuff either," Gideon laughed along with her.

Then suddenly she turned silent, and gave Gideon a long penetrating gaze, the same one she had been giving him since they both discovered they were made for each other. Then she bit her lip yet again. Now all Gideon wanted to do was lean over the table and start kissing her. The new totally honest Gideon wasn't supposed to hold back. The idea of kissing her was the only thing on his mind. And so the new totally honest Gideon knew there was but one thing to do at that very instant. And that was to kiss her.

He leaned in across the table, their eyes locked.

"Wait!" Thurp blurted, "My lip."

Gideon looked at the almost gangrenous canker between her lip and gums.

"I have a sore," Thurp said, "That's why I keep biting it. The medicine doesn't work."

"Uh...oh," Gideon looked to gather his senses, but thank goodness Thurp was there to help him make a smooth transition.

"You mind if I let my hair down?" the tone of her voice was smooth and low and resonated through Gideon's system.

"No. I was gonna say..."

Thurp then detached the ponytail hair extension and dropping it onto the table. She ran her fingers through her short uneven buzz cut. It was as if some small child took a pair of scissors to her hair and just began to lop off huge sections at a time.

"I have to wear it for work. I actually found it. You know the lady in the big office? The one overlooking the fashion square? It was in her waste basket. You'd be surprised by what I find there. I have found tons of stuff. Like there was this sandwich with like two bites in it. I didn't find nothing wrong with it."

Gideon winced, "You ate a sandwich out of someone's trash can?"

"No. Only Half of it. The other half I gave to Durk."

"Durk?" Gideon wondered, "Is that...is that your boyfriend?"

The notion of Durk being her boyfriend seemed to trigger something within Thurp who started to wheeze as she laughed. This just increased exponentially.

Finally, Thurp saw the waitress, instantly stopped laughing, and began to order food.

"Do you guys have... what's that stuff that you put on the peanut butter?"

The Waitress guessed, "Jelly?"

"Yeah! Gimme some of those little, tiny jelly things. The kind you bring to the table if someone orders bread."

"You mean a Jelly caddy?"

"Yeah, but I want just one," Thurp then realizing she was sitting across from Gideon, added, "Say...are you paying?"

Gideon could do nothing else but to say yes.

"I'll have bread. The entire loaf. And five jellies."

When the Waitress was gone, and Thurp turned to Gideon, she began staring at him again. And was back to biting her lip.

There was nothing worse than making a vow and having to go back on it, but then again, there was an even bigger concern for Gideon than that. How exactly was this person a perfect match for him? He heard her clear her throat and her voice raised two octaves, only to listen to her explain that when she drinks the blue fluid in the janitor supply her voice goes down and gives her that nice smokey voice. But when she's not drinking whatever the blue fluid was that they kept on the shelf next to the bleach, her voice raises, and she hoped one day if she drank enough of the stuff, her voice would be permanently sassy. Gideon kept asking himself; how exactly was it that the Match Meter said they were a perfect match? What part of that blister under her lip did the Match Meter think reflected his spiritual essence? What part of the toilet plunging and the high-pitched voice did the Match Meter see in him as the ideal partner?

It was true. His life with Helinka was a total fraud. But it was also true that his so-called "perfect match" was completely disgusting. Maybe the machine was broken, or she found it in the trash. None of it was starting to matter though, as Gideon watched as Thurp practically inhaled the entire loaf of bread in one bite. She took the five jellies and jammed them into her pocket — beside the Match Meter, Gideon presumed.

Thurp suddenly began to change colors.

At first instance, Gideon thought the cause might be the lighting from outside, and the passing NAMP agents who were patrolling the streets. Then he blamed it on the fact he hadn't slept in almost two days. But he soon came to the conclusion that her skin was actually changing from a nice rosy peach to a pale grayish green.

"What's wrong? Are you okay?" Gideon saw sweat streaming down her face.

"I'm...I'm fine..." she gasped, her eyes rolling up into her head.

"Are you sure? You look...." Gideon gulped, "...Terrible..."

"I'm not...I'm not..." she was now all but choking.

"I'm not what?" Gideon was waving down the Waitress.

"Supposed...to... eat...bread..."

And with a thud, Thurp collapsed on the floor.

Gideon began screaming to the Waitress for help.

When the Emergency Disposal Squad arrived, they wanted to speak with Gideon about the events that occurred that had brought the innocent young woman to such a dismal and untimely end. Although not exactly dead, but not exactly alive either, they had decided to take her away nonetheless, figuring it was better to be on the safe side and avoid having anyone on the streets that was anything less than fit. Plus the Waitress had put a claim on her body in with her Credeth Plus Account so the Emergency Disposal Squad felt that was enough to tip the balance in favor of immediate containment. Gideon was moving toward the exits when one of the Emergency Disposal Technicians noticed him. When the technician detained him, Gideon played dumb, like he had no idea what the procedure was when you came across a dead or dying body. They took his name. Then took his name again. Then they filed a preliminary report with Credeth so they could review and determine any violations that may have been committed during the night's proceedings. His name would now be forever linked with Thurp. Or Thrips as her friends used to call her. Somewhere in the mainframe of the super computation device that retained all this sort of information, information that would come in handy for later use, would show that he, Gideon, had bought a cup of coffee for a young woman on the lower end of the social stratum while engaged to be married.

After confirming his address, the full name of his fiancée, and taking witness statements, they finally released Gideon on his own recognizance. Walking through the icy streets off in the distance, between two mirrored buildings, a team of NAMP agents dragged three dead wolves out of the city on hooks. And the sun began to rise in the East.

CALL ME

In her terrycloth bathrobe, Helinka sat snug beside Jules on the sofa like they were two robins in a nest. She listened graciously, trying not to move the slightest bit to her left or to her right. Jules sat legs crossed with his hands folded in his lap and his head tilted to the side like an inquisitive terrier. Neither Helinka nor Jules attempted to betray their valid suspicions as Gideon tried to explain away the $17,000 bill the Emergency Disposal Squad had delivered into her hand for the disposal fees for a 17-year-old blonde girl who had been "left comatose after having a cup of coffee with her fiancé" in the middle of the night.

Both Helinka and Jules were particularly amused by his explanation of how he was trying to help a janitor make ends meet, that he had seen she was looking sickly and pale, and how his company values acts of charity. All the executives at The Startling Concern took part in charitable causes, and that he was simply interested in dedicating time to underage girls, or janitors more specifically, that is, underage female janitors who were afflicted with gangrene. Gideon went into great detail about the lip wound the janitor had that turned a viscous yellowish color, and then he said he had actually saved the girl's life before she died, or something along those lines.

It wasn't so much that Helinka didn't believe a word he said, her concern was whether she was too obvious about the fact she didn't believe a word he said. The last thing she wanted was another audit and more hefty fines for sincerity violations within her morality portfolio. It was best to just keep a straight face and think of something mind-numbing like cold oatmeal in order to do so. This was why she wasn't about to bring up the hotel bill that had arrived just moments before Gideon arrived home. The bill for a one night stay with extra fees tacked on for the torn pillow, a smashed up lamp, and a shattered bathroom window.

The sooner Helinka could extract herself from the discussion, she thought, the safer she was. It was better to just move on with her day. There was a lot to do, and getting to work was a good way of throwing Gideon off the scent that she felt deeply betrayed and knew better than to believe a word he said.

"Coffee anyone?"

Helinka decided to get up and press the service button for breakfast. She was about to press another button for coffee service, but then thought better of ordering coffee. The last thing she wanted was to end up being dragged off by the Emergency Disposal Squad like the poor nameless girl in the report.

"Hot chocolate, Jules?"

She changed the subject.

The new drapes were coming in today. The old drapes were going out. She considered mentioning something about her big day. How she was on the verge of a huge breakthrough at work that would finally hold up her end of making them amongst the richest couples in the country. Instead, she got up and went to the bathroom where she turned on the shower so he could wash off all the slime from his body.

"You look really tired," she told Gideon.

Maybe Gideon could get some sleep on the super train to the Holey Land in the hopes of at least not looking as though he had stayed up all night…helping people.

She sat down and ate breakfast next to Jules with the radio off.

Thinking that there was a chance his instincts were wrong, that Helinka didn't think he was completely and utterly full of it, Gideon had taken the clean towel she handed him as if there was nothing wrong and pretended as though he believed every word of what she said, and shut the door. He stared at the mirror as the fog consumed its edges. He did look tired. He'd have to try and get some sleep on the train. Helinka was right about that. Maybe it wasn't over, he thought. Maybe there was still a chance they would get married, he thought.

Jules sipped his cocoa. He kept repeating to himself. Say nothing. Say nothing. Just be there for her. Act as though he was lockstep with all her sentiments without saying a word. This would help keep her from breaking down, it would help give her the courage she needed, and allow her to get on with her day. This is what he did, this is what a Synoid was, he confidently reminded himself.

So Jules went to her closet and pulled a silky green blouse and a black pencil skirt from the closet and laid them out on her bed.

The first slide from the projector flashed the image of a headless body in the park holding an acoustic guitar. The second slide featured the headless body of a security guard leaned up against a lichen-covered tombstone. The next slide was of a headless body curled up behind a dumpster with a pair of binoculars and bird seed spilling from his pocket. As the slideshow continued, Vintner Vowell brushed his mustache, curling the ends into sharp points in the most subconscious manner.

The NAMP had their hands full with all these mysterious deaths. There was not one morality violation reported in the vicinity of any of the decapitations allowing them to link the perpetrator to the crime. So the NAMP were having a difficult time understanding how exactly someone could be walking around the city decapitating people and leaving no trace of the heads without some morality violation being recorded somewhere. But there were none. The only people who weren't under morality provisions with financial institutions like Credeth all lived deep in the jungles of Malaysia. Or rumored to be hidden away in ice caves in Antarctica, but that was just a rumor, and it was a violation to even consider it. There was absolutely nobody from the jungles of Malaysia anywhere near the crime scenes around Merletown that night. If any Malaysian was in town, the NAMP would be the first to know, they were sure to reassure Vintner Vowell. Then they thought the killer may in fact be a night beast. Like some huge overgrown animal with razor teeth. Maybe it was the ravenous wolves that had escaped the gladiator arena who might have done it. But it wasn't the ravenous wolves. Those had tracking devices. And they were nowhere close to where the decapitations had occurred. Plus if it was the ravenous wolves, where were the heads? It made no sense. It was at this impasse that an agent named Nils recommended calling in a great white hunter to try track down the killer.

"When we saw they had no heads we instantly thought of you," the Warden of NAMP was sure to make perfectly clear.

Vintner Vowell made a low rumbling noise that shook the slideshow projector from its base. The agents all waited as Vintner Vowell paced the room. When he turned to face them, he said in his earth-shaking baritone that he would need five of the top NAMP agents to assist him, and an assurance that when he tracked and bagged the perpetrator that he was guaranteed the trophy for his wall. Done. Handshakes ensued. A bottle of fine brandy was opened and poured on the ground to honor Vergath, the god of nutrient rich antioxidant foods, in order to celebrate of the beginning of a successful campaign.

More handshakes.

Vintner Vowell was now on the trail of the head-snatching subhuman killer.

Gideon had never been hoisted above the heads of men, but there he was on a gilded board with satin cushions and hot beverage service as four men carried him on their shoulders while running. The palanquins were reserved for societies upper crust, and it was Cloreen's favorite mode of transportation. So it was only natural for The Startling Concern's corporate concierge to arrange that her replacement (Gideon) be taken to the train station the exact same way. Moving through the financial district to the Merletown Station, Gideon was able to truly appreciate the awkwardness of the clothes he was wearing. Neon plaid knickers and shimmery salmon-pink overstuffed vest. If he happened to fall overboard into the sea, he knew the vest would surely keep him afloat and would be a beacon to wayward ships for miles around.

Gideon had never golfed before. It always looked so silly to him. But there he was, trying his best to get acquainted with the differences between each club. There were so many. Then the bumpiness of the ride made it impossible to focus in on anything else but not tipping over. He hoped his inability to purchase the Cobrastrikes wouldn't negatively affect his popularity on the course. He wasn't able to get the RTX Cobrastrikes as he had hoped, and was forced to settle for the Viperlofts X33s.

Arriving at the train station, Gideon was eventually lowered to the ground. One of the bearers informed him they didn't accept tips. They were all more than happy to carry premier members of Credeth on their shoulders in exchange for all-day access to the corporate gymnasium, where they would feast on regulated feed consisting of protein chaff and fine fruits, and use all the pressed oil they wanted. There was plenty of wrestling matches and leisure time at the swimming pool. It was a great life, they said. So much so it was their custom to actually tip the passenger. Handing him a bag of injectables, one of the palanquin bearers squeezed Gideon's arm saying he looked a bit soft and he was welcome to join them at the gymnasium.

He politely declined the invitation, but as Gideon stepped directly onto the 1st class train car from Platform 6, he checked his biceps. Lumpy but definitely not soft.

"Do you just have a ham sandwich?" Gideon asked.

The Waiter looked perplexed. Gideon went on to explain that all he wanted was a slice of ham stuck between two pieces of bread. But the more he explained the more perplexed the Waiter became, until Gideon gave up explaining entirely and just agreed to the raw cormorant sashimi and stinging nettle salad with the toasted bark beetles, as the Waiter had recommended.

As Gideon sat watching the depths of the ocean whip past at supersonic speeds, Gideon's mind began to assault him. It was the sandwich at first. The image of Thurp and Durk, whoever he was, sharing a partially consumed sandwich from the waste basket. He cringed at the thought of those two and the permanent stain their worthless lives would leave on his important one.

A hollow feeling in the pit of his gut quickly overwhelmed him. Helinka. His mind continually replaying the look on her face when he told her the fiction about what had happened the previous night. It didn't matter if the Credeth audit would come back to her showing him free and clear, exonerating him of all guilt. And he would certainly leave the clean report on the kitchen table for her to find along with the other bits of mail. And he was indeed thankful for the secret immunity he carried within his Palladium account status. But actually none of that mattered anymore. Gideon knew that she didn't need some report to tell her whether or not he was or wasn't lying. The look in her eyes told the story. And those eyes spelled doom for any future they had together as husband and wife.

The Waiter returned with the tapir hock broth starter.

Gideon was thinking of repair. He could send flowers. But flowers might imply guilt. They also sent flowers to funerals. So he scratched the thought of flowers. He thought about picking up some souvenir in the Holey Land, but the non-sequitur would just compound his distance in her eyes. There was no really good ideas. Maybe brutal honesty, he thought. Maybe he should just be the true Gideon he had imagined he'd be with Thurp, and could just be that with Helinka. He could tell her that he wasn't some premier anything, no upper crust of society. That he was just a thief. Now a double agent for the last Jewish man he knew of in existence. The whole Match Meter results that said they were a perfect match were a total lie, set up by The Startling Concern. That she was only cover for a larger business endeavor. But before she began to throw things across the room and break out in rage, he could try and explain all he had memorized from the seven volumes of books he stole, and his work with Jotham, that marriage was anything other than perfect. That it was full of suffering and struggle.

That it was the will of the one true God that despite these differences they stay together and fight to merge opposites. Like how God merged night and day. That they could learn to know each other for who they really were and come together as one to create a new life. The truth was they didn't need some machine to tell them if they were compatible or not. But he knew the truth. Jules would be there. Jules would be there to whisper in her ear if he wasn't already. Maybe he could borrow one of those shotguns Cauzzie Rob and Cauzzie Roy left lying around and blow a hole through Jules' head. That wouldn't go over well if he was trying to commit to Helinka, destroying her life's work. Maybe it was best if he just tried to make friends with Jules. Get on his good side. That way he'd whisper other things in her ear. Like how nice he was. And how dependable he was. And that they were in fact a perfect match. But then he realized Jules would probably just say how much better he was than Gideon. Every single thought, every single idea, just fizzled out. Even if he got rid of Jules somehow, or made friends with him, it made no difference. Maybe he could tell her the truth about Thurp that he was smitten by her and vowed never to look back. Gideon stared at the hock broth. He leaned in to catch a whiff of the soup's dank odor of used socks left in the hamper too long. Suddenly jarred from all considerations other than total self-preservation, he determined that being brutally honest was too brutal a path to take. He'd have to join some charity groups he thought. Pad the story. He would make inquiries at The Startling Concern about all corporate philanthropy the moment he got back. Those pamphlets would arrive to the apartment, and he'd set them on the kitchen table too so she could find them along with the other bits of mail.

With his non-Cobrastrike golf clubs slung over his shoulder, Gideon stepped off the train onto Platform Z and moved with the crowd beneath a massive sign welcoming all Credeth account members, Level Sterling and Above, to "The Holey Land, a Sindon Smile Corporation For-Profit Enterprise."

All the running from ravenous wolves, lack of sleep, and the supersonic train ride left Gideon feeling a bit wobbly. Stepping to the lookout point, Gideon set down his golf clubs and took a quick rest. Jerusalem was now completely entombed in a pale, green colored, rubber-like substance, as if a synthetic lava flow had covered every bit of the ancient city. The thickness varied in depth. In some patches Gideon could see what looked like green rubber TV antenna sticking out of the ground. In other places the substance looked 40 feet in thickness. Gideon glanced at a plaque which detailed all the innovations that made The Holey Land the world's premier outdoor attraction. The substance that covered Jerusalem, he found out, was called Elastipoxycone.

There was a special thanks to the patron god Chazuble and their matron goddess Manipple, along with their child, the moon goddess Abakus, for making the dream of covering an entire metropolis with Elastipoxycone possible.

Even though it was totally unknown to the visitors boarding the trams, Gideon knew that underneath the everlasting layer of synthetic goo lay Jerusalem. He tried to see if he could make out any sign of the Western Wall, the Tower of David, the Mount of Olives, the Temple Mount, or anything that Jotham had told him about. But the stimulated environment of The Holey Land was so disorienting, almost by design, he couldn't help but feel like he was someplace other than planet earth.

Before boarding the tram, Gideon showed his credentials to the three Greeters dressed head-to-toe in argyle who stood at the entrance of the machines that carried passengers along an elevated path straight to the Holey Land Clubhouse. Seeing his name, they seemed to be impressed.

On the tram, Gideon stared at the fake trees that swayed in the fake breeze, with fake birds singing fake songs that unnaturally gave Gideon the sense of story book enchantment. Passing the bungalows, he thought at first they were life-size gingerbread houses with peppermint shingles until he saw a pair of visitors walk into one with their pet cat. A cartoon character bird with goat horns dressed-up like a Scottish highlander seemed to be the Holey Land's official mascot. Gideon gathered the mascot's name was "Bogey," by all the signs accompanying his face that pointed to "Bogey's Bistro" or "Bogey's Bungee Jump." As the tram moved along the elevated path, he could see in the distance what must have been one of the 18 golf holes, where mechanical crane lifts with huge crystal like wheels roamed across the undulating surface. There were also strange floating machines that looked as though they had four sets of wings, fluttering about the crane's lift platforms. But before he could get a really good look, his view was blocked when the tram went through a tunnel or around some former building that was now just a green rubber mound.

The Holey Land Clubhouse was a huge geodesic golf ball structure with a volcano sticking out of the top that periodically erupted the green rubber substance into the air. Gideon was now awash in hundreds of shimmering banners announcing the "1st Annual Pro-Am Golf Tournament benefiting The Health of Wellness Internment Camp and Hospice." The banners draped down from poles, lamp lights, and clear wires hanging across the elevated path. Soon Gideon realized Supentus had invited him to take part in a corporate charity event that looked to benefit the less fortunate of society which the banners made obvious with all the smiling elderly people with mildew-laden tubes up their noses and the sallow children with dirty crutches.

At the Holey Land Clubhouse there was a warm welcome as Gideon marveled at the tremendous dome structure. He also wondered why nobody was dressed in the latest golf fashions and felt a little self-conscious about his puffy vest. Moving to the check-in counter he was handed a basket of rotting pomegranates with instructions, and they directed him to the mouths of Chazuble and Manipple, the god and goddess of promised tithes delayed due to other more pressing payments.

Step one. Throw the two pieces of fruit in the mouth of Chazuble and the other two pieces of fruit in the mouth of Manipple. Step two. Bow your head to the floor while placing your right hand out before you and your left hand on your wallet. Step three. Shout as loud as you can, "I implore the wombat-faced deities, let me score well enough to impress those around me, but not too good as to embarrass those who I serve." Step four. Get up and leave.

The 1st Hole. Gideon saw one of the crystal-wheeled crane lifts waited the next pairing. The winged machines fluttered in the air above it. They looked like large metallic yet vertical dragonflies. A strange whooshing noise accompanied their constant hovering.

At the tee, Gideon thought he saw Supentus in his mummified-skin tracksuit with the name "Shishak" sewn on the back in an Old English typeface. But the closer he got, he saw it wasn't Supentus, but a tall, gaunt, and silver-haired man. Looking around for his boss, he quickly realized that Supentus must have shape-shifted into an older more distinguished man for the sake of the charitable event. Gideon walked up and happily greeted him.

"Hello Sir. You weren't lying when you said this was an amazing place," Gideon offered his hand.

The man looked a bit puzzled. Then an unseen voice.

"Great to see you Gideon, I see you've met Sindon."

Gideon spun around to see Supentus standing there in a similar mummified-skin tracksuit but with the name "Thutmose IV" printed on the back.

"Hello, Sir. Yes, we just met," Gideon played it off as best he could.

Supentus could see the confusion written on his face about in the matching tracksuits, "We have the same tailor."

Gideon laughed uneasy, "I see. Yes…uh, those aren't… they're not too common…"

"No, my Tutankhamun is on the hanger," Supentus confirmed.

Gideon was lost.

"We not only have the same tailor, but we have the same handicap, don't we CJ?" added Sindon with a devious smirk.

Supentus turned to Gideon, "He's just buttering me up, I've lost the last three rounds to this pillar of humanity you see standing before you."

"Who's buttering who up now?" Sindon said with a nudge in the arm for an old friend.

Whizzing up beside the trio, a teen boy in white hospital gown wearing a turban pulled up in an electric wheelchair, followed by an old woman around 85 or so with an oxygen mask hobbling with a cane, and lastly an armless kid not more than 8-years-old with a vacant expression. They were the pitiful picture of human wreckage.

"Speaking of handicaps!" Sindon exclaimed.

Sindon handed the teen boy in the white hospital gown a plush Bogey doll. They shook hands, made small talk. Then Sindon explained to Gideon how The Holey Land was a place for the sick and elderly to rest.

"I wanted to find a way to give back. And what better way to give back then to solve the world health crisis, Gideon. To gather together all those around the world with infirmities and nobody to care for them, and provide a future filled with hope. Like Pablo here. Pablo was rounded up in the raids on San Salvador, I forget exactly when but that's not important, dates and times. What's important is that he's finally home and in our care. His family back home is thriving now, isn't that right, Pablosito?

The teen boy nodded his head nervously, "Si, señor."

"See! Since Pablo here has been in our care we have fitted him with this robotic wheelie device and he's zipping around. It is a joy to watch. He'll be your caddy today, Gideon. This here is Magdelana," Sindon moved beside the old woman in the oxygen mask. "Magdelana was acquired on the streets of Cartagena, isn't that right Magdelana?" he continued off her nod. "Yes, well, she was begging for pesos, can you believe it, pesos?! Her family had sent her out to knit those little wrist bracelets to sell to tourists. She's been one of our finest success stories. Her lateral agility has proven to be quite impressive. Sometimes, I wonder if Magdelana has a little something extra in her oxygen tank. Do you have something extra in that oxygen tank of yours, Magdelana?"

"Si, señor," she responded with a faint grin.

"See! See!" Sindon moved beside the 8-year-old armless kid. "This one. This one here is Yassir. He's my little miracle boy. Now you might think he can't move very well but you'd be surprise what Yassir can do. He's actually from right under our feet. After we had poured the foundation for the parking lot and convention center, he crawled through the Elastipoxycone screaming, and we pulled him out. He was forced to sever his arms to climb out of two bear traps. With his teeth, mind you. He's a great kid. Being an orphan all the monies raised by you Gideon for each hole you win will go to benefit the HFMS fund. Helping From My Sofa has done such great work for us over the years and this inaugural year they've really stepped up, Gideon. CJ here knows all about the work we do. That's why he's trying to launch a hostile takeover."

Hearing this Supentus sniffed, and corrected, "Not exactly hostile, Sindon. More like belligerent. Or hateful would be more accurate."

Sindon smirked smugly, and turned back to Gideon, "You'll be meeting many caddies today hopefully. The whole point of The Holey Land is to benefit charity. We are poised to be the most profitable charity on the planet by the year 2101."

Then they both turned their attention to Gideon's golf bag. "What's that you got there?" they asked.

"These?" Gideon wondered, "These are my golf clubs."

Sindon burst out laughing, "By golly they are, golf clubs! Jolly good show!"

"That's brilliant, Gideon. Brilliant," Supentus was laughing so hard he squawked like a pterodactyl roosting on its young.

The two CEOs patted Gideon on the back as if he was an old college chum in on the inside joke.

"You'll have to let me use that one, Gideon! Golf clubs. Jolly good show," Sindon took a handkerchief and wiped his mouth from laughing so hard.

Gideon took it all in stride, as if he knew why they were laughing. He had no other choice than to laugh himself because he was totally clueless as to what they thought was so funny. A gloved attendant graciously took the golf clubs from Gideon's arm and rushed them away for safe keeping.

The two CEOs were still laughing at the joke when they stepped toward a crystal wheeled crane lift machine.

"We can use some of that zip over here at Sindon Smile Corp, CJ."

"Well Sindon, sign my generous proposal and I'll put him on your team. Exclusively."

Gideon remained silent as he listened to the friendly banter between two rival CEO's.

"The work we are doing here at the Holey Land is too important to risk putting in the hands of The Startling Concern. The Holey Land is my life's work. It's where I chose to put my name."

"Nobody wants to see you retire, Sindon. I just want to own you outright. Like a slave or a drunken mule. I want to ride you around like a pack horse. You'd remain active, trust me. But you'd also be amongst the richest men in the world," said Supentus, as if these were words were somehow consolation in the face of a hostile corporate takeover.

"It sounds tempting, but I am already one of the richest men in the world."

"On paper. You're stretched pretty thin, Sindon. One false move, one bad year and you'll be running to me, asking to make a deal. When that happens terms may not be so sweet."

"Your point is well taken, but you know very well with the gladiator games losing all their gladiator assets and are well into their reserves, they won't be the only show in town much longer. They'll be out of business by Spring. And the Holey Land is ready to take full advantage. We'll be the only game in town. We have room to grow. Scaleability is what we have. We'll be rivaling your Vacatican any day now."

Gideon had memorized his part. Like an actor with a the script. A script written by Jotham. It was only for him to memorize the lines. Asking Supentus the questions Jotham needed the answers to, so that he could overthrow the pagan powers that had for so long negated God's Divine providence. These were questions like, what were The Startling Concern's future investments? Who was on their mailing list? What were the plans for the Panama Canal re-branding project? Asking these sorts of things was tougher than it looked, and Gideon was unsure how exactly to bring any of this stuff up. How was he supposed to just ask, "Hey, Mr. Supentus, Sir, who else do you have on payroll that my friend Jotham can turn into a double agent like me?"

Jotham never prepped him for being the third wheel with two of the most powerful CEOs on the planet. It was ludicrous to think Gideon was somehow going to be able to interject anything other than total utter silence. It was best not to talk, and Gideon blanked on the script.

It was time to board the Meccatee 800 Module.

Gideon knew it wasn't going to be your average round of golf when the crystal-wheeled crane lift rolled up with four massive tires the size of a single story ranch house in the suburbs. It had a huge green platform attached to a massive hydraulic arm that would lift them up in the air and in all directions.

The Meccatee 800 Module was what Sindon called the greatest invention of his generation. An exclusive mobile golfing command center with state-of-the-art clubs and the finest service buttons on the market. Sindon pressed a lever and out of a small door on the Meccatee 800 Module's dashboard a silver tray emerged with three La Quintain's Majesty's Reserve cigars. Gideon knew these were the most expensive cigars in the world. He had to keep his hands from shaking.

From the sapphire command chairs, looking up at the floating robotic seraphim flapping their mechanical wings, Gideon suddenly had a vision of Ezekiel standing on the river Cheber. It was Jotham who had said he would never share the secrets of the Merkavah to someone like Gideon. That the secrets were too powerful for someone like his profane mind to contemplate. And this might have been for all intents and purposes true. The admonishment didn't keep Gideon from continuing to wonder.

"I see you made this like Ezekiel," said Gideon, "Like the whole thing is like the Merkavah. God's chariot."

Sindon mused between puffs, "Merka-vah? What is that? Merkavah? Is that that Greek yogurt bar in Hiroshima?"

"Oh, I thought…the chariot…" Gideon stumbled.

Supentus seemed to understand what Gideon was saying so he graciously chimed in, "He wants to know about Bopal. The architect. Tell him about your architect, Sindon."

"Ah yes," stuttered Sindon, his mind suddenly refreshed, "Well, I conceived the whole thing with the famous architect man Bopal. He came up with the design. But it was my concept. I wanted the course to look timeless but yet completely futuristic. Bopal will meet us on the 5th Hole. He's always there to say hello."

Gideon buckled himself into the sapphire command chair which seemed to swallow him whole, resolute more than ever not to say another word.

With the Meccatee 800 Module rolling down the course, Sindon got on to talking golf swings. They were all sitting at the controls of the new Cobrastrike Mecca-Command Center. Gideon was surrounded by all sorts of buttons, levers, blinking lights, and monitors.

"Gideon. Since you are not familiar with the Cobrastrike Mecca I'd like to point out a few things to help improve your swing."

Sindon pointed to a row of buttons labelled Woods 1-4 and Irons 5-11, with one button marked with the letter "P" for putter, adding, "Here are your clubs. And you enter the coordinates here."

Gideon saw the dial complete with barometer and wind speed measurements.

"Just watch us and you'll get a hang of it," Supentus reassured Gideon.

Sindon agreed, "Keep your back straight, Gideon, is all I am saying. Trust your clubs. Trust your clubs."

The Meccatee 800 Module seamlessly rolled across the uneven green rubber terrain toward the 1st Hole. The flapping machines followed them overheard. Ever in the promotional mood, Sindon explained that despite the 1st hole's photogenic looks there was the 500-yard-plus carry over water, cliffs, and treacherous bunkers, tight confines, the blind dogleg-right fairway with its elevated green at a front-to-back roll, that the par-5 etc., and it just went on and on.

Gideon stopped listening, not only because he had no idea what Sindon was talking about, but because there were three people standing on the tee, who suddenly started to run as fast as they could down the fairway of the 1st hole.

Sindon explained it was Pablo, Magdelana, and Yassir.

Since Pablo rolled in the wheelchair he quickly outdistanced both Magdalena, who appeared to have a limp, and Yassir, who definitely had a limp. Despite the differences in speed, they continued to encourage each forward. Almost as if their lives depended on it.

Supentus being up first at the tee, moved levers up and some down, pressed green and red buttons, waited for blinking lights to start and to finish blinking. Then with all the dramatic flare he could muster, he raised the Meccatee 800 Module's arm up until the platform rose 150 feet off the ground.

"All right boys, watch and learn from the master."

Suddenly a golf ball the size of a grapefruit shot out of the front of the Meccatee 800 Module. It began soaring totally off course. No problem, the flapping-winged machines got into the action immediately, flapping their metal wings so hard that they sent little gusts blowing the ball back on course where it dropped about 15 yards ahead of Magdelana. She made a lateral move to her right just as the golf ball exploded sending shrapnel into her arms and legs. She buckled to the ground, started screaming, then got up and grabbing her arm, started running again.

"Great shot!" Sindon exclaimed.

Gideon watched in horror as Magdelana was drenched in blood and continued to move down the fairway toward the distant flag that stuck out of the distant green.

Yassir jumped headfirst into a sand trap.

Sindon moved the levers, pressed the buttons, and waited for the blinking lights to finish blinking, then adjusted the Meccatee 800 Module's arm to raise to about 200 feet and swung, sending the huge golf ball straight to the bunker where Yassir was hidden. The flapping machines made only slight adjustments to the ball's trajectory that caused it to land about ten yards in front of the sand trap. As it exploded, two crutches went flying in the air along with a cloud of sand.

"Oooooooh!" Sindon whooped. "Was that a hole in one?"

It wasn't. After a few moments Yassir climbed out of the sand trap and continued running as fast as he could toward the flag.

Supentus laughed, "That was a good stroke. Maybe more loft next time."

Sindon agreed.

Now it was Gideon's turn. He watched Pablo zip away around a water hazard and straight down the fairway. He had seen what Supentus and Sindon did, and memorized their shots thinking emulating them was the best course of action. But now seeing that they were sending military ordinances at human beings, he decided he'd do the complete opposite of whatever they were doing. The last game he ever wanted to win was a game where they were killing humans for sport. Watching was one thing, but actually doing was a completely different matter. So as he gazed upon the control panel, he knew the last thing he wanted to do was to be good at this game. Gideon went about trying to sabotage his own game.

He moved the levers in the opposite direction, pressed all the other buttons, and didn't wait for the blinking lights to finish blinking, then adjusted the Meccatee 800 Module to about 100 feet, quite lower than his two CEO opponents, and pressed the swing button.

Gideon was so happy to see the ball flying viciously off course, but then the flapping machines pounced on it, blowing it back towards the fairway and directly into the path of Pablo.

When the ball landed, it took one giant bounce, then landed square in Pablo's lap and instantly exploded into a million pieces. It was such a brutal direct hit, nothing was left but two burning wheelchair tires.

Gideon turned ghostly pale.

Sindon started clapping and hollering. Supentus began hooting and stomping his feet.

"Hole in one! Hole in one!" shouted Sindon.

"Fantastic shot! You're a natural kid," exclaimed Supentus.

Magdelana and Yassir scrambled to the green in tears and took hold of the flag which spelled that they had made it through one hole. 17 more to go. Magdelana and Yassir were lowered to safety for transport to the 2nd Hole.

Sindon's enthusiasm for Gideon's miraculous shot continued, telling him, "Praise be Manipple! Praise be to Chazuble! What a shot! I'll never forget it, Gideon. The Holey Land is all about future histories and you've given me something completely cherishable to forget. And their lives! Pablo is no longer in any pain. Praise be to Manipple! Praise be to Chazuble! And because of you, Gideon, their family, wherever they are, don't have to worry about their snack bill for the next three months. And they have 40 days free cable."

Sindon began to laugh like an exotic vulture gloating over roadkill. Gideon had to cover his ear to keep from having his eardrums burst open.

The 2nd Hole was a par-4, 200-yard penal hole with a gorge of broken glass as the primary impediment to the green.

Teeing off last, Gideon watched Sindon lay up in the rough and Supentus miss by a mile.

Gideon's turn. And his nightmare only got worse.

Marcel was an elderly French man in a grey cardigan who had become an unnecessary burden to his family when he developed "old man smell," which they described as a stale decaying musk, and was thus donated to the Holey Land. Marcel shook Gideon's hand and tipped his cap, happy to be his new caddy. Gideon tried to tell him to run away and never look back, but his French was so rusty that by the time he put a few words together, Marcel was off and running down the fairway.

Gideon had some decisions to make. He didn't want to go the extreme opposite like he did his last shot. That backfired terribly. So he decided to do his best to avoid the flapping machines that so accurately corrected his first shot and instead fire his golf ball low across the surface.

He watched the golf ball whizz past the flapping machines thanks to its low trajectory and begin bouncing off the surface, gaining massive amounts of speed as it continued straight down the fairway.

Sindon was amazed, "It's a skipper!"

Nobody had seen anyone shoot a skipper before, it was the impossible shot, only a few master golfers had ever pulled it off. The golf ball literally skipped over the course gathering more and more deadly momentum forward with each bound off the fairway.

"I've never seen a first timer hit a skipper!" Supentus shouted.

Gideon had no idea what a skipper was. But he kept hoping Marcel would turn around to see the ball heading his directly at him and maybe try and duck, or get out of the way somehow, anything but continuing his run in its deadly, skipping path.

Then to everyone's amazement and Gideon's abject horror,

it became clear why the shot was called the "skipper." A pair of razor-sharp knives popped out of the side of the golf ball and began to spinning through the air like a buzz saw.

Marcel turned around at the worst possible moment. He might have avoided being cut in two if he had just thrown himself in the bunker, but instead the blades caught him at maximum rotation.

The two CEOs couldn't believe their eyes. It was high-five after high-five. Gideon's face went up on the jumbo screens. It was the "skipper" of a century even if there was only one year left in the century. The replay monitors couldn't get enough, showing the shot over and over again on monitors for all to see. It was the talk of the snack shack. They were practically erecting a statue of Gideon under the Sycamore tree.

A gaggle of photographers met them on the 3rd hole tee.

At the 3rd Hole, Gideon was introduced to Thirstin, an articulate and charming man who's only ailment was the fact he had adult acne. Gideon thought he looked fine. Regardless, Thirstin promised Gideon he'd run like the wind and was thankful for the opportunity to be a part of such a wonderful charity. When Gideon told him to run and hide, Thirstin laughed, as one does when they don't understand exactly what one is saying, and then he took off running. Thankfully Gideon's shots did no serious damage to Thirstin who made it to the flag in one piece. That didn't stop the idol worship. Crowds continued to show up to just touch the corner of his fluorescent puffy vest.

At the 5th Hole, Sindon introduced everybody to Bopal, the golf course's chief architect. And then it became totally apparent what Sindon meant when he said Bopal always met you at the 5th hole. It was because Bopal was dead. Encased and suspended in a twenty-square-foot blue transparent plastic mold, his lifeless body was perpetually preserved and completely intact. The substance was called Florb. Sindon informed everyone Florb had no other commercial attribute other than keeping human bodies in a complete state of incorruptibility. He was hoping it would catch on with the young kids in the new year.

Gideon couldn't help but note Bopal's agonized facial expression and the unsettling blue wizard cape he was wearing.

Sindon informed him again that Bopal would always be there to greet you at the 5th Hole. Specifically, between the hours of 9am to 6pm every day, except Wednesdays when they take him in for cleaning.

Gideon wondered why they felt it necessary to mold Bopal in plastic for all time, but thankfully, Sindon answered him without the need to even ask.

"He knew where the doors to the tomb are hidden," Sindon remarked. "So we had to kill him. Mold him, I mean. He volunteered matter of fact. He volunteered for molding. Which he did as you can see here. Very well. Carry on."

On to the 8th Hole par 4, Thirstin died uneventfully after shrapnel from Gideon's hooking wedge shot exploded 10 yards from where he was hiding. It wasn't the most glorious shot. Sorta "lucky" as Supentus put it. Nevertheless, what mattered most to all betting parties was his phenomenal score that was holding at -12 for the day.

Then they arrived at the 14th Hole, or what was dubbed Mount Cyanide.

It was a 380-yard par 4 with pools of cyanide replacing water hazards, and a fake mountain spewed dense fog and shot sparks out of the hole. Gideon made another terrible shot. By this time, Gideon learned how to work the controls. By firing his ball and having it sink into the water hazard was the best shot he could hope for. Because when the ball exploded, or shot out a hundred knives, or a thousand volts of electricity, or darts filled with biological agents, or whatever the horrible things decided, it would do so underwater.

Gideon's shot landed exactly where he wanted it to, right in the center of the water hazard. But the splash coming from his ball landing dead center in the pool of cyanide doused Fecundo head to toe with the corrosive solution. Gideon had to watch as Fecundo's skin liquified off his body in wafts of green smoke.

"Fantastic shot!" Supentus shouted.

They couldn't believe their eyes.

"Look at that cyanide eat him away!" Sindon rejoiced.

"Cyanide shouldn't burn someone's skin like that..." Gideon tried to keep his composure, but he knew cyanide wasn't corrosive, "Cyanide's a salt extracted from an almond, it's just a salt, it can't eat away your skin like that!"

Sindon looked at him nonplussed, "Cyanide doesn't burn your skin you say? Well, now it does! But not the bones. We are working on it though. Maybe we'll perfect it for the Second Anniversary Tournament. I'm sure you'll be rejoining us soon, Skipper."

Gideon looked down at the maintenance crew in hazmat gear shoveling Fecundo's dripping bones into a wheelbarrow.

24 hours earlier, if you had told Gideon he'd be walking off the 18th hole with a nine stroke lead on two of the most powerful CEO's on the planet, with the flash from photographers popping in his face, while adoring fans were chanting your new nickname "Skipper! Skipper! Skipper!" he'd have thought it were a dream come true. After all, Gideon had even closed his eyes on the train ride over, praying to Jotham's invisible God. Asking to have some sort of miracle, and be the best golfer he could possibly be.

So there went the Skipper walking down the gangplank towards the reception at the Clubhouse.

Gideon was unable to avoid watching replays of all 8 of his "master shots" because the Clubhouse was surrounded by huge monitors. Even the tables and chairs were television screens.

When Supentus got up to go to the restroom, Sindon handed Gideon his business card, whispering, "I like you Skipper. Call me anytime you want to move up the corporate ladder. I can offer you Credeth Level Black-Fire-On-White-Fire. CJ's never gonna offer you that. The most you'll get out of him is Level Palladium. Call me. We'll talk."

After munching on the buttery cracker on toast, Supentus insisted he and Gideon dine together later that evening.

Later that evening at a private table, a stocky Waiter with slicked back hair listened as Supentus placed his order in fluent French. When he was done going through the menu, the Waiter bowed, made a sharp about face, and strode off to the kitchen.

"I hope it's okay Gideon that I ordered for us?" Supentus asked politely.

"Uh, yeah, it's fine," Gideon had heard things like braised antelope shanks, deep fried osprey talons with cream of horse, and thought it sounded sort of edible compared to what he had been forced to endure so far with his newly elevated Level Palladium status.

Supentus poured them both a glass of wine, "You're going to love the appetizer. It's a Singapore delicacy. Flaming fallopian cubes."

They were still flaming when they came to the table.

"Those guys in the kitchen say it's a top-secret recipe, but I can tell you, Gideon. The secret is citrus peel and nori."

Supentus waited for Gideon to sample the fare.

Naturally, Gideon hesitated. When he finally put it to knife and fork he cut a small section off that wasn't as squiggly as the rest and slowly brought it to his mouth. Expecting the worst, he began to chew.

Supentus continued to watch, waiting for Gideon's verdict when a Holey Land Official approached the table with all due cordiality.

"Excuse me, Mr Supentus. Mr. Gideon," said the Official bowing his apologies for the apparent interruption. "You've raised so much money today for charity, Mr. Gideon, that the families wanted to present you with this special Holey Land keepsake."

The Official proceeded to place a bag of fingers on the table that belonging to Pablo's right hand. The Official then bowed, and bowed, and then bowed again, before excusing himself.

Seeing the gruesome trophy, Gideon instantly turned a ghostly pale.

Supentus noticed his change in complexion.

"Is it your first time?" Supentus asked.

"Yeah…" Gideon tried to compose himself, seeing the fingers up close and personal made him realize he had actually murdered eight people in the most brutal of fashion, "I've never ever…ever…ever…ever…"

Supentus was surprisingly sympathetic. "Ah. Yes. Don't worry, Gideon. I was like you at first. But don't worry. You get used to this sort of thing. It's what people in power learn to accept. That these things are a part of life. It comes with the territory."

Gideon forgot what he was chewing and swallowed.

"Like I said, it's your first time. Every chef is different. Some tend to overcook the finer cuts of meat. But I'm like you, it took me a few times to really taste the citrus peel."

Gideon was now completely confused as he thought Supentus was talking about all the needless death at the Holey Land not the subtle flavor profile of pig uterus.

But "Uh…uh…yeah…" was all Gideon could stammer.

Supentus took a few bites and turned to Gideon.

"You're right. It's missing something isn't it. Not just citrus peel. Something else. Style maybe. This whole place is missing that secret something, isn't it? Like a secret ingredient. Style. Look how he steals my style. He was my tailor before he was Sindon's. Guess where he got that idea from? Me. He got it from me. That secret ingredient is me. Seriously. I'll say this for the man, Sindon is a starter. And he's trying. He's got that going for him, Gideon, he's a starter. But he's not the man to lead anything though to its full purpose. Toward its ultimate end. This place has potential, Gideon. But with Sindon steering the ship, it's not going to sail the seven seas. It'll founder in some tranquil bay. My offer is sensational and he knows it, but he still won't sell. He'll break eventually, but not soon enough. I need to find a way to force him to sell. Throwing more money at him won't help. It's just made him more confident, more stubborn. I'd start my own Holey Land, but I wouldn't get far with Sindon controlling all the contracts with the hospitals. And those retirement home things. No. I want this land. It's not just the golf course, it's the land I want. I want the land. It's the bridge between Africa, Asia, and Europe. It's an ideal location. Centrally located. It would make The Startling Concern the most powerful conglomerate in the world. If I could just get my hands on it. I want to set up my office here. Our headquarters. It's perfect. I want you to help me steal it."

This was the moment Gideon was waiting for, the chance to sneak in all the stuff he had been schooled to say, "I have an idea."

"An idea. What kind of idea?"

"I know how we can put him out of business, or at least get him to agree to sell. For pennies on the dollar."

Supentus seemed open to suggestions from his protégé. "I'm listening, Gideon. Tell. What is this idea of yours that will make him sell for pennies on the dollar? Tell me, I'm listening."

"Look at what's happening to the gladiator arena. Like Sindon said himself, they're losing all their inventory. And unless the gladiator arena figures out how to stock up on more gladiators, they will be out of business by Spring."

"When it does, I may increase my shares. Or even take it over."

Gideon thunked the table with is hand, "Well, we'll do the same to him!"

"What do you mean?" Supentus snorted.

"Our invisible god. The all-powerful god that rules all."

Supentus stirred in his chair.

"What we do is simple," said Gideon. He covered the bag of severed fingers with a napkin, and continued, "We say the poor are the salt of the earth. We say the poor are the face of god. Our invisible god! We say that because the invisible god made you and feeds you, and clothes you and shelters you, that cause he does all that for you, you need to be like him and clothe, feed, and shelter the lowest of mankind."

Supentus thought that he understood what Gideon was suggesting, "So what you're saying is we make sick people into something with social value, not just to be sent away or exterminated for sport like the gladiator arena or…here. We convince people that they can gain merit and earn points by helping poor people and not killing them? And you do this all as the way of thanking our invisible god?"

"Yes, the sick and elderly too. Taking care of them is a way to score points with the all-powerful god himself, not on some golf course. This way, the poor will have an option, they can have themselves exterminated at the Holey Land, or they can find refuge and redemption with the one true god. Our god. The one we own. And that's how we get around any of his hospital contracts or whatever Sindon's got his claws into. Then we will control all the poor and all the sick and all the dying. When that happens, he'll be forced to sell. There won't be any more caddies for him to play golf with."

"It sounds logical, Gideon. Although, this flips everything on its head. This sort of thing is beyond any current thinking we have today. It's beyond reason."

"Our god operates above reason. Until the world can learn how to raise the lowly up, then he isn't going to like you. It's not only behaving and treating others well that are like you, its about raising up those less fortunate. And if you do this, then it will remember it, and then when you have violated some Credeth morality clause, you don't get punished because of the good deeds you did. It's sort of like a better reward system too. With our invisible god, you get great financial points and could also use those points to avoid future punishment. So our payouts are smaller too. This is how we beat him, CJ."

Gideon couldn't believe he had said what he said, let alone called his boss "CJ," but instead of lashing out, he watched Supentus slowly begin to take ownership over the idea. It was clear he liked what he heard.

It would be a monumental project, but the concept was so simple. So clean. So easy.

An invisible super god who rewards you for being kind to the poor, the widow, and the sick, for financial points to future purchases or future forgiveness. A god of love and compassion. One that forgives your violations. You keep the morality based financial reward system with the added benefit of zero to no penance. This was what a loving super god would offer consumers. The more Supentus tried to tear it to shreds in his mind, the more the idea seemed to have legs. He liked what he was hearing.

Gideon watched Supentus chew on it over the braised antelope shanks. He watched Supentus kick the concept around over the terrine of deep-fried osprey talons. He watched him mull it over the bowl of creamed horse. Then finally, they were on to dessert.

"I like it Gideon," Supentus was sold. "But what do we call our invisible master god? I am thinking Zaxon. Or Azyx. Something like that. With a Z. I'm thinking like rarely used letters. And we do an alpha and omega type thing, what do you think?"

Gideon smiled, "None of those."

"None? What then?"

"How about just god."

"God? Like just god?"

"Yeah. Just god. There's no room for any other god. Just god," Gideon's confidence was growing, moving far beyond anything Jotham had told him to say, almost to the point of forgetting Jotham even existed. Gideon started feeling an overwhelming rush of creativity, and he continued, as if it was all his idea riffing off the top of his head, as if it was all his conception from the beginning, he began to get excited.

"He has a real name, but you can't say it out loud or you die. Like if anyone hears you say it, like two witnesses hear you say his real name, they can stone you to death. With rocks."

Supentus liked this suggestion, "Then we can offer rewards where you get to travel to one of our resorts and can say his name without dying. You know what I mean."

Gideon totally understood what he was saying. It would be a great way to attract members to reach for a super bonus objective outside of just material items. And saying the invisible gods ineffable name wouldn't cost us a dime. The Startling Concern would be making 100% profits by the utterance alone. The options were seemingly infinite, Gideon was sure to say.

"And when we buy out Sindon and take over the Holey Land for ourselves, we build a giant temple where everyone in the world will have to come to offer gifts to the god. It will be the Temple to replace all other temples. We'll make it illegal to have a temple anywhere else but the Holey Land, like bamot, and like three times a year, everyone in the world has to come and offer up gifts so that it is on everyone's mind, it's like their main concern day in and day out, and then nobody in the planet will ever forget who made them and who owns them — our god. "God. The invisible all-knowing all-seeing god that fully examines your heart and mind. And he will punish you and reward you accordingly. With the pilgrimages we can build new roads, new trains, new hotels, and we can offer worship packages. We can call them festivals, and these festivals are built around the harvests, or better, they are built around our production schedules, like stuff we are doing at The Startling Concern, like whatever products we are selling. Like the stuff with the Panama Canal thing, whatever that is.

"Oh, and we can even make it illegal to worship other gods! And if you worship other gods then you get condemned to the gladiator ring. You'll have to buy that in Spring, and we can reopen it, and we can also make those people who illegally worship others gods, they will become the new caddy! Not the poor! The poor inherit the earth! And when we have everyone believing in the one god, the invisible god, then eventually we can make him show himself. But not him, he's too powerful and if you look at him you'll die, so he'll like send his son, some powerful man who comes down from the sky to walk the earth and show everyone the new rules, like a new law, and you'll have to bow to him because he'll be the king of kings forever and ever. And he'll live right here! In the Holey Land. And we will change the name to Holy, like as in Sacred, the Holy Land! And we'll control all of it!"

He finally took a breath.

Supentus poured out the last of the wine.

"I have to say. I am impressed, Gideon. To think this whole time, I thought you were just a decent car thief. I am glad I rescinded your liquidation order."

"My what?" Gideon thought he heard right, something about having a liquidation order lifted...

"Don't worry, Gideon. Your protégé Shim. He took your place. Never mind all that, let's focus on this other thing. I mean, the ideas you have just seem to pour out of you. It's quite impressive. I've haven't seen anything like it for, I don't know, a hundred and eighty years or so."

Gideon heard the compliment and liked it, "Thank you, Sir."

"I want you to call me CJ from now on."

"Thank you, CJ."

"Those books that you memorized. The ones we had you acquire from Smith Smith. You seem to have such a better grasp on the contents than my clerics do. They are all confused. These are the best and brightest you know. That's what they tell me. But I'm starting not to believe it sitting here with you. Do you know they just recently found out the books were written backwards? This whole time they have been deciphering the thing and it's been completely backwards the entire time. The Hebrew is backwards, Gideon. Can you believe that? It's been weeks wasted. An entire program set behind months. Maybe years. But you. But you, Gideon. You knew the words were backwards the entire time, didn't you? The whole time."

Gideon suddenly got a shiver. What had he walked into just now. He wasn't exactly sure, but he said it in a strange way that made a shiver run down his spine. Suddenly Gideon had nothing to say.

So Supentus stepped in and hissed, "I think you know even more than they do at General Worship. You know about them don't you? General Worship?"

The way he said this gave Gideon goosebumps.

Supentus wiped away crumbs from the tablecloth and onto the floor, asking without eye contact, "Do you happen to be chummy with a the Lead Investigator of General Worship? His name is Jotham. You know about him?"

Suddenly Gideon remembered where he was. He suddenly remembered who he was talking to. His confidence disappeared in an instant. Whatever spell he was under that made his tongue take flight was suddenly cut in half and left to squirm on the floor. The spark of foreboding sweeping over him quickly caught the dry withering trees and the dry bones of the village until it was a fearsome inferno. Gideon went through his memory bank, trying to recount everything he had said in his moment of unholy inspiration, and knew he couldn't blame it all on the wine. He had promised himself he'd keep his mouth shut. Stick to script, but that was all over now. There was no script. There was no keeping to himself.

"Jotham?" Gideon asked nervously, "Yeah, I think I've heard of him."

"Well, I think you know far more about this sort of thing than even he does. And I thought nobody knew this God stuff better than Jotham. But here you are!"

Gideon tried not to give himself away. He was a spy after all. So he did what he thought a good spy would do, he shut his mouth and just nodded.

"Yes, Sir."

"CJ!" said Supentus, slurping the last drops of wine in his glass and leaned in. "Gideon, I like this idea. I like it all. This idea of yours, the invisible god. I like it a lot. I like the idea of the poor and sick being turned into a new kind of asset, all the stuff about a single Temple stationed at the Holey Land, and all this other stuff about the son, all you said. Here's the rub, see. I still need to be able to have strict rules. You see, I need strict rules not only for the masses to follow explicitly to the letter, but also for myself. You see, I am the one that gets to interpret the rules. I can't afford for there to be anyone else giving their two cents, if you know what I mean."

Gideon again just nodded, "Yes, Sir."

"I want to make sure there's no schisms going on. I want things to remain completely whole. That there is no, like, I'm not sure what exactly you'd call them? A Messiah for example. If there's going to be a Messiah. And this Messiah is going to eventually walk the earth, I want to be the one that tells him who to heal, when to cure, how to pray, you know, even down to what you eat and what you drink. I want to be the one who tells them when to go back down and when to come back up, and that sort of thing. Do you think with all your infinite knowledge, with all your insight, with your brain so far out ahead of the curve, do you think this going to be a problem for me to accomplish?"

Gideon shook his head, "Uh...no. Not at all, Sir."

Supentus smiled warmly, "CJ. Call me CJ."

ON THE BRIGHT SIDE

The office intern was splashed in black dusty ink. The custodian said a piece of copy paper had gotten stuck up inside one of the rollers, but despite trying to loosen it with a straightened wire hanger he was unable to unclog the jam.

One of the secretaries managed to grab hold of the paper's edge but when she tried to pull it out, the paper just ripped. Someone suggested they send the folders to get printed and bound at a copy store, but when they searched the phonebook the nearest copy store was located in Flin Flon, Manitoba. So they scrapped the idea. The Duodenary Office Manager never liked the idea of printing out folders for such a solemn occasion. The Octonary Office Manager said with great pride that as long as there was an Enkeling Futures and Prosperities in existence all folders for all high-level inter-corporate meetings would be printed. It was only when the Secondary Office Manager signed off on scrapping the folders because of the busted copy machine that the debate officially ended.

The high-level inter-corporate meeting between Enkeling Futures and Prosperities and Ghana Princely Projects on the subject of Gladiator Arena Spring Failure 2100 would proceed without printed folders.

The wall-to-wall glass office overlooking the Merletown business district had been kept locked up and sealed up until that day. The room was practically empty except for two potted snake plants with phosphorus deficiencies. There had never been a board meeting on the oval shaped black onyx conference table. Some workers who had been with the company its entire twenty five years of existence didn't even know there was a "Conference Room of Sadness" in the building.

But there was a "Conference Room of Sadness" and its door had officially been unlocked for the first time that day when the seven board members for Ghana Princely Projects filed in one after the other, their heads down, dressed in grey and black patterned dashikis, while the seven board members for Enkeling followed behind in similar fashion one after the other.

The offerings to the gods and goddesses were made without ceremony. Both chairmen exchanged pleasantries and small gifts of esteem. But nobody unwrapped the boxes. They had snacks, but these too were all snacks in the darker color schemes. Black coffee was poured. The blinds were drawn. A small handheld flashlight was lit and placed under the table. And the meeting ensued in an orderly fashion.

Meanwhile, downstairs in her lab, Helinka was binding her fingernails with scotch tape from the desk drawer of one of her technicians. She had nervously been waiting the results from the initial incubation when she was told she had blood on the end of her mouth. Seeing her nails being gnawed to the quick, and hoping not to look mad, she began hunting for bandages. Then the numbers started coming in.

Everyone rushed to the table to see that the numbers that had arrived were good. Better than expected. They were happy to see the test results proved they were at the exact same level they were when the test results came back for J.U.L.E.S. And Helinka loved Jules. How much more so would she love her latest, new and improved version? She was eager to find out, hence the nerves.

Hours later when the growth stimulation machines were hydrating the Synoid embryo hidden away inside the huge steel cylinder, she waited even more nervously. Her mind knew anything short of miraculous numbers would most likely spell the end to her career. And as a result, the end of Enkeling Futures and Prosperities. The only one to blame would be her. That wouldn't play well with her Credeth account. The plasticky noise her taped up fingers made when tapping them on her desk, was a constant reminder of how important this reveal was. Her entire career rested on C.N.A.B.L.

C.N.A.B.L. was the accumulation of everything Helinka had to offer.

She had spent countless hours perfecting every aspect of its personality, of its appearance, of its behavioral responsiveness. She had fine-tuned its growth potential processors in order for it to quickly adapt to any situation presented with both skill and aplomb. Her time with Jules had given her marvelous insights as to how exactly to improve upon her original breakthrough. Gone was Jules clinginess, his desire to always over-please. Gone was his propensity for jealousy and his desire to be the leader of the house regardless of who was actually in charge. Gone was his obsession with flannel pajamas and dark 90% Guatemalan cocoa with steamed, never boiled, cream. Although all these idiosyncrasies were things she adored in Jules, she had begun to associate them with being hers, and hers alone. Jules was far too personal to have ever been a marketable success. Therefore, she knew in order for C.N.A.B.L. to succeed where her other Synoids had failed, she'd have to put aside her personal preferences and think first and foremost about the masses of people out there that just wanted to be served, that just wanted to be entertained, that just wanted someone to adore them, without it costing too much or requiring too much of them in return.

Hence the C.N.A.B.L. project got started.

Gone were her reservations about making the Synoid too attractive. Who was she trying to save? The queen? There were no more queens. She had even forgotten that Merle Jennings Jr. Jr. Jr. was the world president. None of that mattered, so why worry about it. Life was meant to be lived. Not to be adjudicated. There was nothing wrong with the physical form, she told herself. In fact, wasn't that what life was all about? Feeling good. Knowing that you're the best, or at least the best version of you. Attractiveness was why there were so many gods and goddesses aligned with looking and feeling your best. Of course, there was nothing vulgar about any of those gods and goddesses and all their unique approaches to health and beauty.

There would be no morality violations just because C.N.A.B.L. was superior physically. She insisted everything was all done with great taste, with emphasis on empowerment and self-realization through the acquisition of personal goods and services. This all made perfect sense, so why not look good doing it. So she began analyzing the square jaw seeking the perfect angles and the perfect indentions. She had a team specifically geared to the structure of the chin. To cleft or not to cleft had become a question that never seemed resolved, although they did end up going with cleft in the end. The more his form came into being, the more she realized that C.N.A.B.L. was going to be a role model for so many people. He'd be the perfect helper to all mankind. He'd be the man you wanted him to be, forceful, decisive, strong, and yet the man you needed him to be, supportive, conciliatory, romantic, and generous. He'd offer you the best of both worlds. He would be able to build cities, empires, and nations, yet be able to wander, dream, and dabble in philosophy. There wouldn't be anything that wasn't perfectly geared to the modern consumer. No longer just considerations of what she thought was good or bad. It was a matter of results.

The numbers continued to exceed all expectations. The

growth stimulation machines indicated maximum hydration at a percentage far higher than that of J.U.L.E.S., coming in at an average of 78% saturation. When the prototype hit the cell development stages, Helinka grew more nervous than ever. One of the technicians was more than glad to offer her a small flask of bourbon he had hidden in the bottom of his desk. It was a slick move. The technician had brought the flask to take pulls during the day to help ease the stress, but hadn't considered his morality clause that prohibited deceptiveness with co-workers and supervisors. So when he noticed Helinka licking the tape of her nails, he pulled the flask from his desk and offered it, now padding his Credeth Silver account status with his consideration clause. After she was done taking a sip, he poured himself a stiff one on the house to even things out.

One of the older technicians who could sense tension had decided she'd wear a funny hat around the office to try and brighten the mood. It worked for a little while, but not long. Someone turned on the radio, but the volume had been turned down drastically when the first set of results came in, and nobody bothered turning it back up.

When the moment of truth arrived, it strangely enough felt as though everything were perfectly normal. All the tension of waiting, all the struggle with keeping their emotions in check, had finally paid off. They had all come to resign themselves to what will be will be. There was nothing more any one of them could do at this point to change the results.

This was especially true for Helinka. And they all wanted to pull themselves together, at least for her. For each and every technician in the room, they would win one way or the other. If it succeeded, they would be rich beyond their wildest imaginations. If it failed, they'd at least be in the running to take over Helinka's job. But at the moment of truth, they saw their success firmly hinged on that of their boss. So everyone was feeling as though they had given it their all for each other, and what would be would be. And what motivated them had nothing to do with their Credeth accounts.

The kill word was always within arm's reach. There had been disagreements about what exactly to have for its kill word. Many insisted it had to continue to go down the next option on the agreed upon list of kill words they had created the previous year, while others insisted it should be something totally new. Not wanting to jinx her project, Helinka let them vote on the subject, and when they had finally picked a winner, they wrote the kill word down. Now it sat on Helinka's desk, ready to be shouted repeatedly at the first sign of trouble.

The moment of truth had finally arrived.

C.N.A.B.L. emerged from the smoke billowing out of the chamber. His firm and muscular leg was the first thing anyone saw. It was a perfect golden tan, just the right amount of sandy blonde leg hair, and what everyone had agreed was the most perfect calves they had ever laid eyes on. Even the men were impressed. When the smoke lifted, the entire room beheld a vision of masculine perfection that, before that moment, they didn't know was possible. C.N.A.B.L. seemed to radiate a golden warmth from under his skin. Nobody could get their eyes off his perfect form. There were muscles that the average human never knew existed, but nothing overt, he was just like a Greek statue that had come to life. When he opened his eyes they were the most mesmerizing blue, like a pale icy blue. With little black dots in the center. And his hair was golden brown with just the right amount of curl.

Then someone asked, "What are those?"

When C.N.A.B.L. moved towards the protective safety glass that separated the prototype from the rest of the lab, they suddenly saw what they were unable to see in the afterglow. A pair of antlers sticking out of C.N.A.B.L.'s head. He was an 8-pointer.

And although it was not what anyone in the room expected, surprisingly nobody thought the antlers were a real problem. They seemed to think the antlers looked really good on C.N.A.B.L. The horns gave him a unique edge that they all agreed made you want to have a pair.

"You know what time it is?" C.N.A.B.L. asked in a smooth silky voice, his comforting hands pressed against the glass.

Everyone was stunned silent. His voice was velvet and melting cocoa butter. Everyone looked at each other wondering what time it was. A technician glanced at their watch, but then it dawned on them that C.N.A.B.L. was being rhetorical — that he wasn't exactly asking for the time.

Helinka decided to end the suspense and pressed the intercom button. "I don't know, C.N.A.B.L. What time do you think it is?"

C.N.A.B.L slowly began tapping his foot to some internal four on the floor. Then his hips began to sway. Then his head began to bob up and down, his antlers moving to and fro. Then he began to click his fingers, and the next thing they knew C.N.A.B.L was swinging and swaying around behind the safety glass.

Helinka observed him in a state of awe and wonder. It looked as though he was dancing.

A technician decided it was time to turn the volume up on the radio again, and as suspected, C.N.A.B.L was in perfect rhythm to the pop music blasting through the lab.

"His ultrasonic hearing, he heard the music even though we couldn't. See," a technician filled in the blanks for Helinka, explaining how although they had turned the music down ages ago, their new Synoid had heard every note and was now dancing to its rhythm.

This news filled the room with a great deal of excitement. Ultrasonic hearing was one of the new additions they had made to their new and improved J.U.L.E.S.

Helinka tried to contain her expectations. She had seen things look so right only for them to go so wrong. Regardless though, she was unable to contain her smile. She thought the antlers were awesome. And if there was a problem they could always offer filing services to the masses. That opened up a whole new market. The cleaning and maintaining of your Synoid's antlers. They could be painted with special polish like your local nail shop. So when the entire lab began to clap, Helinka couldn't help but join in.

C.N.A.B.L's moves were playful and flirtatious, and he flashed his irresistible smile. His brilliant white and flawlessly aligned teeth instantly captivated, charming both man and woman alike. Then C.N.A.B.L. began to bust out all sorts of retro disco moves to the sheer delight of the crew before seamlessly weaving in the electric slide, the humpty dance, the bus stop, and even breakdancing classics like the egg roll and the freeze. He even threw in his own version of the funky chicken in such an effortless manner that his overwhelming joy at being born immediately became infectious, and the somber atmosphere dissipated into a party-like atmosphere in a matter of minutes.

For Helinka it was fast becoming her absolute finest hour, and she tried to take cerebral recordings as sort of mental mementos to keep on hand for all time. As C.N.A.B.L. did a series of windmill cartwheels across the incubation chamber floor, his antlers sparking off the concrete, followed by a series of acrobatic backflips, she wondered how exactly it would test out in other categories like recognition and repetitive learning, knowing that his dexterity and flexibility appeared off the charts. C.N.A.B.L. had instant charisma though, and she could see all the women on the team pressing themselves against the glass for a better view of their creation. Almost losing a bit of inhibition. Heck, she noticed the men were pressed up too, looking for their chance to chum it up with the ideal wingman for a Friday night on the town. When she looked up next, C.N.A.B.L. was walking like an Egyptian.

Someone in the room popped a bottle of warm champagne.

Suds went flying.

Helinka determined if it proved to be an issue moving forward, they could just shave down the antlers.

Up in the Conference Room of Sadness things were shaping up to be the polar opposite of how things were going on downstairs. They had unanimously agreed to move up the closing day for the gladiator arena from mid-April to late January. This way they could use up whatever remaining assets they had, or could acquire, in one last huge finale. They would charge a fortune for tickets that the fans would gladly pay. But then after that it would all be over.

When they had reviewed what those remaining assets looked like, the room felt like they had all been kicked in the stomach. It was insult to injury. The stark reality of being left with only a raving Rasputin look alike, a 70-year-old Capuchin friar, and of course Cloreen, was gut wrenching to say the least. That didn't spell "huge finale" to anyone.

The reports about how their last-minute hopes of opening up the gladiatorial battles to select members of the audience, bringing in weaponized ostriches, armored robots, and even killer jellyfish shot from air cannons, were all quickly shot down for reasons that varied from logistical concerns to zoning issues.

When the legal consultants tried to apologize for heaping layer upon layer of extra sadness onto the proceedings, they were all quickly reassured that nobody was blaming them for the dour ambience and reassured them their contributions were more than appreciated.

Nevertheless, they continued to wonder if there was a way to bring back the ravenous wolves or some form of defective beast. When some inquiries were made they were told all issues with the failed German conservation lupus projects had been corrected. When asked if there was a way to un-correct the issues, they were told that it was not only unethical, but even if they could uncorrect the issue for huge sums of money, the soonest they could deliver more defective beasts would be late July or early August. That would be too late.

Someone in the room suggested they order lunch, but hot food cold and cold food hot so as not to unduly raise anyone's spirits.

Helinka had one of her Assistants draw up a memo. Although she didn't want to be premature, she thought that the board deserved to know the initial good news. This being that so far the new prototype was performing beyond all expectations, and that she was extremely pleased.

With the music still pumping away, C.N.A.B.L. was now reciting Proust to one of the interns through the security glass while simultaneously making shadow puppets on the wall. First he made a flamingo, then a horse, then a jackrabbit. The fact he didn't stoop to making the all-too-common flying bird shadow puppet was noted by the technicians as a clear indication of C.N.A.B.L.'s superior intellectual prowess.

The entire lab raised their hand in unison. All except for Helinka, who somehow hadn't heard the request. By the time she looked up, the female technicians were almost jumping up and down like schoolgirls, going, "Me, me, me, me!" Even the men got into the act, if for no other reason than to rob the women of the privilege.

Unsure what was happening, Helinka furrowed her brow and asked one of her assistants what was all the fuss was about, before seeing for herself C.N.A.B.L. puckering his lips against the glass.

C.N.A.B.L. wanted a kiss. But not from any intern. Only from the one woman responsible for bringing him to life, she's the one that had C.N.A.B.L.'s heart. He even breathed on the glass and drew the shape of a heart in the vapor. Of course, the woman responsible for bringing him to life was Helinka.

There was a sense of anger that coursed through her at that very moment. Why in the world were those technicians daring to claim that they were somehow responsible for bringing C.N.A.B.L. to life? But they were all claiming they were Helinka. The techs were just so carried away with the team's apparent success they were forgetting themselves and taking credit for what was truly her achievement. She knew they had worked their tails off, but she was also equally aware that it was her entire career that was on the line, not theirs. And that if anyone was going to be giving C.N.A.B.L. a first kiss it was going to be her.

Helinka quickly caught herself though, realizing she was on the verge of some serious fines if she were to act on her initial urge to clear the room in order to have C.N.A.B.L. all to herself. Plus, it was completely inappropriate for her, let alone anyone, to behave in such a manner. Realizing that the entire problem was instigated by the Synoid making inappropriate overtures, she calmly stepped to the intercom.

"C.N.A.B.L. please step back from the safety glass and take a seat on the chair."

The Synoid stepped back almost immediately.

She continued, "Thank you. That's a good Synoid. I'd like to go through a few initial tests with you. It's all rather routine."

Helinka asked one of the technicians to turn off the music.

The mood in the room changed from celebration to seriousness. As well it should be, and Helinka made it clear that from here on out, that things needed to get back to being professional. And speaking of being professional, the team had a serious problem on their hand. That problem was the fact C.N.A.B.L. made an inappropriate request for physical contact. A kiss of all things. And a kiss that half the room wanted to provide. This would have to be adjusted immediately. There was no way she could put anything on the market that made unwanted advances on human beings. This was as verboten as it could get, she said. C.N.A.B.L. wasn't meant for breeding. It was meant for industrial applications and environmental services with some domestic possibilities when they figured out what to do about the antlers. But they had to do something about C.N.A.B.L.'s unwanted advances first, since these behaviors clearly threatened people's morality portfolios.

Walking to the file cabinet for the 35-blue logs so that she could initiate the protocol and isolate the thought processes that initiated such a request, she heard a collective gasp. She turned to see C.N.A.B.L. standing in the middle of the lab, his smile glistening, his skin even more radiant now that it was visible for the first time without obstruction from the wall of safety glass.

"Now how about that kiss, sweetheart?" suggested C.N.A.B.L. sliding closer to the technician with the funny hat on her head.

Helinka froze. She was trying to figure how he was able to pass through three feet of bomb-proof safety glass without a sound or a scratch whatsoever. There was no break, no crack, there was absolutely no logical way to have gotten past the barrier.

A shocked assistant told her he just suddenly materialized through the glass; another assistant shouted that C.N.A.B.L. moved through it like a ghost.

The thought that her Synoid was just an apparition went through her mind, but when he playfully took the funny hat off the technician and then placed it on his head, she knew he had a true physical form.

"Step back! Don't get any closer!" Helinka shouted to C.N.A.B.L. who was running the back of his hand along the technician's cheek.

The technician failed to heed the warning.

Who knows exactly why she leaned in to kiss C.N.A.B.L. against all her good sense, maybe it was a wave of emotions, a combination of too much work and loneliness, marriage instincts or unbridled desire — nobody was sure. But the moment the technician leaned into C.N.A.B.L., her eyes closed and her lips extended, expecting the kiss of a lifetime, what she got instead sent everyone into a full-fledged panic.

C.N.A.B.L.'s jaws unhinged like a rattlesnake's jaw, and his kiss was more like a giant vacuum when he planted his gaping mouth on hers and began to inhale all her internal organs, skeleton, lymph system, and nerves, leaving her body nothing more than a deflated beach ball.

"The kill word! Get the kill word!" Helinka screamed as she ran for the piece of paper they had so thoughtfully placed on the desk, but before she could get there, C.N.A.B.L.'s teeth began to glow a brilliant white and without warning emitted a pulse of blinding light that blasted everyone in the room off their feet and sent them hurtling against all the walls.

Picking himself up off the floor, a technician who was well versed in the kill word began to yell, but all he got out was the sound of the letter "A" when C.N.A.B.L. ran him through with his antlers.

Crawling on her hands and knees toward the desk, Helinka reached up to grab the piece of paper with the kill word, but C.N.A.B.L. hurled the impaled technician off his antlers sending his lifeless body slamming into the desk so hard that all the papers went flying.

Helinka knew it would be impossible to find the paper in time to prevent C.N.A.B.L. from destroying everyone in the lab.

"Someone! Say the kill word! Hurry!"

Someone tried. But all they were able to enunciate were the letters, "AL" when C.N.A.B.L. snatched her by the throat and crushed her larynx. As he began consuming the body with ruthless efficiency, Helinka watched as C.N.A.B.L. started to flicker with a strange pulsing energy. There was another blinding flash, and everyone was thrown across the room in every direction yet again. Glass shattered, chemicals went flying, compounds ignited, and the entire room went up in flames.

When Helinka opened her eyes in a daze, she saw what they all saw, C.N.A.B.L. was growing. His muscles were expanding into every direction, his antlers had more points and were longer, his skin was a darker more golden tan, and his eyes turned an even more mesmerizing shade of pale blue.

C.N.A.B.L's methods for consuming humans were the "Greatest Hits" collection from all her other Synoid failures combined. C.N.A.B.L. liquified one Technician, roasted another with beams that shot from his eyes, while another was skinned from head to toe. Each time C.N.A.B.L. ate an employee, it continued to grow both in size and strength.

Helinka was thankful it wasn't decapitating people like Jules, until it snapped off one of her assistant's heads before vanishing through the wall and into the administrative section of the lab.

"ALARM! ALARM!" shouted Helinka, hoping maybe alarm was the kill word.

But it wasn't.

Helinka chased after it, following as best she could, trying to keep pace, but whereas she was being bound by physical barriers like walls and doors, the Synoid could move through matter leaving an unpredictable path of destruction.

C.N.A.B.L materialized in the break room where his now 8-foot-tall bulging muscular frame leaned up seductively against a water cooler where he flashed his brilliant white smile towards a brood of secretaries mindlessly chattering during their lunch break.

"Now which one of you lovelies wants a kiss?"

To say they all dropped their pre-packaged sandwiches, their salty romance novels, their cups of lukewarm hazelnut flavored coffee and instantly ran towards C.N.A.B.L. ready to submit to his every lustful whim would be an understatement. But C.N.A.B.L.'s idea of love and affection centered totally on eating human flesh.

Helinka had maneuvered her way through countless offices

and down a labyrinth of hallways when finally she burst into the break room where she saw C.N.A.B.L. sloshing through the puddles of gore, broken vending machines, and toppled tables. She was too late to save anyone, and she knew she'd continue to be too late unless she was somehow able to guess the kill word.

"ALGEBRA! ALGEBRA! ALGEBRA!

Still nothing slowed C.N.A.B.L. down.

Materializing through another wall, C.N.A.B.L. burst into the male executive washroom where all the up-and-coming executives in their two-piece wool-polyester blends stood before polished porcelain urinals all craning their necks in unison to see the 9-foot-4 inch golden-haired Adonis materialize in front of their faces. Then they looked at each other. Then down at their hands. Then back to each other. Then back at C.N.A.B.L. as if they had just met their dream selves face to face in some sort of dream.

"Yo, bro," said one executive.

Another asked, "Yo, bro. Where's your gym?"

"Are those quadra-lats?" said another fixed upon his pulsing thigh muscles.

C.N.A.B.L. smiled and asked, "Who wants to bring it in for a bro-hug?"

The men looked to each other. Then down at their hands. Then back to each other. Then back at C.N.A.B.L.

Helinka was almost out of breath when she burst into the male executive washroom to see C.N.A.B.L. had grown 12-feet tall, looming over the sinks washing his hands from all the blood. It taking a few mints from the dish.

"ALEXANDRA! ALI BABA! ALASKA! ALCATRAZ! ALKYLINE! ALPACA! ALUMINUM! ALUMNI! ALIVE! ALIVE! ALIVE!"

Nothing Helinka shouted seemed to be effective in stopping the rampage.

The rampage cleared floor-after-floor of the Enkeling

Futures and Prosperities corporate offices, until C.N.A.B.L. was maxing out at around 14-feet tall. But despite his cap height, nothing was slowing down his appetite for flesh. He continued up floor-after-floor with his powers to hypnotize victims never seeming to slow down; everyone stopped whatever they were doing to throw themselves at his feet. It didn't matter if they saw their friend getting chewed to pieces in the process.

When C.N.A.B.L. finally materialized through the walls at the Conference Room of Sadness, Helinka was running close behind, shouting every word she could think of that started with the letters A and L. All the while witnessing the horrific spectacle he left in his wake on each successive floor.

"ALLIGATOR! ALTAR! ALMANAC!" Still nothing.

The Board Members didn't exactly know what was happening when C.N.A.B.L. entered the room. With the only light coming from the flashlight hidden under the table, all they were able to see was the creature's pulsating movements and a faint golden outline of this huge swollen body. Most didn't even realize he was there. But when C.N.A.B.L. smiled his brilliant white grin, it cut through the darkness in such a way that there was no mistaking an otherworldly presence had entered the room.

Then they heard the music. The pop beat was irresistible.

The board members from Ghana Princely Projects were under the impression this was part of some larger presentation. The board members of Enkeling Futures and Prosperities thought it was someone from the Parcel Delivery Service who had made the wrong turn down the hallway. But why was it so large, so imposing? And why was the music so good?

The Ghana Princely Projects board members started to clap to the beat.

The Enkeling Futures and Prosperities board members started bobbing their heads in time.

By this time, Helinka was trying to force herself into the Conference Room of Sadness but the door was locked. She looked around for something to smash through the glass. Finding a potted snake plant, she threw it against the glass, but it just broke into a hundred pieces, making absolutely no impression whatsoever on the glass. She began banging on the partition to try and get their attention, to try and warn them to run for their lives, but nobody inside was able to hear her shouts above the music. And if they were able to hear, the last thing they could do was take their eyes off of C.N.A.B.L.

"Your wildest dreams are about to come true," announced C.N.A.B.L. in his smooth silky voice.

Then he flipped open the mini blinds overlooking the Merletown business district and bathed the room with daylight. When everyone's eyes finally adjusted, they realized they were gazing upon the most impressive physical specimen they had ever had the pleasure of gazing upon. Antlers included.

It was all so breathtaking. And C.N.A.B.L. knew it. He could see how powerful he was in all their collective faces. So he thrusted his hips repeatedly, and began tossing his head back and forth, then took a running leap onto the black onyx conference table, sliding halfway across it before bouncing to his feet where he started rocking his body to the music in gratuitous and overly provocative ways.

But nobody averted their eyes.

"You wanna dance?" C.N.A.B.L. extended his hand to an Enkeling Board Member who blushed, practically melting in his smoldering blue eyes. "Don't be bashful. All you need to do is let your body move to the music. Go with the flow," it advised.

C.N.A.B.L. wasn't about to take no for an answer.

Taking her by the hand and lifting her onto the table in one fluid and effortless motion, they began dancing together. She was shy at first, but the rest of the board members encouraged her with supportive hoots and hollers. C.N.A.B.L. pulled her close, but only being 5' 7" she only went up to about his thigh. But that didn't stop C.N.A.B.L. from putting on all the moves.

Outside the door, the Enkeling Security Forces had finally caught up to the rampage. They quickly moved Helinka aside despite her objections and took a battering ram to the door.

The carnage that followed could only be described as catastrophic. C.N.A.B.L. emitted the most devastating energy pulse from out of his flaring nostrils that turned all the Enkeling security force inside out. The few members of the security force, who regardless of their guts being exposed to the world, that managed to continue fighting the 14-foot, antlered, master of all masculinity, were then quickly ripped to shreds by C.N.A.B.L.'s vice like, square jaw, and thrashed about the room. The room was now painted red with blood. The last security agent by Helinka knew he was all that stood in the way of utter destruction, and rushed into the room firing his shotgun into C.N.A.B.L., but with each round of buck shot, he simply flexed his abs, and the blasts bounced harmlessly off his body. The security agent was thrown out the window where he splattered on the street seventy stories below.

Now C.N.A.B.L. free from all distraction, turned his attention back to the Enkeling board member who he had so dashingly swept off her feet. Wiping the blood from off the side of his mouth, he resumed his enchanting smile.

"Now how about that kiss, sweetheart?" C.N.A.B.L. knelt down on one knee.

The room was stunned silent.

The board member thought she had just been teleported into some bawdy daytime drama, but regardless of knowing what she was about to do was totally wrong, she somehow knew romance had no rhyme or reason. It just happened. Spontaneously. So regardless of the fact she wasn't wearing lip gloss, she closed her eyes and parted her lips slightly, going in for the kiss.

Before he could chew off her face, Helinka ran in screaming, "ALBATROSS! ALBATROSS! ALBATROSS!"

C.N.A.B.L. slumped over in sleep mode.

The Synoid's rampage was now officially over.

The board member opened her eyes, immediately coming to her senses.

The rest of the board members looked on in even more stunned silence. Some with looks that were indistinguishable with those of terror and exhilaration.

Helinka realized all eyes were on her and her now sleeping Synoid. She figured she'd try and explain herself the best she could before getting hauled away to be incarcerated for an unknown period of time.

"Hi everybody…sorry about…" Helinka hesitated. A gust of wind from the shattered window blew into the room. She thought she could smell fresh baked bread wafting in. "Sorry about the window…"

Before she could say another word, one of the board members for Ghana Princely Projects began to clap. And it was infectious. Soon the entire room was giving her a standing ovation.

"This has got to be the greatest presentation we have ever seen!" the chairman for Ghana Princely Projects declared.

Never before had anyone witnessed what it actually felt like to be inside the gladiator arena. It was like they had all gone on a roller coaster ride with a quadruple corkscrew and were just now trying to regain their balance. And it suddenly made perfect sense to everyone in the room. All their dreams had come true, just like the Synoid said. They had their inventory all along, right under their noses. The gladiator arena was saved. But not just saved, it had all of a sudden elevated to the next level of entertainment. They had just experienced something they didn't even think was possible. It was thrilling, captivating, moving, heroic. It was all those words smushed together in a violent bloody rapture. They began to laugh and became almost giddy with excitement. Just moments early they had been lamenting the loss of trillions of dollars in revenue. And now, in a matter of minutes, they were clamoring together, making plans, talking future strategies, exploring marketing plans, formulating souvenir ideas, speculating on sponsorship deals, all to make a gazillion dollars in revenue. Maybe more. All to be split down the middle, 50/50. It was the greatest singular comeback of their lives, and they owed it all to Helinka.

The chairman turned congratulating Helinka. "When do you think we can launch?"

She wasn't 100% sure, but when she began going over with the board the initial production schedule, prospective release dates, and the inventory of defective Synoids they were keeping in the basement, she thought that she heard one of the board members refer to her as "sweetheart."

CLEAVE

A memory book, he decided. It was personal, it was quirky, it would be something he would have to make with his hands. You couldn't just go out and buy it. That meant it was special. So giving her a memory book made perfect sense. As soon as he had made up his mind, Gideon began to wonder which memories he'd put in the book. Did they even have any, he wondered.

Record success stories, goals, dreams, and more!

That's what was written on the instruction guide. And he began to think. They had success stories, goals, and dreams. So this was good. And thanks to Helinka's recent promotion to Chief Gladiator Monster Maker Outfitter and his rise to Product Development Chief & Right-Hand Man of The Startling Concern CEO, they were now officially two of the richest people in the world. That, he thought, definitely accounted for what people would consider success stories, goals, and dreams, all in one.

What was the "and more!?" He wondered. The more he thought, the more he knew there were no "and mores." There were no photos of them at the Vacatican. That trip was abruptly cancelled. There were no photos of anything really. Come to think of it, they were introduced by professional colleagues at someone's birthday. Their match meters went off — PERFECT MATCH.

They had coffee a few times. Got engaged and got promoted.

He knew the only memories they had were about making money. So the more Gideon thought it over, he decided to scrap the idea of a memory book. It was idiotic to try so hard to give her a gift that money couldn't buy, only to have money be all the gift was about.

A song. That was about as personalized as you could get. And it cost as close to nothing as anyone could imagine. There was no photo album to buy, no images to have to be printed. All you needed was a title, some lyrics, a melody, and wham, you were done. Sure, he didn't have the best voice, but this would only help make him sound that much more authentic and vulnerable. The instructions on how to write a song seemed simple enough. "Me and You." His first step was done. He had picked the title. Then he thought it sounded as if the relationship was all about him, so he switched the title to "You and Me." That title sounded presumptuous, he thought, the last thing he wanted was to give the impression he could speak for her. They were partners after all. He settled on "Us." By step two Gideon hit a snag. It required he "write down all your emotions connected with your song title." He couldn't think of any emotion that was worth mentioning in a song.

The song idea was then promptly discarded as well since the idea of writing a song about anxiety and dread was about the worst gift of all.

Going up and down the aisle of Craft Depot, he thought maybe painting a painting of her would be the perfect expression of personalized devotion. He passed on that idea too. There were too many colors to choose from. Plus, the only color he was certain about was gray. He had settled on the idea of buying the heart-shaped pillow kit where he could stitch their names on it. *Gideon + Helinka 4 Ever!* He had even had it in his shopping basket. But by the time he had to check-out he had only purchased odds and ends like scotch-tape, scissors, some adhesive foam, glitter paint, and a sheet of googly eyes.

Hours later, Gideon was staring at a pinecone with foam hands and feet, googly eyes, and a light accent of silver glitter. But he knew it looked stupid, and there was no way he could give this to Helinka and her parents as his bridal price. That didn't stop him from trying to figure out some thematic tie-in, in hopes of justifying his pinecone man. All the options he had explored were unsatisfying. At that point, he reckoned the easiest and safest thing to do was just to hand over a chunk of his Startling Concern shares to Helinka's parents and call it a day. But that would be too easy. That's what everyone was expecting. He wanted to knock everyone's socks off. But time was running out.

By the time time ran out, the engaged couple stood front and center at the Credeth Wedding Pavilion's Premium Planning Acropolis making their final selections on all the minute wedding details that had up until that point gone undecided. Gideon also knew after all those details were signed off on, they'd be presenting their dowry and bridal price, thus making the wedding date official.

Helinka stared across the rack of the newly released Gus Van Brackish jewel-encrusted sapphire and bdellium flats, and it dawned on her that there was nothing keeping her from having them all. There had always been something special about selecting the superior slipper, sandal, or pump, searching high and low, stretching her final cent, or by simply giving in to her heart's desire. The Murkel line was no different. Carnali Blanc had no sway either. Maybe if Jules was here, she thought, he'd help her with that discerning eye of his. Maybe he could help her regain what she seemingly lost when she gained everything. But without some sudden rush of adrenaline, she realized she'd rather be anywhere else but there. Then right when she was on the verge of giving up all hope, she saw the pair she wanted.

"Excuse me, Miss," Helinka waived down the stock girl she had spotted out of the corner of her eye moving invisibly behind a row of curtains.

The stock girl was unsure what to make of this wealthy woman staring at her sterile industrial-pleather clogs.

"Yes..." she squeaked.

"How much for your shoes?"

On the other side of the Credeth Wedding Pavillion's Premium Planning Acropolis, Gideon was having his measurements taken for his new line of executive loungewear by the famous tailor, who on his boss's recommendation, flew in from Lower Canada just for the occasion. With his aforementioned promotion to Product Development Chief & Right-Hand Man for The Startling Concern CEO, Gideon was allowed to forgo the Bedouin tent apparel and go back to his favorite sweats and hoodie. The tailor had something more special in mind though, insisting that cotton wouldn't do for a man of influence arising from his success, achievement, and rank. So Gideon perused the sample book of human leathers that the famous tailor was so adept at working with.

Gideon had never seen a bog man in real life before. Nor had the thought of wearing the skin of an ancient sacrificial victim, preserved in a bog for over two millennia in acidic soil, ever cross his mind. But he found himself torn between the leather skins of Clonycavan Man and Croghan Man.

As his fingers felt the blackish-tan skins and listened to the tailor explain how less quality human leathers didn't possess the same patina created from the tannins produced after so much time underneath a peat bog, he began to imagine himself walking through the office, or on the streets, or in a restaurant, knowing that nobody else in the world was able to wear what he was wearing. Except for Supentus, of course. But like the tailor explained, he wore Pharaoh skin which wasn't available to Gideon. But the good news was that bog man leather was not only a triple-kill sacrifice to the three goddesses of fertility, sovereignty and war, which of course made them the most desirable, but they were missing nipples as a sign of servitude to the king. So his new loungewear would not only make the statement that he was one of the richest men in the world, but it would let everyone know he also humbly served his boss. Gideon chose Croghan Man but also ordered a set of athleisure pajamas to be sewn from the Inca Ice Maiden.

The Eternal Union Coordinating Executive personally came down from the 32nd floor to personally confirm Gideon and Helinka's wedding plans. This was quite the honor, but the least she could do for such prestigious clients as Gideon and Helinka. When she arrived there were smiles galore and scripted small talk they had approved the previous Fall. They signed every form in triplicate and dotted every i and crossed every t, making all the paperwork officially official. The next steps, she explained, were simply formalities.

"Man and woman expect certain things of each other even before they marry."

The Eternal Union Coordinating Executive read from an old book, adding, "After marriage, some husbands and wives cannot satisfy their partner's expectations. They may become disappointed and unhappy with each other and have problems within their marriage. A married couple may argue about almost anything. Such as how to spend their money, how to spend their recreation time, or what type of implement to use when disciplining a child. If they do not work out their differences, they may find it difficult to be friends, romantic partners, or good parents. Couples with marriage problems should seek help from a trained marriage counselor. Marriage counselors need to be licensed. Using an unlicensed "street" counselor can lead to fines and jail time. A couple can obtain names of qualified counselors in their area from the New Australian Association of Marriage and Family Counselors, 225 Yaal Avenue, Claremount, Newer

South Wales, New Australia, 71333."

Gideon and Helinka checked the box that said they understood.

The Eternal Union Coordinating Executive shuffled papers about within a manila folder, "I just need to go over the form one last time and just hear it from you directly. Are you both aware that your Credeth Palladium status only allows for monogamy?"

They both answered, "Yes."

"You are aware that your status also requires strict endogamy. That means you may only marry within the same status of finance and worship. If and when your status changes, we will have to reassign one or both of you to a different class grouping and that will mean forfeiture of certain privileges as outlined in your Credeth Palladium advantage plus plan.

"Yes," Gideon and Helinka confirmed in unison.

"We have your clearance from General Worship. Everything looks good. Please sign here."

They both signed.

"Okay now finally. The good stuff," the Eternal Union Coordinating Executive clapped her hands twice.

Gideon could hear Helinka's father's disapproving baritone grumbles long before they had even entered the room. Helinka rushed up to her parents and squeezed them both enthusiastically, peppering them with kisses.

Vintner ignored Gideon's handshake choosing to acknowledge him with some inaudible warble before sitting down with his wife next to Helinka.

"Greetings! We are here to reveal the gift exchanges. Helinka's dowry and Gideon's bridal price."

The Eternal Union Coordinating Executive had a TV monitor rolled into the room. When they plugged it in and set up the cables, she invited Helinka's parents to present their dowry.

Pressing play on the monitor, the screen flashed a few seconds of static, some color bars, timecode, then appeared a breathtaking helicopter shot moving swiftly up a pristine coastline with baby powder sand and turquoise waters splashing upon a remote, spotless beach. Electronic inspirational music with synthetic wind chimes began to rattle from the speakers before the shot landed on a beach front estate that looked like a cathedral of wall-to-wall glass. As the shot moved in on the gigantic house, the setting sunlight flared off its futuristic facade. Perched on a rocky shore overlooking the endless vistas, the helicopter hovered around the house, which gave the audience a panoramic view of the architectural monstrosity from every possible angle. The presentation ended as abruptly as it began with the camera zooming up a storybook picket fence where both their names, "Helinka & Gideon," could be seen emblazoned in gold letters at the gate. Moving closer on the front door, revealed an oversized red bow wrapped around it. The door opened into the house, and everything faded to black. The End.

Helinka with tears in her eyes, turned, hugging her mom and dad.

Gideon stared at the empty monitor in disbelief. Not only was that the greatest house he had ever seen, but he was sure that his hand-made presentation would never come close to something like that. Before Gideon could ask the Eternal Union Coordinator Executive if it was possible to change his gift to all the stocks he owned in The Startling Concern, she pressed the play button on the TV monitor.

"Now for your bridal price."

It was too late, the presentation began. The voice of an English narrator welcomed all in the room.

"*Tally ho. Tally ho! There was once a man who met a lady, and they fell in love.*"

Images of Gideon walking the streets of Merletown in deep contemplation.

"*What to give the perfect woman who has everything? A house? That's too easy, only someone not trying would give a gift like houses or money.*"

Gideon shrank in his seat.

"There are some things that money can't buy."

The monitor began flashing images of Gideon decorating a wedding cake. First spreading the frosting with the help of an expert wedding cake baker. Another image showed the baker instructing Gideon how to make fondant flowers with a pastry bag. Another image showed Gideon hand painting the bride and groom statues on the top of the cake.

"And that's the gift of eternal love."

Some random staff worker wheeled in the wedding cake. It was seven layers tall, with over seventy different frosting colors used in the flower decorations, and even had a row of blinking lights flashing around its base.

Gideon didn't want to open his eyes. He knew seeing their collective shock due to such a drastic letdown as having to behold his amateur wedding cake would technically spell the end before it even began. He continued to keep his eyes shut. But the longer he did, the longer the silence matched him step for step. Suddenly, the urge to at least confirm his worst fears began to slowly overpower his desire to hide his shame. He slowly opened an eye lid just enough to qualify for a squint.

Instead of seeing a room filled with disappointed faces, Helinka and her parents were admiring the wedding cake.

"You did this yourself?" asked Helinka's Mother.

Vintner's guttural grumbles were slightly less earth shattering. They almost sounded like he was impressed. Helinka stared at the intricate work he did on the bride and groom statues. Gideon tried to gauge her face. She was neither excessively happy nor excessively sad. He began to straighten in his chair. At least she was present. That was good. He realized that it wasn't going to be so bad after all. After all, it was just the beginning of a lifetime together. You plant a seed. You watch it grow. You wait seven years. Then you can partake of its fruit. At least that's what he remembered reading in Jotham's book. Or maybe it was five years. So how would it be any different in a marriage? You'd have to toil. And it was his responsibility to get up early and get to work. Making sure they were prepared for the harvest. It would take time, but it would grow. It would grow, and he'd make sure of it. Gideon brightened at the thought. He kept a close eye on Helinka. He began to admire her. Almost for the first time. Not as some acquisition. Some prop. He began to admire her for being a human being, although completely different in every way, physically, emotionally, and mentally, they would soon become one. Bone from my bone, he thought. Flesh from my flesh.

In the car home, Vintner Vowell confirmed to his wife that although he would much rather have preferred stocks of The Startling Concern, the whole wedding cake thing was actually something special. It was a nice sentiment, he determined. Vintner Vowell even told his wife he might even think twice now about Gideon. He might even invite him on his next hunting expedition to the Dark Continent. Heck, he may even learn to call him son one day.

The beach house was everything anyone would ever dream of.

The setting sun bathed the massive living room in an orange glow. The water reflecting a deep grayish blue with sparkles of sun flitting across its surface.

"The ocean looks like its crying. The water looks like tears," said Helinka standing beside Gideon who was gazing off at the view.

"Oh, I know this. See along the horizon. The waters were separated at the beginning of time. That's why the lower waters, the ocean, cries."

Helinka listened closely as Gideon nudged his shoulder next to hers.

"Why though?"

"Why do the lower waters cry? Because they got separated. And because the sky was closer to heaven, whereas the ocean was left behind on earth, they began to cry. And that's why the ocean is filled with salt. Cause of all their tears."

It was a romantic thought. And she contemplated it as the sun began to dip below the horizon.

"What about when it rains?" she suddenly asked in a quiet voice.

"The rain?" Gideon searched his memory banks. "I guess the sky misses the ocean. But when they are united in the end times, they'll both stop crying. The sea will stop its tears, and the sky will stop its sobbing. They'll be united. No more tears. No more sadness. No more separation. They'll be united together… like in Holy matrimony. Like us."

Gideon gave her a kiss on the cheek and put his arm around her as the sun disappeared into a small infinitesimal dot before sinking below the horizon and out of sight.

Helinka thought about her Synoids. And how they were destined for the gladiator arena. They were supposed to change the world for the better. She thought about how all her dreams had come true. The sunset was spectacular in its kaleidoscope of brilliant oranges, reds, and purples. The antique, hand-carved French limestone tiles under her feet were the vision of perfection. She looked up into the western sky and caught sight of a waxing moon beginning to emerge in the absence of the setting sun. She thought about how she had made all these extraordinary plans to become this power player in society and how those plans were completely out of her control. Sure, she was rich, she thought. That was all good and all, but you make plans to become married. You know that you plan on being married forever, but how are those plans going to work out? Who has dominion over all this, the water, the sky, the moon, she wondered. After staring at the waves crash over and over again on the infinite grains of sand, she spoke.

"My parents, I think really liked your bride price."

Gideon let out a nervous laugh. This was news to his ears,

"Well, I really like our dowry, I mean this place is…it's…"

As Gideon searched for the right adjective, Helinka continued, "About your little cake painting."

The tone of her voice gave Gideon pause. "What do you mean? My little cake painting?"

"The thing you did that my mom and dad like so much."

Sensing something wasn't quite right, Gideon faced her. "What's wrong? Did you not like it?"

Helinka let out a singular disconnected laugh. Then composed herself.

Furrowing his brow, Gideon continued to look at her inquisitively.

She finally looked up at him. Cold and distant, "I just have one question for you."

"Yeah…what is is?

"The bride and groom statuettes…"

"Yeah…?"

"Where was Jules?" she asked.

Gideon stepped back not quite sure what to make of hearing the name J.U.L.E.S. Jules? He thought, what does that thing have to do with any of this? He was under the impression that her tests were over, that that thing was bound for the gladiator pits with the rest of her inventions. He wanted to throw a brick into the giant windows as he swelled with rage at the thought. She was suggesting he should have put a cake statue of Jules along with the bride and groom. That was a ludicrous thing to suggest. His eyes couldn't leave hers. She had this strange expression as if she had asked some question she knew the answer to, as if there was something that he had done to deceive her. As if this was all some willful affront. His mind raced, searching instantly for the proper reply. Anger would just make her distant, confusion would just make her stronger, apologies would justify her. The only thing he could do was be rational. Plant the seed. Watch it grow.

"But it's just us, Helinka. You and me. Husband and wife."

Gideon stepped in for an embrace, but she pulled away with a daring look in her eyes.

"But it's not," Helinka said smiling.

Gideon shook his head, "It's not what?"

"It's not just you and me."

"Are you saying…?"

"It's not. It's not just you and me."

Helinka slowly turned and walked off, presumably to resume her house tour.

Gideon stood watching her climb the spiral staircase and disappear into the maze that was the second floor.

The waves never for an instant stopped crashing. And the pristine and secluded beach was lit up in the night.

PARTLY CLOUDY

The forecast indicated sunny, partly cloudy skies, with a high around 78.

His mirrored pants reflected something else entirely as he sat waiting upon the lichen-covered wall. The day was in fact rather gray and slightly chilled. A few light drops fell intermittently across the pavement. A few hit Jotham in the face, and he wondered why he had left his coat in the car.

He knew there was a lot to discuss with Gideon. Things may even get heated. Although he was hoping to avoid that. The key in his mind was threading that fine line between rebuke and encouragement. Finding a way to get through to Gideon that didn't require lecturing him about how much was at stake, or filling his head with theoretical notions of right and wrong which seemed to be so ineffective. It had become clear that whatever conviction and clarity he thought he was imparting to his spy, it all seemed to melt away as soon as Gideon was faced with any overpowering situations. Whether it be intimidating board meetings or grueling rounds of death golf with two evil CEOs, for example. Gideon was crumbling time and time again. Doing the exact opposite of helping take down their wicked empires. He was in fact helping them in ways he never thought possible. The idea that The Startling Concern was turning everything about his God into a monotheistic idol was far worse than anything the Cauzzies had gotten wrong under his same tutelage.

It seemed to get chillier by the second.

Jotham had decided to take a different approach this time around. He thought he had found a way to power Gideon through any challenging situation with something other than abstract calculations. The idea materialized in a roundabout way. Jotham knew he was letting himself down too, not just Gideon and the Cauzzies, who had seemingly gone Christian rogue, but with himself and his own people. With Rabbi Eliyahu Ben Yechiel especially. So trying to find his own reserves, he reflected upon his role models. The Patriarchs. He knew that Abraham wouldn't have run away quite like he had. Abraham hadn't run away from the five kings. He hadn't run away from the covenant of circumcision. Sure, he had made a few miscalculations like saying Sarah was his sister instead of being confident enough to risk his life by claiming her as his wife, but nobody was perfect-perfect. But he was 10 out of 10 for trials. Jotham knew he surely wasn't close to being 10 out of 10. Not even close to 3 out of 1000. The last thing he wanted to do so was fill Gideon's head with what he would do in his shoes. That certainly wasn't working. After willingly sending Rabbi Yechiel to the torture chamber there was no doubt that the answer lay elsewhere. He'd have to rely on real life examples. He'd have to be more like Abraham. Like Isaac. Like Jacob. Maybe if he could convince Gideon to look towards these role models and do what they did, he'd be better able to perform under equally treacherous circumstances.

Grabbing his jacket suddenly became more than an option as the wind began to pick up. Jotham looked down the path in both directions. Still no sign of Gideon. Checking his watch, he decided the world wouldn't end if he went to his car and grabbed his jacket.

The dark emissaries were waiting.

Their black sheets draped over their heads looking as though they were almost posing for a picture. Two of the dark emissaries rested their elbows on either side of the doors while three others arranged themselves in different positions on the hood of car. Jotham's instincts told him to run. That this was bad news. The best thing to do was run for his life. They must be on to him. There was no other reason to explain the ominous tableau he saw before his eyes. He continued to move towards them, step by step, as if everything was right with the world. He thought about Abraham. Abraham rose up and defeated the five kings. He thought about Isaac. Isaac dug more wells until his enemies were compelled to make peace. He thought about Jacob. Jacob wrestled Esau's angel and received the just blessing. Whatever happened, he would himself take a different approach this time. He'd rely on his role models with the hopes of performing well under what was sure to be treacherous circumstances.

"You're interfering with an investigation," Jotham announced with his trademark ruthless and unmerciful persona. "Consider yourselves on report. All of you."

The mysterious heads under those black sheets looked back and forth at each other. Jotham imagined their wicked grins hidden away underneath their dark shrouds, so amused by his apparent bravado.

"Silence," one exclaimed, smoothly sliding off the hood of the car to face off with Jotham. Then they all circled him at once.

Jotham stood his ground, "What's this? Have you all lost your minds?"

"We have some questions to ask you. Please come with us."

The office at General Worship seemed far more frigid than anything he had experienced outside. Rabbi Eliyahu Ben Yechiel was a beyond a shadow of his old self. There was so much yellowish bruising and unhealed slashes peeking out from the rented rags he wore that his purple swollen eyes looked like an afterthought.

Two NAMP agents stood at either side of Jotham who stood obstinately with his arms folded, listening to the dark emissaries coaxing the now complying Rabbi to reveal all he had told them.

"Please tell us again, you are speaking too softly," one of the dark emissaries urged as he pushed the tape recorder closer to the Rabbi's trembling face.

The Rabbi finally spoke seeing his friend standing in the room, "Jotham…is that you?"

"Much better. Please repeat for us what we already now. Louder!"

The Rabbi shook his head; he didn't understand.

The dark emissary raised his shrill voice, "About being a Jew. Tell us what we already know! Is Jotham a treasonous Jew?!"

"He would never…not treason…never…" the Rabbi muttered.

The dark emissaries turned their veiled attention and accusing glances at Jotham, "We have been on to you for some time. You have made yourself quite apparent. You thought you were being smart, but you were quite apparent. Now this prisoner has helped us confirm what we have suspected for some time. That you are a nefarious Jew. We thought your kind was extinct. But here we are. With yet more of you in need of immediate extermination."

"Whatever you think you know, you're wrong," Jotham said calmly. "You are interfering with an investigation, and you will all regret what you have done."

"Noooooo!" a dark emissary squealed.

"It is you, Jotham who will regret what you have done!" belched another. "We will not kill you right away but will hang you from a tree for many days. For many days." A wet spot of saliva formed around the black sheet as he shouted venomously.

Yet another dark emissary scoffed under his black sheet, "You thought we wouldn't know! That you could outsmart us?!

Look at these!"

Photograph after black and white photograph began piling up one after the other upon the metal desk.

There was an image of Jotham meeting privately with the Cauzzies at Lee Land #3. A set of blurry shots featuring Jotham dragging kosher meet up the elevators. One image was particularly hard to explain away, it showed Jotham praying with a phylacteries. Another with him wearing a prayer shawl taken through the window of his apartment. Then there were the photos of Jotham meeting Gideon. They had lots of those.

Jotham looked away, trying to seem totally unimpressed.

But it was pretty clear they were building their case for quite some time. And they weren't done explaining their evidence. So with intentionally menacing voices, they laughed off the notion that Jotham was conducting some private investigation. They knew that was a blatant lie.

"The coat rack. You think we didn't know what that was? It was a crucifix!" Cackles seemed to punctuate every word that oozed from their lips.

Jotham began to realize how foolish he truly was. Not only trying to convince anyone moving forward of his innocence, but the thought he could actually succeed in bringing about the recognition of Divine providence and the one true God.

"You're an infiltrating Jew. And we can prove it!"

They had documented the entire transaction with the law firm of Ygnwie, Erasemus, and Sumer. How Jotham insisted that there was no code violation of Article 87, when they showed there were repeated violations. And on face value, that added up to nothing more than blatant obstruction. They had him dead to rights. But they wanted more. To prove that Jotham was more than just guilty of bad decision making. To build that case it looked as though they had gotten exactly what they needed from the Rabbi.

The Rabbi. Jotham watched him rocking back and forth in

the chair. As he did so, he felt deep in his bones that time was up. He had failed. Sure, he could stretch things out with due process. Maybe for a month. Maybe for a year. Sure, he could publicly denounce the fact he was a Jew. He could make the case go to court. He could even renounce his God on an international stage. But in the end, he knew it was just delaying the inevitable. Everyone in the room could see Jotham was bound for the gallows.

So he kept his eyes fixed on the Rabbi.

It was now time to take inventory, he thought. His mind mulled over the Cauzzies and what they would do when he was gone. They'd most certainly try and find a priest to perform the Eucharistic rites in their basement church; they'd get in some shotgun battle with the NAMP, but just end up slaughtered or thrown into the gladiator arena. Yup, that sounded about right, he thought.

Gideon. What would happen to Gideon, he wondered. Gideon would most likely continue to impress the heads over at The Startling Concern, and then with the news of him being arrested by the dark emissaries and losing his power as Lead Investigator of General Worship, he'd just pretend nothing ever happened. He'd probably go on to become one of the richest people in the world and usher in the first monotheistic invisible idol in the history of mankind. Yup, that sounded about right too, he thought.

So now it was just him and Rabbi Yechiel. He wondered how much longer the Rabbi could hold out before falling over faint or dead. He reminded himself of their internal torture timeline that said if a man can talk, he has a month. If a man couldn't talk, he has three weeks. If a man keeps his eyes closed, he has a week. If a man urinates lying down, he has the morrow.

There was nothing more to do, he concluded. So Jotham pounded his hand on the table so hard the mirrors on his sleeve could be heard shattering beneath the blow.

"You're making a huge mistake!" he shouted.

As the dark emissaries found his protests amusing, and while they heckled him back and forth, what they failed to see was Jotham's sleight of hand as he palmed the sharpest shard in his grasp.

Then the Rabbi gathered the last bit of his strength, "Jotham…"

The dark emissaries shoved the tape recorder close to his face, "He's going to say something else! Speak up old man. Speak! Speak!"

The Rabbi lifted his eyes, "Take me home…"

Jotham readied the razor-sharp mirror fragment and smiled, "Let's go."

The first NAMP officer hit the ground with his throat slashed from ear to ear before anyone in the room could even blink. Jotham pounced on the second NAMP officer as he lifted his shotgun to fire, slashing open his arm, the errant blast blowing through one of the dark emissaries hovering over the desk. Jotham snapped another's neck, dropping him in an instant. Another emissary began shrieking the alarm, but Jotham silenced him with a vicious combination, then threw him into another knocking them down like bowling pins.

Taking Rabbi Yechiel on his shoulders, Jotham grabbed the shotgun, kicked open the door, and began running down the hallway and straight for the exit. One blast, and then another, took care of two pursuing emissaries blowing huge holes into their flowing black sheets.

Jotham got halfway across the parking lot before he was struck in the leg by a bullet. Another grazed his shoulder, while others zinged past his head, even more bullets sent up clouds of dirt and rocks into the air as they skipped across the blacktop. When he neared the tree line the machine guns opened fire strafing Jotham diagonally across his body. As he fell to his knees, he saw that the Rabbi was already gone. Whether by the beating he had endured or the bullet that was lodged in his neck, it would remain a mystery to Jotham. Lifting him back up on his shoulders, he was determined to make it into the safety of the tree cover when Jotham took a bullet in the back of his head. Falling forward into the dirt, he lay motionless.

They stood over him and fired another round in the back of his head for good measure. Then kicked him in the ribs to make sure he was dead.

Wearing white cotton gloves, he adjusted the takedown screw and took the barrel in his grip and turned it counterclockwise a quarter turn. Pulling off the barrel he set it down on a torn Australian flag beach towel. He collected all the springs and small pins and nuts and carefully placed them into a mug with a chipped handle. You could barely read the words "World's Best Dad" under the thick layer of coffee stains. Peering down the barrel with his large Invasive eye, Cauzzie Rob inspected the fouling. He opened a pack of cleaning swabs and got to work removing the loose particles with a utility brush. He made sure to take his time knowing there would be lots of repetition. Breaking for a smoke he was told they had finished wiring all their car's gas tanks together into a bomb and handed him the detonator. He set it in a drawer and resumed cleaning the action, the bolt, the receiver, the frame, and the chamber. With a bronze brush he ran it through the barrel until it was spotless. He lubricated the worn action bars on the pump action. Then the bolt lugs. Wiping down the stock with a dry cloth and pausing to chug a can of beer. Setting the crushed can aside, he began to reassemble the shotgun.

If there was going to be a showdown, and if they were going to go down in a blaze of glory, nobody was gonna say the Cauzzies didn't keep their guns clean. This Cauzzie Rob made perfectly clear to his compadres. So he leaned the finished shotgun against the wall along with the three other clean ones and got to work disassembling the next. He adjusted the takedown screw and took the barrel in his grip and turned it counterclockwise a quarter turn.

Wiping down a silver bowl, Cauzzie Roy looked at his upside-down reflection. He started making faces and laughing at his distorted features. After burning a good thirty minutes doing that, he drank a beer, and melted two sticks of butter on one of the car's exhaust manifolds. Carefully opening up forty-six sugar packets he placed them into the silver bowl. With the butter melted, he let it cool for a few minutes before adding it into the bowl. His wrist began to ache as he whisked it together while simultaneously cranking the Christopher Cross from his tape deck. He pulled out the eggshells that had fell into the mixture after he had tried to crack them both with one hand. He claimed he had seen it done on a cooking show and wanted to give it a try. He gave up trying to master it after seeing he was running out of eggs. He beat everything together, then eyeballed the flour, and other ingredients, and began to stir. A brown roach crawled across his hand and fell into the batter. Cauzzie Roy looked around the room. Nobody saw anything so he continued to stir. It was the ideal consistency. Lining the cupcake pan with paper liners, he began to fill them in with a slotted spoon. He baked them under the car's catalytic converter. Then frosted them on top with smiling Cauzzie faces.

They covered the beat-up coffee table with all their desserts: chocolate chip cookies, fudge brownies, cupcakes, caramel popcorn balls, a lime jello mold, a gallon of milk, and a bowl of sugar in case anyone wanted more sweetness. Cauzzie Roy knew it was a nice spread. If there was going to be a showdown, and if they were going to go down in a blaze of glory, nobody was gonna say the Cauzzies couldn't bake goods like grandma.

There were a few more preparations before their guests arrived. Everyone pitched in tearing down the Bruce Lee and

Scarface posters, which they burned outside by the storage containers. They made the final touches on their underground chapel; dusting the altar and placing the four folding chairs they had inside and wheeling in the Lazy Boy. They placed all their sacred books on a shelf. Looked around, seeing nothing else needing to be done, they moved to the cooler, cracked beers, and waited.

When the NAMP Taskforce rolled up in their unmarked vans, they wondered if they had arrived at the right place. The photos of Invasive Designate R showed it was supposed to look like a slaughterhouse, but all the agents agreed it looked like an old 20th Century building hit by a tornado. Then someone pointed out the bell tower and said it must be some sort of slap happy temple. Then one of the representatives from Ygnwie, Erasemus, and Sumer pointed out signs of the slaughterhouse peeking out from underneath the white church facade. Whatever it was they were looking at, they all seemed to agree it was one massive building code violation. The representative agreed, and even told Erasemus esq. that if they wanted, they could hand the Invasives an additional violation if they called in the Central Building Inspector. Although he had considered it himself, Erasemus esq. said they were there on bigger business.

Barristan esq. esq. esq. agreed and simply advised everyone to "Watch your heads."

The vans were stashed under the bows of the huge oaks that lined the road to Invasive Designate R. The agents strapped on their helmets and threw on their battle gear until they looked like moving pieces of charcoal. They positioned themselves around the perimeter, then burrowed in for an ambush. They checked their machine guns for ammo and switched them off safety. When everyone was ready, they gave Erasemus esq. and Barristan esq. esq. esq. the go sign, and with that it was show time.

The doorbell rang.

Cauzzie Rob gave explicit instructions not to answer on

the first ring. They wanted to look casual, business as usual like, not too eager. Appearing as though they were just going about their daily business would be good for negotiations. So when the doorbell rang a second time, he answered it.

"Oi! Welcome to Lee Land #3. My name is Cauzzie Rob," he offered his hand.

When they failed to take it, he wiped it on his parachute pants and offered it again. This time Barristan esq. esq. esq. reluctantly shook it.

"I'm Barristan esq. esq. esq. and this is Erasemus esq. and we are here by the authority of the World Governing Council to talk to you about violations of Article 87."

"Right right! Come on in," Cauzzie Rob stepped aside allowing them to enter.

Cauzzie Roy escorted them down the labyrinth of steps leading to the recreation room explaining, "We shut off the methane pumps for your comfort. We also opened the windows and washed down the slaughter yard. We wanted you to feel at home."

The attorneys couldn't help but notice the discolored walls where the Bruce Lee and Scarface posters once hung, but simply kept silent, stoic, all business as they carefully descended the winding staircase.

"You humans need to refresh, we never do, we're always fresh," Cauzzie Roy explained. "You always decay. We never decay. We smell like flowers; you smell like boiled pork, but not wanting to get you thinking this is anything other than facts. Facts. Here, smell."

Barristan esq. esq. esq. hesitated when Cauzzie Roy presented his underarm for him to take a deep whiff. Seeing him hesitate, he encouraged him, "Come on, smell, mate."

Reluctantly Barristan esq. esq. esq. sniffed his underarm.

"What's it smell like, mate?"

Barristan esq. esq. esq. was a little surprised that it didn't smell bad at all, "Geraniums."

"Geraniums! That's right, mate," Cauzzie Roy slapped his knee.

Cauzzie Rob chimed in as expected, "Yeah, we don't have that boiled pig scent you humans have. Decay. Decay it is."

Leading them to their seats inside the recreation room, Cauzzie Rex stood sentry as commanded beside the sofa, next to the row of cleaned and polished pump action shotguns.

"Refreshments!" Cauzzie Roy exclaimed. "Fresh baked refreshments. You humans need to refresh yourselves all the time. So here are your refreshments. Enjoy!"

The attorneys decided to get down to business, opening up their briefcases and taking out stacks of files. They didn't even seem to bother to consider any of the baked treats that overwhelmed the coffee table and set their papers anywhere they found space.

Erasemus esq. explained the issues at hand — their desire to renegotiate Article 747 in light of the Article 87 violations committed by the Invasives of Invasive Designate R.

The Cauzzies sat back and listened to Erasemus esq. explain that if they removed the language that enabled them to go on shooting rampages and steal whatever fit into their bag, they would in exchange forgo prosecuting them on the Article 87 violations.

Cauzzie Rob nodded his head. He understood their proposal. After consulting with Cauzzie Roy they presented their counter proposal. The Cauzzies would remove the language that enabled them to go on shooting rampages and steal whatever fit into their bag if the state would first off, acknowledge that they in fact had a religion that they called "Christianity." Secondly, deliver the Capuchin monk the gladiator arena had in custody so he could perform services at their altar, and thirdly, allow them to build a brewery and/or supply them with truckloads of beer.

Erasemus esq. and Barristan esq. esq. esq. nodded their

heads and whispered into each other's ear. They'd need to make some calls.

The Capuchin friar showed up about an hour later.

The attorneys agreed to contain their excitement. They had anticipated unreasonable negotiations with subhuman slime. Instead, they thought the demands were beyond reasonable and looked to lock things down quickly. They drafted up a new version of the agreement with the following changes: instead of calling it "Christianity" their religion would be labelled "Invasive God," that there would be a stipulation requiring the Invasives to register with General Worship all rites and liturgies for the record, and in lieu of a brewery, they'd offer forty cases of beer a month for seven years. They presented a good offer with the hopes there'd be no need for hardball tactics, and if they were lucky, they could be back at the office by lunch.

The Cauzzies agreed to contain their excitement. They had anticipated unreasonable negotiations with the human dogs. But when they agreed to the forty cases of beer it was beyond anything they had hoped. Cauzzie Rob had only demanded it as a future concession not thinking for a minute they'd actually agree to a monthly supply of free beer. They agreed to the re-labelling of "Christianity" to "Invasive God" when it was clarified the name change was just for legal documentation, and that the Cauzzies were free to call their religion whatever they wanted when nobody was looking. They agreed to the stipulations to register with General Worship since they considered this an act of validation amongst the nations.

Cauzzie Rob and Cauzzie Roy pretended to have a heated argument as if they weren't beyond thrilled with the negotiations, then for the sake of looking like they were playing hardball, they informed the attorneys they needed an 8th year of beer deliveries or no deal.

It was a deal. All that needed to be done now was to have it reviewed and signed off on by the World Governing Body but that was all a formality. They all knew they had a deal. And it all was about as painless a process as anyone could have hoped.

The Cauzzies handed over two years advance on their required tissue cultures in their glass test tubes as a sign of good faith.

The Attorney's handed over the Capuchin friar as a sign of their good faith, who the Cauzzies quickly brought into their fold.

"Can you perform the Holy Sacrifice?"

"Yes. I am an ordained priest," the friar said with a thick Nigerian accent, adding, "But I'm not a Capuchin. I'm a regular Franciscan. OFM. My name is Dan. Dan Anuba they kidnapped me from Nigeria and I was —"

Cauzzie Rob interrupted, "You're alright by me Danny boy!"

They showed Father Dan to his room.

Cauzzie Roy showed him everything they had prepared for his arrival, "Here are some Nilla wafers, non-leveled. Here is your salt, some frankincense, and this here is special Exodus blend — it's incense mate. So you should be all ready to get to work. Oh, here's the Holy Bible, mate. RSV."

The attorneys checked their watches, but surprisingly were in no hurry to leave. They inspected the baked goods. Erasemus took a bite of a cupcake. It had a peculiar texture.

"Crunchy," Erasemus esq. observed chewing.

Cauzzie Roy realizing he must have bitten into the baked-in cockroach tried to play it off, "Yeah, the flavor checks in but it never checks out."

"Delicious," Barristan esq. esq. esq. confirmed.

Cauzzie Rob cracked a beer and offered one to Barristan esq. esq. esq. who thought about it for a minute then said to himself, why not? The attorneys proceeded to revert to their frat house days and the next thing you knew they had downed three consecutively. Everyone was having a good time, but now when they checked their watches, the attorneys knew it was time to go.

There were handshakes and more handshakes. With both parties having feared the worse and made their preparations accordingly, it was like they had no plan for what to do when things went perfectly smoothly for both sides. So they just laughed and joked and suddenly showed interest in the other in a way they never thought they could.

Barristan esq. esq. esq. even handed Cauzzie Rob his personal contact and acknowledged that while doing business together might be a conflict of interest moving forward, he said any assistance they needed in the future, with legal questions or just plain old advice, to feel free to give him a call. Cauzzie Roy on the other hand gave Erasemus esq. an unedited copy of both Scarface and Enter the Dragon along with a box of frozen T-bones and the recipe to his cupcakes, sans roach. When the attorneys looked over the steaks, they were amazed by the marbling.

A fist fight broke out between Cauzzie Roy and Cauzzie Ralph over who was going to ring the church bell first. Father Dan quickly intervened, separating the two.

"See!" Cauzzie Rob rejoiced after seeing cooler heads prevail, "Father Dan is already making it a better day! Peace be with you! And peace be with you!"

"Peace be with you!" a buzzing Barristan esq. esq. esq. exclaimed.

High-fives ensued. More handshakes. Another high-five. Even Father Dan was actually adjusting well to the idea he was going to be spared the gladiator arena in exchange for breaking bread with Invasives. He politely refused a beer though.

When the attorneys stepped out of Invasive Designate R, they signaled a double thumbs-up for NAMP Taskforce to stand down and emerge from their ambush positions. When they did, they began to stretch their aching muscles and pass around bottles of water. The stand down order was passed along the line.

Cauzzie Roy climbed the ladder to the belfry. He looked out

over all the NAMP Agents gathering on the road.

"Oi!" he shouted down at Erasemus and Barristan.

The attorneys looked up squinting. Blinded by the glare, they shielded the sun with their hands and saw and heard Cauzzie Roy ringing the church bell. The melodious clanging carillon of the bells was simply joy to hear. And the more he rang the bell the more it sounded like a magical old hymn, and the attorneys couldn't help but watch the tribute with broad smiles on their faces.

Suddenly Cauzzie Roy lost his balance. Tugging the rope slightly too forcefully, the church bell grazed his face, and upon reflex, he inadvertently stepped back against the railing which hadn't been properly anchored. He began to wobble. Fearing he was going to go toppling over the side head over heels, Cauzzie Roy grabbed the flared end of the bell as it swung back toward him. And he began holding on for dear life.

A screw fell at the foot of Erasemus esq. He looked down at it, then back up to see Cauzzie Roy holding onto the end of the bell as it slowly gave way.

Erasemus screamed.

The NAMP Taskforce took evasive measures.

And Cauzzie Roy came crashing down, taking the church bell and the steeple with him.

The sound of the bell landing square on the heads of Erasemus esq. and Barristan esq. esq. esq. made a distinctive deep and resonate thud, and to all watching it seemed like the bodies exploded as if an obese man had bellyflopped into a swimming pool filled with blood. There were a few NAMP agents stung by bits and pieces of bone hitting their faces from more than twenty yards away.

With his neck properly snapped in two, Cauzzie Roy twitched in the dirt for a few seconds before turning a strange grayish-brown color and began to shrivel into the earth.

There was no other way for the NAMP Taskforce to

interpret what they saw other than a willful act of aggression and went into full tactical assault mode.

Alarms began to wail. Followed by the sound of guns of all calibers, shape, and size, being locked and loaded.

There was no other way for the Cauzzies to interpret what they saw on security monitors showing waves of black-clad militiamen in full tactical assault.

Alarms began to wail. Followed by the sound of shotguns being locked and loaded, a few Hail Marys.

And a blaze of glory.

Vintner Vowell was on the trail. A tweed blazer with leather elbow patches. His elephant gun over his shoulder. A looking glass at his side.

He had tracked the beast all the way through regional park, up the dense trail of thorny underbrush and into the grove of sycamores which were directly across from the Omicon Bank's parking lot. Arriving by the money dispensing machine, he thought the trail had gone cold, but picked it up again outside of the dry cleaners on 31st Avenue.

Looking straight up he saw a set of iron emergency stairs leading to the roof of a brick apartment building. Vintner knew he wasn't in his 20's anymore and took the elevator to the building's roof access. There he saw fresh sign that the beast had been crouched down by a heating vent overlooking the adjacent apartment building almost as if it was watching something. Or someone. A few lights were on, and he could see what looked to be an argument between a man and a woman, but the angle prevented him from seeing more than bodies moving back and forth somewhat frenetically. Another apartment had the curtains drawn open and a man sat by the window wondering. A book at his side.

He looked behind him suddenly, thinking the beast might

have lured him up in an ingenious trap to throw him off the side but there was nothing. Just an empty rooftop. Where could it have gone, he continued to ask himself as he walked along the roof's edge.

A footprint of an athletic shoe on the ledge convinced him the beast must have leaped to the other building. The track clearly showed evidence of the beast having launched himself at a standstill. It must have taken extraordinary strength to make a cold jump at that distance, he knew, and instantly looked down expecting to see a body splattered on the blacktop far below. But there was no body. No beast. Just a rivulet that was catching all drainage that ran down the middle of an alley. It was dark. Maybe he missed something. But when he spied through his looking glass, again, there was no indication what had leapt from the ledge had fallen. There was no way he was going to jump so he spied the opposite roof through the looking glass for anything out of the ordinary but saw nothing.

The trail had run cold.

Vintner lit up a cigar and got the sense that whatever this beast was, it wasn't going to be easy tracking it down. His mind thought back on Bucharest 2096. It was shaping up to be a repeat of the same encounter, he was telling himself, when something out of the corner of his eye caught his attention.

Across the way, on the opposite rooftop, was a figure cloaked in shadows slinking across the perimeter. Vintner knew it was the beast. He carefully loaded his elephant gun, took a bearing, and fired. It looked like a plume of feathers erupted into the night air. He couldn't have missed. He never missed. The idea of a feathered beast in humanoid form captivated Vintner. How thrilling that would look on his trophy wall.

He always claimed to be in better shape than any young man out of the Academy but couldn't help but feel his age when he finally made it down the six flights of stairs, through the lobby of the apartment building, and out the double glass doors, past the alley and into the opposing apartment lobby. Trying to catch his breath, he pressed the door to the elevator. Expecting to see a headless body fall out, he was almost surprised to see it empty. Pressing the top floor, the doors opened up onto a well-lit corridor. Vintner stepped out in one smooth effortless movement and methodically made his way to the roof access door. Up a short flight of steps, he aimed his elephant gun at the open door. Stalking his prey, he took cover behind a roof A/C unit that rumbled and rattled away. Although he felt he had made a direct hit on his target, he was still overtly cautious. There was that time in Veracruz, when they thought the nun was down and how that came back to haunt the entire expedition. So he moved slowly and deliberately around the A/C, his gun pointed and ready to fire without a moment's hesitation.

The feathers were everywhere. White and grey. Then others accented with drops of blood.

Vintner did in fact hit bullseye. But just not the beast. One of his headless victims instead. By the looks of it, a teenage boy tending to his pigeons in the coop he kept on the rooftop. Vintner moved in for a closer look. A few birds flapped about. A few others had flown out the open door and were perched on TV antennas. All still waiting to be fed. A bag of Growfazz birdseed blend still gripped in the teenage boy's hand. A trail of blood led off to the ledge. Whatever it was, it had gotten away again. Leaping across the next building and clearly on the run.

When NAMP arrived, they agreed that the beast must have been in the process of ripping the pigeon keepers head off when Vintner fired, shooting the boy instead of the beast. Again, there was no sign of the head.

Later that evening, in the dead of the night, when the city was sound asleep, Vintner found the beast's trail again. A feather. A drop of blood. It led East. The neighborhood looked familiar to him, like he had been there before on some previous occasion, but as he tried to place when he had seen the street before his thoughts began to wander to this beast he was chasing. How ruthless and cunning it was. Whatever it was. The wonder, he amused himself thinking, that this beast collected heads as trophies. And soon he would be collecting its head for his wall. How apropos. How apropos.

The trail went cold right when the sun began to rise.

Vintner lit up another cigar, looked around, and knew he had been in the neighborhood before. It was eerily familiar. But the hunt was over. The beast had slipped through his hands yet again. He tucked the feather into his pocket and headed back to camp. A sleep and a shave. A cup of brandy. And maybe it would come to him. This place that seemed so familiar.

"No, I don't think I can...No."

A pain arose from Helinka's subconscious. She swiftly withdrew her hands as an unfamiliar pain slowly crept silently into her senses and rested in the pit of her stomach. It was a vulnerability and despair she hadn't known for an eternity. It was there though, she felt it, swimming beneath the surface and far, far below, where for the first time, she saw it reigning undisturbed in the abyss. Her eyes desperate now, looked up to the room filled with strangers she had just moments ago been amongst, comfortable, conformed, capable, and now her hands were trembling seeing that this thing, this unknown thing that stirred within her had finally breached for all to see. A tear ran down her cheek.

It was only a few hours earlier when Jules first sensed something was wrong. If the white clogs weren't obvious enough for the Synoid's brain to comprehend, when she showed no interest in the purple velveteen pumpkin pillows by Batoush he knew he had to ask.

It wasn't that she wasn't enjoying herself, she explained, it wasn't like she wasn't having a nice time with Jules. Spending time together was everything it was supposed to be, light-hearted, easy-going, and completely effortless. The conversations never got old. Sure, there were those lulls in conversation, but they felt natural and always appropriate in that little space and time, like it was all scripted to be unscripted. And she was having another one of those nice days today, she explained, but there was something so unsatisfying in all of the selections she was making, like thread counts for Turkish linen, calculating how many sets, the variations of off-whites, figuring not just on her bedroom, but guest rooms also, and eventually the kids' rooms, when they got around to having kids. Were they going to have kids? Do you plan that far ahead? There were comforters, duvets, decorative pillows to consider. Then she had to consider a whole lot of other things too, like wedding invitations. And all that sort of thing, she said.

Jules listened to her tell him how the guppy pedicure was so much fun and the tasting menu at Volga was exquisite.

"What about that thing in the living room?" Jules knew what that thing was in the living room.

"What's that?" Helinka heard him just fine.

At first Jules thought the 200-cubic-foot roll off dumpster in the middle of the living room overlooking the sea was the latest sculpture by Goria. Then he thought it might have been a forgery of a Goria when he noticed a discrepancy on one of the steel rollers. The pattern of rust was different. And there was a cough drop wrapper pressed into it. It didn't take him long from there to check his contemporary art archives in his Modus-Aparatix and realize that it was just a rented dumpster.

"For trash," she told him as if it weren't totally obvious.

He knew it wasn't just for trash though. Well at least not technically. When Jules had peeked inside the dumpster, he didn't think he saw trash. How could the new drapes they just ordered be trash? The new settee was inside but with a huge slash across the fabric. It didn't make any sense to him, and he was concerned.

Jules scanned his memory banks. All the valuable information Helinka had personally inputted within his brain. Looking for an explanation for the strange human behavior he was witnessing subtly evolve in-front of his face. He was alive because of her. He reminded himself of this every day. This was never lost on Jules. He could see her little kisses planted all across his thoughts and facts, his information, statistics, calculations, and experimentations, and all his stiff-necked ways. When the results of his inquiry came back from his mental Corpus Commutium processor the datum was clear yet completely surprising to Jules. Helinka was in full meltdown mode. This wasn't the result he was expecting. Cold feet at the worst, he assumed. But full meltdown mode? Then the more he thought about it the more it wasn't so subtle. He determined what was next was how to fix her. Shopping was not the answer, he knew that. Food wasn't the answer. He was drawing blanks. Formulas and calculations weren't working. He wasn't finding the answer he was looking for. Then he thought about himself. What would Jules do? If she created me, and I am her creation, then wouldn't that make my thoughts, her thoughts? Since she wasn't currently capable of thinking straight, if he could just do the thinking then they'd be able to get out of the trouble they were in.

Jules knew he learned by experience.

"I want you to come with me."

"Where?" she asked.

"I can't tell you until we get there. But you have to promise not to get mad at me."

Helinka winced, "Mad at you?"

It was too much to explain he said, and they took a palankeen through a maze of back alleys and cavernous concrete monoliths of the city she had never before stepped into. Not that they were somehow rundown or derelict, they just weren't for going into. They were just there. Something had to fill the space between where she started and where she was going, after all. But to venture inside was never a consideration. So she looked to Jules ever more inquisitively, wondering where exactly he was taking her. Each and every time Jules shook his head or reminded her what she promised. She wouldn't get mad at him.

The building was nondescript. Some steps and a door. Looking up through the haze of midday the structures appeared like desert outcroppings. There was a current of warm air blowing from some obscure direction that she couldn't quite figure out if it was coming from the vents blowing down on the wet cardboard stacked in front of the import export building or the neon sign shop next door.

Jules pressed the doorbell. A man answered. Jules handed him a card and the man disappeared inside. This was too much for Helinka to just keep quiet.

"Where are we? Jules. Jules? How do you know about this place? And, and…What is this place?!"

Jules put his finger to his lips. Helinka couldn't help but laugh, the audacity of this creature to tell her to shush, but whatever anger might have colored her initial indignation swiftly faded into a strange blend of excitement for whatever unknown lurked behind the door and that there was a part of her in Jules that knew exactly where they were going.

The waiting room was small. She noticed a square picture frame on the wall with the dimensions 12"x12" printed above a stock family photo. The pall of dust on the side table was highlighted by a half-moon void where the vase had been recently moved two inches to the left. The reception desk lay on the other side of a glass partition with a slot to pass documents back and forth.

Baron Grel was what Helinka envisioned a fine Englishman to be. Refined. Always nice to listen to. His voice imparting a tradition and order that always seemed so difficult to achieve with an accent that was all your own. A sound which lingered in your mind just a little longer than her lazy tongue could ever hope to achieve. He was both reserved and welcoming. So much so that she thought they were in an English manor house instead of a dusty waiting room.

Jules and Baron Grel caught up on old chatter, and she understood he had already made arrangements for her to be here, long ago. Although from the sound of it she was there sooner than either had expected. Helinka wondered to herself, what else was Jules planning that she had no idea about. What else was he arranging for her when they weren't side by side. And when weren't they side by side?

"So what exactly is this place," Helinka asked.

"The Happy Place, you mean?" Baron Grel corrected, "It's a sanctuary. A state of mind. A zone fully free from judgment. Here there is an absence of status and rank. A getaway where nobody has to worry or be penalized for being vulnerable. For being open. Imperfection here is the goal. It is the prize we seek. Here at the Happy Place there are no violations. We are your refuge. Here you can remove the mask you present to the world, the one that satisfies its rigorous demands yet fails to represent your true individuality. My job is to be that fishing hook deep within the most mysterious recesses of your soul and to draw that truth into the light. How does this sound?"

Helinka looked for the right word, "Frightening…no wait." She thought some more. "Portentous."

Baron Grel's smile exuded satisfaction at her response.

"Helinka, my dear. On the other side of those doors, you will come face to face with your true self. On the other side of that door, you come face to face with you. When you step through those doors there are no rules, regulations, or things like the law. So what do you say? Shall we?"

Without hesitation, Helinka beelined to the door, but when she tried to open it, it was locked.

"Oh, the door, it's locked."

Baron Grel slid a clipboard through the window's slot.

"We'll need you to sign off on these disclosures and liability waivers first."

"You said there was no law."

"These? These are just ordinances."

"Oh...I see."

So there she was. With the pain that had arisen from deep within her subconscious. She swiftly withdrew her hands as a tear ran down her cheek.

The others began to shout encouraging words, urging her to let go of the fear, while Baron Grel kept a close eye on her.

"You're doing wonderful, Helinka."

Helinka didn't feel wonderful, she felt discombobulated.

"Tell me what you see, Helinka," Baron Grel urged. "Tell me!"

Helinka didn't want to say.

"Release yourself!" he said, his arms outstretched theatrically.

Helinka looked away, trying not to face it.

"You can do this!"

"It's..." she finally began to build up the courage, "It's... brown."

"Yes, yes, what else?"

"It's, it's...orange."

"Yes, yes, now tell me, Helinka, what is it?"

"Sweet potatoes and hash browns..."

"YES!" Baron Grel shouted. But now he had more work to do, he continued to pry it out of her, "Now! Now what are you doing!"

Helinka looked at the strange rubber blue gloves on her hands. They had a synthetic smell to them that she was unable to place. The thing in her hand was a small rectangle, on one side was yellow and soft, the other side was green and rough. The bubbles were everywhere filling up the sink.

"I don't know," she muttered almost under her breath.

Baron Grel was now up in her face, knowing she was on the verge of the breakthrough, "Yes you do. Tell me! What are you doing?!"

Helinka squeezed the small rectangle in her hand and saw the suds ooze from the tiny caverns and onto the plate.

"The dishes…I'm doing dishes."

"How does that make you feel?!" orchestrated Baron Grel.

It was embarrassing. It was shameful. It was confusing. It was disgusting, she said to everyone's collective appreciation. She was suddenly amongst friends. Seeing this gave her pause. She started to breathe again. The tear was wiped away. And she reflected on the spotless plate that her hands had brought to a polished shine. It was fun, joyous, invigorating, and surprisingly satisfying, she remarked. The room lit up with like smiles. They had all been where she was now standing. Helinka held up her plate and the room broke out in applause.

The group session quickly followed.

Helinka along with all the other participants, each one from different sectors of the society who had so vigilantly carried upon their backs the norms, artifacts, and assumptions that served the world in all its greater glory and allowed it to thrive as a single morally upright unit, were now standing before their own personal sink, waiting for Baron Grel to distribute their own tubs of dirty dishes from the recent lunch rush at the upstairs Chinese buffet.

The plates were filled with half-eaten egg rolls, cold remains of chicken chow mein, crusted remnants of sweet and sour sauce, piles of discarded broccoli from an order of General Tso's, to flecks of beef and stray mung beans from a chop suey platter.

Helinka scraped each plate in her bus tray and took her soapy sponge and wiped each plate down before setting it into the water to soak. Baron Grel suggested she remove the rubber gloves to feel the warm water, the slippery suds, and the squishy remains of consumed food. Hesitant at first, she found the courage and removed the gloves. The whole sensation of holding the plates with no barrier between her skin and the dirty dishes made her feel exposed as if something was going to seep inside her and contaminate her intellectual values she had cultivated since birth. But here it was different. The group thrived.

At first when she saw her fingers shrivel and wrinkle up, she thought she was dying, that her perfect skin and perfect self had leaked out into the water and she naturally started to panic.

Baron Grel explained the phenomena. Osmosis, he said, is purely normal and that what she was seeing was the water drawing the salts from your fingers into the water. That she was indeed giving up part of her essence. The other participants who had experienced this before and become accustomed to it all showed her their wrinkled hands. More broad smiles. A few laughs. Helinka's confidence grew again. It was all the perfect outlet she thought. The idea of thinking versus feeling. She had been such a grand thinker and such a poor feeler. There was an understanding within her that she had forgotten about that other side, the one that governed the emotional, that culture that affected the values and norms and artifacts and assumptions of people which her thoughts knew it best to suppress. The emotions crept out in her facial expressions, the way she drummed her fingers on the table. But they were never part of her. They were locked away. Deep in the abyss.

As she finished cleaning her last plate and set them with the others, everyone stood back and looked at all they had accomplished. The session was closed with a group vow to keep everything they had experienced strictly guarded in The Happy Place.

Jules listened to Helinka as she told him all about it. How she had to scrub and scrub a weird sauce off the plate with her finger and how she broke a nail. She showed him the proof. It was indeed a broken nail.

"I'm gonna leave it like this. I'm not getting it fixed. I like it!" said Helinka taking Jules by the arm as they strode down the serpentine alleys toward more familiar grounds.

"Thank you, Jules. That was so thoughtful. I'm going back next week. But shhhhh. Don't tell anyone."

Thanks to the admonition of the Happy Place, they had new inside jokes and code words about it that were all their own. And when Jules' veiled words about liquid soap began to sound a bit too explicit, she playfully shushed him again, pulled him closer, and matched him stride for stride all the way home.

Jules watched Helinka closer. She moved around the apartment freer now. This was good to see. But he knew the mission set out in his Synoid brain was to fix her, and although she was clearly responding better to the idea of shopping for succulents and had even booked a table for two at Wame, he knew there was more to be said.

They had just finished their appetizer when Jules spoke.

"I have something to say."

Helinka had noticed something about Jules the moment she stepped out of the Happy Place, like he was holding something back, or like he had something on his mind. She tried to do her best to reassure him with all the affection she could, assuming it was the fact he was unable to participate in the fun of The Happy Place because he was a Synoid, and that Synoids don't have these kinds of issues, and that maybe Jules wanted to have them too. She wasn't sure. But now seeing that he was about to open up, she set her fork down and took his hand.

"What is it Jules?"

"You're not cured."

"What do you mean? The thing?" Helinka referred to the experience at The Happy Place in code, "You mean that?"

"Yes."

"I don't get it? What do you mean not cured?"

Jules mustered his courage, "This idea that you've released

this, this emotion that has been pent up inside you, that this was some emotional outlet, this, how do I say it? This isn't the answer to anything, Helinka."

Helinka wasn't sure what he was getting at, after all, it was him who had taken her there and she was feeling better about things. Now here he was with all this seriousness.

"I don't understand. Why'd you take me there then?" she asked.

"So you would see the truth."

"I don't understand. What truth? I finally feel, I don't know how to say it, I finally feel free. Work and all this stuff, this living the perfect life, I just, I just finally feel better. I feel free, Jules. So what truth is it? What truth am I missing here?"

"Emotional freedom for the sake of self-indulgence is no better than servitude to some moralistic culture. Freedom for the sake of self-indulgence rather than responsibility toward others isn't true freedom."

Helinka was speechless. How to respond to this, she wondered. She processed his words.

"Jules. Are you suggesting..." Helinka thought she had formulated her thought, but soon realized she was still in the processes of taking in what he had said.

"Helinka. You think of me as your son, as a child that you have raised to take on the world. Some creation so that your status as some goddess would be assured. But I see you differently. Not as my creator necessarily. Although I embrace that will all my heart. The thing is I see you in another way too. As a partner, as your other half. I want you to consider that an emotional outlet isn't the same as an emotional connection. What you need is that emotional connection. I want you to be responsible to me, but in another way. A more meaningful and fulfilling way. Not mother to son, but in that other way. Do you know what I mean?

Helinka knew what he meant.

Jules seeing this added, "You can wash all the dishes you

want to the end of time, but until you face the fact that you made me, and that you are also made for me, then neither of us will ever be truly happy."

The candles flickered and the entrees were served. And they sat in unspoken stillness. Their eyes occasionally finding each others. Each pretending that nothing so earth shattering as being together forever had been said. They scanned the dessert menus, hoping that there was some other way out.

"That's Gideon!" Supentus rejoiced upon seeing the 12"x12" black and white print, shot through a telephoto lens from the back of some suspicious van.

The dark emissaries sat across from his intricately carved ivory desk, and although they were fewer in number due to the damage inflicted by their former boss, they still maintained their flowing black and ghostly shrouds. The only difference was hidden. The black armbands they wore underneath their robes in honor of their fallen comrades.

"That he is indeed," rhetorically squealed one of the dark emissaries.

Supentus tried his best to listen as his visitors let him in on all the gory details. But their heavy breathing was distracting. While they went on about things like double agents, infidels, and stolen secrets, all he heard was the sound of wind whistling through a warped window. Then Supentus changed his mind. He thought the dark emissaries sounded more like frayed violin bows run across strings of greenish-yellow phlegm, or an ill-tuned snakeskin shanshin from a Japanese junk shop, or maybe it was more like a bent and broken bayou banjo.

"Did you hear what we are saying?!"

Supentus was thinking of ordering takeout and a shot of wheat grass, replying, "Every word."

"Gideon is a spy!" The dark emissaries were flexing their

perceived muscle, adding, "As soon as he walks off the elevator we will apprehend him! You seem to find it amusing that he is stealing The Startling Concern's secrets! Upending the natural order and all the institutions we've all sworn by their lives to serve and uphold!"

"He's been a valuable asset to our company," said Supentus.

"INFIDEL!" they shrieked.

"Yeah, well, not everyone's perfect."

The dark emissaries sat speechless. This was devastating news they were bringing him, and they had anticipated much groveling on the part of the powerful CEO. They were at a loss as to why he wasn't groveling at their feet.

Seeing their apparent dismay, even under their black sheets, Supentus let them in on a little secret. When he was finished there was a long unbroken silence. Then finally someone decided to speak.

"What do you mean, you knew about Gideon all along?!" the dark emissaries writhed.

Seeing he needed to elaborate, Supentus swiveled his chair toward them, cleared his throat, and began filling in the blanks.

"The whole thing with Cloreen being caught by Jotham with the Eucharistic host, I knew it was set-up from the start. I could have put a stop to the whole thing then, but if anyone was going to excel in the gladiator arena it was Cloreen. So I wasn't concerned. I was more curious what exactly your dead boss, this Jotham of yours, was planning with my little car thief. So I played along to see what this 'infidel,' as you say, had on his mind. And look it's all turned out for the best!"

"So you knew all along!? How'd this turn out to be the best?! You should have reported this!" they shrieked once more, a twang of desperation lurking in, being slow to adjust to the idea that there would be no groveling as expected.

"Hey, it sounds like you knew all along too. So we're even," said Supentus winking at them like a seasoned gameshow host.

"Look, we both have our reasons for doing what we do. But here we are now, all gathered around the table, so let's talk turkey. Shall I ring for snacks?"

There was some momentary grumbling, but the dark emissaries were never ones to refuse snacks.

After some light noshing and small talk the tone of the meeting lightened enough to where they once again got down to the business at hand. Supentus took the lead.

"I appreciate you coming down and giving me a heads up, I really do, because this gives me a chance to let you in on a little thing I've been up to. Get your perspective on things."

The dark emissaries made staccato noises from underneath their black sheets that seemed to indicate they were most pleased with having their perspectives heard, especially by someone as powerful as CJ Supentus.

"We are about to launch our new Invisible Super God and I want you in on the ground floor!" offered up Supentus.

The dark emissaries were unsure they had heard what they had all so clearly heard, "Invisible…Super God?"

"Yes!" exclaimed Supentus.

"Ground floor?" they all looked stunned.

"Yes! I'm talking one single all powerful and invisible god to replace all other gods!"

"Just one god? Invisible?!"

"Yes!"

After a long pause, the dark emissaries spoke in almost a whisper, "That would mean…"

"Yes! You know what that would mean!" Supentus didn't hesitate making his pitch, "I'm talking 15% of all gross commissions for every single one of you. For an eternity."

"Eternity…" the dark emissaries couldn't believe what they were hearing.

"If you decide to back this project, you know what that will mean for every one of you?" continued Supentus. "That would make you all the richest people in the history of mankind. Except for me, of course. But it's just me, and there are all of you. I think if you do the math you'll see it's more than fair.

The dark emissaries were doing the math.

"15% for eternity for just doing what it is you do, you know, as the new Lead Inspectors of General Worship. You know what I mean?"

The dark emissaries commiserated amongst themselves. Were they hearing this right? Was this all too good to be true? But they immediately brushed aside those concerns when they realized where they were at. They were all sitting in the office of the CEO for the Startling Concern, one of the most powerful conglomerates on the planet, if not the most powerful. And at the same time, they remembered who they were, the new Lead Inspectors of General Worship and the power they held in the palms of their hand. This kind of partnership had the potentially to be one of the most lucrative of all time. Therefore, the dark emissaries quickly deduced that if taking over the world was remotely possible, this was the exact time and place in order to do so.

"Tell us more about this Invisible Super God," they asked.

"Yes! Absolutely!" exclaimed Supentus smiling. Then handing them a sheet of paper, "But not before you sign these NDA's."

A DARK TURN

It was a tower.

On display in the middle of The Startling Concern executive board room was a scale model of their proposed Godgod Prayer Tower that would extend 50 miles into the the sky, scraping the top of the mesosphere and just inches away from the thermosphere.

The new Head of Product Development walked Gideon and Supentus through how the design team envisioned the tower to work. He explained how all your dreams, hopes, and desires travel up the tower in the form of prayers and are then transformed into holy ions and spewed out into the thermosphere where they escape through the exosphere and into space where they are then absorbed by The Startling Concern's infinite, invisible "Godgod," as they were calling it. The Godgod would then collect the holy ions and send his responses back down through the atmosphere like the dew fall, and into the tower where The Startling Concern's new "Super-Power-Computation-Transmission-Altar" would receive the responses, translate them, interpret them, and then distribute the commands to the trillions of customers around the world.

The new Head of Product Development explained how the focus groups showed the customers were having a difficult time relating to a deity that they weren't able to see, hear, or touch, when they themselves were in such a limited physical confine. The tower enabled them to have a visual conduit to this new infinite and all powerful ideal. A way of linking heaven and earth, and thus helping them transition from worshipping winged jackals to the new infinite and invisible Godgod.

"High fives!" shouted Supentus as he gave everyone a high five. "Fist bump!" Supentus gave everyone a fist bump with an exploding hand gesture before suggesting a slight alternation, "Let's find a word other than customers. It sounds a bit unromantic. Maybe, guests? Oh wait, no. I got it, how about 'true believers.' I love it!"

"Excellent! True believers. Got it!" replied the new Head of Product Development jotting the change down in his notebook.

"I love it. Don't you Gideon?" asked Supentus not even waiting for his answer; he was talking a million miles a minute. "Let's build this thing right outside of the Holey Land. Like right outside the gate. Have it loom over Sir Sindon. So he has to look at it everyday! I think we should have two, one at the Vacatican and one outside the Holey Land. Wait. Scratch that. No wait. I was right. Two towers is actually a good idea. You can't have Godgod without a pair. Two is better than one. You know Gideon, like they had two of those golden calves, right? One in Dan and one in Beit El? The whole Jeroboam thing? Or maybe you don't know about that, or you haven't been coached up by your friend, the one that got his brains splattered all over the parking lot, anyways, I'm just spitballing here, so what do you think? One outside the gate of the Holey Land and one at the Vacatican."

Gideon was hung up on the brains comment, "Uh...what was that about..."

"You know, Gideon, you're my official right hand man," exclaimed Supentus. "Officially. We're connected now for all-times sake. By the way, I love your new bogman leathers. Those are pretty sweet. Nice stitching. We almost match now. Of course, this track suit is my second Mentuhotep. Like as in Mentuhotep II. My Mentuhotep I is at the cleaners. Anyways, did my tailor treat you well, Gideon? He always complains about my shape shifting, and having to deal with all those variable measurements, so he must have been thrilled to see you. Just in your one size. Hmm. I do admire a good bogman. Excellent taste you have. Don't you love the Tower concept? I love it. By the way, The Lead Inspectors for General Worship are on board. You know those guys with the funny outfits. They remind me of giant veils. But black. Not white."

Gideon was hoping he had heard wrong, "Isn't the Lead Inspector for —

"— Anyway, the tower idea really helps with the transition, you know what I mean?" interrupted Supentus, before adding, "There's a lot of moving pieces taking customers from graven images and animal deities, and all that, to something totally mind-altering like the invisible and all knowing, infinite Godgod. You know what I mean? Of course you do, Gideon, you inspired all of this! It gives the customer, oops, I mean, the 'true believers' something to focus on when it comes to our infinite being. I think it just helps unify everyone into one single idea, you know what I mean? It helps focus the imagination. It reminds me of my early days. The tower. My apprenticeship days. Ah, yes. You know, I've always done exceptionally well with towers. And giants. Some of my previous work is still with us today. Did you know that? Wait, of course you wouldn't Gideon, you're just a car thief. Towers. Giants. Towers again. It all works. It's timeless. Feet on the floor, head in the clouds, I always say."

Gideon had zero time to process what was happening let alone what was being said, so he tried to play along, but right when he was about to open his mouth to say something, Supentus would cut him off.

"I know what you're thinking, Gideon," he continued, "I

went ahead and did all the work without you. I hope you don't mind. I just got excited, that's all. I hope you understand. I'm so excited about this. To think I was so busy making everyone happy I didn't even bother to think about ripping off God himself. Like just blatantly ripping him off. I've had great success converting God's whole shtick into little fragments, but never just taking over Divine Providence itself. It's genius, Gideon. Pure genius. Let me show you this!"

Supentus took Gideon by the arm and brought him to a shoebox-sized diorama of a modeling clay skybridge with orange and red triangles made out of cardboard underneath it.

"I know it's a little bit hard to see here, but this is gonna be inside the tower. I riffed off that idea you came up with for hotels and vacation packages, and thought it would be great to incorporate some of our other investments into the whole Godgod concept. See this is gonna be a huge glass skybridge that will look like ice. And underneath it will be this huge crevasse with lava. That's what those triangles are. So it's a whole fire and ice thing."

Gideon tried to act like he understood it all, "Uh, yeah. I see"

"Do you, Gideon?" asked Supentus with a strange look on his face. "I want to make absolutely sure you do understand. You remember Cloreen right? The one you replaced? She negotiated a hostile takeover of Fontanel Integrated Research. So this is a perfect example of how to bring our subsidiaries into the fold. Do you see what I mean?"

"Uh, yeah…but…"

"Babies. See we sell the true believers the babies, do the whole finance thing, and they sacrifice them into the lava flow," explained Supentus as he hoped to clarify his vision.

Hearing this, Gideon was horrified, "You mean babies? Like real babies, like human babies?"

"I know it's totally 'Molachian' but you can see how awesome this is, so like let's say you wanted to get extra points with Godgod, or merit a promotion, or merit a better command to come down from the whole tower thing. I mean the options are endless. We can offer a load of exciting vacation packages with other holdings, like the Vacatican, or extra bonus miles on your travel rewards points, or a free mocha with proof of purchase type thing, I mean, I haven't thought this all out completely, but we can tie in a bunch of deals with our hotels, restaurants, entertainment, and it's all just feeding the machine. It's brilliant. What do you think? I wanna hear your thoughts."

Gideon tried not to panic, the idea of killing babies for free mochas was never part of the deal, "I am not sure that the one true God —"

"— You mean Godgod?" Supentus interjected.

"Uh…yeah, Godgod. I mean god god is a kind and loving God…god… and I think that family is something he wants, he'd want to preserve, not destroy, and…"

Supentus cut him off.

"Is that what Jotham told you to say?"

Gideon was stunned silent.

Supentus continued off his shocked expression, "Sacrificing a baby is totally kind and loving, Gideon. Didn't you learn anything from your boy Jotham? Sacrificing a baby isn't losing a baby. That's where so many people get sacrifice so wrong. When people hear the word sacrifice, they think they are losing something, but that's totally not what it means. You are actually gaining something. What you are doing is making that thing you sacrifice holy. Look at the word itself, Gideon. Sacrifice is from two Latin words, 'Sacer' which means holy, and 'facere' means to make. See. To 'make holy.' So we aren't destroying anything. You see? Gideon? Gideon? Gideon, you look a little pale?

Gideon grabbed his head, the movement ripping a seam in the sleeve of his bogman leisurewear, "Jotham? Is he…?"

"Dead? Yes. Brains blown out everywhere. I saw pictures.

They showed me. Gruesome. He didn't stand a chance. Tried to break for it, and they gunned him down. Brains everywhere. I hope you don't get those same ideas Gideon and try and run."

Gideon looked as though he had been hit in the gut with a sledgehammer and just continued to mumble, "Jotham... dead..."

Supentus asked one of the executives to bring a glass of water, then took Gideon by the shoulders, reassuring him, "Gideon, just because I don't really need you anymore doesn't mean I am going to turn you over to the dark emissaries who killed your friend."

"It was never my idea...any of this..." Gideon tried to save himself, and this was his feeble effort.

Supentus gave him a compassionate look, like a parent forgiving their toddler.

"Don't sell yourself so short, kiddo! Here drink this," Supentus handed Gideon the glass of water, then added, "Look, Gideon. I knew all along. I mean, when I heard you mentioning all that stuff about the Tetragrammaton, and then the Merkavah, this is heady stuff, Gideon. It never sounded like you. So I knew. Did that stop me from promoting you, did it? No? So I don't want you to start worrying. Like I said, you're my right hand man. You're in this with me and you still have a job to do. Got that?"

Gideon shook his head no.

Seeing the need to speak with Gideon in private, Supentus clicked his fingers.

When Gideon opened his eyes he found himself sitting in a theater chair in the middle of a private screening room. The room was entirely black and faced a huge projection screen.

"Did you like that, Gideon?" said Supentus laughing, "That's an old trick I learned from the Count of the Szekeys back in Gorgeny before the Turks took it over. But that's another story. I saw you were having a little breakdown and thought it would be better to talk in private instead of with all those people around, I hope you don't mind?"

Gideon was speechless. Motionless. He had told himself so many times before to just keep quiet only to open his mouth. But now it was different. He was scared stiff. If he wanted to run his legs wouldn't let him. If he wanted to scream, his brain was unable to send the signal. He was for all intents and purposes a ghost.

Supentus wasn't expecting Gideon to answer whether or not he minded suddenly teleporting from the board room to a private screening room. He knew what to expect with someone in his situation. He knew how Gideon was coming to terms with the the realities of his situation, and those terms were fear. 100% total and absolute fear. So he just allowed Gideon to sit there in his catatonic state while gently trying to talk him back to the world of the living.

"I've known all along," started Supentus, "But unlike you, I haven't forgotten. It's just I've been so close to it for so long, sometimes you just lose perspective. But you gave me back that perspective I needed. You could say, I've been so busy converting this whole morality thing I forgot all about the job I was hired to do. I'm here for one reason and one reason only. And that's to take the tools I've been given with nature and make a case for mankind. It's that simple. And what better way to accomplish that goal than to become like God himself? This is what you reminded me of. You and your big memory."

Gideon's lips began to move, "Are you going to kill me?"

"Heaven forbid I would do such a thing, Gideon," laughed Supentus. "I'm all about fun. That killing stuff, I'll leave to you and those Cauzzie friends of yours. I just want to be your role model, Gideon. And I want to be the best man at your wedding. You asked for Helinka, remember? And I authorized that didn't I, remember? Your match meter didn't just miraculously show up as 'perfect match,' remember? That was me who gave her to you. So now that your Jotham friend is gone, you'll need someone to fill his shoes. I can fill his shoes! I can fill everyone's shoes. Even his. I'll be your best man," said Supentus pointing to the heavens. "This world may be his footstool, but I think it works better as an ottoman."

Gideon put his head in his hands.

Supentus kicked his feet up on the chair in front of him.

"Are those tears Gideon?" Supentus knew they were. "Don't cry Gideon. You've done really well. Really well. Here, this might cheer you up."

Supentus clicked his fingers and the theater screen lit up with the flickering of a home movie. A toddler in a high chair being fed by his mother.

"How cute! Is that you, Gideon? As a baby? It is! It's baby Gideon" asked Supentus as he suddenly started munching on a bucket of buttered popcorn.

Gideon peered out between his fingers.

"Is that you and your parents at Ayers Rock? You look so cute. I like your nappies."

Supentus was more than happy to provide the captions as images of Gideon as a toddler flashed upon the screen. Everything from him and his family camping in Kosciusko, a birthday party, to playing catch with his father in the backyard of a modular home. It all brought Gideon's head out of his hands, his tears dried up almost instantly. It was him. Those were his parents. And as Gideon began to get lost in the visual presentation a smile crept into his expression, a bit of wonder, a bit of nostalgia as he recognized things like his stuffed turtle he called Blublub.

"Blublub," Gideon smiled.

"Look Gideon! Is that you at seder?" Supentus pointed to the screen in awe, there was Gideon not more than five or six, asking his father a question. "Look Gideon! You were a Jew!

I wonder what tribe you are from. Definitely not Issachar. My guess is Gad. You look to me like the too many cows type of guy. Wow. Look at that. A Jew. Does any of this ring a bell?"

Gideon's face tensed up. He turned and stared at Supentus.

"I can see it in your eyes, Gideon," mused Supentus, "You're not sure if this is some conjuring, if it is real or not, but it's not easily dismissed. But don't look at me. I remember. You've clearly chosen to forget. I think you should watch closely."

Gideon turned back to the screen. It was a funeral.

Nothing felt like a home movie anymore. Erased was that layer of celluloid that added that special separation. No, that was gone. And now Gideon felt as though he was there. Sitting alone in the front row of Brown Brothers Funeral Home with a tidy black suit and kippah. An 8-year old Gideon keeping his head down, only occasionally lifting it when relatives came by to tend to him, offering condolences. Gideon moved to the caskets, looking in.

"So so tragic," said Supentus in a sad voice. "The hatred. The violence. It was such a troubling time."

Running down a street with this fellow 4th-grade hooligans looking for mischief, he throws a stone at the last remaining window pain of the abandoned bakery, but missing wildly. The pack joins in and finally shatters the last remaining pain of glass. It's a collage of adolescent destruction, across train tracks, behind unsuspecting supermarkets, in the hills above the town. Trying to smoke cigarettes on an industrial park rooftop. Plucking at a Korean-made pawn shop flying-V guitar in the living room of a two bedroom apartment, he makes strange noises off untuned strings, the complete opposite of whatever King Crimson song was blaring from the faux-oak Fisher stereo system. It was Uncle Dovi in the kitchen, Gideon noticed. Uncle Dovi! He couldn't quite see what he was preparing, a sandwich maybe. Whatever it was required slamming the refrigerator door a few times. A glass of wine posing as a cup of coffee at noon day, Uncle Dovi turned on the tele. He was a lanky fellow with that unkept beard of his and always wearing a promotional cigarette T-shirt. It didn't matter what brand. Marlboro, Camel, Chesterfields, his former partner in the liquor store left the box of T-shirts on the table but nothing else the day he ran off with their stock. Then young Gideon roused from his sleep. Throwing back the action figure comforter he had thought he had outgrown, rubbing his eyes as he checked the digital clock's red beady eyes.

4:12 AM. Nothing good happens at 4 in the morning he'd come to learn as he shuffled through the hall, as the breaking of plates echoed through the darkness, or was it a lamp — it was too dark to see. The darkness mixed everything together. It was just noises. Just yelling. A woman shouting back things he couldn't make out or quite understand. Something about a promise. A screen door crashing off its hinges as it took all the abuse it could endure from two passionately intoxicated 24-hour acquaintances.

The day brought out the sound of cicadas. The smell of dry grass wafted through the warm air. Flat on his back, Gideon chewed on a stick of Wrigley's, as Uncle Dovi in cramped quarters under a car chassis banged away as the Salem 100 dangled from his lip, ashes falling into his beard. It was now Gideon's turn, as Uncle Dovi handing him a pry bar, Gideon handed him the torque wrench as if on cue. Uncle Dovi reached up and continued to struggle with the part. Yes. A light seemed to flood into the forefront of Gideon's mind. It was the 1987 Buick Grand National. Although it was missing most of its parts, Gideon laughed recalling how that fact never stopped Uncle Dovi from telling you it was the "full midnight package" with dark factory additions like the power dome hood and spoiler, although he had never himself seen the power dome. The missing T-tops didn't keep them from taking the rumbling rebuilt 3.8 liter fuel injected V6 turbo down to the Ampol servo in less than tropical conditions. That's what the fleece in the backseat was for, Uncle Dovi would explain.

Uncle Dovi explained to the newly minted teenage Gideon, now pulling double duty with both bubblegum and cigarette, the tools. Five clip leads. Electrical tape. His Bryce Canyon souvenir pocketknife. A screwdriver. Then he explained the craftsmanship required, the evaluation of a car's ignition, the battery, all the components. Showing him all the wires crammed under the dash. Walking him through the voltmeter, untwisting the bundles of wire, red wire, yellow wire, whatever other color. Once the engine started, how to remove the starter lead and to kill the engine by unclipping the 12v from the ignition lead.

The stack of manuals made a booming sound as they hit the kitchen table. They were to be memorized. Each and ever one. All the wiring diagrams. From beginning to end. He didn't want Gideon to skip a beat. In and out in a matter of minutes. You could only do that if you could remember, Uncle Dovi said. Gideon could remember it now, like it was yesterday, "Remembering will save you." It's what Uncle Dovi would say. He got it out of *Dr. Masterson's Methods of Memorization Techniques* paperback. It still had the library card inside from when Uncle Dovi must have shoved it down his corduroys when he permanently checked the book out. He watched as his uncle tore off his kippah from his head, smacking him repeatedly over the head with it. And Gideon's improvised karpas was no match for the Waste King 300. There would be no more seders. Forget about seders.

Gideon sat on the porch sipping a Fosters with his uncle while identifying all the cars passing by. Anything turn of the Century was of considerable interest. It was a 1996 Plymouth Breeze. It was a JA-body cloud car, just an upscale Chrysler Cirrus.

Playing lookout, Uncle Dovi leaned up against the door mumbling under his breath to get a move on. Gideon knew exactly what he was looking at. He knew exactly what to cut and where. Gideon remembered the exhilaration. Fencing it at Fresno Joe's, splitting the take. All the memories were rushing back now, everything from the Saab 900 to the silver Cadillac Catera that he tried to keep, and almost got caught if he hadn't spotted the military cops trying to break the theft ring. It all got too hot.

So the letter was no surprise when the 13-year old Gideon found it on the kitchen table. All the beer and cold pizza having been taken from the refrigerator leaving him only a half loaf of Wonder white. The envelope was light. It was a short note. "See you around, kid." That's all the note said.

"Where he go?" asked Supentus. "Geelong? Lots of opportunities at the time. The post-war building boom was a lure for many. Or was it the red-head woman?"

"The red head," spoke Gideon with a slight rasp.

Supentus nodded and looked back to the screen with apparent empathy.

All of the memories came flooding into Gideon's mind all at once. The visions moved rapidly along the surface, he could taste them, the hair on his arms like a million tiny antennas, every sense stirred alive into the present, as if he was there, all over again, and he couldn't help but wonder to himself, where had these memories all gone off to in the first place?

Somehow despite the urge to move through his later teens, he kept circling back to his childhood. Before the interruption. That cataclysmic event horizon that seemed to be the only thing he could surmise that could swallow his memory whole. Had he himself hidden all this way, he wondered. The fact his parents were brutally beaten to death by a mob while shopping for Samsonites. Why hadn't he remembered this of all things? How was this not the number one thing on his mind all day and all night. No matter how much he tried to uncover the secret he was unable to explain it away other than that it was he who chose to forget. The dreaded irony seemed to sink his spirits to an even greater low. Here he was the master of memory having forgotten who he was. A Jew of all things. How could this happen, how could he let himself get so badly turned astray.

Supentus started to laugh seeing Gideon struggling to find the answer.

Gideon turned and saw sitting beside him, Supentus shape-shifting into the form of none other than Uncle Dovi himself.

"I hope this helps, Gideon," said Uncle Dovi before clicking his fingers one last time and disappearing out of sight, "See you around kid."

Gideon went down the list of countries. Bolivia. Burma. Bangladesh. Then scratched them off his list. It was going to be more difficult than he thought to find a place where The Startling Concern didn't have some tungsten mine, some rare metal processing plant, or some forbidden outpost within arms reach.

The thought of hiding in plain sight crossed his mind once or twice. But where would be a good "plain sight?"

Maybe just spin a globe and wherever your finger lands that's where he'd go. But where to find a globe?

There was the thought of fleeing to some exotic island like Celebes or Curacao and living the rest of his life shooting underwater wedding videos for unsuspecting tourists and eating the daily catch. That sounded good. But if he was stuck on an island how would he escape if he had to escape, and the odds were that there'd come a time where he'd have to escape. That would be extra difficult being trapped on an island.

Then there was Helinka to consider, she'd most likely want to go somewhere that her parents could visit if things eventually cooled down. The Congo came to mind. Her father loved hunting humans in the Congo. Or was it Cameroon? He wasn't sure which. Either way, he wondered what would that humidity do to her hair? He tried to think if humidity was good for hair or not. His first thought was that it was. So maybe Cameroon. And there was Jules to think about too. Not that he wanted to consider Jules, but he knew how much she liked him. Did

Cameroon have cliffs? He'd throw Jules off a cliff and pretend it was an accident. They'd go hiking — or better yet, they'd go foraging. Then he'd run back to the tent all panicked explaining to her how one minute Jules was there and the next minute he was gone. When he thought about it deeper, he realized if they found the body, she'd find some way to check its brain reports, and she'd find some recording of him pushing Jules over the abyss. Then their marriage would be over. That was too risky. He couldn't risk losing her. Not now. Maybe a snake bite. Like dropping some venomous mamba snake to slither through his bedroom and bite him in the neck. But what if they were all forced to share a bedroom?

Gideon threw down the atlas in disgust having seen no good options on the list of countries starting with the letter D. Did he really think that Helinka, let alone Jules, was going to run off with him to some remote location, giving up all the creature comforts for wild harvested roots and semi-poisonous berries? What a joke, he thought. How was he going to convince Helinka of all people to leave it all behind, all the money in the world just to live in a tent. Even if the tent was made from fine gold and positioned perfectly on some baby powder sand beach, how in the world was she going to "forage?" The chances were slim if not impossible. But the alternative, he thought, the alternative of staying another day with CJ Supentus as his best man was even more of a remote punchline.

Denmark. Dusseldorf. Derbyshire maybe.

When he finally burst into the apartment, he saw that Helinka and Jules were already packed. A set of crocodile suitcases sat in the foyer.

"How did you find out?!" exclaimed Gideon, pleasantly surprised upon seeing their bags packed. This would save lots of time. It was perfect in fact, no long explanations, no long drawn out debate as to what were the best options. For whatever reason they were ready and willing to go with him to the ends of the earth.

"How did I find out?" repeated Helinka, thinking that Gideon was referring to why she was breaking off their engagement and leaving him, "I think I've always had a feeling, Gideon. From the very start."

"What? Wait. No. Don't say anything. Let's just get going," he said, taking a few trash bags and tossing in his personal possessions he knew he'd need for a life on the run. Toothbrush, toothpaste. An alarm clock. Socks. Clean underwear. Pajamas.

Looking under his pillow for his pajamas, there was Helinka's mysterious list that he had always wondered about. He read the latest entries.

Y.K.O.V.V. — Kill word, Catch-pole. Acid sea cucumber man, talons.

P.K.N.K.Q. — Kill word, Thorn. Winged worm man, corrosive bile.

Helinka ripped the list from Gideon's hand, growling at him, "How dare you!"

"How dare I what?"

"Read my personal things."

Gideon resumed looking for his pajamas, "You keep it under your pillow! Every night I come across that list, what's it for? Normally people sleep with a gun under their pillow, or pajamas, but not some list. What's kill word mean anyway? No! Never mind, we gotta get out of here, you can tell me later. Have you seen my pajamas?"

"That's my research, Gideon! And no, I haven't seen your pajamas."

"I said we can talk about this later!" pleaded Gideon. "Right now, let's just get on the next train out of town. Then a hovercraft. Or some sort of boat. I have enough cash, we just need to get to the harbor. We should be able to find a boat. Something with a motor."

Helinka looked at him like he was out of his mind, "What's

wrong with you, Gideon? I'm not going anywhere with you."

"What? You want to stay? That's suicide! We have to run. I'm telling you, it's not just the dark emissaries we have to worry about, it's everyone, I mean Supentus, he's not what you think he is, let's just talk about it in the car, no, let's talk about it on the bus, I think public transportation is the safest bet."

"Have you gone mad?"

"Mad?!" Gideon pointed to their bags, "I'd think if you knew what kinda trouble we were in you'd have packed for me too, I'd call that mad!"

"Knew what?" asked Helinka unyielding.

"Jotham! He's dead! They murdered him! Supentus! He's mad! I mean madder than mad!"

Helinka sat back down beside Jules calmly, "Who is Jotham? What does any of this have to do with me?"

"What? You're my wife!" slammed Gideon.

"Your wife? All you and I have is a wedding date. And I'd actually like to talk with you about that."

"We can talk about that in the car!" yelled Gideon as he threw in a pair of sneakers into the trash bag now pulling double as his suitcase, looking around. "Have you seen my sweats? My favorite ones? You know the ones…?"

"I'm not going anywhere with you."

Gideon finally set his panic aside and stopped. Staring into both their faces, he saw flight, but a different kind of flight. This sort had courage and calm. Nothing like his kinda flight which just meant grab what you could and take a car, a bus, a train, a palankeen, a rickshaw, or anything out of town before they knew you were gone.

"What do you mean you're not going with me? Jules can come. I'm okay with that, if that's what's worrying you. Right Jules?"

Jules looked down at his shoes.

"I don't think this is a good idea, Gideon," said Helinka

approached him with enough compassion to give the impression of no hard feelings. But not much more.

"You mean? Us?" It had finally dawned on Gideon who she was talking about.

"Yes, Gideon. Us."

Gideon shook his head, "No, no way, this is, look, if things were, I don't know how if you fully understand things, if things have been a little strange lately I can explain why, but I think we need to just get going."

He took her bag in his hand and opened the front door.

Jules stepped forward, "You're not listening, Gideon."

"I'm not talking to you! You robot! I'm talking to my fiancée! Get out of my way!" shouted Gideon pushing his way aside and setting her bag in the hallway.

"I don't want to get married, Gideon. Not with you," said Helinka a bit more forceful.

Gideon shook his head, "No, no, you're making a mistake. It's okay. I'll explain everything."

Helinka took Gideon in her arms, "No, Gideon. I was making a mistake, but not anymore."

Gideon pulled back, hoping to reason, beg, anything, "But, but our Match Meter…"

"I'm overriding the Match Meter," Helinka informed him.

"Overriding the Match Meter? You can't do that? Can you?" he stammered, seeing he was left with no other options but to beg, Gideon got down on one knee, "Please Helinka, don't do this to me, please. I need you. I need you otherwise, it's all over, please not now, let's just talk about this, please."

The muzzle of an elephant gun pressed up against the back of Gideon's head.

It was Vintner Vowell.

Standing behind him were so many NAMP Agents they virtually clogged the apartment hallway.

Vintner pulled back the hammers and in his low resonating

voice bellowed, "I'd put a hole through you, you beast."

Helinka seeing her dad and having no idea why he was there, pushed the barrel aside and stepped in between him and Gideon.

"Daddy! What do you think you're doing? I can handle this!" Helinka exclaimed, bewildered as to how her father knew she was leaving Gideon.

Vintner lowered his gun then motioned for two NAMP Agents, "Block the windows. That's its egress."

The NAMP Agents fully armed with automatic weapons entered the apartment and proceeded to guard any escape by way of the windows.

Gideon slowly got to his feet, absolutely dumbstruck as to why The Startling Concern, or General Worship for that matter, would have thought to send Vintner Vowell, his future father-in-law (no matter how up in the air that was at that moment) to keep him from escaping.

"You Sir!" rumbled Vintner, "Are under arrest!"

Gideon seeing no other alternative put his hands in the air.

Helinka took hold of her father, "Daddy, I don't want Gideon arrested, stop being so, so silly. How in the world did you find out I was leaving him?"

Vintner's eyes narrowed, "I should say you are leaving him! He will be arrested, sent to jail, plead guilty in a court of law, then I will have his head, stuffed and mounted on my wall."

"Nobody is stuffing anybody!" insisted Helinka, still clueless as to her father's true intentions.

Vintner emitted a deep roar that practically shook the room. "I have tracked down my prey to your apartment, I know for a fact it is him, and I will have my trophy!"

Gideon started to realize that this had nothing to do with The Startling Concern or General Worship, and looked to Helinka in outrage, accusing, "You told your parents you were leaving me?! Your psycho father! You told him before you had the decency to tell me? You want to leave me and you want me dead too?!"

Helinka turned and faced Gideon, "I did no such thing! Just because I don't want to marry you doesn't mean I want to see you shot!" Helinka turned to her father, "Daddy, I want you to get those men out of here and leave at once."

"Darling, you fail to see what is happening here. This man!" Vintner pointed his boney finger just inches from Gideon's face, continuing with dramatic flare, "This man is a decapitator! A night fiend! Prowling through the city and ripping off heads!"

As Helinka was hearing this, she couldn't help but put two and two together, the news that her father had tracked what he called a decapitator to her front door, and hearing the accusation that someone had been prowling the city at night ripping off heads, she instantly turned to Jules.

Jules looked down at his shoes.

Vintner continued in full husky obbligato, "Your fiancé is a mad man!"

Gideon burst out laughing. There wasn't much else he could do, between his perilous situation, his fiancée leaving him, and now being accused of being a "decapitator." He had had enough. He needed to go. And as far away from there as possible.

"You guys are all mad! Everyone. I am thinking I'm the only one sane around here. Gimme that!" yelled Gideon taking his trash bag from out of the hands of one of the NAMP Agents, adding, "I'm packing my things and walking out that door!"

"Only place you are going is with us!" barked Vintner.

But Gideon wasn't having a word of it, he moved to the bedroom closet to pack the rest of his stuff and hit the road. "You Helinka, hopefully when cooler heads prevail, we can talk, but between you and your father, I think you're right, maybe it's best we call it a day. As for you, Vintner, you have zero proof of anything! None! Zero! Nada! I'm no more a 'decapitator' than I am some kind of god! Now out of my way. I'm getting my stuff and going. I don't know where, Luxembourg, Yemen, Zimbabwe, who knows, but anywhere but here."

A feather floated down on Gideon's nose, he tried blowing it away, but it seemed to just hang in the air in front of his face. He swatted the feather away with his hand.

With one last parting shot, Gideon decided to finally let loose, "And one last thing! Those Match Meter results! They were fake!"

Gideon yanked open the closet door to get his stuff, and the moment he did, he was buried in an avalanche of severed human heads. Over 30 grotesque, unattached heads, all with decaying mourning faces. Most were covered in dirt as if they had been buried for weeks, a few random ones were stuffed into plastic zip lock bags, and the remainder just days from mummification. Not knowing what hit him, Gideon sat up and looked around him at the pile of decapitated heads and started screaming; trying to get them off as he kicked and shoved them in all directions. The more he tried the more they seemed to roll back into his lap, and seeing the blood all over his hands he panicked.

"We got him red handed, men!" shouted Vintner to his military escorts.

Helinka shrieked then immediately turned to Jules who, anticipating all this, looked back at her with resolute and defiant eyes, and took hold of her hand.

She had been wondering to herself all along what he was up to, but now finally knew the full extent of his plans. Those plans consisted of getting rid of Gideon. So she turned to see Gideon freaking out, slipping in the gory mess, and the NAMP Agents yanking him up violently by the arms and slapping on the handcuffs; then her father Vintner vindicating himself and proclaiming his manhunting savvy, and she knew all she needed to do was open her mouth to tell everyone in the room that it wasn't Gideon who was reeking havoc across the city, decapitating innocents just wanting a neck massage, but that it was her Synoid all along, Jules. And that it was him who had stashed those heads inside his closet in an elaborate rouse to frame Gideon for a crime he didn't commit, just so Jules could have her all to himself, as husband and wife. But she hesitated. Giving up Jules would be the same as condemning herself.

She had a choice to make. There wasn't a second to lose. So she watched silently as they dragged Gideon down the hallway, kicking and screaming.

GLADIATOR ARENA

Her badge said "All Access." The security guard checked her credentials and thanked her for her patience. The disclaimer was brief and to the point, along the lines of: *the area you are about to enter may expose you to things normally kept hidden away and out of sight and that you acknowledge by entering in that you forgo the illusion of happiness that is presented for that singular purpose in the gladiator arena above.*

Helinka told the Security Guard that she understood and was thusly allowed to pass through the huge double doors shaped like a monster's mouth. The jagged-edged teeth that hissed open gave Helinka the sense that she was being swallowed alive. The stairs leading to the catacombs were designed to look like a blistering esophagus. The deeper she went, the more she felt as though she had stepped into an anatomy class with green pulses of light coming from a strange thyroid structure and the spinning spectral tunnel of the vena cava.

She had come to make a confession.

It wasn't the way she had hoped things would go down. Seeing Gideon fighting for his life on account of both her creations, Jules and now her menagerie of Synoid mutants. It wasn't her conscious design. These creations, these extensions of her hands, heart, and mind, now aligned themselves to grab hold of Gideon, rip out his aorta, and put an end to any ideas of salvation. But before she could make this admission, she had to perform the perfunctory duties as Chief Gladiator Monster Maker and make the rounds so that her time with Gideon wouldn't appear to be the primary motivating factor for descending into the pits.

Inspecting her "Monster Mutants," as they were being billed to the world audience, she couldn't help but be overwhelmed by their vast array of shapes, sizes, and slaying symptoms. How it all came from that single sample. Joey, she thought. It had all been because of Joey, a half human, half Cauzzie kangaroo abomination. How else could things turn out?

She laughed as B.L.E.K.S smashed his gaping toothless gums into the glass wall separating her from her creations. She wasn't so much amused by B.L.E.K.S's attempts to gum her to pieces as she was the realization that she had been so single-minded in her attempts to create the perfect alternative to the Cauzzie, that she hadn't ever reflected on where it all began. She recalled the first day on the project, going over the tissue sample and all the feelings that went with it, excitement and trepidation. And as she moved on to another example of her Monster Mutants as it disappeared and reappeared within the confines of its cage, at times even appearing as a burst into a blue fireball before reappearing back into its humanoid form, her thoughts teleported back to when it all "all" began.

She thought back to the day the obscure Australian biological firm decided to create the global warming solution and save all mankind from destruction. First patented as "Autonomous Florae Carbon Conversion System" and later labelled as the Invasive, which then became known as the infamous Cannibal Aussie. The holotype, she amused herself, that organism's single specimen designation that established what would be known forever after as the "Cauzzie," had finally evolved into this. The ultimate entertainment spectacle for the masses.

The tour of the contestants was an alphabet of the damned. With each soon-to-be victim spelling out a litany of transgressions from accounting fraud to zoning crimes. Unlike her Monster Mutant creations, she noticed, who seemed so dead-set on their singular service, the contestants consistently looked for any alternative that would allow them the chance to be anywhere but where they were. A perfect example of this was the stammering middle-aged blonde woman who had scratched so long at the walls for a way out that her fingernails left blood streaks all along the length of her cell. This repeated itself over and over again.

There were a few exceptions. Father Dan was confidently praying. Cloreen was sitting down sharpening a small diamond shaped-blade that she kept hidden in the palm of her hand. When their eyes met, Cloreen smiled as if they had bumped into each other at some high-end fashion boutique. She seemed without a care in the world. They made small talk. Cloreen loved Helinka's cute sandals that she said were perfect for the occasion. And Helinka loved how Cloreen had done her hair in an upbraided twist. Helinka complimented how tone her arms had become wielding a sword. Cloreen complimented how much more happier she looked than the last time they met. There was some giggling, a splash of gossip, and the greeting ended with Helinka wishing Cloreen the best of luck and that they should do lunch when their schedules permitted.

Then there was Gideon. Pacing the length of his cell. Dressed in a sparkling silver jumpsuit with fancy letters on it proclaiming him the "Decapitator." If there was a can he would have been kicking it. As he reached one end of the wall and turned, he caught sight of Helinka standing there with her green tunic and designer genie-inspired pants. Gideon smiled, then catching himself he let the smile fade into a veiled absence of expression.

"Hello, Helinka," said Gideon.

Helinka pressed her forehead onto the glass and waved hello. Gideon took a few steps closer. His appetite for yelling had long been satiated by the possibilities of what to do with those final remaining hours. The straight face was for her behalf, otherwise he'd still be smiling. That last thing he wanted to do was make her feel guilty for not saying anything to the NAMP when she had the chance. Sure, if there was a lifetime ahead of them he'd have let her have it. But he had hoped to see her again. And seeing her standing there was at least something he had wished for mercifully granted. At the perfect time too, as the drum beats from above began to thunder down to below.

Helinka was the first to say anything, "I have a confession to make."

"Yeah. So do I," replied Gideon.

Helinka spoke after their long pause, "Who wants to go first?"

"I'll tell you what," Gideon smiled, "I'll tell you this since I'm about to get turned into cat food. Or pâté. Anyway, the point is I've always loved you, from the first moment I laid eyes on you. And just cause I only figured this out twenty minutes ago doesn't mean I'm no less in love with you now. Sure, I'm incapable of being true, and for that I deserve to die. I've made mistakes, and although you're out there and I'm in here, I know for certain that this is where I belong. At least I'll get a shot at going out in style. What kinda style that is, only God knows. What I'm trying to say is that although we weren't meant to be husband and wife, I have always loved you. As a friend. As a person bound in this struggle the same as everybody else. And I'm sorta happy to be here condemned to die. At least I have a few moments just to be the person I've always wanted to be. No matter how horrible that is. So…uh…that's about it."

"You're surprisingly calm about all this," she said.

"Yeah well, I have something now, that's how do you say, better than all those calculations and figures you are so good with. I have someone to emulate. My friend Jotham. He showed me how to do what I need to do. It's about dedication really…

Anyway, to explain would be a long story that I can't get into now that I'm on schedule for the chomping block, but it has to do with role models, Abraham and Jacob, but, what have you got to say, I can't wait, what's your confession?"

Helinka took a deep breath and said, "I was the one who stole your sweats. And put three holes in them."

Suddenly Gideon abandoned his composure, "You! Do you see what I've been wearing ever since! Look at me! Sequins. They have me going to my death in sequins!"

"I can explain!"

"Please do! I'm waiting."

"I had hoped to make a Synoid version of you. My plan was to take everything I loved about Jules and just throw in that part of you that I loved, and if I was able to do that, then I'd have everything I ever wanted. So I had to take your sweat pants. It was the only way I could get all the samples I needed at once without asking you. But it all went so terribly wrong. Instead of being the perfect creation, it was a strange eye-thing that spits out bolts of electricity, it didn't really have any form, it was monstrous."

Gideon recoiled at hearing that his sweat pants did that.

Helinka continued, "I wanted a part of you in that perfect life-form. But with that tiny bit of you in it, everything just fell apart. I just want you to know that I did honestly want you to be in it. It's just that the only perfect life form I was able to create was all me. So I couldn't let them take Jules. Them taking Jules would be a death sentence for two of us, not just one. But here is the good news, and why everything is going to work out for all of us. You know my list?"

"The one you keep under your bed?"

"Yes!" Helinka calmed down realizing she was a bit too enthusiastic; in a softer voice she continued, "I know a way to save you. Your memory, Gideon. Your memory."

"My memory? What about it?"

Helinka explained how the kill words worked, how they were

the failsafe for all her failed prototypes, and by simply shouting the word out loud, any opponent he would have to face in the gladiator arena would be instantly rendered incapacitated, thus allowing him to slay his adversary in total safety. Matching the opponent's description with the corresponding kill word would allow him to win every battle and go undefeated, and thus escape the curse.

And here was the best news of all, she said, "If you go undefeated, you'll win the billion dollar prize money and get to leave a free man!"

Gideon recalled the list in his mind, "So you're saying if I see an 'Acid Sea Cucumber Man' with talons I yell 'Thorn?'"

"Exactly! This is the only way I could think of where we'd all come out as winners."

Gideon saw the entire list perfectly clear in his memory, as if he was holding the list in his hand.

"Just, whatever you do," she added, "Don't say the kill word twice, that brings them back to life. I won't be around to reprogram them."

He smiled again, "Why are you doing this for me?"

"Like I said, I don't want to marry you, but I don't want you to die," said Helinka, adding, "Plus who knows? Your perfect match might be in this building right now. Or at home watching on the television. You never know."

"My perfect match," agreed Gideon. Mulling it over, he smiled, "Yes. My perfect match."

Things got off to just the kind of start you'd want if you were the Enkeling Futures and Prosperities executives. The ratings were astronomical. According to their initial numbers, which were on the conservative side, the entire civilized world had tuned-in to see the blood letting. And nobody, executives and sponsors alike, was disappointed with the initial battles as the

Monster Mutants lived up to their billing and wreaked havoc on the contestants leaving behind a cocktail of mashed organs, bile, and blood in the soaked sand.

A driver of a modified Zamboni with street-cleaner parts attached tried his best to purify the arena's sand between each adversarial encounter between human and defective Synoid, but the ancient machine could only manage to turn the arena into a muddy pit of despair. That along with the stench of blood did nothing to tamper the rabid enthusiasm of the spectators who filled the arena to the rafters. The drums continued their incessant percussive barrage making the assault on the senses so comprehensive the audience was almost liable for blood guilt.

By calling any of these displays a "battle" you were essentially using a euphemism for all-out-slaughter. A fan favorite was the timely demise of Father Dan who refused to fire his crossbow and began to scream at the top of his lungs to "Stop in the name of Christ." This however turned out to be barely audible over the cacophony of drums, chanting, and cheers, and was being reported by the announcers as him asking "Stop I want some fries," which was then quickly followed by Father Dan being roasted alive by flame-thrower carrying R.G.F.X. What ensued after the battle was a rush to the concession stands for French fried potatoes with a side of ranch.

The librarian put on a good show with a lucky swing of her battle ax that chopped off one of the four Siamese quadruplets belonging to S.M.L.E.'s squirming body, only to be violently halted by a squirt of bloody from one of its ventricle that landed directly on her face, leaving her stunned just long enough for the Monster Mutant to return the favor by chopping her in half with a swing of its Samurai blade.

A shadowy human figure standing over ten-feet-tall stepped into the arena. It was M.D.U.L.A.. And as the spotlight hit the Monster Mutant everyone let out a collective gasp as they beheld a human brain, but not in its normal ball-like form, but in the shape of a man with the grayish-pink jellylike grooves and folds covering the entire surface of its body: its head, its torso, arms, fingers, legs, and toes, with a fissure down the middle and a snapping spinal chord for a tail. It looked as though a giant had climbed into a rubber suit made up entirely of gray matter.

The crowd held its breath in stunned silence.

Cloreen wasn't expecting anything like the thing she saw squishing its way to the center of the arena, sizing her up with its opaque bubbly eyes. She had taken on thousands of Barbarians, countless dissidents, criminals, and even rabid wolves, but she had never before seen the likes of a human brain man. It struck her as odd, though, that it had come to a sword fight empty handed.

"Not too smart of you to walk in here without a weapon," she let it know.

M.D.U.L.A.'s voice transmitted throughout the arena as if through a set of reverberating loud speakers, communicating by its telepathic mental powers.

"My weapon is my intellect!"

Cloreen thought this was hilarious, "So you think you're going to kill me with your mind?"

"I don't think. I know," said M.D.U.L.A. as it began to emit intermittent frequencies almost like a radio scanning for a station. When he found the wavelength he was looking for, M.D.U.L.A began his mental assault, "I know how you are going to die."

"Oh really, do tell."

"First, you will plunge your hands into your face and scratch out your eyeballs; you will tear your tongue out and begin to peel off your skin, then you will feel an itch within your internal organs and you will search for it and by the time you have found it, your intestines will lay in a pile upon the sands. Then you will look up to me and beg for mercy. And there shall be no mercy. For I will consume your intellect with this!

M.D.U.L.A. pulled out a bendy straw.

"You're going to suck my intellect out with a straw?"

"Not before I expose you for what you really are!" Another of his brain frequencies scanned Cloreen, "I know all about your life. The one you have so desperately tried to hide. Yes. It is true. I know all about you."

Cloreen raised her sword and moved in preparing to strike, "All I know is I have a sword and you have nothing."

Challengingly, M.D.U.L.A. stepped closer, "Are you sure about that?....Laura."

Laura. Hearing that name froze Cloreen cold where she stood. Her expression was a whirlwind of disbelief, shame, and horror. She threw her sword into the sand and grabbed her head, covering her ears as if hoping that would make the memory all go away.

"No, don't say that name!" screamed Cloreen.

M.D.U.L.A. reveled in his superior intellect that was now on display for all to see. With his simple reveal of this name Laura that he had exhumed from the underground cemetery of her mind, he had so instantly defeated her. And he began laughing to himself as he kicked aside the sword and drew near to her. The confidence in his overwhelming mental powers growing along with the crowd's total and utter disbelief that their once so formidable matron of doom had fallen to her knees by the mere mention of a name, Laura.

"Please! Kill me now, just, just don't repeat that name!" she begged.

"Why so soon, Laura?" said M.D.U.L.A., now savoring every minute. "We haven't given this fine audience what they came for. I want to inflict maximum damage. I want to humiliate you and expose the truth about what you truly are."

Cloreen shook her head as tears ran down her face, "No... please...kill me now."

"You have lived your whole life trying to sterilize your existence, Laura, trying to scrub yourself clean from your past, to leave that life far behind. Like your husband!"

"Noooooo!"

"YES!"

Cloreen began to roll around in the sand in agony as M.D.U.L.A. stalked around her ready to inflict more wounds with his walk down memory lane.

"You were never like the others! So unladylike, so much a tomboy. You could never fit in. Remember the country fair? How you left little Cassie in the balloon?"

Her cries to stop had turned into guttural moans.

M.D.U.L.A. raised his victorious hands to the crowd as if to have them confirm his omniscient mental prowess.

"Shall I continue?" it belched.

The crowd remained silent.

M.D.U.L.A. turned back to Cloreen, "Such a heartwarming, wholesome, pleasant life you lived on the farm. Far far away from the glitz and glamor of Merletown. In fact, you can't get farther away from the Downtown Social District than…Minnesota! Yes! You were just a little girl in pigtails, with a furry dog. Jack! How Jack died in your arms. Your first and only friend. Then there was Bandit. Your father, remember him? What about your parents you left behind for your husband who you abandoned at the school for the blind? Everyone loved him, Charles was his name? Remember?! And your sweet mother Caroline and your sister Mary? You never compared to Mary! And that's why you wanted to escape, so you left for the Dakota Territory, to teach at the school of the blind, and you met Almonzo!"

Cloreen looked up at M.D.U.L.A., but gone was her strained expression begging for kindly forbearance. Her tears were now that of laughter.

M.D.U.L.A. wasn't expecting this, continuing after a stutter, "And you lived in a little…"

Through the derisive laughter, Cloreen was more than happy to finish M.D.U.L.A.'s sentence, "A little on house on the prairie?"

M.D.U.L.A. watched in confusion as Cloreen rose to her feet and dusted herself off.

"I can't do this anymore..." she said, "It's too much, I can't keep a straight face."

"What? What are you laughing at?!"

"Look, I got you good. You're talking about Laura Ingles Wilder from that TV show they are playing on Channel 5. Haven't you seen the reruns?"

"No...no...I, I don't watch TV. TV is for the feeble of mind. For the low intellectual capacity..."

The crowd erupted with cheers and roars of laughter seeing that Cloreen had turned the tables on the intellectually superior brain man.

Cloreen by then had stopped laughing long enough to get down to the business at hand, "Who is humiliated now, you big pompous brain? Everyone has seen how stupid you really are, getting fooled in public by fake characters from a syndicated TV show!"

"I'm not stupid! I'm smart!" shouted M.D.U.L.A. growing desperate.

"Okay, then if you are so smart you know what to do next, don't you?" asked Cloreen.

M.D.U.L.A. nodded yes.

"Then get to it, brain."

M.D.U.L.A. sank his hands into his head, and began tearing himself apart piece by piece until there was nothing left but a steaming pile of pink goo.

Cloreen walked up, took the bendy straw in her hand and took a sip of the gelatinous pile of remains that was once M.D.U.L.A.. After giving the flavor a second or two to register with her taste buds, she turned to the massive crowd.

"Way too salty."

The crowd began to chant her name, "CLOREEEEEN, CLOREEEEEN, CLOREEEEN!"

She walked off the arena floor, brushing aside the swarm of reporters, her arms in the air all the while thinking of Laura.

Now a word from our sponsor, Godgod.

The Startling Concern's new Godgod, the invisible all-powerful super god was finally unveiled to the capacity crowd on the jumbo monitors. The commercial was quite impressive, and for a moment there the mesmerized audience had totally forgotten they were at the gladiator arena waiting for the finale (who was none other than Gideon himself). They sat in amazement as they beheld the new Godgod tower reaching up to space to transmit their personal prayers directly into the appropriate constellations, where the all powerful and invisible god would personally answer every single request, assigning you a divine purpose, raining down dignity, financial freedom, creature comforts, coupons, happiness, and vacation perks, all for zero down. The offer of instant returns and 50% cash back on all acts of devotion really got the crowd in a lather. The repentance package was a mind-blowing prospect, that of course being Gideon's hidden contribution. Not to have to go through audits, confessionals, and penance, but getting to walk away from all morality violations by merely saying you were sorry was a huge hit. But what really brought them to their feet was the skybridge and the sacrificial upgrades for infant newborns thrown into the lava river. The special effects were even more graphic, gory, and spectacular than anything they were watching live that glorious day, and everyone was on their feet wanting more. Godgod was a hit, and everyone would have dashed to the gates looking to sign up if it were not for the need for inaugural blood.

Gideon was all that stood in the way of everyone's dreams coming true. It was his sacrificial inaugural blood, the advertisement made so sure to stress over and over, that would kick off Godgod and a life of serenity and grace for all mankind.

Again with zero down, free gifts, and instant cash returns. And coupons, we can't forget the coupons. Gideon's dead body would be harvested for every drop of blood to splash on the base of the Godgod Tower, the one right out side the Holey Land, in order to inaugurate the god of all gods. Godgod.

The ovation for Godgod almost rivaled the one Cloreen received after killing the human brain, and when the lights went out in the arena, everyone went completely off the rails in anticipation of what was about to come next, which of course was the big finale.

The announcer made sure to emphasize this point through the PA system, which was now cranked to maximum distortion, *"Say goodbye to your old deities and say hello to Godgod, now all we need to get this party started is some bloooooooooood!"*

The audience was binge eating this all up to the point where their vomitus screaming and whistling no longer sufficed, therefore leaving only one avenue for the rabid horde to adequately express its ravenous unity. And that was by stomping their feet in a grim rhythmic cadence so that it sounded as if a billion drums were announcing the arrival of an unseen Viking onslaught, which was to come in the form of the crowd itself. They had come to see Gideon die, and for the first time this truth penetrated the primal thoughts of the sacrificial victim himself. It was one thing to pace back and forth in your cell in fatalistic anticipation, and something totally different to be thrown into the middle of the arena with the lights off and the black heartbeat of doom raining down from the rafters.

This would have been a good time for Gideon to reflect on his life and the fact that every single action he had ever taken had led him where he was, in the middle of a gladiator arena with the top billing over his former boss Cloreen. This would have been something to ponder as to whether or not it was finally the promotion that he had always sought, and it would have been a good time to ponder the ironic nature that the Godgod he had helped bring to life, would only come to life after his bloody death. But it wasn't a good time for Gideon to do anything but actually reflect. Literally. We're talking about his sequin jumpsuit.

A single spotlight pierced through the darkness like a shooting star descending from the rafters, sending a spectrum of light bouncing off Gideon's reflective battle costume. It was as if the gods of gladiators had exclaimed "Let there be light." The dizzying kaleidoscope of colors shown fifty rows deep in all directions. This just invited an unrestrained trifecta of pandemonium that included stomping, cheering, and screaming, from the already maniacal multitude.

Gideon tried to pick up his sword and prepare for whatever one of Helinka's failed creations would come bursting through the gates, but found he was unable to lift it. Maybe it was his trembling hands that he hadn't noticed until then, or the sheer weight of the weapon. At that moment he sort of wished he had taken up the palankeen bearers on their offer to pump up his weak and soft biceps. But there was no time to think thanks to the announcer who decided it was time to not only throw huge amounts of gas on an already blazing inferno, but to fill in the blanks when it came to Gideon and his blood being the key to all mankind's spiritual liberation at the hands of Godgod.

"All gods and goddess bow to the one true invisible Godgod, and you will too the minute Gideon's sacrifice is complete! So give a big Merletown welcome for COOOOOORRRRRYYYY!"

As if in honor of his sweatpants and their genetic contribution to Helinka's Monster Mutants, it was none other than C.C.O.R.Y. who appeared from out of the tunnel. Its crystalline reptile yoke hovering menacingly above the ground, and seemed to suck all the air out of the arena as it slowly made its way towards Gideon.

The lack of human form immediately put an end to the trifecta of pandemonium, downshifting into random, disembodied gasps as they all beheld the strangest sight they had ever seen. Silvery-white radioactive bolts shot out from its semi-transparent membrane. Some would later go on to say it was a jellyfish with plasma scales, others thought it was living breathing eggs-over-easy blue plate special, others thought it appeared to be a deflated weather balloon being constantly struck by silver strands of lightning.

If the arena had lost their singular ability to think straight thanks to the vision of C.C.O.R.Y., it was a thousand times worse for Gideon. He let go of the sword as he tried his best to keep from losing his lunch; a ham sandwich on two slices of Wonder bread.

Gideon didn't need to look around to understand that escape was hopeless. Neither did C.C.O.R.Y. for that matter, who didn't seem to be in a big hurry, the creature simply inched closer and closer taking its sweet time, happy to emit streams of radioactive energy and melt sand into globs of glass as it went.

The Enkeling Futures and Prosperities promotional team was well aware of C.C.O.R.Y.'s ability to melt sand into glass and were looking to capitalize on it by selling the globulars as souvenirs of the day Gideon died in the arena, and his sacrifice being the start to Godgod's omnipotent reign over creation as the one true and invisible god.

Just when Gideon recovered enough of his senses to reach down for the sword, C.C.O.R.Y. sprayed the arena with a pulse of radioactive fire. One of these pulses caught Gideon's sword, causing it to start glowing a vibrant green. It fell from Gideon's hand on impact. Just like the mysterious Match Meter reading that pulled up "perfect match" with the likes of Thurp, Gideon wondered what in the world was in his sweatpants DNA that could turn something so physically perfect as Jules into something so abominable as C.C.O.R.Y. What part of its lizard yoke and crystal structure, which couldn't stop spitting out gamma particles at Gideon's feet, have to do with his own genetic makeup? And at that brief moment, Gideon thought the world might just be better off with him dead than alive. He was clearly incompatible with everything by the looks of the approaching abomination. Might as well die while he was on top, and not just the fact he had top billing. It's all he could think of as he watched C.C.O.R.Y. move in for the kill. Thankfully at that moment he was finally who he was — a Jewish man in the midst of sacrificial service to the one true God. Not some Godgod lie, but the one true God. To him that was tops. So why not go out on top? This notion only lasted for a brief moment, because suddenly Gideon remembered he was a thief. The last one left alive (for the time being.) As a thief, maybe it was possible that with the top secret corporate information he had stolen stored up in his brain, that list of kill words specifically, maybe it was possible for Gideon to steal a few more minutes of life. So he scanned the list as the giant yoke reached out with its radioactive tentacles to strangle the life out of him.

"FLINTLOCK!" shouted Gideon.

C.C.O.R.Y. suddenly transformed into scrambled eggs, splattering onto the arena sand as if smashed with a frying pan.

"Whooo hoo!" hollered Gideon through the stunned and silent arena. He was jumping up and down and pumping his fist, completely beside himself that the kill words worked so well. He was able to incapacitate C.C.O.R.Y. with just a single word. Gideon moved his arms and legs so spasmodically in celebration that some fans in the audience thought he was suffering from the aftereffects of electrical shock.

"Ah..........ugh," the announcer sputtered in the microphone, summing up the entire arena's unified frame of mind, having seen Gideon defeat the scariest Mutant Monster as of yet with a single word.

The Enkeling Futures and Prosperities executives looked at each other thinking there must be some kind of glitch. The executives from Ghana Princely Projects winced wondering what kind of voodoo spell had saved Gideon from what was supposed to be a moment of celebration. Whatever they were wondering throughout the entire arena, it had left them all speechless.

Gideon hearing his whoops echo back at him, and with a renewed sense of confidence that it was possible to take down the entire Mutant Monster arsenal with the kill list filed away in his mental vault, took full advantage of being center stage and decided to make a speech.

"I propose a challenge!" shouted Gideon. "If they can't kill me, and my blood doesn't splatter on their god god idol, that means it's all a lie, right?!

The crowd looked at each other completely unsure of what kind of challenge Gideon was proposing. Sure they had heard him right, but they hadn't exactly fully comprehended the full scope of his intention. So someone in Row 3400 Aisle 1012, Seat 55Y had enough sense to shout out, "What exactly are you talking about?"

It was a challenge. Gideon's one true God versus all the gods and goddesses of the world's social and financial institutions combined.

"Including this new Godgod," replied Gideon. "It's just one big lie! I should know! I'm just a thief and my whole life has been one big lie!

Finally Gideon was able to spill his guts. But not just to Helinka or the likes of Thurps, but to the entire world. He explained everything from his parents murder, Uncle Dovie, to his life as a thief, his ability to memorize vast volumes of secret corporate information, and his deceptive life within The Startling Concern. In effective soap opera cliffhanger fashion, Gideon had them all on the edge of their seat as he explained the failed Smith Smith robbery, how the Cauzzies blackmailed him, the efforts of a true hero, Jotham, and his hidden mission to take down the entire idolatrous world. Gideon explained his role with the creation of Godgod that had everyone's ear. Even the Enkling Futures and Prosperities executives were hearing the ringing of the telephone as The Startling Concern itself was putting in call after call to do all they could to stop the bleeding, or should we say start the bleeding — Gideon's bleeding.

"If I'm the sacrificial blood that this new and invisible Godgod needs, a god who is supposedly more powerful than all the gods in existence, that means if they're unable to kill me and splash my blood on their ceremonial altar that will prove it's all a lie!"

The crowd murmured amongst itself; what Gideon was proposing sounded reasonable enough. If the the Godgod required Gideon's blood, and if they couldn't kill Gideon, that obviously meant it had no power.

"Okay! We follow...so what's the bet?" shouted the lady in Row 9088, Aisle XB134443, Seat 2.

"I stand for the one true God," shouted Gideon. "The God of Abraham, the God of Isaac, the God of Jacob, and the remnant that's keeping this world going. And I am here to work a hidden miracle in this arena today! So if I can kill all these Mutant Monsters with just a single word, that means there is only one word and there's only one word that counts. And that's the word of the one true God. So if I remain standing, that means all your idols are just one huge lie and we have to tear it all down to the ground. So are you up for the challenge? My God versus all their gods. Winner take all?"

The approving applause started with just a few smattering claps and then began to build into thunderous wave of unanimous agreement amongst all those present to hear Gideon's challenge. So it was on, officially yet unofficially.

The gladiator arena had taken on a whole new dimension when it came to "winner take all," not only was it a billion dollars cash prize, plus your freedom if you managed to conquer all, but now there was an additional "winner take all" battle, one between spiritual truths and corporate lies. It gave an entirely new dimension to the gladiator arena that the bloodthirsty crowd hadn't quite expected when they paid astronomical prices for their tickets. But suddenly everyone felt as though they had gotten the bargain of a lifetime, a two for one deal. Nobody was able to remember a more exciting showdown than the one that was about to transpire in front of their collective noses, but that was primarily because nobody had any memory anymore. But if they did, they agreed, it would rank right up there at the top. So the crowd settled in and thus began the renewal of their thunderous chants, ear-piercing whistles, and virulent noise making, all for the sake of a good show.

"Bring it on!" shouted Gideon, with all due zealousness.

Although he may have spoken too soon.

The Enkling Futures and Prosperities executives were eager to have their last say. They weren't impressed with the speech or the wager, and even more horrified that they'd be losing out on a major sponsor in The Startling Concern if they didn't do something and do something fast in order to ensure Gideon's blood in a basin by midnight.

K.K.L.R.'s chameleon tongue shot out of its mouth the moment it emerged from the tunnel. The lizard tongue instantly wrapped around Gideon's neck, strangling him before he could even utter a word, which brought the Enkling Futures and Prosperities executives to their feet with their own special celebration, which also included strange arm and leg movements along with a thousand exploding fist bumps.

Having one's larynx crushed wasn't exactly in the cards for Gideon.

He had expected gamma rays, of course; arrows and spears and swords, sure. And any of those preconceived scenarios which would allow for him to search his massive memory and bring to mind the kill word, thus incapacitating his opponent. But he had never taken into account a lizard tongue choking him and making it impossible to speak. But there was Gideon, slowly being reeled into the gapping mouth of K.K.L.R. like a guppy caught in a trawling net. Making matters even more deplorable was the fact

Gideon recognized the tongue and flashing double-row of fangs were that of K.K.L.R. He knew this almost immediately. And his vocal cords wanted to scream "Brazil," his foggy brain wanted to yell "Brazil," but all could muster was a faint wheeze. Dragged ever closer, Gideon struggled to break free, taking hold of a fist full of sand that just spilled out between his fingers. Forget the suffocation, K.K.L.R.'s breath practically put an end to Gideon. Now just feet from being swallowed whole, thus ending the challenge before it had really gotten started, Gideon felt the handle of his green glowing sword graze his hand as he slid across the sand. Grabbing hold, he thrust the sword out ahead of him, allowing for his momentum to bring the sword straight into K.K.L.R.'s soft underbelly. The split second the chameleon tongue loosened its grip on Gideon's throat, dropping him to the sand, he shouted, "Brazil!"

Gideon was now 2 for 2 as the chameleon beast keeled over into the sand. He felt as though he had just been slathered with gravel and microwaved on high when M.A.A.R., the part human-looking red demoniac creature, who literally spoke backwards, leaped into the arena shouting, "I know you Gideon, you're nothing more than cat meat as far as I'm concerned," but it sounded more like, "Denrecnoc ma I sa raf sa taem tac naht erom gnihton er'ouy, Noedig uoy wonk I!"

"Kamikaze!"

It was all Gideon needed to say in order to down the red menace, putting him at 3 out of 3 for the day.

B.L.E.K.S. shot his crossbow from out of the shadows, cutting a groove in Gideon's shoulder. It was a near miss and not so honorable. But that didn't keep B.L.E.K.S. from continuing to take pot shots from the shadows. "I'm going to skin you alive and use you for upholstery. I have a settee in mind that I think would be perfect!" gummed B.L.E.K.S. from the safety of the tunnel, continuing to conceal himself long enough to get off a second deadly shot.

But Gideon recalled Helinka's extensive notes on B.L.E.K.S., specifically its desire to skin her alive and turn her into a lampshade. So he shouted, "Parable!"

B.L.E.K.S.'s body fell from the shadows into the light of the arena sand.

Gideon was now 4 for 4 and gaining momentum. The crowd was starting to rally behind him thinking that it might just be possible for this meek looking man to carry the day.

When A.L.K.K. appeared spewing cadaver worms from its organs while swinging a battle ax, the sight was so hideously disgusting that Gideon vomited in his mouth, it was the pickle that went with the ham sandwich. It almost kept him from uttering the kill word, "Flypaper!" Despite it sounding more like "Fwypoopah," A.L.K.K. completely shut down until all that was left was a sleeping, squirming mess.

He was now 5 for 5.

Gideon had so captivated the audience they began thinking he might just be a god himself; or a man god, either one. It wasn't hard for them to believe that he was some sort of savior come to free them from the yoke of bondage and liberate them from out of their proverbial prison of self-deception, and thus shepherd them into a new world of vision and light. It wasn't hard to imagine Gideon was some sort of magical intercessor that would put an end to all the darkness. Turn the moon into the sun and the sun into the moon. That he may be the "light giver." This was especially true since he wore sequins. I mean why else would you wear a sequin jumpsuit if not for shining the light of the one true God into the world? All this made perfect sense to the entire audience. And some began to wonder if they could mold Gideon in gold, or better yet, if they could cast him permanently in Florp. Sealing him in Florp would practically make Gideon eternal, just like Bopal at the 5th hole of the Holey Land. Everyone was getting excited about the prospects of this new God of Abraham, Isaac, and Jacob, as well as molding their spokesman in a block of Florp.

There was lots of time to ponder these notions, since more and more Mutant Monsters were being dispatched until the crew chief warned the executives about their shriveling stock. Gideon was starting to feel the burn as well, but still, he had seamlessly and flawlessly worked through the "Year of Darkness" and was sitting at 112 out of 112 when the Enkeling Futures and Prosperities executives picked up the "Geetz Geerts" memorial walkie-talkie and ordered the crew chief in charge of handling the Mutant Monsters to release "all of the beasts at once" in the hopes of killing Gideon "once and for all."

The executives' reasoning was simple — maybe by releasing all the remaining Mutant Monsters it would be possible to overwhelm Gideon, allowing for one of the creatures to get in a lucky strike before he could utter any of his magic words. It made perfect sense to them. So they approved the last ditch effort and put a call into the crew chief in the hopes of bringing an end to Gideon.

The crew chief listened closely to their request. After they had finished, he calmly tried to explain that releasing all the Mutant Monsters at once would make rounding them up next to impossible, and thus put everyone in the arena at risk of becoming "collateral damage." After the executives looked up the meaning of "collateral damage" they walkie-talkie'd back to the crew chief saying that if any innocent people died they would simply claim "force majeure."

And so it was settled.

The crew chief calmly informed his wranglers, and all the assistants down to the guy who cleaned the latrines, to run for cover. Releasing all the safety mechanisms to the holding cells as requested, the crew chief set the locks to open in five minutes in order to give himself enough time to grab his Thermos from the break room and make it to the parking garage in time for a clean getaway. So he hit the switch and took off running.

Gideon heard a strange noise. At first it was faint, almost a whisper. Gideon didn't know what to do other than remain perfectly still as he tried to make heads or tails of the strange pulsing noise. The music continued to grow and grow louder and louder, and appeared to be coming from the tunnel. Then the crowd caught wind of the mysterious push-button melody and thumping drum machine and thinking it was a rather catchy tune, started clapping along with the beat.

Then they saw the antlers.

As they emerged from the tunnel everyone began to "Oooooh."

It was none other than C.N.A.B.L. himself, and it was clear by the mesmerized crowd that he had lost none of his physical appeal. The audience, man and women alike, thought they were witnessing the birth of a new Adam, with Cain and Abel mixed in, to make one perfect human specimen. This was a Monster Mutant though, how could they all forget? Being a Monster Mutant obviously meant that C.N.A.B.L. wasn't a real human, because real humans didn't have antlers, and they weren't eight feet tall either, nor did they have perfect hair and flawless abs like the kind they were gawking at so intently. Nor were humans able to emit electronica music out of their ears as if he were a boombox. All these obvious facts didn't stop every living soul in the stands from wondering how exactly they could find a pair of antlers just like them — either that or at least have C.N.A.B.L. give them a kiss.

C.N.A.B.L. hadn't come for the audience though, he had come for Gideon. What nobody could know because the crew chief had sent them all running, was that down in the dungeon all the Monster Mutants had taken a vote to see who would be their representative in negotiating a deal with Gideon who could kill with a single utterance. The volunteer was C.N.A.B.L. So there he was flashing his pearly white teeth and busting his moves as if the bloody sands of gore were nothing more than a disco dance floor. The sequin pants were a nice touch, and you'd think Gideon and C.N.A.B.L. were dance partners instead of gladiatorial combatants. This was all part of C.N.A.B.L.'s plan to make nice, he figured if anything was going to cause Gideon to pause just long enough to keep him from uttering his kill words it would be the sight of his antlers.

Upon seeing those same antlers, Gideon realized there was a slight problem when it came to C.N.A.B.L. He was nowhere to be found on Helinka's list. It didn't mention anything about a Synoid with any characteristics like "antlers," "disco dancer," "pearly whites," "yellow fro," "bronze tan," nor did it mention anything about "six pack abs." There was absolutely nothing he could utter, because there was no kill word. Gideon realized he was helpless. So he did the only thing he could do in a position of total helplessness. He stood and watched. C.N.A.B.L.'s interpretive dance had the crowd on its feet. Gideon wondered how did a person get danced to death. Murdered by "the hustle" or the "the Charleston" would look rather interesting on a tomb stone, Gideon thought.

Suddenly C.N.A.B.L.'s eyes began to glow red and smoke began to ooze from the corner of his perfectly angled eyelids. It didn't take a genius to figure out what was gonna happen next. Especially if you were already familiar with any of Helinka's creations. It would be either acid, some kind of green ooze, or radioactive lasers, which were about to shoot from out of C.N.A.B.L.'s pupils, thus destroying Gideon where he stood. Surprisingly, it wasn't just one, but all three at once. Acid, glowing green blood, and lasers, all intertwined together, which came shooting out of C.N.A.B.L.'s eyes in a triple beam of destruction. Gideon waited for the big splash, but it never came. C.N.A.B.L. had set his targets on the Mezzanine level executive box seats were he doused the Enkeling Futures and Prosperities executives all in the face. The executives weren't expecting to be the target of the triple death beam, so when their skeletons started to glow under their skin they tried to run to the exits, but when they grabbed the door knob their skin melted off into a puddle of acid and goo, then the green blood coagulated whatever was left into neat fleshy mounds.

The triple whammy of ocular weaponry was the Mutant Monsters way of offering up a sacrifice in honor of their new leader, Gideon. The Synoids figured it made perfect sense that the rightful owner of the remaining slaves would be Gideon. Their creator Helinka was engaged to be married to him, but she rejected him for Jules, and they were created by Helinka but were also rejected in favor of Jules, so it made perfect sense for the king of rejection to reign over the slaves of rejection.

So C.N.A.B.L. threw himself at Gideon's feet. His antlers almost buried in the sand as he pleaded for mercy on behalf of all the mutant Synoids.

"I want to kiss you and show my supplication," pleaded C.N.A.B.L. "But if I kiss you I'll end up sucking all your liver into my mouth and I don't want that. I want to blow you a kiss, but if I do that only flames would come out and you'd be burned alive. That leaves me with only one way to for me to show full and total submission and that's to grovel."

"You don't have to grovel," said Gideon, realizing that they had come to make peace.

"Please, oh powerful one who kills with a word, please spare all of us remaining Monster Mutants. We don't want to die,

"And I don't want to hurt you either."

"It's just our nature to kill," said C.N.A.B.L. getting up on one knee. "But we see you have the power of life or death in your words. We are your slaves, at your disposal."

Gideon know knew how he was going fulfill on Jotham's original mission, "It's not me who has the power of life and death. It's not me. I'm just a washed up thief, that's all."

"If it is true what you say, then spare us for the sake of your one true God," replied C.N.A.B.L. With this, the remaining

Monster Mutants slowly emerged from the tunnels and filed in behind C.N.A.B.L. hoping to be granted reprieve.

"I can do better than that," shouted Gideon. "You're gonna need an army to do the work I've planned for you. Flintlock, Kamikaze, Parable, Brazil, Flypaper, Hong Kong, Fingernail, Hopscotch..."

And the list went on and on until all one hundred plus Monster Mutants were reanimated before everyone's eyes. The likes of C.C.OR.Y., B.L.E.K.S., A.A.K.S. M.A.A.R., and the entire list of deadly acronyms immediately followed the lead of their official spokesman C.N.A.B.L. to bow to Gideon in servitude.

The only one that failed to rise was K.K.L.R.

"I'm sorry about your friend, K.K.L.R.," apologized Gideon. "It's just it shot its tongue out of his mouth and I had no choice... Forgive me. And another thing. I don't want any of you to change. I need you to do what you were made to do. Kill."

"Tell us how we can serve," confirmed C.N.A.B.L.

"You're idol smasher now," commanded Gideon. "Now go! Destroy every single idolatrous temple, smash every evil altar, rip down every ashera tree, kill every one of those demonic priests with their pointy hats, if anyone gets in your way, shoot lasers! Burn down every strip mall and all their idolatrous temples! If you burn down a pizza parlor next door, let it burn! It's now your sworn duty is to wipe all idols off the face of the planet. And when you're done you can live in peace in Antartica or the Lower Canada, whatever works for you. Do you understand the command I have just given you all?"

C.N.A.B.L. looked to all his resurrected mutants then confirmed they all understood their kill order, "We will do as you have said."

"Then go!" shouted Gideon to his newly minted mutant army, "Go you idol smashers! Tear down that Godgod tower! Go! Pave the way! You have purpose now. So go! Fulfill your destiny. Go!"

Unleashing 100 plus former Monster Mutants onto the streets of Merletown was the equivalent of turning the entire world into a gladiator arena, complete with electronica dance beats.

It was now Gideon's turn to send everyone out to pick up the pieces, reminding the stunned crowd all about their wager, "The challenge is over! They couldn't kill me! So you know what that means, it means you need to go out there and start being humans. Human beings! Not slaves, but go out there and start being real human beings for once! And one more thing, if you welch you die!"

A good curse was all that was needed to seal the deal.

But they weren't going to leave until giving Gideon a standing ovation. The entire arena stood up to serenade his miraculous performance, the one they had all witnessed with their eyes, a performance they'd never forget.

Gideon knew better than to think the victory had anything to do with him. All he could do was remember his parents, his grandparents, and his entire bloodline stretching back to the beginning of time, which he was determined to get to know more about somehow, someway. Gideon was about to go free and be a billion dollars richer. Maybe it wasn't enough to buy a mega mansion but good enough to help a few people out. And how could he forget Jotham? And all the rabbis in his apartment, they were now free to teach everyone all about the stuff they conveniently had forgotten all about. Even Helinka and her botched attempts to create the perfect partner, finally had Jules. He wouldn't have been able to do anything if it weren't for Helinka. And then there were the Cauzzies. Cauzzie Rob, Cauzzie Roy and the entire gang. The Cauzzies deserved all his gratitude. They were the ones that broke in and robbed him of the future he thought he wanted, a life at the top of the heap. The ultimate contributor to the grand money machine of death. But thanks to those green buggers he was fighting at the bottom of the barrel for life. They were all such noble thoughts.

And then the crowd stopped cheering. And an eerie silence fell over the arena. Nobody was going anywhere, least of all the exists.

"So it looks like it's just you and me now, Gideon," she said, laughing rather ruefully.

Gideon had forgotten all about Cloreen. But there she was with her sword in hand, having just finished her warm up exercises and all her pre-battle breathing techniques, waiting to make her contribution to his list of noble thoughts.

"It's you and me now, Gideon," she said. "We're the perfect match."

There was no kill word for Cloreen. And unlike C.N.A.B.L., there would be no bowing in servitude, either.

The audience was buzzing as they all found their seats, ready for another bloody encore.

"Run if you must, Gideon."

It was as if Cloreen was reading Gideon's mind. He tried to take a step backwards, but this was harder than it appeared considering his legs were trembling. When his back slammed up against the arena's glass enclosure, he suddenly realized he had met the limit of his boundaries. There was no where else to run. In just a few short strides Cloreen was on top of him, slashing down one handed. Gideon felt the edge of her sword graze past his head removing a lock of his hair.

"A souvenir of our affection, Gideon," said Cloreen, letting the lock float into her palm before tucking it away, adding, "You know a lock of hair is still a popular trope in the realm of romantic genre, especially before an impending separation. You get it, Gideon? Separation. Will it be your arm? Or your leg?"

Scurrying away on his hands and knees, Gideon naturally tripped over himself, sending him plowing face first into the grimy sand. Rolling over on his back, he lifted his sword to fend off her charge. But no charge came. Cloreen wasn't going to do away with him just like that. She wanted to savor a few more precious moments to pair up with newly acquired lock of hair.

"I think I'm going to separate your head from your neck, Gideon" said Cloreen, tracking him as if he were some wounded beast.

Gideon knew he'd have to fight if he wanted to live, but when he tried Cloreen simply sidestepped Gideon's attempts at swordplay, glowing green sword or not.

Despite seeing how easily Cloreen was toying with Gideon, the crowd never stopped cheering him on, thinking that this was all part of his master plan. Of course it was no such thing. And Gideon tried another wild swing, but again, Cloreen just moved to the left. Two more dismal efforts zapped whatever was left of Gideon's strength and he knew things were about to get real desperate.

"This is where I'm supposed to critique your swordplay, Gideon," taunted Cloreen. "You know, like how the superior swordsman always mocks the inferior opponent. I'm supposed to let you know how your fear is throwing you off balance, or how your Mugai-ryu technique needs work."

With an effortless snap of her sword, Cloreen slashed Gideon across the stomach, not deep enough to kill but certainly enough to entertain. Blood began to ooze from the edges.

"Is this where I play up the old cat and mouse game, Gideon?" asked Cloreen. "Me being the cat, and you being the mouse. But it's such a cliché, Gideon. I'm not sure how I feel about it."

Gideon reeled backward, seeing the blood he clutched his stomach expecting his lower intestines to come pouring out and was surprised to see when they hadn't. She was true to her word, playing cat and mouse. He being trapped.

"Me," Cloreen laughed, "I'm a personal fan of violent impalings, stabbing eye-sockets, skullers, twain hangings, wrath-hewing, and that sort of thing. I hope to show you all I've learned since you took my job and so skillfully arranged my departure. It's because of you that I came by all these superior skills."

Cloreen slashed at Gideon's left arm. A little deeper this time.

"Yes, Gideon. You're not the only one to be sent to the gladiator arena for something they didn't do."

Gideon's prediction of real desperation was accurate, he took off running in a vain effort to release the pressure. Cloreen's footwork closed the gap in a matter of seconds. Again, there was no escape. Pushing him up against the barricades, she feinted a strike sending Gideon cowering like a frightened turtle. She could have easily cut his head off right then and there, but instead stood over him, looking down at his complete and total helplessness.

When Gideon realized his head was still on his neck, he scurried away as fast as he could. It wasn't a good look for Gideon, and the collective moan that crept down from the audience made sure to emphasize that point.

Clearly Cloreen had done what she had come to do. Turn the tables as she had done so many times before within the arena, you could even say turning the tables was her specialty. So with everything in flux, she felt it was finally time to win back her fickle fans. There would be no more feints, no more cat and mouse. She was just going to chop off Gideon's head, stick it on the end of her sword and raise it to the rafters. And then when she was done with her victory lap, she'd hurl his head into the crowd for some lucky sod to take home as a souvenir. She'd be victorious yet again, gain her freedom, and spend a billion dollars on shoes and a one-way ticket to Caracas. It was time to collect her paycheck and go home. So she moved in for the kill.

Gideon, on the other hand, picked up the message loud and clear, and the instant he saw Cloreen advancing on him, he remembered Jotham. So he knew he couldn't go down without fighting back.

Cloreen brought her sword down with such force that she was sure Gideon's head would be cleanly separated from his body, but instead, it was only the clank of cold metal against metal that rattled her bones. And to everyone's amazement, including Cloreen's, the battle was now fully joined. Gideon and his glowing green sword had repelled the fatal blow.

Now Gideon countered, going on a fearsome attack, striking with great power and precision. And it looked as if, for a single moment, Gideon was a master swordsman. He was forcing Cloreen back into a defensive position. In fact she had never retreated in her entire career as a gladiator. The crowd went wild as Gideon continued to put her on the back foot, with slash after slash and blow after blow. With the tide of battle swinging to Gideon he forced Cloreen back into the wall, their swords in constant contact. Now with his rage growing, his distorted face gripped with uncontrolled anger, he served up terrific blow after terrific blow. Sparks flew with every strike, one catching Cloreen across the shoulder, drawing blood.

Cloreen couldn't let this go unanswered, and soon the swordplay was furious; Gideon attacking, slashing, hacking away; Cloreen was parrying effortlessly, and while doing so was elegantly defensive. Gideon continued pressing forward like a raging bull with a wondrous skill he never thought he had in him, but still, none of his blows seemed to be causing any real damage. Cloreen was handling Gideon's onslaught without any overpowering difficulty, and never losing her balance for a second. Gideon had given all he had, done everything he could possibly do, above and beyond all reason, yet despite his best and almost miraculous effort it wasn't enough to make Cloreen even break a sweat.

Then it was her turn to counterattack. Moving with grace and speed, Cloreen dodged, lurched, whirled, and slashed while showcasing her perfect footing.

Gideon knew it was only a matter of seconds before she penetrated his defense. His arms felt like rubber bands, and each one of her devastating blows took their exponential toll. Cloreen seemed to be perfectly aware of his faltering stance too, so she pressed forward sword against sword. Gideon tried backing away, he was horrified, the terror was written on his dilated pupils — he had tried everything and it wasn't enough.

Then it happened. With a two-handed swing, Cloreen brought her blade down onto Gideon's sword with so much forced that it shattered in two. It was a violent clank that echoed through the arena as the force of the blow shook Gideon to the core. The glowing green sword crumbed from his grip like a fistful of sand.

"I'd kiss you goodbye too, Gideon, but I might smudge my lip gloss," the smirk on Cloreen's face left Gideon cold.

"You don't have to do this..." murmured Gideon, backing up step by step as if there was someplace he could escape to, or something that he could say to dissuade her from taking his head.

"I was going to throw your head into the crowd, Gideon. But now, for what you just said, I think I might keep it as a paperweight. Or give it as a gift to your boss over at The Startling Concern."

"The Synoids, the Monster Mutants," shouted Gideon, "they are destroying Credeth and all those dreams of Palladium status as we speak, there won't be anything left of The Startling Concern when they are done. It's all over Cloreen, killing me won't change a thing. So don't do it!"

"What? And ruin my undefeated streak? I don't think so, Gideon," she said moving in for the kill.

"It's true, Jotham set you up, I know," he confessed. "But it's Supentus that has been manipulating this entire thing from the start, he could have freed you but he didn't, he wanted to keep you here to fulfill some diabolical plan! He's been ruining my life since my parents died, he's manipulated my entire life to bring about his own evil plan, he's the devil! You and I are just pawns! We're cogs in his evil master plan. But we can change that! We can stop it! Just don't kill me!"

Gideon could retreat no further, although it wasn't the barricades stopping him but the remains of K.K.L.R..

Seeing he had no where else to run, Cloreen slowly lifted her sword, "I'll bring up your concerns to my hair stylist, and see what he recommends, Gideon. But we really can't disappoint the audience now, can we?"

While Cloreen was talking, Gideon remembered K.K.L.R.'s special attribute. His deadly chameleon tongue. The same chameleon tongue that shot out of K.K.L.R.'s mouth and wrapped around his neck keeping him from shouting the kill word. It was worth a shot.

"Say goodbye, Gideon," remarked Cloreen. "You've met your match."

Just before she was able to take his head off, Gideon jumped on K.K.L.R.'s head with so much pressure it turned into a giant squeeze doll, opening up its mouth and shooting its chameleon tongue and striking Cloreen in the face with such force she went flying across the arena, sending her crashing into the barricades. She was out cold. Possibly dead.

As the packed arena erupted in sheer madness, Gideon picked up her sword and seeing that she was just out cold, waited for her to regain consciousness so he could talk some sense into her. Or propose marriage whichever came first.

"Show's over everyone!" yelled Gideon. "It's time to go finish what we started. Go! It's all over now. It's your turn now."

After the uproarious five minute standing ovation the audience lingered only long enough to make sure Gideon was serious about what he said about not killing Cloreen. When they saw that Gideon wasn't lying, that there was no way they were going to get to see her die, they shrugged their collective shoulders realizing the show was therefore truly over. But not exactly. With this revelation dawning on their singular mind, they all brightened up at the prospect that the battle had switched from the sands of the arena into the stands of the arena with all the fans. It was this realization that each one of them needed to get out there as a single body and claim victory the same way they had seen Gideon do it, by defying all odds to pull off the impossible win; by staying true to his one true God of remembrance. This God was their God now. They had lost the bet. And while others would still keep their options open, that was their privilege to do. If they wanted to welch, that is. Gideon had won the challenge fair and square and now it was their turn to pay up. So with this understanding in mind, the mob made for the exits in a wiliful, steady procession.

When Cloreen finally came too, she saw Gideon standing over here with a sword just a hair's breadth from her jugular.

"Kill me. Quick," she hissed.

"I don't decide who lives and dies," replied Gideon. "The evil you and I have committed in our lives has been carried by something far greater than either of us and it was done all for the sake of future good. Well now its time for you and I to choose to do some good for once."

A single tear ran down her cheek.

"You said we were a perfect match," added Gideon, "And I know what you meant, the most poignant duel to the death. But let's defy death, you and me. What do you say? Imagine what we could do together. Maybe we are the perfect match, Cloreen, but as husband and wife. You'll be first in command and I'll be your backup, just like old times. We'll change the world, you and me. For good."

Gideon extended his hand,

Cloreen gazed up at him without blinking. Without moving a muscle.

"What do you say, Cloreen? What do you say if you give me your hand. And we both walk out of here. Together like we're supposed to do. Just like how it's written."

Seeing Cloreen wasn't about to move with a sword at her neck, Gideon hurled it across the arena.

Relief and wonder swept over Cloreen's once blank lifeless expression.

"Give me your hand," urged Gideon.

Cloreen was unable to keep herself from smiling. It wasn't the biggest grin, but just enough of one. Gideon's selflessness was so beyond anything she could ever conceive, in fact she was having difficulty processing the possibilities of life with Gideon in lieu of violent death. The idea of her and Gideon reshaping the world, as husband and wife of all things, with him and his words of wisdom and her with her gift to wipe it all clean. It would surely be a thing to behold, she knew.

Gideon watched her eyes wrestle with the idea of them together for the rest of their lives, and all the wonderful possibilities that lay before them, "We're going to do this, Cloreen. Together. You and me."

Cloreen fought off the emotions which continued to bubble to the surface until she finally stopped fighting. Gladiators, Monster Mutants, or tears for that matter.

"Okay Gideon. You win," she said with her eyes fixed on his. Resolved now.

Reaching up to take hold of Gideon's hand in hers, Cloreen felt the end of the diamond-shaped dagger she kept hidden in the cusp of her palm with the end of her ring finger, just to remind herself it was still there.

CJ Supentus slumped ungainly in his executive leather chair. Suffering from what they call the thousand yard stare. But the look in his eyes was even farther reaching than that and almost penetrated a distance of light-years and possibly beyond. The ticker tape was detailing the destruction being wrought by the riots led by the Synoid raiders, all the massive fires at the temples burning out of control, the looting and destruction of every idolatrous entity, the financial institutions like Credeth having been burned to the ground. It was the kind of news that CEOs of major corporations never want to hear. It was the end of everything they had built. Brick by brick it was all being taken apart, thanks to Gideon and his merry band of Synoids.

His hand covered his mouth in such a way that the grey men in the pointy hats weren't exactly sure what he had said in response to their question. They were too wary to ask him again, and just looked at each other in the hopes one of them would have the wherewithal to know what to do.

Then, when all looked hopeless, Supentus opened his mouth, "Sell."

A flurry of action ensued. Some jumped on the radio giving commands to their underlings while others flipped through the ledgers making marks and stamping orders. When the flurry subsided, another grey man in a pointy hat approached Supentus, genuflecting.

"My lord, we are anticipating a decrease verging on abandonment and huge losses over the course of the the unforeseeable future with RX Ventures, holders of the god Blazerus, the sub-deity Vespirs, the goddess Floxum —"

Supentus abruptly cut him off, "SELL!"

The sell off continued as another grey man approached, "TXHR Industrial Holdings with the portfolio of goddesses Avuncku, Cotubus, Sporium, and the minor god, Oleum, are anticipating large drops as the exotic meat industry is on the verge of collapse. We suggest total and utter liquidation."

"Sell," Supentus confirmed.

"The pagan bus tours of the Vacatican has seen substantial drops putting at risk all our expansion projects with the Holey Land tram tours so the consensus seems to be —"

Again Supentus interrupted, his voice tinged with disdain, "Sell."

The movement seemed to pick up the pace as more calls were made, more ledgers opened and closed, more investments scuttled and sold.

Then fully prostrating himself on the ground, another grey man in a pointy hat approached with a green ledger in his hand.

"My Lord. We need your official approval, if you please."

With a flick of his hand, Supentus motioned him to get on with it.

He continued, "Thank you, my Lord. We have a payment of 4.2 billion dollars, an 18% commission rate on all future Messianic endeavors, a new luxury apartment, a private palankeen, private train car, as well as her previous job back. All to be paid out to Cloreen for quote, 'taking a dive' unquote."

"Approved," suddenly Supentus was perking up.

Another grey man approached, "Shares in the agriculture firm Grains of Paradise Wheat and Barley Makers Incorporated are dropping badly. What do you suggest we do, my Lord?"

Supentus rose from his executive chair, "Buy! Buy! Buy! We're gonna need to make a lot of bread."

And with that final declarative statement, Supentus put an end to the meeting and began to walk toward the exist, shape-shifting as he went, morphing into an olive-skinned Judean man with beautiful flowing brown hair, a long beard, and piercing blue eyes. His mummified tracksuit materializing into three thousand year old Middle-Eastern robes. On his feet, a pair of dusty sandals.

"We're going to need a lot of bread."